Genevieve's War

PATRICIA REILLY GIFF

Holiday House / New York

HOLIDAY HOUSE is registered in the U.S. Patent and Trademark Office.

Printed and bound in February 2017 at Maple Press, York, PA, USA.

First Edition

1 3 5 7 9 10 8 6 4 2

www.holidayhouse.com

Library of Congress Cataloging-in-Publication Data

Names: Giff, Patricia Reilly.

Title: Genevieve's war / by Patricia Reilly Giff.

Description: First edition. | New York : Holiday House, [2017] | Summary:
"In August 1939 Genevieve makes an impulsive decision not to get on the train
to take her by boat back to New York and must spend the duration of
World War II with her grandmother in a small village in Alsace, France,
where she becomes involved with the French resistance."

Identifiers: LCCN 2016027038 | ISBN 9780823438006 (hardcover)

Subjects: | CYAC: World War, 1939–1945—Underground

Movements—France—Fiction. | Grandparent and child—Fiction.

Self-reliance—Fiction. | France—History—German occupation,
1940–1945—Fiction.

Classification: LCC PZ7.G3626 Ge 2017 | DDC [Fic]—dc23

LC record available at https://lccn.loc.gov/2016027038

Genevieve's War

———⋅———

For George Nicholson, beloved friend.

For James Matthew Giff, beloved son.

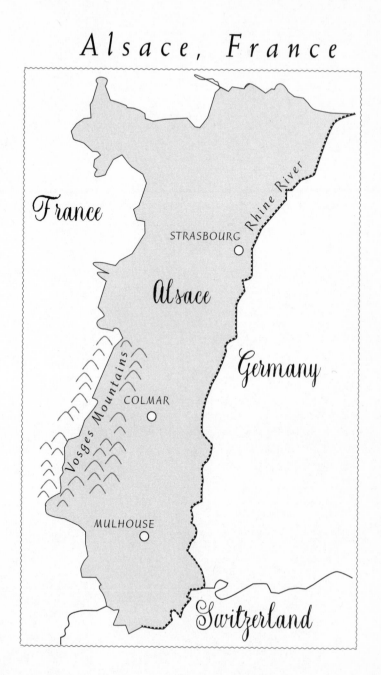

Alsace, France

France

Alsace

STRASBOURG

Rhine River

Germany

Vosges Mountains

COLMAR

MULHOUSE

Switzerland

THE END

My heart drummed against my chest, my throat so dry I couldn't swallow.

Mémé and I crouched on the dirt floor of the farmhouse cellar, our dog, Louis, huddled beside us. The sounds of the mortar and bursts of artillery seemed to go on forever. We were trapped in the middle: the Americans on one side of us, the Germans on the other.

It was freezing without heat, and dark! I'd burned our only candle down to a nub; then it had sputtered and died.

"I have to go upstairs," I told Mémé. "We need quilts and sweaters."

I felt her reach out. "Don't, Genevieve. I'll go."

My grandmother, braver than I!

"It's all right." I stood and ran my hands along the wall to find my way to the stairs.

A tremendous boom. The house shook.

We knew the cellar was the safest place in the bombardment, but suppose the house came down? We'd be buried under stone and timber with no one to help us.

Was that happening right now to the shops in the

village, the school, the farmhouses along the way? I stumbled over something that rolled and clattered, and then I went up into the daylight, blinking.

Everything looked so normal. I passed the hall table with my father's picture, the living room chairs.

But nothing was normal. In the kitchen, windows were shattered; shards of glass that must have been a hundred years old covered the wide sills. My feet crunched against pieces on the stone floor.

The three-colored cat, half hidden under the table, peered out at me. She hissed when I tried to pick her up, and backed away. Poor thing, as frightened as we were. I'd have to leave her for now.

Another boom.

No time!

I yanked open the drawer for candles, glancing outside quickly. The gravel driveway was torn up, a tree split, the winter fields gray with patches of snow.

Head down, the candles in my pocket, I ran to pull the quilt off the bed, sweaters off hooks, the sounds of the battle so much louder than they had been in the cellar.

I threw the quilt and sweaters down the stairs to

free my hands. Then I lighted a candle with shaking fingers as the cat dived ahead of me.

Who'd said the war would be over someday?

We'd all said it! It would be over and there'd be peace.

Someday would never come.

BEFORE

one

"*Gen?*" André's voice was loud.

I leaned over the hall table to peer out the window; one elbow knocked my father's picture to the floor.

André beckoned from the barn. "Look what I found. Hurry."

I put the picture back on the table, wiping off imaginary dust with one sleeve. Who was he anyway, my father with his grim face, his hands balled into fists?

My wooden sabots clattered on the stone floor as I sped through the kitchen.

"Don't slam—" Mémé began over her shoulder.

I caught the door just in time, hopped over the three-colored cat on the stone step, then crossed the gravel path to the barn, with its sweet smell of hay.

Inside, André pointed: two ancient bicycles leaned against each other in one of the stalls. Bits of hay covered the seats and cobwebs stretched across the spokes.

Bicycles! We could pump the tires with air and ride away from the farm, pedaling up one hill and coasting down the next, arms out. I smiled, remembering when André had taught me to ride. *"You'll speed along as if you've been doing this forever, Gen,"* he'd said.

For the first time in days, I'd stop thinking of him sailing home to New York, leaving me with our disagreeable grandmother, Mémé, to weed rows of cabbages and pick bugs off the beans, to speak Alsatian or French every minute, and never hear a word in English.

I'd be here for another two weeks!

And then, home. But not to Aunt Marie, not to our house in Springfield Gardens, not to my old school in September. I brushed my hair away, determined to brush my thoughts away too.

André was filling the tires, so I wiped off a few dried spiders, as old as the bikes. Then, zigzagging along the path, the gravel spitting out from under the wheels, we called to Mémé. "Going for a ride."

We didn't wait to hear what she'd say.

We flew! André led the way, going east, past farms and woods filled with evergreens.

Someone was yelling at us!

I glanced over my shoulder and slowed down. Rémy, younger than André, a couple of years older than me, pedaled toward us, waving.

Rémy had been the best part of this summer. Rémy with blue eyes and curly hair! Rémy who towered over me and made my heart beat faster!

"Some bikes!" he called.

His wasn't much better; I had to laugh. "Race you to the top of the hill," I called back.

André pulled to one side, watching. I rode past with Rémy behind me, letting me win.

André caught up, and later, we stopped at a grassy meadow to see an ancient stone tower. A messy storks' nest rested precariously on top. "The white storks of Alsace," André said. "With long legs like yours, Gen."

Rémy grinned at me, a tiny scar at the corner of his mouth dimpling. He made me smile too. If only he lived in New York!

I shaded my eyes to see the mother bird's head and a hint of her folded black wings, but her babies were hidden deep in the nest.

"If I were here this winter," André said, "I'd climb the tower and see the world."

Rémy said, "Sure," and I sputtered, "Really!"

But André could do almost anything. He was my best friend and a great cook. Now he was going home ahead of me. He'd spent the summer here working in the village bistro. Last summer he'd been in Basel, the summer before in Strasbourg and Colmar, working in restaurants. Now he'd study business in college so he could open his own restaurant someday. "I'll call it Genevieve's Place," he always said. "And you'll be the star."

"Some star, with skinny brown braids," I always said.

But now, I bit my lip: my brother, skinny, with coal-black hair, leaving. André, who laughed at everything, who cared about me.

He read my mind. "I'll visit you at Cousin Ellen's. And I'll bring you a red parasol to make you happy." He stopped when he saw my face. He knew what I was thinking. Cousin Ellen! My mother's friend. I hardly knew her.

Aunt Marie, my mother as long as I could remember, was teaching in Canada, so far north that even letters would be hard to get.

No choice, she'd said, *I have to work in this little*

village for the book I'm writing. It'll make all the differ-ence to us. But we'll be together by Christmas, I promise.

Did I say something aloud? Rémy looked at me with sympathy. "Don't go back, Gen. Stay."

Stay with Mémé, who complained about every-thing? I shook my head.

We rode along and passed a half-timbered house, a chestnut tree shading its windows. It was blue-gray, a beautiful color. Then a farm filled with vegetables and plum trees. Rémy pointed. "I wish it were mine," he said. "Someday I'll farm."

"What about your parents' pharmacy?" André asked.

Rémy grinned. "I'll leave that to my little sister, Céline. She's three. On her way to growing up."

We stopped too far away from the Rhine to see the water, but I knew it was there. And beyond that, Germany!

"They're coming, Gen," Rémy said. "The Ger-mans will run right over us."

I felt a quick tightening in my chest. André's face was serious. "They want to take Alsace back and gob-ble up the rest of Europe."

He reached over and touched my hand on the

handlebar. "You'll get out before they come." He frowned. I knew he was thinking about our father and grandparents, who were born here. "I hate to desert Mémé," he said.

I thought of her stern face, the lines that crisscrossed her forehead. Born in 1876, she was in her sixties but seemed like a hundred. And what I knew of my father would fit in a thimble. I thought of his picture: Gérard Michel, a stern man glaring into the camera.

I didn't care one bit that we were leaving Mémé and Alsace. It couldn't be soon enough for me.

At that moment, the sky turned from blue to charcoal gray. Lightning streaked across the sky and a clap of thunder followed. "Let's go!" Rémy shouted.

Rain beat on our heads and shoulders. Heads down, we pedaled along the way we'd come. At last, Mémé's farm was ahead of us. We waved as Rémy kept going toward his parents' pharmacy in the village square.

We were soaked, our clothes dripping. We wheeled the bicycles into the barn, dried them off, and covered them with old drop cloths, and again, I thought of André leaving.

I put my hand on his arm, but before I could say anything, he glanced toward the kitchen window, where

Mémé stared out at the rain. "She'll be alone without us," he said.

"She's been alone for years. She'll be glad when I'm gone."

And I'd be glad too, more than glad.

two

@Mémé and I pulled weeds, our nails broken and lined with soil. How strong I'd become this summer. In the field, at first, my face had blistered, but then I tanned until I could spend long hours in the sun. My arms and legs had new muscles.

Mémé stretched, one hand rubbing her back. "The Germans are coming soon," she said, almost echoing André's words before he'd left, hugging me to him.

"But not yet."

And not for me. I'd be on the *Normandie* traveling west. At the railing, I'd watch the rolling sea, and in the dining room, I'd order petits fours thick with fondant icing.

If only I hadn't dreamed about Cousin Ellen last night. She was kind and friendly and when Aunt Marie asked if I could stay with her, she'd said, *"I'd love it."*

But I wouldn't know one person in Flushing, wouldn't have one friend, instead of being home in Springfield Gardens, where I knew everyone. Now I'd even be leaving my new friend, Katrin, who lived on the next farm, the best friend I'd ever had.

And Rémy. Oh, Rémy!

This was my last day. My ticket lay on the edge of the bed upstairs. Madame Thierry, who was a neighbor at home, and almost as old as Mémé, would meet me at the train station.

"You can't go alone," Aunt Marie had said in June after André had left, her face worried. *"Madame Thierry is going to Alsace for the summer too. She'll take care of you both ways."*

I had to smile. Madame Thierry was the one who needed care!

"You have less than an hour," Mémé said. "This ship may be the last to cross before the war. If you miss the train you may not reach it in time."

War! That was all anyone talked about. "Less than an hour," I repeated to Mémé, as if it didn't matter one way or the other. I could be as tough as this old woman, who, bent and limping, still managed to run the farm alone.

Lines pleated themselves above her lips. "Finish packing, Genevieve. We'll take the cart to the railroad station. Your holiday is over."

Holiday. I pursed my lips the way she did. Holiday was Jones Beach on Long Island, the waves smashing onto the shore. It wasn't digging in Mémé's fields, all the way across the Atlantic, stuffing sausages, or boiling jars to hold beans and plums.

It certainly wasn't sleeping in the upstairs bedroom where my father had spent his childhood. The ceiling sloped low over my head, and the straw mattress crackled when I moved.

Most of all, it wasn't spending a summer with Mémé.

But what had Aunt Marie said? *"You and André know about your mother, but what about your father? Your grandmother? The farm that will be yours someday?"*

She'd told me that she and my mother had gone to Alsace, that Mom had seen my father in the village. *The two of us with French parents, able to speak French ourselves,* she'd said. *Your mother fell in love.*

I knew so much about my mother. She'd been skinny like André and tall like me. She wore Evening in Paris perfume and loved to dance with me in her arms.

I could almost see her.

But all I could see of my father was a face that looked as if he'd eaten a lemon!

How different everything would have been if they hadn't taken the train to the mountains when I was a baby. If the train hadn't jumped the tracks. If they still lived.

I threw a bunch of weeds toward the wheelbarrow but missed. Mémé muttered something behind me. *Clumsiness,* probably. I had a quick thought of Aunt Marie, who called me Flyaway Girl. *Things just fly away from you and are lost,* she'd say, and laugh.

I walked across the field, wanting to dance across. *Last time,* I told myself. Dozens of cabbages would be ready to harvest soon. But not by me!

The three-colored cat was sunning herself on the path; she reached out with one paw to give me a little scratch as I passed.

Inside, I trailed my fingers over the massive kitchen table. The room was dark, with a huge fireplace; copper pots hung on hooks, and vegetables simmered on the stove, almost ready for the jars on the counter. A crusty loaf of bread covered with a tea towel was on the table, and I cut myself a slice to munch on.

Louis, the shepherd dog, padded in behind me.

"He's a watchdog," Mémé had told me a dozen times. "Meant to be kept outside at night."

I'd forgotten to close the door again, but it wasn't night! I bent to hug him, his rough fur against my cheek. "Good dog." I slipped him a chunk of bread too.

After I walked him outside, I climbed the stairs, my hand raised over the banister, which bristled with splinters, and scooped up one of my knee socks from the top step.

It didn't take long to fold everything into my suitcase: underwear and socks, skirts and blouses. I stared at the books I'd brought with me. I'd read them over and over, myths and folktales, and a French book about a lost dog, from my friend, Katrin. Aunt Marie, who loved to read, had taught me to read too, when I was only three. I'd have to carry the books in the string bag I'd made this summer, a bit of a mess.

I changed into Sunday clothes, sliding into patent leather shoes and leaving the wooden sabots under the bed.

Did I have everything? The dresser drawers were warped and so hard to open that I hadn't used them. But just in case, I checked.

They were empty, except for the bottom one. It held an old photo of Mémé. How pretty she'd been, young and smiling a little. How different from the sour old woman she was now. I turned the picture over. *Miel* was written on the back. Honey! More like vinegar, if you asked me.

No one would have written *Miel* on the back of my father's picture.

I pulled my things down the stairs and outside.

Sister, the horse, was tethered to the cart. I rested my hand on her chocolate side. Her skin rippled under my hand, and she looked back at me as if she knew I was leaving. Mémé stood on the other side of the cart, leaning against it. A surprise. She never leaned against anything.

"The poor horse doesn't even have a name yet," André had said in June. *"How old is she, Mémé?"*

"Twelve."

"I christen her Sister," he'd said, *"in honor of my sister."*

"Me?"

"Her legs are long. And her huge brown eyes are like yours."

"Mine are gray."

He'd grinned. "Doesn't matter. Her feet clop just like yours."

I'd looked quickly at Mémé, at her faint smile. No one could resist André.

I gave the horse another pat. I'd miss her and all the animals, even the cow André had named Elsie. *"Elsie?" Mémé had echoed.*

He'd laughed. "It's a cow's name."

"An American cow," I'd added.

What would happen if I dashed into the barn and said good-bye to the cow, or to the hens that pecked at seed in their pen?

But Mémé was frowning, impatient. No detours!

Her lips chewed on themselves as she stared at the side field with its rows of squash, and beyond them the potato plants with their purple flowers.

Did she care that I was leaving? That she'd be alone this fall, to pull all that from the earth, to fill dozens of jars of food, and store potatoes and apples in the cool cellar? Only one person would eat them all winter.

Louis circled the cart, wanting to come with us. I ran my hand over his head and kissed his gray muzzle. "I'll miss you," I whispered. I climbed up, but Mémé still stood on the other side of the cart.

I saw then how pale she was, her wrinkled face dotted with perspiration.

"What is it?" I asked.

"Nothing." She held on to the edge of the cart as she climbed up slowly, dragging her left foot.

"What?" I asked again.

"It's just twisted . . . ," she began, and didn't finish.

I looked down and saw a line of blood on the hem of her long dress.

"How did you do this?"

"Stop, Genevieve. We'll miss the train with all your questions."

She flicked the reins lightly on Sister's back. Then we were on our way, leaving the house with its red shutters, the cow, the chickens, the pig, the three-colored cat and Louis, whose thick tail wagged uncertainly.

three

Cypress trees lined the road on each side of us. Sister's bells jangled, and with every step she took, I heard, *Summer's over.*

Nearby, the woodcutter was sawing in the forest. Sometimes I'd caught a glimpse of him, straps over his bent shoulders, pulling his cart along, with new wood piled high. He'd raise his hand in a gentle wave, then duck his head.

We passed the Moellers' farmhouse, where Katrin leaned against the window, waving. Yesterday we'd said a long good-bye, crying a little, hugging, promising to write and to be friends forever.

Katrin was funny and warm. Her cheeks were round and covered with freckles, and her hair was a halo of curls. She never stopped talking... some of it about America, and all of it mixed up. She'd lean forward:

"Do you see cowboys in New York City all the time?" Or "How about buffaloes? If I'm going to be a writer, I have to know these things."

I looked back over my shoulder until she and the farm disappeared at the turn of the road.

Next to me, Mémé faced straight ahead, her lips in a thin line, her jaws clenched. What had she done to her foot?

We made our way into the village square. Baskets of red and white geraniums were everywhere. Shop doors and windows in the upstairs apartments were open against the heat.

Three old men in berets sat at a table in front of the bistro. They'd been in the same spot every day since I'd come, voices raised, arguing over one thing or another.

"Let's stop at the pâtisserie," I said.

Mémé twitched one narrow shoulder, as if she were asking why.

"I want to say good-bye."

She pulled on the reins, and I tumbled out of the cart before she could change her mind.

Inside the pâtisserie, I breathed in the smell of plum tarts baking in the oven. My mouth watered as I glanced at shelves filled with cakes and éclairs plump with whipped cream.

Madame Jacques wiped her floury hands on her apron and reached into the case for a meringue for me. "My favorite," I said.

"Ah yes. Your father's favorite too."

He loved meringues? My father with his grim face?

"So, Genevieve." Madame Jacques wiped her warm face, her cheeks like soft dough. "Summer is over, and you leave before the Germans come."

I nodded, the sweet meringue melting on my tongue.

She tilted her head. "I think you will come back. Maybe not soon. It will be a long time." She tapped the wooden floor with one foot. "The Germans remember that Alsace belonged to them once. They want us back."

She smiled then. "My son, Claude, is still sleeping upstairs. Lazy boy. Otherwise he'd say good-bye to you too."

From the window, I saw Mémé frowning at me. Madame Jacques gave me a kiss on each cheek. I went out the door and was barely onto the cart when Mémé snapped the reins again and the horse jolted forward.

On the other side of the square, Monsieur Philippe lounged in the doorway of his shop, books piled up in the small window next to him. He looked at me impassively. His lips were impossibly thick, his teeth nut brown. He was nothing like Madame Jacques, who laughed at everything, touching your shoulder as she did.

As we passed the pharmacy, Rémy stood at the open door. He mouthed something. Was it *I will miss you?* Did he look sad, thinking we wouldn't see each other for a long time?

As the horse labored up the hill, I looked back at the fairy-tale village. The houses were half-timbered, their stone walls painted yellow or pink, or green and the church steeple rose above all of it in a thin point.

I remembered the ancient stone tower with its messy storks' nest. *I hate to desert Mémé,* André had said. Did I say it aloud? She turned to stare at me sharply, but I pretended to glance at the field. We didn't speak for the rest of the way.

At the station, I pulled out my suitcase and the string bag of books. I tucked my purse under my arm, wondering where I'd left my gloves. I jumped down, and with my hand gentling Sister's back, I glanced at

Mémé. "Thank you," I managed. What else could I say? "The farm is beautiful." I realized it was true: the field in the morning, green and washed, the Vosges Mountains in the distance.

She leaned forward. "You may come again after the war, Genevieve."

I blinked in surprise, then glanced down. Her foot turned in and there was a drop of blood on her sock. But before I could say a word, she was turning the cart on her way back to the farm.

four

$\mathcal{D}ust$ rose from the cart. I watched until Sister trotted around a curve; then I dragged my heavy suitcase and the books into the station.

Inside, the wooden benches were filled. People leaned against the walls or sat on the cement floor, boxes and bags at their feet. A buzz of voices rose and fell like angry bees.

The four Grossmans, a Jewish family, the mother and father and two children, were pressed together in a far corner. Katrin had told me they were leaving for safety. How terrible that the Germans hated them. And why? I waved but they didn't see me.

Madame Thierry sat on a bench, eyes closed, mouth opened, asleep.

I stood nearby, next to a stanchion. The ceiling was

open to the sky; pigeons flew back and forth, wings whirring, feathers drifting. A cloud changed shapes: an old man, an angel's wing, a giant shoe.

I closed my eyes. *The train to Le Havre, the ship. Then New York. The library, black-and-white ice cream sodas with Aunt Marie!* I swallowed. No! I'd have to find another library near Ellen, Aunt Marie would be far away, and André wouldn't be scrambling eggs on Saturday mornings. *Gen, you're my best customer!*

Next to me, a woman was eating a buttery crêpe. It was folded in four, and sugar dotted her dress. My mouth watered. I had a few francs left, so I went to find one at the shop.

I returned to my place, a warm crêpe in my hand. Katrin had taught me to make crêpes, but she was so busy talking she'd burned the first two. If only she lived in New York. Ah, Katrin!

And Rémy.

I brought the crêpe to my mouth; I smelled the butter, but I didn't taste it.

The first snow in New York. Christmas! Aunt Marie would be home by then, and André for the holidays. And I'd be there.

A family sat on the bench next to Madame Thierry, surrounded by packages and even an empty birdcage. The man's feet rested on a metal trunk. Their daughter, maybe five years old, inched her way closer, her eyes on my crêpe. She held out her hand, but her mother reached for her. "*Non.*"

"It's all right," I said, smiling at the little girl.

The mother leaned down toward her. "She's saving her crêpe for later."

Why couldn't I eat it?

I heard the chug of the train, the shrill whistle. People rushed for bags, for trunks. Someone called, "Where are you, Charles? Hurry."

I tapped Madame Thierry on the shoulder. "Time to go."

She jumped. "I've been looking all over for you."

Sure! "Sorry," I said as I helped her to her feet.

The train pulled in, and pigeons flew up, feathers floating.

I remembered leaving Katrin. "*I've always wanted to see a buffalo. I'm going to write books,*" she'd said. "*Tons of them.*"

And Rémy: "*Don't go back, Gen.*"

But Mémé!

How had she managed to hurt herself before I left? I didn't love her. I didn't even like her. I felt a stab of anger. But could she have broken a bone? That miserable woman would have to harvest the beans, the squash, the cabbages by herself. But suppose she couldn't do all that? What would she eat this winter? I ran one hand over my arm, summer muscles.

Ridiculous.

Suppose there really was a war? I shivered. Maybe, maybe not.

Why didn't I hurry? Why didn't I take those steps as the train door opened?

Aunt Marie! *"It's not always thinking of being happy. Doing the right thing will make you happy."*

I handed my crêpe to the little girl, the lump in my throat choking me.

The train began to fill and the platform emptied. Madame Thierry walked ahead.

Still time.

"Genevieve?" she called.

I waved. "Go ahead. I can't . . ."

She didn't wait to hear the rest. Shaking her head, she stepped onto the train. The doors were closing.

Grab everything, I told myself. *Run!* I didn't do that; I stood still.

The train began to move slowly, to pick up speed. I put my arms around the stanchion as if it were alive, as if it could comfort me.

five

How could I take that endless walk back to the farm?

Folle, Mémé would say. *Crazy.*

The sun beat on my head as I dragged everything along. At the top of a hill, I moved aside as a cart lumbered by. If only I'd spent those francs on something to drink.

I'd have to leave the suitcase and the books, but not where anyone could see. I walked farther and found a spot for them in a wooded area, dotted with evergreens. I'd come back tomorrow with Sister and the cart.

I sank down next to an old tree and leaned my forehead against the bark. I saw Aunt Marie's face, her small glasses framing her blue eyes, her dark hair in a pageboy.

One day when I was little, I'd noticed our glass

doorknobs. *"Diamonds,"* I'd whispered. *"We must be rich."* Aunt Marie had put her warm arms around me. *"Any house is rich if you're in it,"* she'd said.

What would Aunt Marie think when she found out what I'd done? *The right thing!*

What would André think?

I walked farther into the woods and sat on a fallen tree trunk. My sobs were so loud that anyone coming along the road might have heard me. I wept until there were no tears left; then I left the suitcase and the string bag with the books under a patch of thick bushes.

I walked for what seemed forever, my feet blistering in the stiff patent leather shoes, the comfortable ones still inside the suitcase.

I passed the school and reached the village square, hurrying now. The shops were closed except for the bistro, where André had spent most of the summer chopping onions and carrots, washing endless dishes, and loving it all. The old men still sat in front, heads together, arguing.

Rémy opened the pharmacy door. "Gen?" In two quick steps he was standing next to me, reaching out to hug me.

For just that second I felt a burst of happiness.

"But the Germans—" he began.

The war! "I have to go." I could hardly talk.

"I'm sorry," he said. "I'm so sorry."

I nodded, then turned and kept walking. From the last hill I saw the tile roof of Katrin's farmhouse. A moment later, she came down the path, arms out. "What happened, Genevieve? Why—"

I held up my hand, out of breath. She led me toward her house. Her brother, Karl, poked his head out the door and smiled. Her mother was shelling beans at the table, her head turned, talking to someone in the next room. Were they speaking German? She looked up. "Genevieve!"

Katrin poured milk for me and I drank it leaning against the counter, gulping it down. "Thank you," I managed when the glass was almost empty.

"Why, Gen?" Katrin began, but I just shook my head. She danced around the table. "I'm so glad you stayed. I'll put you in the first book I write. In the meantime, we'll celebrate the fall together."

I was filled with homesickness, but when I listened to her, I felt better. I held the cool glass up to my hot forehead, then drank the rest.

The church bells chimed the Angelus.

Six o'clock!

I jumped up. "I have to go. But thank you for the milk." I backed out the door. Mémé might be sitting at the kitchen table, a thick stew in front of her, Sunday's leftover chicken shredded into it, with a handful of juniper berries for flavor.

What would she say?

I went along the road until her farm was in front of me: the house with the pointed roof, the barn, Sister in the field, the filthy pig rooting nearby.

Louis barked, his tail thumping, telling Mémé I was home. I knelt down beside him, my head on his, my arms around his thick fur. I hopped over the three-colored cat on the step, then went inside.

Mémé wasn't at the table. She was stretched out on the long bench next to the hearth, her foot raised. When she saw me, her hand went to her mouth, my long-dead grandfather Victor's ring loose on her finger.

I sank onto a chair, easing off my Sunday shoes, wiggling my toes in the heavy stockings.

"What are you doing here?" She almost bit off the words.

What could I say? "Your ankle?" I asked.

"You've missed the train, the ship. Headlong! Do you ever think?"

The tears in my eyes were tears of rage. "I came back to—"

"Help me?" She blew air between her lips.

I wouldn't give her the satisfaction. "No!"

"All that money for tickets," she said. "Wasted!"

I caught my breath. Aunt Marie saving money for months, all for my trip. But not for André. He'd used his restaurant money. Why hadn't I remembered that? I felt sick to my stomach.

I stamped over to the hearth and heated two bowls of chicken stew. I sawed off two slabs of bread and brought hers over to the small table next to the couch.

"You'll have to write to the cousin," Mémé said, not touching the stew.

I wanted to cover my ears. I slammed my bowl down on the large table. I sat with my back toward her, so I couldn't see her angry face, and spooned in the salty stew, suddenly not hungry.

"A disruption in my life," I thought I heard her whisper.

At home, André cooked every Sunday, thick beef

stews in the winter, cold tomato soups on hot summer days. We'd sit around the kitchen table, the three of us, talking, laughing.

I had to stop thinking of it. I couldn't let myself cry again. I left the kitchen a little later, seeing that Mémé hadn't touched her food.

Upstairs, I threw myself on the bed. A piece of straw poked through the mattress, and I pulled it out. At home every night, I'd hear the mournful wail of the Long Island train as it passed the Higbie Avenue station. I'd cuddle deeper under the covers, cozy and warm.

André would have put his arms around me and told me not to cry. *Everything will be all right,* he'd have said.

But it wouldn't be all right. I turned my head into the musty pillow. I'd made a terrible mistake.

six

It was barely light when I threw on a dress I'd forgotten to pack and scrambled under the bed for the wooden sabots. No more feeling sorry for myself! No more thinking about the ship sailing west. There was nothing I could do about it but write to Cousin Ellen. I'd tell her I was staying in Alsace. I'd say that Aunt Marie would be happy that I'd be with my dear grandmother. *Dear grandmother.* Such a lie!

I'd write to Aunt Marie too, a letter that would stay in the mailbox at home for months. I'd remind her of doing the right thing. I'd promise we'd be together by Christmas. After all, how long could a war last? A couple of weeks? A month or two?

André's note would be easy. He always understood everything, so I'd barely have to explain.

Louis lay on the rag rug, his dark eyes following me as I moved around the room. "Oh, Louis," I said. "I forgot to put you out last night." I was glad, though. I was beginning to love this dog!

We went down the narrow stairs together. No matter how early I'd been up all summer, Mémé was always awake, dressed, her hair in a tight bun. Elsie would be tethered out back, already milked. Sister would be frolicking in the field after her quiet night in the barn, and the pig would be wandering around, snuffling and snorting.

But not this morning. Mémé still hadn't moved from the bench, and the stew had congealed in the bowl.

"You can't lie there forever," I said, ready to ask how I could help her.

"You're thirteen years old. Don't tell me what to do."

Impossible.

I tried again. "Can I get you something for your ankle?"

She stared out the window. "The animals," she said. "The horse, the cow . . ."

I nodded. "Do you need a doctor?"

She shook her head. "It will heal by itself."

I grabbed a chunk of bread, slathered it with jam and went outside. The three-colored cat stared up at me with her great yellow eyes. I grinned at her. "Not too friendly, I see, but how about a quick pat?"

I reached out, but she was having none of my friendship. Claws unsheathed, she raked my hand.

"Next time," I said over my shoulder, and hurried to the barn. I gave Sister her oats and scattered seed for the chickens. Slop went into the pig trough, and I managed to milk the cow. I wouldn't have known how to do any of it early this summer. Still it took half the morning.

"Genevieve," Katrin called, and trudged up the gravel path.

I went to meet her and we sat on the stone steps outside the kitchen door.

"My poor friend," she said, her face earnest. "You're the best person I know. Staying here for that old woman."

I glanced back at the window. Had Mémé heard?

But Katrin was on to something else. "Wait until you see Monsieur Henri, the history teacher. He's in love with himself and his swept-back hair."

School! I'd forgotten that too. New teachers, new kids.

"You'll have to learn German," Katrin said.

I shook my head. Aunt Marie was a language

teacher. At home, she spoke French to us one day, Alsatian another, and sometimes, she threw in an afternoon of German. I'd have no problem with that.

"*Guten Morgen*," Katrin said. "Know what that means?"

"Good morning. I'm not a complete idiot." Then it came to me. My clothes. My books. How had I forgotten them? I scrambled up.

"What?" Katrin asked.

"I left my things..." I hurried along the driveway and burst into the kitchen. Mémé was up, leaning against the table.

"Could I take the cart?" I rushed through the rest of it: my heavy suitcase, the string bag, the woods.

"Go ahead," Mémé said, and under her breath, "Why am I not surprised?"

In the barn, I harnessed Sister to the cart. Imagine Aunt Marie seeing me do that! Before I came to Alsace, I'd never seen a horse or cart up close, much less a harness.

We came around the driveway, and Katrin climbed up next to me. "We'll drive toward the railroad station," I told her.

As we passed the village, Madame Jacques was at

the pâtisserie window, shocked to see me. She raised her hand to wave.

Katrin and I searched, staring at trees, at bushes, climbing off the cart and wandering through the woods. But as the sun went down, we had to give up.

Mémé had managed to put a plate of cheese on the table, with cold sausages and bread. She was sitting at the table. We ate silently, but then I began, the words almost forced out of my mouth. "I have nothing else to wear, Mémé."

"You didn't find your suitcase." Mémé chewed on her lips, a miserable habit, especially since I'd noticed I did the same thing. "I've resigned myself. You are head-strong and forgetful, and I will have to live with that."

It was unbearable to think that I was one bit like her. "I'm not," I blurted.

Mémé raised wispy eyebrows and motioned to me to help her take the steps to her bedroom upstairs. I opened the door thinking the room reminded me of her, everything neat, the quilt soldier-straight. Only the coral necklace looped across the top of her dresser seemed out of place.

Mémé sank down in the chair next to the window,

and I saw then that she'd managed to wrap a cloth around her ankle.

Across the room where she must have seen it every morning was a painting. I knew nothing about art, but I could see how beautiful it was. I couldn't stop staring at it: two girls wearing red skirts, blouses with puffy white sleeves, and huge black bows in their hair. They stood in a field, with woven baskets of plums in their arms; the light from a late-afternoon sun streamed over their shoulders.

I wanted to stand there and drink it in forever. "The painting," I breathed.

"I'm on the right, an old friend on the left. Gérard always laughed at the bows."

I couldn't believe it: that beautiful girl, her soft dark hair flowing under the bow, her smooth hands grasping the basket. *Miel. Honey.* And my father laughed? A surprise!

"Open the armoire door," she said. Dresses hung in a row, shoes marched along underneath. "Choose."

I shook my head. "Whatever you want to give me."

"Humility doesn't become you."

I took a thick knitted sweater off the top shelf, then

slipped two dresses from their hangers. She had sewn them by hand, as she had all her clothing. Her stitches were tiny and even, not like my own when I had to make an apron in school last year. "Mile-long stitches wandering all over the fabric," Mrs. Rizzo, the sewing teacher, had sniffed.

"Ah, something else," Mémé said. "I'd forgotten about this. Gérard's notebook is there too. Take it."

"I'm really sorry," I said. If only she'd say she was grateful I'd stayed. "Please tell me what you did to your ankle."

She hesitated. "A fall in the field. It will heal." She pointed to the dresser. "Underwear in the drawer."

I took a couple of pairs, bleached and clean, fit for a woman over sixty.

"I'll just stay here now," she said, so I bundled everything in my arms and nodded thanks.

She held up her hand. "It's all right."

I knew it wasn't all right, but I kept going down the hall and into my bedroom.

I sat on the bed, the straw crackling, to open the notebook. What could that grim-faced man have written? But maybe not a man! Maybe a boy who liked meringues and laughed over huge bows!

As I opened the book, I saw that he wasn't a very good student. Pages were marked with the teacher's red pencil: *poor, terrible work, Gérard, be more careful.*

In the back, doodles! And on the last page, he'd drawn a picture of a girl with loopy curls and a long, skinny neck. There was a big X over her. *Suzanne talks too much. She tells the teacher everything.*

I had to smile. My father's notebook was just like mine when I was in third or fourth grade. His Suzanne was just like Ruthie, a girl in my class whose hand was raised every two minutes to tattle on someone.

I fell asleep wondering if Suzanne, grown-up now, still lived in Alsace, and trying not to think about home.

WAR

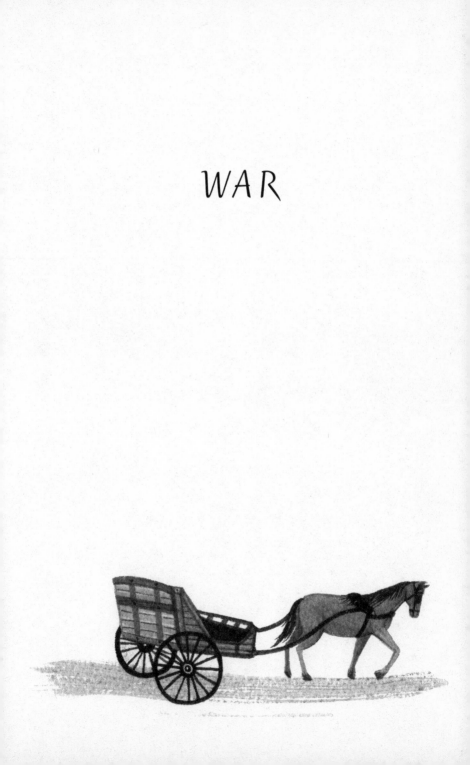

seven

Every day I waited for mail. Still nothing from André. He hated to write, I knew that from summers before. And when he did write, his letters were short and... "Useless," I'd told him.

Mémé spent most of her time at the kitchen table, and when she walked outside, I could see what an effort it took. I was beginning to realize how frail she was.

"You'll need socks," she said, unraveling the wool from old socks and knitting new ones.

Managing the animals was becoming easier. I loved the smell of hay in the barn, Elsie looking back at me as I milked her, and the hens clucking in their pen. I learned how to hang the herbs from the small garden on hooks so they'd dry. The kitchen smelled of thyme, and rosemary, and dill.

One morning, when I came downstairs, Mémé was

listening to the radio play the French national anthem. She looked up, her bony fingers knotted together, gray wool on the table in front of her. "We're at war." She stared at me. "You know now what you've done."

I raised my chin, but I couldn't think of anything to say.

News of the soldiers fighting farther west came during the next few days. The Germans had barreled through the massive trenches the French had built, and even gone around them in their tanks and jeeps. Everyone along the German border was evacuated for safety, and we were all given gas masks.

I was afraid, but Mémé said only, "We're lucky to be five miles from the border. I couldn't bear to leave the farm."

That fall was chilly, with drenching rains. School was closed; Monsieur Henri and some of the other teachers were in the army. "It's the best thing to come out of this war," Katrin said.

And it gave me time to do the chores. Mémé worked hard, I knew that, but everything was an effort for her, and I scurried around, feeding animals, pulling up cabbages, trying to do what had to be done, even though she was as miserable as ever. The cat still glared at me, and I'd given her a name now, Tiger.

Then it was December. Why had I thought the war would be over before Christmas? *Aunt Marie coming down the attic stairs, balancing boxes of ornaments and garlands to trim the tree. Presents for each other.*

Aunt Marie would be home now, knowing what I'd done.

She wrote a tearstained letter. *You say I told you to do the right thing. What I meant by that was doing your homework and cleaning your bedroom. I am so angry, Geneviève, and terrified for you. I am frantic for your safety, but there's no way I can think of to get you home. Be careful. I love you so much.*

In bed I stared at the crack that ran along the ceiling. Aunt Marie had never been angry with me before. Not once, as long as I could remember. "Homesick," I whispered. It really was a sickness; my eyes burned, my chest was tight. I fell asleep to dream of our tree last year with its ornaments and silver tinsel shining like thin icicles.

And then it was Christmas Eve. That day, a small goose lay in a roasting pan, and a box was at my plate. Mémé turned from the sink. "Open it."

Inside were small wooden figures: a horse with a flowing tail, a cat, a dog like Louis, a reindeer with antlers, and a house that was a miniature of Mémé's. "Jean, the woodcutter, carved them for the tree long ago," she said. "Except for the cat. That was your father's work." She held it up. "He was sixteen."

The cat was a mess, one leg shorter than the other, an ear missing, its wire whiskers bent. I grinned, and even Mémé smiled a little.

In the center of the table was a wooden shoe, almost the size of my foot. "My father made it for me when I was ten," she said. "Leave it at the hearth. Perhaps Père Noël will have something for you." She piled ingredients on the table: nutmeg and ginger, flour, a few eggs, a pitcher of milk, and a tin pan shaped like a boy.

Gingerbread!

Later, from the window, she pointed to a small tree at the edge of the field. "Chop it down," she said.

"You think I could chop down a tree?" I could hear the surprise in my voice, and without thinking, blurted, "You want a Christmas tree?"

"Christmas trees began in Alsace," she said, as if she couldn't believe I didn't know that.

"I found it in the woods." He grinned, his eyes dancing. "It was open, so I went through it. . . ."

My underwear? My face was hot.

"American clothes." It was almost as if he knew what I was thinking.

I swallowed. "Thank you. I'm so glad to have it."

"Merry Christmas, Gen." He went along the gravel path, waving back at me.

It wasn't until later that I realized the string bag with the books was missing.

Had someone taken them? I wondered.

eight

School began after the holidays, when I'd hoped to get through the year without it. "Don't worry," Katrin said as we walked; she linked her arm in mine. "It will be fine. You'll see."

I looked at her smiling face, her plump cheeks. She was almost like the sister I'd never had.

And she was right; it was fine. The schoolyard was filled, and in two minutes she'd pulled me over to a couple of girls. "This is Genevieve," she said, "a new friend."

They grinned as Katrin pointed to each one. "Liane plays the piano, even in her head," she said. "Aline is the best at math, and Yvonne is so shy, she barely talks."

I saw Rémy on the other side of the yard and he raised one hand, waving.

Then it was time for classes. Not so different from home! The days went by with homework and chores. Mémé taught me to cook spaetzle, a pasta I'd never tasted before, and spicy bread with dried pears. Snow came and then thawed. I tried to coax friendship from Tiger with tiny morsels of chicken. Then the sun grew warmer. Home seemed forever away. But by the time school ended for the summer, I didn't have to worry about school anymore, and I'd made friends.

I had something else to worry about. Something much worse! In June, Paris fell and France lost the war. What would happen now? But those who had been evacuated from the border began to wander back, and everything seemed the same in the village.

The strawberries were ripe, lettuce grew in rows and asparagus fronds waved in the breeze. Overhead, bees flitted among the peach blossoms. Katrin and I sat on the steps, waving our hands to keep them away.

"Loud, aren't they!" she said, her face to the sun.

Too loud.

"Not bees," I said.

The rumble grew louder. Katrin tilted her head. "What could it be? Motors?"

I clutched her arm as we stared down the road. "Germans!"

She patted my hand. "I'm not afraid."

I turned to the window. Mémé was behind the curtain. "Come inside, Genevieve." She tapped the pane with her thimble. "Come now."

"You too, Katrin," I said.

She shook her head, her curls flying. "I'm going to watch."

"Genevieve," Mémé said urgently.

Motorcycles with sidecars came down the road, sending up clouds of dust, the drivers' faces half-covered by helmets. I edged my way inside and peered out the window with Mémé. A jeep stopped in front, and one of the soldiers motioned to Katrin. My mouth went dry as she walked toward him.

The soldier pointed, and Katrin glanced back at the house. They talked for a moment before he roared away in his jeep. I held the door open for her, but only a few inches.

"What did he say?" I asked.

"He wanted to know who lived here and how many rooms there were. He said he liked the house and he'd be back. Exciting, isn't it!"

Mémé's back was rigid, and I felt a tick in my throat. But gradually the motors died away, and Katrin went out through the field to her house.

Mémé and I sank down at the table. "The soldiers are here to stay," she said. "Officers might want places to sleep."

"Will they put us out? Where would we go?"

"There's that." Was that fear in her voice? "Maybe they'll just take a room or two."

Nazis in the house? Here with us?

In the next few weeks, scores of people came down the road. The Germans were deporting Jewish people and families of men who'd fought against them in the Great War. Some of the people carried children, others staggered along with bundles in their arms or pulled small wagons piled high. They looked hot and tired.

"They weren't even allowed to take their money, or gold, or jewelry, not even their wedding rings," Mémé said bitterly. "They have nothing left. Their homes are gone, all their things."

I pictured myself on that road, walking, not knowing where I was going. I tried not to think of soldiers invading our house.

nine

Summer was almost over. I saw jeeps going by, but the Germans didn't bother us.

"Not yet," Mémé said.

The fields were bursting with vegetables ready to be harvested. I did most of the chores, but Mémé helped as much as she could, her jaws clenched, never complaining.

I'd been here more than a year. A second tearstained letter had gotten through from Aunt Marie. With every word, I could see how frightened she was for me. I kept writing to her, though, hoping my mail would arrive, telling her I was sorry but that I was all right and I'd come home when I could. Most of all, I told her I loved her.

These days I was up earlier than usual, rolling out of bed, my eyes still half-closed, my back and shoulders

"How did they know? Who told them?" I asked.

Mémé's face was stony. "We always have a pig. Everyone knows that."

"Yes, everyone," Katrin said. "We lost our pig to them yesterday. And the cow too." She leaned forward, whispering. "We're hiding food now, as much as we can. I think everyone will be doing that."

On the way to school, I couldn't stop thinking of the pig and the meat that wouldn't be ours this winter. I thought about how all of us would manage to hide food.

We reached the square and stopped. The Germans had toppled a stone statue of a French soldier from the Great War. A cloud of gray rose from the base, and small chunks were scattered underneath.

I wondered if we'd be late, but it didn't matter. Everyone was still outside the school, gathered around a paper taped to the wall: it was a long list with a huge black VERBOTEN printed across the top. *Forbidden.*

We couldn't speak French anymore. Our names and street names would be changed to German. Wedding rings had to be worn on the right hand in the German way.

Katrin twitched her shoulder. "Not important."

I stared at her.

"Many people here speak German all the time, especially those who were alive when Alsace belonged to Germany. Now we'll all think German, speak German. We'll have to be German."

She pointed to the list with one finger. "Listen to this. Radios have to be turned in to the village hall. And something else . . ."

I leaned forward. On the bottom of the list I read: *All books not written in German must be burned immediately!*

Where were my books, one in French, the others in English, and my name in all of them? Who had them now?

All I could think of was that list and what it meant. I wouldn't be able to keep my French name, and André had told me that Mémé had never taken her wedding ring off. Now she'd have to change it to her other hand.

Inside after art class, the principal came in, with a man following. The principal spoke in German: "Welcome your new history teacher, Herr Albert."

"Where's Monsieur Henri?" someone asked. It was what all of us were wondering.

There was no expression on the principal's face. "He is no longer with us."

The new teacher spoke up. "In prison, of course. He was a soldier, after all."

The new teacher's sleeves didn't cover his wrists. His pants were baggy. He snapped his feet together, then raised his arm in the Hitler salute. *"Guten Morgen."*

"Guten Morgen," we parroted back, and sank into our seats as the principal went out the door.

Herr Albert asked our names, pointing from desk to desk. Immediately after the last student spoke, he repeated them, all of them correct. Herr Albert might look sloppy, but his brain was sharp. He wasn't finished, though; he changed some of our names on the spot. Yvonne became Helga; I became Gerta.

He glanced at the tricolor flag hanging in front. With one motion he pulled it down and dropped it into the wastebasket. "No need for this anymore." He ignored the gasps that came from the back of the room.

He reached into his valise and took out the Nazi flag with its swastika like a black spider. He unfolded it and, reaching up, threaded it into the holder.

Liane looked down at her desk and moved her fingers, playing an imaginary piano. Claude looked furious, and my chest felt tight, almost as if someone were squeezing me too hard.

Herr Albert rubbed his hands together. "We'll begin our study of history now." He pointed to the wall map. "Alsace is a strip of land between the Vosges Mountains and the Rhine River," he said, as if every five-year-old in Alsace didn't know that. "It was German from 1871 to the end of the First World War. Then, sadly, it became French."

By this time he'd lost us. Katrin and I passed notes back and forth, choosing crazy names for everyone in the class. I jumped as I realized Herr Albert was standing in front of me. "There's no time for gossip in my room." He leaned closer. "In the seventeen hundreds you would have to walk through the village wearing the Klapperstein."

What was he talking about? Katrin looked as confused as I was. But he went on. "A huge stone. Gossips wore it around their necks, weighing them down."

Laughter bubbled up as I thought of our wearing it, inching our way through the village. Katrin bit her lip, trying to look serious.

Herr Albert's face changed. No longer did he look like a messy teacher, but more like someone to fear. "We are German now," he said. "And you will see change all over Europe."

I swallowed and looked down at my desk as he crumpled Katrin's note. If only this terrible day would end.

ten

$\mathcal{The}$ next Saturday, I came into the kitchen carrying cabbages, almost like babies, from the wheelbarrow.

Mémé locked the door behind me. "We have things to do."

I nibbled at a square of cheese from the table as she dropped a rubber mat in front of the armoire. "You might as well know about this," she said. "I'll let you help me."

She was impossible, I told myself for the hundredth time. I pushed back my chair and stood up as she straightened the mat with one foot. "We must move the armoire, and the stone floor can't be marked."

What was she talking about? How could we move that huge cabinet? How could I do it? She had no strength left.

"I moved this in the Great War with Gérard," she said. "Push, Genevieve."

Inch by inch, I managed to open a space behind the armoire, wide enough to squeeze through. I stared into that dusty space, almost the size of the pantry.

"But why . . . ," I began.

"A place to store food, to keep us alive. Do you think I'd let the Germans come in here and take everything?"

I raised my hand to my throat.

She handed me a rag and I slid inside to wipe down the shelves. We went from pantry to armoire, filling them.

"Take only half. We have to eat, after all."

Almost finished, I kept looking at the shelves. The vegetables inside the glass jars were almost like jewels, the green beans, the golden pears, the red peppers. I tripped and the last jar of tomatoes slipped out of my hands. Mémé wasn't paying attention, though. It was as if she hadn't heard the glass smashing, or seen the red swath spreading around the broken jar. She pinched my sleeve. "We can't trust anyone. Tell no one, Genevieve."

I thought of the people I'd met here: Rémy, Madame Jacques at the bakery, her son, Claude, even

Monsieur Philippe, the bookseller, with his thick lips and unfriendly face.

Katrin and I talked about everything: how much money the bistro owner had hidden under his mattress, how many tarts Madame Jacques ate every day, how many hours Liane played the piano.

And Mémé. Of course, Mémé.

I knelt to pick up the shards of glass.

"You'll see," Mémé said. "There are those who are French, and others who are German sympathizers."

I nodded uncertainly.

"Promise me. Give me your word."

"All right." I crossed my fingers. I didn't bother to look at her. Surely it was all right to tell Katrin.

Slowly I pushed the armoire back into place, thinking of my father doing this so many years ago.

There was only the half-filled pantry to tell us what we'd done.

A mistake. I knew it right away, and maybe the young soldier did too. He bent his head.

"Ah." The officer laughed. "I'll just borrow them both."

"Please," I began, but I couldn't stop him.

He climbed the fence, whistling for Sister. She came immediately, hoping for a sugar cube or an apple slice, and he opened the gate for her. He snapped his fingers at the young soldier. "Get the cart from the barn. Harness her."

The young soldier's face was red, his freckles standing out. Did he feel sorry for me?

Moments later, Sister and the cart were gone, rattling up the road toward the village. I felt tears of grief. What would André have done? Worse, what would Mémé say? I flew upstairs. She was in her bedroom, a mop in her hand. "Oh, Mémé, he took the horse."

She looked up. "What are you talking about?"

"And the cart. An officer."

The mop slid away from her. "My horse?"

Would she yell at me? Cry the way I was crying? Instead she clenched her hands into fists. "An old horse." She raised her head. "A rickety cart."

eleven

𝒥𝓃 November, a mild wind swept over the field. "A good day to air the quilts," Mémé said.

I came around the side of the house with a quilt to hang, and stopped. An officer stood there, medals weighing down his uniform. A soldier stood behind him, his face covered with freckles; he must have been André's age.

I hugged the quilt to me. Where was Mémé?

The officer pointed, his boot resting on the bottom rail of the fence. "There's a horse in the field."

I glanced toward Sister.

He smiled with perfect teeth. "As long as we're all Germans, we have to share everything. What's the horse's name?"

"Sister. No one rides her. We just harness her up to the cart..."

"Why are you saying that? She's a wonderful horse, and without the cart we can't go far."

"There's nothing we can do," Mémé said.

"Could we complain to someone?"

"Better to keep still. We don't want to be noticed."

It was too late; we had been noticed. Toward the end of the day, another German came, riding a motorcycle. He left it in front and strolled around to the back of the house, his boots heavy on the gravel.

Mémé was still in her bedroom. I called her from the stairs. "A German is outside."

"I'll be right there," she said.

She came down a few minutes later, but she didn't wait for him to knock. "Can I help you?" she said as she opened the door.

"You have a big house, with only the two of you?"

She barely nodded.

How did he know that? And then I realized. He must have been the German who'd spoken to Katrin!

"You have extra rooms, then," he said. "Perhaps . . ."

He went past her, through the kitchen into the hall. "The stairs?"

"There's a room down here," Mémé said, the German words sounding strange on her tongue.

"I wouldn't want to disturb you. Let's see what's on the second floor."

What could we do? We followed him upstairs, Mémé walking slowly as she'd done all year. We watched as he opened doors and stopped at her room, his hand on the molding.

The painting was gone. A pale square against darker paint stood out on the wall. He noticed it too. He walked in, circled the bed and stared, his hands clenched behind his back.

Mémé started back down the hall toward the stairs.

"Frau," he called after her, his voice sharp.

She turned, waiting. Louis padded up the stairs and stood close to her. Even the dog knew something was wrong. Mémé put her hand on his head.

"Is the dog vicious?" the soldier asked.

"Certainly not."

"Yes. We wouldn't want to get rid of him."

My heart was pounding. First Sister. Now Louis?

"What hung on the wall?" The German ran one finger over the pale square.

She didn't hesitate. "A mirror. Shattered."

He glanced at me, and my eyes slid away from him; I

stared down at the floor. Was that the edge of the frame just under the bed?

He stood at the dresser now, running his fingers over Mémé's necklace. "This room will do nicely. I'll bring my things this afternoon."

We couldn't look at him. He'd just changed our lives.

"Perhaps I'll see the shards from the mirror later," he said as he went downstairs. "But in the meantime, hang something pleasant to look at."

Mémé leaned against the wall, and I bent to bury my cheek in Louis's fur. "It's under the bed," I whispered.

"Yes. But first, we want to be sure he's gone. He can guess the painting is valuable."

I went down to the hall window, and she was right. The motorcycle was still there. I edged my way along the hall, peering into the kitchen.

He was standing at the massive sink. I backed away and up the stairs. Moments later, I heard the roar of the motorcycle. "He's gone."

"We'll use the space overhead," Mémé said. "It was meant for workers a hundred years ago. A pull-down stair went up from your bedroom, but Gérard plastered it over during the Great War, so there's only one way to get there."

She slid the painting from under the bed and wrapped it in a pillowcase. "You'll have to go out on the roof from your bedroom, Genevieve."

How could I do that? The drop was terrifying. She stared at me, almost daring me to say I couldn't do it. I knew what would happen. She'd try it herself, never mind the ankle that still gave her trouble. There she'd be, a bag of bones rolling down the slanted roof and hitting the gravel far below.

We went into my room, and I opened my window, staring out, trying not to look down.

"Climb onto the sill," Mémé said.

It was much wider than the one at home. I put one knee up, then the other, crouching, moving outside, my hands glued to the bottom of the frame.

"Reach up, Genevieve. You'll feel the ledge at the top of the window."

I leaned back, one hand still clutching the frame, the other reaching . . .

And grasped it. It took forever to make myself stand on the top of the ledge, three stories above the ground.

The wind pulled at my dress and hair; behind me came the steady tap-tapping of loose tiles.

I touched the window above and, stretching, managed to shove it open, my heart fluttering.

"Good." Mémé held the painting up to me, the pillowcase flapping.

Then, the rumble of a motor. Was the officer back? He couldn't have gone far.

I pushed the painting inside and saw him at the end of the gravel path. I scrambled into a small room, the dust thick on the floor, cobwebs like fine net stretched across the corners. I huddled there, shaking, the painting in my arms. Vaguely, I heard Mémé shut the bedroom window below.

After a while, I rested the painting against the wall, careful to avoid jutting nails. On the floor was a thin straw mattress, and I crouched down on it, trembling. "All right," I whispered, "I'm all right."

I ran my hand over the dusty floor at my side, feeling grit under my nails. And then I felt something else. Deep cuts had been carved into the wood, almost the size of my fists. I ran my fingers over them, realizing they were letters, *G.M.*

My father's initials, for his name, Gérard Michel. My initials too.

Without thinking, I patted the carving almost as if I might be patting Louis's broad head. For the first time, I didn't visualize a grim-faced man with a beard. I saw someone my age, kneeling there, carving.

The initials had been here all this time, almost as if they were waiting to find me.

And something else. As the sun began to set, it threw light on the opposite wall so I could see stick figures of two girls wearing enormous bows, and the face of a boy with a huge smiling mouth.

My father? A boy. Not the funny drawing of a grumpy man. I felt warmth spread through my chest. But I went back to thinking of the German soldier invading our farmhouse. Wouldn't he want to know where I was?

twelve

Wrapping my arms around my waist, I tried to keep warm. I kept sneezing from layers of dust, but I must have slept.

I dreamed of a house, roses growing in front. Our own house in Springfield Gardens. Home.

I awoke to the sound of wind, stronger now. Outside, there was almost no light. I stood up, but I couldn't see if the motorcycle was still on the path.

Was the officer in the house? I'd take a chance and slide down the roof, leaving the painting safe against the wall.

I could do it.

I climbed out backward, leaning hard against the sloping roof. I found my window ledge with one foot, crouched and grabbed it with both hands, my feet sliding down to the stone sill.

Mémé was there. She steadied my legs, then held my waist, guiding me into the bedroom. "I told him you were resting, that you had a headache," she whispered. "We'll go along the hall quietly, past my room, where he stares at a terrible painting I've placed on the wall, and soils my quilt with his boots. We'll tiptoe downstairs and fortify ourselves for whatever we'll have to deal with."

What we dealt with first was arranging the extra bedroom beyond the kitchen for us both, pulling quilts and pillows out of the chest. We'd leave upstairs for him.

At the kitchen table, I made myself eat. I was worn out, and so glad André was safe at college in New York.

"One more thing." Mémé spoke as if the words were being forced out of her. "Louis must go."

"Please, no." He was under the table, his muzzle on my instep. "He'll be quiet. He's such a good dog, so gentle."

She peered up at the ceiling as if she could see the German officer on the second floor. "The dog needs to be safe." She hesitated. "I would take him, but I don't want you alone here with the German."

"Louis loves us."

She raised one hand to stop my words. "You'll go through the field, over the wall, and find Jean, the woodcutter. He's a kind man. He'll keep Louis close so he can't come back to us. Maybe someday . . ."

I was crying again. Everyone I loved was disappearing, everyone was flying away.

I went to the door, and Louis followed me outside, almost as if he understood what was happening.

Tonight there was only a sliver of moon. I hesitated until my eyes became used to the shape of the field and the forest beyond. We walked slowly, Louis leading me now, until we crossed the low stone wall.

I stopped, hearing voices. I reached for Louis's collar, but my fingers slid along his back and he kept going.

"It's the Michels' dog," someone said.

I knew the voice.

The woodcutter answered, "Yes, his name is Louis."

I went forward to see Rémy crouched on the ground, petting the dog. The woodcutter turned as he heard me.

"My grandmother asked if you would take Louis for us," I said.

"A good dog. But why?"

"A German officer is going to stay at the house. He doesn't like dogs, and we're afraid . . ." I couldn't finish.

Rémy looked up at me, his eyes burning. "What kind of a man dislikes dogs?"

The woodcutter put his broad hand on my shoulder. "Tell Elise . . . . Tell your grandmother . . ." He shook his head. "She'll know." He reached for Louis's collar.

"I'll bring back food for him," I said.

He waved his hand. "No need, I'll take care of him." Then it was almost as if he and the dog melted into the trees, in front of me one moment, gone the next.

"I'm sorry, Gen," Rémy said. "Really sorry you're not back in your New York." He smiled. "But think how lucky you are to be at your grandmother's beautiful farm."

I had to smile too. I lifted one hand, then went across the wall to Mémé, wondering what Rémy was doing there.

A few days later I was on my way to meet Katrin for school when the German officer cornered me at the end of the path. "Where's the dog, *Fraülein?*"

I stared at the ground. Mémé and I should have decided what to say to him, but we'd never thought he'd be interested enough to ask.

Digging my toe into the gravel, I tried to think. "He ran away."

"An old dog like that?"

"He does that sometimes."

"Then he'll be back."

"I don't know."

But he'd lost interest in Louis and me. He straddled his motorcycle and sped away.

Katrin waited for me at her gate, ready to talk, but I raised my hand, saying, "Wait," while I thought about how I'd tell her what had happened.

We kept going, but finally I held up my hand again. "Listen." I was almost whispering.

Katrin turned, her head close to mine. "What is it?"

By the time we saw the school, I'd told her everything I could think of: the attic room, the painting, Louis.

I wondered what Mémé would say if she knew. But she wouldn't know. Katrin would keep our secret, I was sure of it.

thirteen

It was hard to concentrate in school. My thoughts wandered to the German officer, who would be looking over our shoulders all the time now, to Louis, who used to pad up to my bedroom at night. I made myself think of happier things: my father's carving, Rémy's smile. I grinned to myself, picturing Tiger, the three-colored cat who reminded me a little of Mémé with her suspicious eyes, her unfriendly face.

At last, it was time to go home. Katrin and I reached the square and saw soldiers in front of the bookshop. Monsieur Philippe came outside with a pile of books in his arms. He dropped them in the street and went back for more.

"French books," Katrin whispered.

Soldiers drenched them with a can of something—turpentine, maybe—and threw a match onto the pile. Philippe stood there talking with them as flames shot up, devouring the books. He kicked one farther into the fire; the pages curled up, lighted and were gone. Didn't he care?

One of the soldiers elbowed him, laughing, and Philippe said, "Enough of the French, eh?"

I couldn't watch anymore. "Let's go," I told Katrin.

At the end of the square, I glanced down the alley to see Rémy with a piece of chalk in his hand. He drew lines on the stone, then disappeared toward the back of the pharmacy. "What was he doing?"

"Drawing the Cross of Lorraine."

"But what does it mean?"

"It's a symbol from the medieval days. Free France!" She frowned. "If you look, you'll see it everywhere. The Germans can't bear it. They're making people wash it off, or paint over it. And if they ever catch anyone doing it, there'll be trouble, arrests and maybe worse."

Why had Rémy taken such a chance?

We walked the rest of the way, both of us quiet. I left her at her gate and crossed the wall. There was just enough ink in my pen to draw the cross on one of the stones.

Free France.

Mémé was in the kitchen, her left finger bandaged,

covering her ring. She must have heard about the new rules. "I won't take it off," she said fiercely.

I slid into the chair across from her.

"The Germans came today. They've taken the cow." She spread her hands wide. "The hens too."

I felt the tears that had been threatening all day.

"They've left almost nothing," she said.

"The bicycles?"

"Still there."

"They were too old, too rusty, I guess."

Mémé stood, leaning on the table for a moment, then went to the counter. "Vegetable soup. At least we'll have that. And the potatoes and apples are still in the cellar rooms."

The German came in then, without knocking. "Soup? I'll trouble you for some too."

How would we ever retrieve the food behind the armoire? The German, whose name we knew now was Fürst, appeared when we least expected him. We watched at the windows for him; still, he managed to surprise us. We had to be careful of everything we did, everything we said.

That evening, Mémé and I went to our room early. We locked the door and pulled the radio out from its hiding place under a pile of quilts, turning it on just loud enough to catch the solemn voice of the newscaster. The news had been terrible all year: so many countries had fallen to the Germans.

Before we had time to listen, a sudden boom rattled the windowpanes. In one motion, Mémé pulled back the quilt and I flew to the window, Mémé right behind me. Beyond the village was a glow of orange, almost as if the sun had risen.

Fürst's boots clumped down the stairs and stopped. Mémé threw the quilt over the radio, but he kept going through the hall and into the kitchen. The outside door slammed, and the motorcycle roared as he sped toward the village.

"What is it?" I asked, but Mémé shook her head.

We watched the glow soften and eventually disappear. We went back to bed, but not to sleep until the night was almost over.

"What do you think happened?" I asked Katrin the next morning.

"My brother, Karl, told me. They blew up the railway station and ruined as much of the tracks as they could."

I thought of the station, the pigeons flying overhead,

the crêpes dotted with sugar. "Why would the Germans do that?"

She raised her eyebrows. "Are you five years old? It was the French, trying to stop the Germans from deporting people, from drafting Alsatian men to fight for them. The Resistance!"

It was the first time I'd heard that word.

We stopped at the square. Even this far from the station, smoke hung in the air with a strong smell of burning, almost like licorice. Soldiers rushed back and forth.

Outside the school, we waited for the principal to call us inside, hearing the word *Resistance* again and again, and another word, *sabotage.*

In our history class, Herr Albert called the roll, staring at each one of us as he said our names. "If anyone knows about the fire, he must tell, otherwise he will be as guilty as the saboteurs."

My heart thumped. He made me feel as if I were in danger, even though I didn't know anything about it. I was glad to escape from his room and go to the science laboratory, where the teacher filled bottles with different-colored water that seemed to be useless.

That afternoon, Mémé sat in the rocker knitting

socks. "Rémy's father has been arrested," she said. "He's been taken to Shirmeck prison. Clara Moeller stopped by to tell me."

I could hardly breathe. "What about Rémy's mother and his little sister, Cécile?"

"They were lucky. A courier will take them to Switzerland."

I could hardly get the word out. "Rémy?"

"Missing. If they find him . . ."

I thought of the Cross of Lorraine, and Rémy at the woodcutter's the other day. Was he there now?

The door opened and Fürst came in. "It's snowing," he said in a pleasant voice.

Mémé turned away from him, and I pretended I didn't see him go toward the coal stove and bend over it. I knew it was cold and empty.

"You'll have to use more fuel, Frau Meyer," he said, using our new German name. "Don't hoard it. We'll all be sick from the drafts."

Mémé's back stiffened.

He saw my eyes. He must have known I hated him. There wasn't enough coal to last the winter. But what did he care? He wanted to be warm now. And later?

Maybe he'd find somewhere else to stay. I could only hope that.

He went up to the bedroom, and Mémé laid her knitting on the table. "I wouldn't ask this . . ."

"You don't have to ask. I'm going to the woodcutter's to look for Rémy."

"Go now. Go carefully, though. It's cold and windy."

I wrapped my coat and one of her old scarves around me and left the house without a sound. Outside, the snow was beginning to cover the ground. I ran, slipping and sliding across the field. I didn't see the low stone wall and went headlong across it. The fall took my breath, and my knees burned, beginning to bleed.

I could almost hear Mémé's voice. "I told you."

I scrambled up. The wind was biting my face, closing my eyes so the world was hidden and everything was disappearing. I peered ahead. How could I find my way to the woodcutter's small house buried in the trees?

fourteen

The woodcutter came forward, his footsteps silent. Louis bounded toward me, his fur covered with snow, his tail waving. I leaned against him, running my hand over his head and his back. So much had happened since he'd slept at the foot of my bed.

I took a chance. "Is Rémy with you?" I whispered. "Is he all right?" If only I could see him smiling at me, or touching my shoulder.

The woodcutter bent his head close to mine. "He can't stay here safely for long." He took a breath. "His arm was burned enough to worry about infection. The Germans will be watching for that. He'll have to disappear." He shook his head. "The poor boy: his father gone, his mother and sister taking that dangerous trip to Switzerland. Even the pharmacy has been shuttered. All the medicines belong to the Germans now."

Oh, Rémy. But I knew what we had to do. Somehow we'd bring him to the house, help him across the roof and into that small attic room. "We'll take him as soon as the German sleeps," I said.

No matter what, I'd see Rémy again!

The woodcutter held Louis's collar, and I turned to stumble back over the low stone wall and crossed the field.

The German officer stood in the kitchen, leaning against the table, his coat over his shoulders. "Where have you been?"

"I told you—" Mémé began, but he raised his hand.

"Let the girl tell me herself."

What had she told him? What could I say?

I barely said anything. "The snow, lovely—" I began, and broke off. "I'm going to be sick." Hand to my mouth, I rushed past him, down the hall, and closed the bedroom door.

It was the best I could do.

Moments later, Mémé came into the room. "You never cease to surprise me, Genevieve."

I didn't tell her that I'd fallen and scraped my knees against the wall. I thought of that stone with its Cross of Lorraine, and no way to erase it. She'd say, "You don't think!"

I sat on the bed and, lips hardly moving, told her what the woodcutter had said.

She stared at the window, nodding.

I went to the half-opened bedroom door and stood, listening, until we were sure Fürst slept. The wait was endless.

"Something else to think about. We need a signal." Mémé worried her forehead with her bandaged finger. "Your father's carved cat!"

I remembered! One leg shorter than the other, wire whiskers. Christmas was coming in just a few days. Another Christmas!

"If it's safe, I'll hang the cat in the window," she said.

I nodded. I'd look for it.

It was almost midnight when I went back across the field; the snow had stopped and a misty moon gleamed overhead. The woodcutter was there waiting to lead me to his house.

Rémy lay on a cot, his eyes closed. He started up as he heard me whisper his name. "Gen!" He tried to smile, and I touched his hand, so glad to see him, but frightened about the terrible danger we were all in.

"Play with fire," he began the old saying, "you're going to get burned."

I swallowed. "I'm sorry," I said. "Really . . ."

"My father was betrayed," he said. "But who was it?"

There was anger in the woodcutter's voice. "We can't be sure of anyone."

Almost Mémé's exact words.

We left quickly, the woodcutter holding Louis's collar and talking gently to the crying dog.

Crossing the field, I watched our window. The cat wasn't there. I saw movement: Fürst, walking around the table.

I put my arms around Rémy to steady him and we sank down in the wet snow to wait. It was almost dawn, both of us shivering, when Fürst banged out of the house. I saw him kick at Tiger, who snarled and raced around the side of the house. Then Fürst straddled his motorcycle and left.

I despised him.

Mémé was at the window, hanging the cat; its wire whiskers caught the light. Her hand was raised, beckoning.

"Now," I told Rémy. We stumbled to our feet and walked across the rest of the field. Inside, Mémé slid a jar of water into my pocket for him. "A small bathroom behind the eaves," she whispered.

We took the stairs, one slow step at a time to my bedroom.

Flakes of snow swirled on the sill as I raised the window. "We have to go out there," I said. "It won't be easy."

"It's all right," he whispered.

We climbed the slippery roof together. It was much harder than the first time I'd done it. But at last, we were in that dusty room.

Rémy slid down on the straw mattress. "Thank you, Gen." His eyes closed, and he was asleep. I watched him, his fine eyelashes, his eyes moving slightly below the lids. He mumbled something—was it *planting*?

I remembered he wanted to be a farmer, to have his own field, like the one we'd seen that summer day.

How tired I was! The night was over and I hadn't slept. I couldn't wait to go downstairs and throw myself into bed.

But first, I worked off his boots and threw my coat over him, seeing that the burn on his arm was covered with torn rags.

I bent to touch my father's initials, thinking how strange it was that they comforted me. I ran my hand over the pillowcase that held the painting; it was streaked with dust. The painting shouldn't have been here.

So many things that shouldn't have been.

I climbed down to Mémé, my knees stiff, wishing I could put the painting back where it belonged.

Wishing!

My head was filled with wishes.

fifteen

Was Fürst back? I heard the sound of a motorcycle, but then it faded away.

Mémé followed me inside the bedroom, carrying a cup of broth, hot and steaming. "Don't sleep," she whispered as if he were standing in the hall.

I could hardly keep my eyes open. The wind outside was strong, the snow blowing across the field. "I have to sleep." I sank down on the edge of the bed.

"You will manage." She barely moved her lips, almost as if Fürst could hear from upstairs. "You will go to school as if everything is normal." She reached out, holding the broth to my lips.

I sipped at it. I could feel myself waking.

"Where is your coat, Genevieve?"

I pointed up.

"Never mind. You can wear mine."

"That would look normal?" In spite of myself, I grinned at her, and I thought I saw her smile. "And what about Rémy? It's so cold, so terrible up there."

"We just have to do the best we can." She went on, her head close to mine. "After school, find a way to delay."

I glanced at her determined face.

"Look at me, Genevieve. You can't let Katrin know about this."

I took a large swallow of broth, so hot it burned my tongue. "Katrin would help, I know she would."

"You don't know."

"All right."

"So. You'll go to Philippe. Tell him you have books but you want something new. He'll know we're sheltering someone, that we need help."

"I can't tell Katrin." I was filled with anger. "But you're willing to let that man know? He burns books without any feelings; he talks to the Germans."

"Genevieve, for once will you listen!"

I didn't answer. We went into the kitchen and I jammed my hat over my head, pulled on her coat and threw a woolen scarf over my shoulders. "All right," I said. There was no help for it. She'd won again.

I spent the day at school, looking out at small cyclones of snow in the air, trying to stay awake. In history, Herr Albert tapped his desk with a pointer. "What is outside, Fraülein Meyer, is not as important as the history I'm teaching."

History! Herr Albert was fascinated by history.

At last school was over. Katrin and I left, our mouths covered with scarves. I hesitated. "Forgot my book." My voice was muffled.

She glanced back toward the school, squinting against the blowing snow. "I'll come with you."

"No, it's too cold."

She nodded. I could see she was grateful as she kept going. When she was just a shadow far ahead, I glanced over my shoulder to be sure I was alone. Then I trudged toward the square.

beginning to wonder if I'd done the right thing. Overhead a clock clicked, five minutes, ten. I rapped on the door.

"Yes? Open," the voice said in German from inside.

I stood in the doorway, nervous. The doctor was rail-thin and didn't seem friendly. I wasn't his patient, after all. I tried to act as if nothing much had happened, that only a small burn from the stove had brought me here. "My grandmother needs something for a burn."

"I can't help you."

"You're a doctor."

"Think of what you're saying. The Germans have been here three times asking just that question: who in this village needs something for a burn?"

I took a breath. I understood. "But just a small—"

He wouldn't let me finish. "If they see you coming from here and find that you're carrying a jar of burn medicine, you'll be in prison, and so will I."

I backed out of the room and closed the door behind me.

It was almost dark now. Tendrils of smoke still rose in the distance from the railway station. I crossed the square, passing the butcher's shop, with empty hooks where once huge slabs of meat had hung and the bou-langerie, closed now, without bread. The pâtisserie

sixteen

$\mathcal{Soldiers}$ were billeted in the village hall now, and some of them marched along the street in pairs. An old woman had to step off the sidewalk to let them pass. I looked toward the shuttered pharmacy, thinking that the medicine Rémy needed was inside that door, but taken now by the Germans.

In front of me was a house with a pointed roof and wilted flowers in the snow-covered window boxes. I remembered it belonged to a doctor.

Suppose I went in and said my grandmother had burned herself cooking, her fingers grasping the pot handle? Why not? He could give me something to help heal that burn.

I went up the path, and saw the door was open.

No one was inside the waiting room, with its chairs in a row like a theater. I stared at the closed door in front of me, came next, with its shelves almost bare. But Madame Jacques had hung a wreath in the window. I'd almost forgotten: Christmas was in a few days. Christmas again!

I heard the loud singing of soldiers coming from the bistro. I veered past, and then I was in front of the bookshop, peering inside. Dim light came from the storage room in back. I could hardly see the books on the shelves. I trudged around to the alley.

The bookshop's small window was halfway down the alley. The back room wasn't nearly as neat as the front. The walls were unpainted, the clock had stopped at two-thirty, probably years ago, and books were stacked in an uneven pile on a table.

Philippe wasn't there. I glanced at the stairs leading up to his apartment and rapped harder. I had to get home to Rémy.

Philippe came downstairs, a napkin looped around his thick neck, looking annoyed at being disturbed.

I kept knocking. *Hurry. Hurry.*

He moved his huge girth slowly, then opened the door. By this time I'd forgotten Mémé's exact words, so I raised my shoulders. "I want a book," I whispered.

He shook his head.

"We have books—" I began.

He took a quick look down the alley, pulled me inside and pushed me onto a chair. "Never talk when you're outside." His voice was fierce.

I was almost more afraid of him than of the Germans.

"I'm Genevieve Michel," I said.

"I know who you are."

"We have books. But I want another one." My mouth trembled; in spite of myself, I was crying.

"You're too old for tears."

"Rémy . . . ," I began.

He frowned, lines creasing his wide forehead, and raised one hand.

"We have him in the attic. His arm was burned—" I bit off the words.

Philippe stared, silent.

"The doctor wouldn't give me anything for the burn."

He made a sound with his tongue. His face was filled with fury. "Doctor? You went to the doctor?"

I backed away from him. It was a mistake coming here, maybe as much as going to the doctor's. I reached for the doorknob; I'd done what I could.

Philippe held up his hand. "Can you manage for a few days?"

I wanted to say *We can manage forever*. I wanted to say *We don't need you*. But I thought of that room, cold and dark, and we did need him, or someone, to help.

He waited for me to answer. I nodded, then turned the knob and opened the door.

"Tell your grandmother I'll arrange things."

I took a last look at the back of the store and left.

Left too quickly, because I'd seen something on one of the chairs at his table. Bunched-up like a charcoal cat was a wool sweater.

I told myself we were all cold these days without enough coal to warm our stoves. But I knew! The last time I'd seen it, André was wearing that sweater.

My thoughts raced. Could Philippe have given André over to the Germans? But wasn't André safe at home in New York? Wasn't he? I shook my head, turned and went back to the bookshop. I peered in, but from where I was standing, I couldn't see the chair with the sweater. Philippe stood there, staring at a cabinet.

I rapped on the window, and he came to the door again. "What is it?" he asked, almost as if he might be saying *What now, pest?*

"The sweater."

He raised his massive shoulders.

"On the chair." I glanced toward it: a pile of books teetered there now.

"Underneath." I went toward the chair and swept my hand over the books, which toppled onto the floor. There was no sweater; the chair was empty.

I frowned up at him. "I know what I saw."

"Go home."

If only I could. "Where's my brother?"

"Hasn't he been gone since before the war?"

"What did you do with his sweater?"

Philippe shook his head, opened his mouth to say something.

"I saw it. Just now." I was trembling, angry.

"You could be dangerous," he said. "My advice is for you to avoid seeing things." He gripped my shoulder, pushed me to the door and outside; the lock snapped behind me. I pictured André, the sweater looped around his shoulders. André laughing, happy with himself, happy with me.

I slipped down the alley again, past the noisy bistro, then hurried along the empty road back to the farm.

Mémé trusted this man. It was wrong. I felt it. I was sure of it.

Where was André? Could he be here somewhere? Taken by the Germans? Had Philippe betrayed him?

But suppose it wasn't André's sweater?

No. I'd seen the pulls in the sleeve, the zipper not quite matching the color of the wool. Aunt Marie had knitted it. It couldn't have been anyone else's. How did Philippe get it?

At the farm, the motorcycle was gone. Tiger slept on the stone step. I stepped around her and, heartsick, told Mémé that I'd tried to get medicine for Rémy. "The doctor wouldn't give it to me."

She looked at me, horrified. "You asked—" She broke off. "What is the matter with you?"

She was right. I didn't think. I lost things, forgot them, and now the doctor!

But what about Monsieur Philippe? I leaned forward. "I think he sides with the Germans. We can't trust him."

She shook her head.

"But you said to trust no one."

She waved her hand. "Don't talk foolishness to me about Philippe."

I didn't say another word. But I needed someone to talk to, someone I could trust.

Katrin.

I was determined to do what I'd promised not to do. I'd tell her everything she hadn't heard so far.

Yes, in the morning, on the way to school. It was the last day before school closed for the Christmas holidays.

seventeen

$\mathcal{The}$ window rattled; someone pulled hard on my arm. I pulled the quilt up higher; I felt as if I'd just fallen asleep.

Mémé? What was she saying?

I opened my eyes and glanced toward the window. Icicles glowed silver in the dark, and sleet peppered the glass.

"Wake up, Genevieve," Mémé said urgently. "The boy is in that freezing room. He needs food and warmer clothing."

Suddenly wide awake, I threw on my clothes, and Mémé handed me two thick sweaters. "Gérard's," she said.

I pulled them on, one over the other; it was almost as if I could feel my father by wearing them. Mémé shoved a chunk of cheese, a wizened apple and a small potato that had been cooked and cooled into one huge pocket, and a jar of water into the other.

She stood at the bottom of the stairs, back rigid. "I would do this," she began, "if only..."

I touched her thin shoulder, then tiptoed upstairs. I heard a sound and turned. Fürst stood in the doorway across the hall. "It's the middle of the night, Gerta."

My heart hammered. Sleepwalking? He'd never believe it. "C-cold," I stammered. "I left my robe..." My voice trailed off.

"Even with those sweaters." He shook his head. "She doesn't give us enough heat," he said, and disappeared inside.

I went into my old bedroom, locked the door behind me and sat on the edge of the bed, shaking. Outside, the roof tiles were slick with ice. Could I open the window without a sound?

But Rémy was crouched up there with wind and cold coming in through the chinks around the window, without anything to eat. I had to do this.

It took forever to raise the icy window. Head down, I

went out; the roof tiles chattered in the wind. I climbed, the sleet stinging, forcing me to close my eyes. I reached up and held on to the sill, fingers tapping on the attic window.

Open, Rémy. Open.

He leaned out to me, his hands colder than mine.

I slid onto the floor, unable to talk, hardly able to move. He put one arm out, hugging me. *Ah, Rémy.*

"Wait." I shrugged off both sweaters. "Put them on."

He shook his head. "You'll freeze."

"Put them on right away." I sounded like Mémé.

He grinned and reached for them, wincing as he pulled a sleeve over his arm.

"Sorry," I said, wincing with him.

He shrugged. "I was too close when the explosion went off. But it was worth it, every bit of it, and it won't be the end. The Resistance fighters won't stop until the Germans are sent back across the Rhine."

If only it would happen.

"In the pockets . . . ," I began, and waited while he sat on the edge of the mattress and ate the cheese and the potato.

He held out the apple for me.

I smiled. "No. What would my grandmother say?" I whispered, even though the walls were thick and the German was on the other side of the house.

He whispered too. "What would I have done without you and your grandmother?"

"Philippe is trying to get help for you." I looked at him carefully. "Do you trust him?"

Rémy shrugged. "We can't trust anyone. But maybe he'll find a courier. He might have been the one to help my mother and sister." He hesitated, his voice thick. "If only they're safe. If only I'll see them again."

"You will. Someday," I said it fiercely, as if I believed this terrible time wouldn't last.

"Someday," he echoed, then said, "My father," and stopped, his mouth unsteady.

I dug my fingers into my own father's initials, and we listened to sleet, like pebbles, hitting the window. How terrible for Rémy to be alone without anyone to talk to, without a book to read!

"You have to go now," he said. He opened the window and helped me out. As I reached with my feet for the window below, he put his hand on my head.

I couldn't look up; the sleet was sharp against my head. My foot slipped on the icy tiles, and Rémy grabbed my hand, holding me until I slid farther down. Moments later, I reached my window, terrified that I'd see Fürst staring out at me.

But the door is locked, I told myself. I raised the icy window and went inside, wiping my hands and legs on the quilt—*Sorry, Mémé*—and spotted the gloves I'd lost last fall under the bed.

Flyaway Girl.

I remembered to pull an old robe out of the armoire and shrugged into it in case the German was in the hall. I unlocked the door, gritting my teeth at the sound.

I went downstairs, the old steps creaking. Without thinking, I threw myself into Mémé's arms at the bottom. She raised her hands to my head and smoothed my hair. *Dear child?* Was that what she said?

I slipped out of my damp shoes and left them in the hall as we went into the kitchen. Mémé made tea without tea. "Even the lemons are gone," she said. "But hot water is beginning to taste fine."

She was right. The steaming water felt wonderful in my mouth, my throat, my chest. And my bed waited for me. Never mind the straw that crackled as I turned. I couldn't wait to sleep.

eighteen

It was warmer the next morning; icicles dripped from the kitchen window, and a pale sun, like a lemon drop, appeared over the back field.

I sat at the table, yawning, as Mémé brought me a cup of cocoa, so weak it barely had color.

Fürst came into the kitchen and frowned. "Certainly not a nourishing breakfast, Gerta."

Gerta! How harsh that sounded.

I didn't answer. And Mémé kept her eyes on the hearth. Didn't he know how little food we had? That we were always hungry?

"That cat," he said. "Always in the way."

Anger filled my chest. Sister gone, the cow, the chickens. And Louis, our beloved Louis. The cat was all we had left.

I clenched my hands into fists and Mémé reached forward, her hands covering them.

He paid no attention. He opened the door, melting snow cascading into the kitchen, and then he was gone, leaving a puddle on the stone floor.

Mémé combed her fingers through my hair. "Oh, Genevieve."

I looked up at her. "Too much. Even though that cat doesn't care one bit about me. She struts around, tail high, as if she owns the place." I tried to smile.

"Sometimes it takes a long time before you earn a cat's trust," Mémé said. "And this cat just wandered in. Who knows what her life was like before."

"Fürst had better not get too close to her. She'll scratch him to pieces. I wish she would."

It was time for school, and I knew I had to be there. "Katrin will be waiting," I said, wiping my eyes.

Mémé nodded. "You found your gloves."

"They were under the bed, waiting for me."

Her lips moved a little. Almost a smile. But she looked as tired as I was.

I went out the door and Tiger darted in. At the end of the path, I looked up, staring at the attic window. Somewhere inside, Rémy waited. I hoped he was warm enough; I hoped he wasn't too hungry.

Katrin came along, books in her arms, her woolen hat pulled low over her forehead.

The snow had melted on the wall, and I motioned to her to sit with me. "Just for a minute." We eased ourselves down on the damp stones, and I stretched my legs out, trying to think of where to start.

She frowned. "Something's happened?"

"Rémy's in the attic."

Eyes wide, she glanced toward the house, even though she couldn't see the window from where we sat.

I told her everything, rushing along breathlessly: climbing on the roof, a courier to take Rémy's mother and sister to Switzerland, that maybe there'd be one for him.

I lowered my head. "But Philippe. I think he's a German sympathizer."

"How can that be?"

"To begin with, I'm almost sure he has my brother's sweater. Why?"

She stared up at the trees along the path. "He might have found it somewhere." She glanced at me sympathetically.

"I'm so afraid . . . , " I began, and stopped. I couldn't say anything more.

We sat there a little longer; we'd be late for school, but neither of us cared.

I saw tears in her eyes. "They're rebuilding the railroad station and the tracks. They're talking about drafting boys," she said. "I can't stop thinking about it. Alsatian boys. My brother, Karl, isn't even seventeen yet."

She stared down at her books. "I thought the Germans weren't terrible. But every day there's something new. My grandfather can't even wear a beret anymore. There's a six months' prison sentence for that." She wiped her eyes. "Berets are too French."

I put my arms around her, feeling how thin she'd become. She was hungry; we were all hungry. "I'm really sorry," I told her.

She shook herself. "But you need help. Who can really trust Monsieur Philippe, now that I think of it? He's always staring out his window, watching what goes on. That old thief. He probably stole the sweater for himself."

I had to grin at her words, *old thief*! But Philippe's head wouldn't even fit into one of André's sweaters!

"We'll just have to watch him," she said. "See what he's up to."

I nodded. "After school."

"We'll go right into the bookshop. I have a few francs. I'll buy a book; you'll sneak around. Why not?"

My mouth went dry. I could think of a dozen reasons not to be sneaking around Philippe's bookshop. I pictured him raising a huge foot and stepping on me.

We were really late, the last ones to slip into the classroom. Herr Albert looked up, tapping his pencil on the desk. "I want to see you both after school today."

"Yes, Herr Albert," Katrin said, answering for us both.

I sank into my seat, terrified. He was a true German, a Nazi. It was almost as if he might have leaned over the stone wall and heard all the things I'd told Katrin. Didn't he say he'd find out everything?

I spent the day worrying about Rémy, worrying about Katrin, worrying about myself. What did Herr Albert know?

"Are you talking to yourself, *Fraülein?*"

I jumped. He stood in front of me. "Sorry," I managed. Everyone looked sympathetic. Liane's fingers curled over an imaginary piano. Claude slammed a book on his desk. And Katrin shook her head, knowing what I was thinking.

As soon as Herr Albert marched to the front of the room, I sank back into my world of worry. What did he want? What could he do to us this afternoon?

At last the day was over. We waited while Herr Albert left the room. He didn't return for at least five minutes.

Katrin leaned over. "He wants to frighten us."

He swooped back into the classroom. "To be punctual is the German way," he said. "You'll each write an essay for me."

That was all?

"You'll call it 'The History of Alsace.' I'll see it the day after Christmas. I'll be here even though the school is closed."

We nodded, escaping down the hall, holding in our laughter. "What happened to 'Merry Christmas'!" Katrin sputtered.

We hesitated at the bookshop, staring at the German books in the window. Two soldiers were inside. One of them was perched on the edge of the counter. He pushed at his little round glasses, laughing at something

Philippe said. The other's back was toward us, his fingers running along, searching for something.

Katrin pushed the door open.

I saw the surprise on Philippe's face as we walked toward him. I was sure he wanted to tell us to go away, to leave him alone with the soldiers. He went to the cluttered table at the side of the room.

Katrin followed him. "You know what books I have, I think."

Philippe barely nodded; he stared at me.

"What shall I get next?" Katrin's voice was so loud that one of the soldiers glanced at her.

"There." Katrin went to a bookcase in the corner. "On the bottom shelf. A book about writing."

Philippe bent down to see where she was pointing. It wasn't easy for him, a large man in such a small space.

Hardly breathing, I ducked behind the curtain into the back room. My eyes swept over the table, the chairs. I slid open one of the cabinet drawers, and then another, all filled with old books and papers.

My hand was on the third drawer when I saw a gray sweater hanging from a hook near the bottom of the stairs. I was reaching out, my hand on the wool, when

I heard Philippe's heavy footsteps coming toward the back.

I pulled the sweater off the hook. If I could just see the zipper and the edge of the sleeves!

Philippe pushed the curtain aside. "What are you doing?"

Behind him, one of the soldiers watched us. "Have you lost something?" he asked.

A soldier with freckles. A soldier who might have been André's age. He was the one who'd taken Sister, the one who'd been sorry. He remembered who I was and smiled, but I looked away.

"I thought there were more books back here."

"No." Philippe couldn't have looked angrier. He glanced at the sweater in my arms. "We don't sell sweaters," he said, and reached for it.

I felt the heavy wool go through my hands even as I tried to hold on to it.

He brushed the collar with one large hand, then hung it back on the hook. He motioned me to the front.

I went past him, past the German, going toward Katrin, who was still at the bookcase, with two or three books in her arms.

The soldier with the glasses pointed to a pile of

books. "Ah, *Mein Kampf,* by Adolf Hitler, our *Führer.* If only more people were like you, Herr Philippe, recognizing our great leader."

I glanced at Katrin and she looked back at me. She put the books on top of the bookcase. "Maybe next time," she told Philippe.

He wasn't paying attention. The German was still talking. I heard him say something, maybe *Let's get together to talk.* I waved at Katrin, wanting to get out of there before the soldiers left and we were alone with Philippe.

She wasn't in a hurry. She pulled her hat tighter around her ears and buttoned her coat slowly.

We started across the square, and she touched my shoulder. "You're right, Genevieve. We both heard the soldier talking as if he were a friend."

And Philippe knew about Rémy, hungry and hidden in our attic!

"Tell me," Katrin said. "Did you find the sweater?"

I shook my head. "A gray sweater. Maybe..." I shrugged. "If only I'd had another few minutes."

It was too late. I might never know.

nineteen

Mémé and I decorated a tiny pine tree for Christmas but left the wire-whiskered cat hanging in the window to guard us. There'd be no goose this year, but Mémé managed potato pancakes and a small bowl of stewed apples with cinnamon for our dessert.

"A feast," I told her, and upstairs Rémy thought so too, wolfing it all down.

Fürst was having a real feast: dinner at the village hall with the other soldiers, pork and sauerkraut, and a flaming peach tart. Eating food that belonged to the farmers, maybe even to us.

The next morning, I finished my essay for Herr Albert and went off to Katrin's so we could bring them to him together.

But she was sick, lying on the couch, coughing, her face red with fever, her voice hoarse.

I'd have to go alone, bringing both essays with me. I dreaded going into the empty building, facing that man who was angry most of the time. Who knew what he'd say about my miserable handwriting, my paper that had three ink blots?

Inside, Herr Albert sat at his desk, reading. He snapped the book shut. "Fraülein Meyer." His voice was sharp and cold.

"I have Katrin Moeller's work with me too," I told him. "She was too sick to leave her house."

He didn't answer. He held his hand out for the papers and read hers first, shaking his head. It was no better than mine, I guessed. And mine was a mess. I'd made up some of the dates, guessed at the rest. He barely looked at each page before he tossed it on his desk.

I stood there, on one foot and then the other, waiting for him to tell me I could go.

Instead he glared at me, eyes narrowed. "Not much thought went into this work."

What could I say? He was right.

He stacked the few pages neatly, then cleared his throat. "You have a German officer living in your house. Not everyone is that fortunate."

I didn't answer. My face must have told him what I was thinking.

"Ah," he said. "Some students would be going through the officer's things, trying to find out"—he shrugged—"whatever they could for the Resistance."

"I'd never do that."

"That would certainly be against the Germans," he said.

What a horrible man he was! "Can I go now?"

He waved his hand. I was almost at the door when he said something else. *"Carpe diem."*

I knew what that meant. *Seize the day,* something Aunt Marie often said. But there was another string of Latin words. I paid no attention. I almost skipped down the hall. I was free. I didn't have to see him; I didn't have to think about school, or *carpe diem,* or any of that nonsense for another few days. I could concentrate on Rémy. If only I were sure Philippe would send help for him. Every day that the Germans didn't arrive to arrest him surprised me. But no matter what I said to Mémé, she stood firm. Rémy would stay with us, and Philippe would find a courier for him.

I hurried back to the farm. Even with the mittens Mémé had knitted for me, my hands were cold.

Herr Albert would still be sitting in the classroom, probably thinking of all the things he could do next week to make our lives miserable!

I stopped short in the middle of the road.

The rest of what he'd said after *carpe diem.*

If only I could remember what Aunt Marie would have said next. Wasn't it something like *Never mind the consequences?*

I began to walk again, slowly now, trying to remember exactly what he'd said.

A strange man. I put my head back, looking at the treetops, black against a pewter sky. Then my hand in the mitten went to my mouth when I realized that he'd been telling me to look through Fürst's things for anything I might find. *Seize the day. Never mind the consequences.*

Sometimes people surprise you, something Aunt Marie said.

I was surprised. More than surprised.

The bare branches grated against each other. *Some students would be going through the officer's things . . . It would be against the Germans . . . it would be for the Resistance.*

Was Herr Albert part of the Resistance?

Marching around the room, putting up the German flag. It was all an act!

I began to walk again; then I ran. For the first time, I cared about doing something for Herr Albert. And something else made my heart sing. He'd believed I'd understand what he was saying.

I went up the walk, the wire-whiskered cat in the window, wondering if I should tell Mémé what had happened.

Maybe not. At least, not yet.

In the kitchen, candles lay on the counter; the cellar door was open. She must be downstairs, and Fürst was off in the village somewhere, so I went upstairs.

His door was locked. Of course. I went down the stairs two at a time and reached into the small kitchen drawer that was filled with keys, some of them black with age. But I knew what I was looking for: the ring of keys I'd often seen Mémé use.

Fürst kept the room the same way Mémé did: the quilt stretched neatly across the bed, his clothes hid-den away in the armoire. I looked under the bed, went through the dresser drawers, opened the armoire doors and went through his pockets. I found only a scrap of paper, written in German: *sugar, flour, butter, eggs, cream, chocolate.*

A grocery list.

Nothing more.

Then came the sound of the motorcycle.

I stood in the doorway, making sure I hadn't disturbed anything. The armoire doors were closed, the quilt straight on the bed.

Quickly, my hands shaking, I locked the door and raced back to the kitchen to put the keys in the drawer. I went down to the cellar to help Mémé with whatever she was doing, probably gathering up the few potatoes that were left. The steps were steep, but she never stopped, never gave up.

twenty

It was a strange afternoon, no school, no outside work, and Mémé had taken a nap. Mémé sleeping in the daytime! But then, her ankle had never healed the way it should have. She held on to railings, to chairs as she passed.

Fürst carried things downstairs; he looped a small case over the handlebars of his motorcycle, a uniform on a hanger; then he sped away.

I spent the rest of the day with Rémy, bringing him food, more water, a third sweater and a book I'd found in Mémé's living room.

He was tired and bored. "What takes Philippe so long?" he asked. "I can't stay here forever."

I bit my lip and left him, promising I'd ask. Downstairs, I read another book I'd found on Mémé's shelf, but it was hard to concentrate.

he attic!" I danced around the table. "And Louis can
e home."

Mémé nodded. "You make me dizzy."

And one more thing. The painting.

Mémé followed as I went up the stairs to my old
oom. I crawled up on the roof, tapping the window,
g Rémy's face, wavery in the old glass.

The German is gone," I called in to him. "You can
inside where it's warm."

e slid down and came into the bedroom, and,
t not believing how daring I was, I put my arms
him, careful not to hurt his burn, which had
to scab over. I danced with him too, both of us
g, as Mémé watched.

nt back up for the painting and managed it care-
til I reached the bedroom window again.

t me," I told Mémé, and smiled at Rémy, who
e edge of the bed.

stood at her bedroom door as I took down the
ercolor of the Vosges Mountains, then slid the
out of the pillowcase, wiping the frame gently
irt. I reached up and hung it on the wall where
d.

d at the two girls, their faces beautiful, huge

Later, I opened the kitchen door to see Fürst at
the table, digging a fork into a plate of potatoes sprinkled with nutmeg. It was probably my dinner, or
Rémy's.

"Ah, Fraülein Meyer," he said. "You're home in
time to say good-bye. I'll be leaving in a few minutes."

I glanced at Mémé, who raised her eyebrows.

"I have a promotion." He waved his hand over the
potatoes. "This is a celebration."

Leaving!

Yes. A small leather suitcase rested on the floor next
to him. It was the beginning of a new year, maybe a new
beginning for us.

"Your grandmother has been a good host." He
shoveled in a huge mouthful of potatoes. "Everything
is clean in the good German way, but she's a little stingy
with the food and the coal."

I thought of the carrots she'd managed to find in the
field yesterday. She'd scraped and chopped them with an
onion she'd saved. "Eat," she'd told me, "I'm not hungry."

Her clothes hung on her; her hands were almost
transparent.

He said it again. "Stingy."

I saw something in Mémé's eyes. Warning me?

Realizing the anger that was boiling up from my chest into my throat?

"She's wonderful!" I almost yelled it, and slammed the book on the table, just missing his plate of potatoes.

He jumped.

I stamped past into the hall.

"An ungainly girl," he said after me.

"No." Surprisingly, Mémé's voice was as angry as mine had been. "I couldn't get along without her during this terrible time." She broke off and began again. "Her father would have been proud of her."

I glanced into the kitchen; her back was toward me, bent, thin, her hair steel gray in a tight bun.

I leaned against the wall.

She'd said no. She'd said she couldn't do without me. I swallowed.

Once, she'd said: You may come again after the war. She'd called me dear child.

And my father. *He would have been proud of me.* Words I'd never forget.

Sometimes people surprise you.

I was beginning to love Mémé.

I heard the sound of a motor and peered out the hall window. A black car, long and sleek, two small Nazi

flags flying on the hood, was parked outsi take him away.

The kitchen chair scraped back, a head to see him shrug into his coat a suitcase under the table. "Thank you, said. "I hope to see you one day. Perha at peace."

He stepped out the door, and the darted inside, and slid under the tab gone, the motor purring as the car sp lucky, we'd never see him again.

Mémé slid his plate into the s ish, Genevieve. If the car hadn't co who knows what he would have de

At my feet, the cat scratched was up and in my lap. I reached her head. I didn't move. I looke eyes.

"Your cat," she said.

"Yes."

I sat there for long minut decided she'd had enough. S let her out.

But I had things to do.

black bows on their long hair, and leaned forward, leaned closer.

"Oh." It was almost a breath.

"So you see it this time," Mémé said.

I couldn't answer.

"Yes," she said. "I realized it the moment you stepped off the train with André that summer."

In the painting Mémé was beautiful, and I knew I wasn't. I hadn't even thought I was pretty, but still, she could have been me.

I thought of my father, then Mémé starving herself so I could eat. I thought of her father, who'd made the wooden shoe. And André's voice one time: *Long ago we were Alsatian.*

"Miel," I said.

Her hand went to her mouth. "Your grandfather's name for me."

We collected Rémy from my room and went downstairs into the kitchen. Before we could sit at the table, Mémé glanced at the armoire. "It's time to move it."

Food!

Rémy and I managed to push the armoire aside. We brought jars of thick white beans, tomato sauce, golden pears and fat sausages to the table.

We didn't talk. Instead we feasted, forks to our mouths, the beans in their rich sauce sliding down our throats.

We sat there as it grew dark outside; then Mémé took Rémy into the downstairs bedroom while I washed the plates and let them drain on the counter.

Mémé came back and stood at the kitchen door, looking out at the darkness. I knew she was thinking about Louis.

"I'll go," I said, and dropped one of the pewter plates. It clattered across the floor and came to rest under the table. "Sorry," I muttered. I scooped it up and grabbed my jacket before she could say anything, and went past her at the door.

It was a beautiful night; a huge moon had come up that was almost orange. It lighted the back of the house and the fields. I walked quickly, though, anxious to bring the dog to Mémé.

I climbed the stone wall and went through the trees until I saw the small house in front of me. The door opened before I could raise my hand to knock.

"Louis heard you." The woodcutter pulled me inside. "Are you all right?"

"The German is gone," I said.

Louis was right behind him, looking up, whining, his tail wagging hard. I leaned over to run my hand along his back.

"Ah," the woodcutter said. "I'm glad. The dog has been sad, wanting to go home."

But Louis had been well cared for. A thick mat was in front of a table, a bowl of water and a plate with bits of food was left in the corner.

The woodcutter had been carving what looked like a chess set. Small figures lay on that table: a queen, maybe, and a row of pawns. I wanted to stop and look, but Louis stood at the door, tail down, worried that he wouldn't get to go home.

"Thank you," I told the woodcutter. "We're grateful. More than you can know."

I leaned over the dog. "Time to go home."

Louis bounded out, looking back at me, almost as if he were telling me to hurry.

Mémé waited at the door, and he rushed to her, crying. Her arms went around him, and I saw that she had tears in her eyes. But she said only, "Time for bed."

twenty-one

For the next few days it was as if the war had never been. School had begun again after the holidays, and I could almost ignore the soldiers who seemed to be everywhere. I couldn't ignore Herr Albert, though. He strutted around the room or stood in front, hands behind his back. I watched him, wondering what he was like before the war when he didn't have to act his way through the day.

In the late afternoons Louis lay under the table, his muzzle on my feet, content to be home, while Mémé crocheted a sweater from old wool, interrupting herself to show me cable stitches for the socks I was knitting.

And yet we were wary. Things seemed almost too quiet. Wouldn't the Germans still be searching for Rémy?

Today I'd managed to stop at Philippe's to find out what was happening with the courier, then went back to Rémy and Mémé. Philippe had said, "Soon. It's dangerous work; it takes time."

My hands were fists. "It's taking too long. I don't believe him."

"Oh, Genevieve."

"Philippe lies. I know he does."

Mémé leaned forward. "What is this all about?"

"He has André's sweater."

"That can't be."

"Oh, it can be. I think I saw it. Really." I waved my hand in front of my face. "Somehow he saw André doing something that summer, and told the Germans. Maybe André never got to the ship; he could be in prison now, right here."

"Ah, Genevieve, your imagination is boundless." Mémé sighed. "Let me tell you about the Great War. Gérard sat exactly where you are. We'd both been up all night. Remember, our village was German then, and the French needed to take it because of the garrison filled with soldiers at the edge of the square. They needed guides."

I sat up. My father in this chair, as tired as I was.

"We waited until it was dark and managed to sneak through the village. Philippe stood at the window, watching. We went toward the mountains, Gérard and I, and two others. We were seen and the Germans came after us, yelling: 'Traitors!' We knew if they caught us . . ."

She broke off, staring up at the ceiling, tears on her cheeks.

"What happened?"

She shook her head. "Another time. We have to have dinner."

We sat there, eating until we were full. But as we finished, I heard the sound of a motor. A truck? Mémé and I pushed our chairs back from the table. Rémy stood, almost like a deer, ready to run.

Mémé pointed. "The cellar."

He moved quickly; his footsteps on the stairs were whispers of sound. His winter jacket was looped over his chair; I threw it under the table.

The armoire was still away from the wall, but there was no time to do anything about it. Mémé slid Rémy's plate under hers. We sat there, frozen, as the sharp rap came on the outside door.

Mémé raised her head, straightened herself, then opened it.

Two soldiers came into the kitchen, looking around. One reached across the table, sweeping plates and food onto the floor. "Where is he?"

Mémé's face was calm. "My husband has been dead for many years."

The other soldier went behind the armoire. "They're hoarding food," he said. "A good find. We'll take it all with us."

At the table, the soldier leaned forward. "We know he's here."

Mémé looked around. "There are only the two of us."

One of the soldiers climbed the stairs toward the bedrooms. The painting!

His partner opened doors: the pantry, the bedroom and then the stairs to the cellar. He pulled a flashlight off his belt and started down.

The cellar was huge, I told myself, and even with the flashlight, maybe Rémy was hidden. I leaned forward against the table, my knees tight together to stop their trembling, my feet on his jacket, pushing it farther under the table.

Across from me, Mémé sat unmoving, her thin hands clenched.

The soldier who'd been upstairs clattered into the kitchen, shaking his head. "We'll find him," he said, his boots on the food we'd been eating. The rest, which would have lasted us until the next harvest, would be gone. But he hadn't seen the painting, or if he had, he wasn't interested.

And like a miracle, the second one came up from the cellar. "No one is there."

They went out the door, the motor started up and the sound of the truck gradually faded away.

I tried to stand, but I felt as if my legs wouldn't hold me. And so we sat at the table waiting, thinking Rémy would appear.

But he didn't come.

Mémé sighed. "Genevieve, perhaps . . ."

On shaky legs, I went down the stairs, calling his name softly. The cellar was the width of the house, with many small rooms almost like caves. I went back and forth, stopping, listening. But even in the darkness, I could tell he wasn't there. And in back, over my head, an open window rattled, pulling in cold air.

How had the German not seen it? I shook my head. They hadn't seen the jacket either.

Rémy had saved himself, and us, and was somewhere outside in the shelter of the trees, or maybe at the woodcutter's place.

Back up in the kitchen, I pulled his jacket out from under the table. "I'm going to look for him," I told Mémé.

She looked doubtful, but she said, "Yes. Go slowly. Watch."

As the sky inched toward darkness, I slipped between the trees, until I saw the dim shape of the woodcutter's house. The door was open.

I stood there, shocked. The woodcutter was gone, and inside the room the quilt had been thrown from the bed onto the floor, the rocking chair splintered, the table with carved figures overturned. Small carving knives were on the floor, along with a cup of blue paint, which had splashed over the table legs.

I thought of the happy day with Rémy and André, riding the bicycles in the sun, the tower with its storks' nest, the blue-gray house nearby.

Shirmeck Prison was in my mind, or worse, Struthof, the terrible concentration camp that people whispered about.

I went out the door, hurrying through the forest, fearful now that soldiers still might be watching the woodcutter's house. *Philippe,* I thought bitterly.

We spent the next hour cleaning up the food on the floor and pushed the empty armoire back against the wall. Then we waited. Would Rémy come back? I was sure he wouldn't.

I hoped he'd found a warm place to stay. But I couldn't imagine what to do with his jacket. If the Germans came again, if they found it, what trouble we'd be in.

I wrapped it in a small quilt that was old and frayed around the edges and stood with it in my arms.

"Bury it," Mémé said.

"Suppose Rémy comes back for it?"

She shook her head. "We'll find something else for him. We can't take a chance."

I knew she was right. I found a shovel in the barn, but outside the ground was rock-hard, still frozen from the snow.

I went back to the barn and climbed the ladder to the loft, pushing the jacket ahead of me, and buried it deep under the hay.

The best I could do, I told myself.

Inside, Mémé was waiting. Tired and worried, we climbed the stairs to our old rooms.

Where was Rémy? Where was the woodcutter?

And then, surprisingly, I slept.

twenty-two

$\mathcal{E}arly$ the next morning, I awoke suddenly, heart pounding. Something terrible had happened. I jolted up, my mouth dry as dust, my knees shaking. *It was only a dream*, I told myself, *only a nightmare*.

Rémy.

The woodcutter.

Not a dream.

I dressed, braided my hair with trembling fingers and went downstairs. Mémé was stirring a few oats in a pot of boiling water.

"We have to tell Philippe," she said.

"Philippe! How can we trust him? He might have betrayed us."

She closed her eyes. "The Great War. Germans shooting at us, your father down on the ground. I knew

I had to have help. I ran to the village, ran as I never had before, straight to Philippe.

"When we got back to your father, blood had soaked his sleeves, his shirt. Philippe carried him to the farm, good, strong Philippe, telling me he wouldn't let him die. 'Hold on, Gérard,' he'd said. 'Almost home.'"

Mémé looked down at her hands. "Here, in this kitchen, we wrapped Gérard's chest with cloths, and Philippe pressed his hands against the wound until the bleeding stopped. Know this, Genevieve. I'd trust Philippe with my life. With your life.

"He made it possible for us to go on with our work. Gérard healed slowly, still in pain, but we were able to lead the French into villages we knew and fight against the Germans."

I sat there, picturing her young, as fierce as I saw her now. I had to do something too. "Oh, Mémé. I have to look for Rémy."

"You can't do that. You have to go to school. It must seem that you hardly knew Rémy or the wood-cutter." She leaned forward, the lines deep in her forehead. "Someone has betrayed them, and us,

just as someone betrayed your father that night long ago."

I closed my eyes.

Katrin?

Was that possible?

"I will go to Philippe myself," she said, "and tell him..."

"I could...," I began. But suppose it had been Katrin? How could I leave her on the way to school to go to the bookshop?

I went outside and walked toward her house. She was the only one who knew that Rémy was with us. Our friendship was over. I'd tell her that.

Katrin called from her doorway. "Genevieve? I'm not going to school today." Her voice was filled with tears. "My brother is being sent to work in a factory somewhere. We'll go to the station with him."

Blowing up the tracks had all been for nothing. The Germans had forced men to repair them.

I ran across the field, back to the kitchen, to tell Mémé I was early, that I'd go to Philippe. And then I was on the road, hurrying to the village square.

The sign on the bookshop door read CLOSED. It was early, after all.

I flew around to the back. Through the window, I saw Philippe at the table and rapped hard enough to hurt my knuckles.

He opened the door; I stumbled in and slid down at the table, too breathless to say a word.

He went back to the window, pulled down the shade and sat awkwardly, almost as if it were an effort to fit his huge bulk in that narrow chair. He stared at me, waiting.

"Mémé trusts you," I said.

"And why not? We grew up together, fought underground during the Great War..."

"They came for Rémy last night."

He leaned forward.

"They didn't find him, I think. But the woodcutter... I'm not sure. They've ruined his house." My voice trembled as I raised my shoulders.

Philippe shook his head. "Perhaps the courier will come. He is on his way back from..." His voice trailed off. He went to the window and raised the shade just enough to peer out.

"Finish what you started to say," I said, stopping myself just before I banged my fist on the table.

"The less you know, the better. How do we know we can trust you? An American—"

I held up my hand to cut him off. "I know what I am."

He sighed. "How old are you?"

"Sixteen." Not true, of course, but I was tall for fourteen, and how would he know what class I was in?

He shrugged his huge shoulders. Then he sighed. "The couriers know the way to Switzerland, or even west to Spain. They've learned which houses are safe. But still, it's dangerous. We just have to wait, to hope."

He went to a small stove at the side of the room and poured hot water into a cup. "Would you like coffee?"

"Coffee?" Where had he gotten coffee? It had disappeared months ago.

"Coffee without coffee." He poured hot water into two cups.

He reached for the door of a cabinet and pulled out a sweater. He shoved it across the table in front of me.

It wasn't André's. It wasn't even the same sweater I'd seen the other day: not a zipper in front, but wooden buttons, no raveling at the hem. It was meant for a large man, a man like Philippe.

"A lie," I said bitterly, pushing the sweater away from me.

"Like your age." For the first time he laughed, a

dry laugh, almost without sound. "Go to school, Genevieve. Forget about war for a while."

I went out to the alley, slamming the door behind me, with enough force that I almost broke the window.

That afternoon, on the way home, I saw Katrin and her mother walking all the way from the railway station. I remembered Madame Moeller saying, *We were Germans before. We'll have to be Germans.*

And their names hadn't been changed. German names: Katrin. Karl. Moeller.

How had I told Katrin everything?

I caught up with them as they turned onto the path toward their farm. "Katrin?"

Her mother kept going. Maybe she was crying.

"Will we ever see Karl again?" Katrin said. "Will we ever see any of them? Dozens of boys on the train platform..."

"You told someone."

"About Karl leaving? Everyone knows that."

"About Rémy and the woodcutter. About all the things I told you."

She looked away. "I didn't tell anyone."

"You're lying."

She turned back to me, her face shocked.

I grabbed her arm, held it hard. "Who?"

She was really crying now. "I didn't—"

"Yes, you did."

"I have to go inside." Her cheeks were blotched. "My mother is waiting for me."

I moved in front of her, blocking the way. "We'll stay here forever, until you tell me."

"You're as bad as the Germans."

"Worse," I said.

"The only one I told was Liane."

Liane, who played an imaginary piano on her desk.

"And maybe Claude."

Madame Jacques's son from the pâtisserie.

"You can trust them," she said. "They'd never—"

I let go of her arm. "Go inside to your mother. You're not my friend. I'll never walk to school with you again. Never tell you..." I took a breath. "Never tell you anything."

I went back down the path. It was beginning to rain, and even in my warm coat I was shivering.

twenty-three

@Mémé was outside, her hair wet, her jacket soaked, staring at the field, which was only now beginning to thaw.

"Come inside," I said.

She looked up, wiping her hands on her apron, and we went across the gravel path into the kitchen. I tossed my coat and hat on an empty chair and my books on the countertop. "I've done something terrible," I said.

She slid the teakettle over the flame and stood there waiting for the water to boil.

"You're not paying attention to me. I've done something terrible."

She turned. "How can I not pay attention to you, Genevieve? You are everywhere. Your books, your clothes, even your bathrobe can be found in every room of this house."

She pulled two of the Strasbourg cups from the

armoire. "In the beginning," she said, "I thought I'd go out of my mind. An old woman used to a neat house, to a quiet house. Instead I have dishes in the sink; there's clattering on the stairs, doors slamming."

I bent my head. I wanted to tell her that at home our house wasn't like a tomb, that Aunt Marie sang, recited poetry in French, that sometimes I had friends over and we made fudge.

I didn't say anything. I didn't have time.

Mémé put the steaming water in front of me. "But after a while, I remembered your father, the noise he made, the messes!"

I closed my eyes: *His notebook with the terrible marks, the doodles, the list of his classmates, Suzanne the tattletale, the initials G.M. cut into the attic floor, my father, meringues his favorite.*

"I told Katrin everything," I said. "And she told Liane and Claude. It's my fault. All of it." I swiped at the tears running down my cheeks.

Mémé bent her head so I could see that stiff part in her hair. "Sometimes things happen that we'd never expected, that we never thought about," she said slowly. "But the important thing is to begin again."

She went into the hall and brought back my father's

picture. "You see how sad he looks. He had to leave everything he loved. Some of our friends had been taken away, but he had managed to escape, and would cross the country to Spain." Her lips were unsteady. "And then to America."

Sad? All the times I'd looked at the picture. *Grim. Angry. Unfriendly. Miserable.* Never once had I thought *sad.* But there it was exactly. His dark eyes staring out, his hands clenched.

My Alsatian father, Gérard. Sad.

"That day, Philippe took his picture with a box camera so I'd have something to remember him by. Gérard blamed himself. 'I must have told someone, Maman,' he said." Mémé shrugged her thin shoulders. "We never knew who it was."

I ran my fingers over the picture. I knew how he felt. If someone took a picture of me now, they'd see the same sorrow, the same grief.

"Drink your tea without tea," Mémé said. "Raise your head."

I couldn't drink, I couldn't speak. My throat felt as if it were closing.

"It is useless to blame yourself." Her voice was harsh. "There is much more to this than Katrin."

I glanced at her. I could almost count her bones. Her dress hung loosely around her. She weighed less than I did now, and came only to my shoulder.

"We do what we can," she said.

And what she could do was run this farm by herself. She had worked in the resistance during the Great War. In this war, she had sheltered Rémy. She had taken in a girl who was forgetful and messy, who hadn't loved her.

She must have known what I was thinking. "A girl who changed my life," she said. "A girl who looked like me when I was young, who acted like the son I loved."

Her arms went across the table. I could see the veins running through her small hands. I reached for them, held them in mine.

We sat there, not speaking; then she gave my hand a quick pat and picked up her cup. "Drink, child," she said. "Your tea is getting cold."

And that's what I did. I raised the cup to my mouth; the water was still hot, comforting.

I sipped it slowly. *We do what we can,* she'd said.

And so I was determined to find Rémy.

in the distance, then closer where the woods led to the village. Rémy was somewhere, I told myself.

The handlebars were freezing! I rested the bike against the wall and poked my head in the door.

Mémé looked up.

"I'm going to look for—" I began.

She broke in. "If the Germans can't find him, why do you think you might?"

"I don't know. I have to try." I could hear the desperation in my voice.

"Eat something first," she said.

I began to shake my head, but I was so hungry. I needed something. Still in my coat and hat, I stood in the kitchen, where somehow Mémé had managed to make warm cereal. I spooned it up, wondering if there was enough for her, or had she given me all of it? If I ever made it home, I'd send her food, tons of food, I promised myself.

She stood there, watching me. "Stay away from the main roads. If you're stopped, you might say you're looking for food. Be home before—"

Was that worry on her face? I waved my hand, cutting her off. "Dark. I know." I wiped my mouth as she reached for the empty bowl. "I'll be all right."

twenty-four

That Sunday, a cold January morning, I woke to find Louis on the floor next to me and Tiger curled up at the bottom of the bed. I lay there, trying not to move my feet; the irritable cat was close enough to pounce on my toes.

And then I remembered. Rémy!

I took a chance, slid my legs over the side of the bed quickly and dressed, my fingers fumbling with the buttons. I had only today to look for Rémy without thinking about school.

Church was first, so I had a late start. Afterward, I hurried around to the barn and pulled open the doors. Tiger darted in ahead of me, ready to search for a tasty mouse or two. I shuddered. I knew Louis was eating rats now.

Enough snow had melted so I could ride the bicycl I wheeled it out, my eyes going to the Vosges Mountai

Would I really be all right? Wandering around in the woods, when the Germans were everywhere?

My fault. All my fault.

I pulled my woolen hat down to cover my ears, then went along the road. Even the Germans weren't around on this Sunday afternoon.

By the time I reached the village, I realized I should have pumped up the tires. Riding up the hills was hard.

I began to see the dark trucks of the Germans far ahead. Where was I going? I wasn't even sure.

I passed stubbled fields, still winter gray, and turned down a side road, which was mostly dirt and gravel with a few patches of snow here and there.

The road came to an end, and almost in front of me was a German soldier, his hand raised. Guarding the field in back of him?

The sign on the fence: VERBOTEN. Forbidden.

I slid to a stop, the old bike veering to one side, wobbling, then caught in the mud. My heart ticked up in my throat. Could I turn the bike and ride away before he took the ten steps to get to me?

I'd never be able to do it.

Then I saw who he was: André's age, freckled face,

the one who'd been sorry about Sister, the one who'd been looking for books at Philippe's.

I straddled the bike. I didn't move, and neither did he. We stared at each other. Over his shoulder, I saw a horse in the field. She tossed her head; her back rippled.

I caught my breath. Sister, looking fine! I remembered André teaching me to harness her. I'd held apples for her. Lumps of sugar.

The soldier walked toward me. "You're not supposed to be here."

I tried to turn the bike, head down. He was German, after all. A soldier. The enemy.

He was in front of me now. "You wanted to see the horse?"

I shook my head. "I didn't know she was here."

He looked past me, along the road. "She belongs to an officer now. But would you like to go to her?"

I felt a flash of anger. "She's my grandmother's horse."

"Of course. And someday, maybe . . . But stay for only a few minutes. The officer will be here soon."

He opened the gate, then steadied the bicycle as I went past him and crossed the field, calling the horse.

She saw me and came toward me, hoping for a treat.

If only I'd had something to give her. If only I could take her out of there and bring her to Mémé.

I ran my hand over Sister's back, reached up to feel her muzzle with its stiff dark hairs. Someday.

"*Fraülein*," the German called.

I gave the horse one last pat, crossed the field again and closed the gate behind me. I didn't look at him as I took the bike and steadied it.

"I'm sorry," he said.

I turned the bike, and he said it again. "I'm really sorry."

The anger burst from my chest. "You're part of it. I wouldn't be here, we wouldn't be hungry, people evacuated, Jews deported..."

I bit off the name *Rémy*.

I didn't bother to look at him as I pedaled away. I knew he was looking after me.

It wasn't until I was past that road, onto the next small path, sheltered by the forest, that I stopped the bike and leaned it against a tree.

I crouched down, my head on my knees, shaking, the anger gone, feeling so sad. But I couldn't stay there for long. I had to keep searching. I had to find Rémy.

The rest of the day went by slowly as I went from

one hidden path to another, almost too tired to keep going on those tires that were almost flat. My feet were sore, beginning to blister.

It was dark by the time I found my way back to the farm. I passed Katrin's house with its red roof and looked away.

Mémé stood in the doorway, her hand on Louis's head, the cat stretching in front of her. "Genevieve?"

I shook my head. "He's nowhere."

I dropped the bicycle on the gravel path, too tired to put it in the barn. Inside, I slid onto a chair, pulling off my shoes, feeling the pain in my feet, my toes. Mémé put a bowl of thin soup in front of me. It held a few cabbage leaves, another carrot and something that looked like grass, maybe chives. She went back to the stove and poured the rest into a bowl for herself, with a little left for Louis.

I told her about Sister, and she turned. "We couldn't have taken care of her as well as they have."

I breathed in the steam from the soup, wondering if Rémy had eaten today, wondering if he might be with the woodcutter. "We'll have to say I've had the grippe, a terrible sore throat, because I'm not going to give up. I won't go to school tomorrow."

"I knew you wouldn't give up," she said. "You remind me..."

I answered for her. "Of my father?"

She turned back to the stove. "No."

I didn't ask. I knew. I looked away from her, smiling just a little.

Sipping at the soup, I thought of that long day.

Rémy was out there somewhere.

Would I ever find him?

I'd keep looking tomorrow.

twenty-five

$\mathcal{I'd}$ dreamed last night, a mixed-up dream of my school at home, with its cornerstone that read *1914*. I awoke wondering what my father would have been doing that year, the beginning of the Great War in Europe.

I slid out of bed, in a hurry to get started, but when my feet touched the floor, the pain from the blisters and the muscles in my legs was amazing.

Rocking back and forth, I knew I'd never be able to get on the bike today. I was filled with anger at myself and that old bike.

I hobbled into the kitchen. Mémé was pulling on an ancient jacket that might have belonged to my grandfather. "I'm going out to the field. Maybe I'll find a vegetable or two." She stopped. "What's the matter, child?"

I raised one foot to show her, and she winced. "Sit."

"How can I look for him?" I said bitterly. "I can't even get as far as the road."

"Rest awhile." She went out the door. Did she ever rest?

Katrin was hurrying up the gravel path, head down, her books in her arms. I didn't want her to see my feet, or to know about what I'd been doing. I pulled my robe around me.

Katrin passed Mémé, who was leaving the barn, and came to the kitchen door. I had no choice. "You can come in."

"Are you sick?"

I shrugged.

"Listen, Gen, just for a minute. I went to Liane. I asked her if she'd told anyone about Rémy."

I wrapped the robe tighter around my ankles. "She probably told a dozen people," I said, forgetting that I wasn't going to say a word to her.

I saw her shake her head from the corner of my eye; then I looked toward the window at Mémé disappearing across the field.

"Liane said she was sorry, that she didn't remember what I'd told her. She'd been practicing a Bach piece for church in her head." Katrin reached across the table, but I moved my hands away. "Liane said she knew I was saying something, but she just kept nodding so I wouldn't be disappointed in her."

I swallowed. It sounded like Liane, paying no attention in school, playing an imaginary piano all day. I had to believe Katrin. "But what about Claude?"

"I saw him after school. He was furious with me for asking. 'Do you think I'd give the Germans one thing?' he yelled at me, his face red. 'Do you think I'm not French?'"

"So it was your mother!" I closed my eyes. I didn't want to see the tears in hers.

"Never! And remember, *you* told me, Genevieve!"

She was right.

"I have to go to school," she said. "But think about it. We said we'd be friends forever."

I should have called her back, but I waited too long. By the time I managed to get to the window, walking on the sides of my feet, she was halfway down the path, running. She never heard me.

For a while, I sat in my robe with my bare feet on a kitchen chair, sipping coffee without coffee. I wasn't even hungry.

I sank onto the cold stone floor, holding my ankles,

turning my feet so I could see the thick blisters. If only I could have gone after Katrin. It was too hard even to go back to the table, impossible to go to my room and throw myself on the bed.

After a while, I slept. Maybe that was why I didn't hear the motorcycle rumble up the path and around to the kitchen door.

The banging was loud. I jumped, opening my eyes. Fürst stared in at me.

My heart drummed against my chest. What was he doing here? Never mind the pain. I stood up and hobbled to the door as quickly as I could.

"I'm back, Fraülein Meyer," he said, as if I'd be glad to see him.

I swallowed, nodding.

"What happened to your feet?" He rested his briefcase on one of the chairs and a suitcase on the floor next to him.

"It's nothing." The pain was so bad I could hardly talk.

"I'll require the bedroom again," he said.

The painting! "If you come back later, my grandmother and I will have it ready for you."

He looked around. "Where is she?"

I waved my hand. "Outside somewhere."

"I saw your dog. I wonder where he was when I was here last." He stared at me. "I wonder too where the boy was."

I thought about saying *What boy?* But it was hard to think. Already Fürst was on to food. "I was told about your hoarding food in an armoire," he said. "Food that I was denied." I could hear something in his voice. Fury?

If only I weren't alone here with him.

He shrugged, took a breath. "I'll drop my things off upstairs and be back for dinner tonight."

"The quilt," I said. "The bed . . ."

It was too late. He went around the table and climbed the stairs, carrying his things.

I took three steps to the table and tucked my feet underneath.

What would we do about Louis? What could we do? He'd have to stay here. There was nowhere for him to go.

And what was upstairs? Were there marks on the windowsill from where I'd gone out on the roof? I closed my eyes. He'd see the painting, of course.

His footsteps were on the stairs again. He came into the kitchen, humming, carrying Mémé's painting.

"Please," I said, before I could think. "It's Mémé when she was young."

He stopped humming. "You hid this from me." He propped it up on the table, where I could see Mémé's lovely face. He stared at it. "A fine work. It really wasn't fair of your grandmother to hang that terrible painting of the Vosges in my room." He flicked imaginary dust off the top of the frame. "Selfish. Don't you know the power I have? How important I am?"

"Please," I begged.

"You'll have some paper. We need to wrap this."

I didn't answer.

"Perhaps you'll look, *Fraülein*," he said. "You know what's in these cabinets."

"I don't know...," I began. I did know. Mémé kept wrapping paper in a drawer on the other side of the room.

His voice changed. "Stand up and look."

I put my hands on the table's edge and pushed back the chair. I managed to walk across the room and open the drawer.

I hobbled back to the table and folded the paper around the painting. Would I ever see it again?

"Let me see your foot."

"It's nothing," I said again.

"Do it."

I raised one foot.

"Burned," he said.

I caught my breath, thinking of the explosion at the station. Would he think . . . "I dropped a pot of boiling water."

Perfect. Boiling water, bare feet.

He picked up the painting and went out, the door closing behind him, and sped away on the motorcycle.

I realized he'd left his briefcase upstairs. I counted to fifty, then took the ring of keys and went up to the bedroom on my knees. His briefcase was there, next to the bed. I fiddled with the lock, and it was open. "Ah, Fürst," I whispered. "Not so careful after all."

I searched, papers, numbers, arrests, all in German, of course. And then the name followed by a word: *Rolf, missing.*

Rolf? Rémy?

Two more names. The first: *Woodcutter. Struthof.* My hand went to my mouth: Struthof, the concentration camp. I'd heard it was the only one in all of France. And then: *Albert, the teacher. His house, school? Today.*

I closed my eyes. Herr Albert would be at school.

I closed the case and sat on the stairs, bumping down each step as fast as I could go, my legs stretched out in front of me.

I didn't stop for my coat. I managed to slide into the wooden sabots, then went to the bicycle, crying out with the pain, pedaling down the gravel path away from the farm.

I was just able to hide at the edge of the woods as I heard the motorcycle: Fürst remembering and coming back for his briefcase?

I waited only for a moment, then kept going, feeling the wetness in my socks as blisters broke.

Past the village, at the school, I threw the bicycle down where it couldn't be seen and peered along the empty hall, hearing the voices of students, of teachers.

At the classroom, I raised my fingers to the little window, and of course, Herr Albert saw me.

I beckoned and he came to the door, opened it a few inches and came outside. "You were sick," he said.

"Go," I said. "Leave. They're coming for you. Don't go home. Go to the bookshop."

He pushed me away from the door so I couldn't be seen, then opened it farther, saying, "Go on with your work," to the students.

Herr Albert! Precise even now!

We hurried out of the school building. He stopped to put his hand on my shoulder. "I'm grateful, more than you know," he said. "But not surprised."

"Hurry," I said. "And please tell Monsieur Philippe that the woodcutter was taken to Struthof."

"I'm sorry," Herr Albert said. "Poor man. Try not to be seen as you go back home."

He took the back road to the bookshop, and I pedaled to the farm, my feet pulsing with pain.

twenty-six

Mémé must have seen me as I pedaled back up the path to the kitchen. She came in from across the field a few minutes later, wiping her feet.

I was at the table, my head down, shivering with cold, in too much pain to find my sweater.

She didn't say a word. She went into the bedroom and hurried back with the quilt, wrapping it around my shoulders. She took her woolen hat off a hook and pulled it down over my head.

"A moment." She put water on to heat and covered my feet with a towel.

"What happened?" she said, still kneeling next to me.

Where could I begin?

The painting!

I tried to get the words out. "I'm sorry. Fürst is back." I swallowed. "He's taken..."

She stared at me. "Of course. He came to the bedroom and found the painting."

"It's my fault."

She looked grim. "You may be guilty of many things, Genevieve, but this is certainly not one of them."

"I know you loved it." My mouth was trembling. "I loved it too."

She put her arms around me. "We will have it back someday. I always meant it for you, from the first time your father wrote and told me how lovely you were. 'A smiling baby,' he said. 'A perfect baby. I can't stop watching her.'"

I began to cry, to sob. "He loved me."

She looked shocked. "Of course. What good father doesn't love his daughter? But more, you and André and your mother had made him happy, so far from home."

She wiped the tears on my face with her small fingers. "Later we'll cry, when this is all over. We'll have roast goose and a plum tart, and you'll go home to the place you love in America."

She stopped. "But you're freezing. Where have you been, child?"

Shivering in her arms, I told her all of it.

"And you blamed yourself?" she said. "Oh, Genevieve. You couldn't have done better."

I thought of what Herr Albert had said, words that made the terrible trip to the school worthwhile: *not surprised.*

I thought of Aunt Marie. *Any house is rich if you're in it.*

And now this: *You couldn't have done better.*

In spite of this terrible war, in spite of Fürst, in spite of Rémy being missing, in spite of the hunger that cramped my stomach, I felt happiness, like syrup in my chest.

Mémé patted my shoulder and, leaning against the table, got to her feet. "I'll bring our things downstairs again. We'll soak your feet in warm water from the stove and then I'll make a meal from old vegetables I found in the field."

Was she smiling? "Yes, we'll eat before the German returns. There'll be nothing left for him. Not a withered carrot, not a sprig of parsley. What did he say about me? That I was selfish? Indeed, that's what I am."

For that moment, I saw the girl in the painting, her lips curled into that smile.

I wished I had known her then.

twenty-seven

$\mathcal{K}atrin$ came to the house the day after I'd warned Herr Albert. Neither of us mentioned our argument. She was full of news. "Soldiers burst into school," she said, "looking for something; looking for someone. But they didn't find anything." She raised her shoulders. "And now even Herr Albert has disappeared. The principal has taken over for him. Strange!"

"Yes, strange," I repeated.

It wasn't until the middle of January that my feet healed. Because of those blisters, those aches, Fürst never guessed I was the one who'd warned Herr Albert. Still, I couldn't wait to look for Rémy again. He was out there somewhere. In the cold? Hungry?

One morning the sun shone into the bedroom. I moved my feet under the quilt and felt like myself.

I threw on my clothes and went downstairs. I hadn't

been in school for weeks; no one would miss me for another day, or even another week.

I tried to decide where to go. And then I realized. Rémy would have been afraid to be near the village, where everyone knew him.

I'd chosen the wrong way. Maybe he'd have gone toward the Rhine, even though it was closer to Germany, the area bristling with soldiers.

Before I left, I stood in the kitchen chewing a small knob of cheese, saying good-bye to Mémé. I pumped up the tires. *No blisters this time,* I told myself.

I pedaled along the edge of the road, stopping sometimes, resting and calling softly into the woods. A German soldier driving a truck came by, splashing through puddles, and slowed down, so I wheeled away from him, wondering if he'd stop me. But then he was gone.

I went farther, and as I squinted at the warm sun, I saw the tower.

I thought of the three of us that summer day before the war. *If I could climb to the top—there must be a way—*what had André said? *I'd see the world.*

Maybe I'd see something, even smoke from a fire deep in the woods.

I rode faster. Another truck passed, and a few motorcycles. I paid no attention to them. I passed farm-houses, some of them empty, their owners scattered across France.

My eyes were on the tower as I went closer. The messy storks' nest perched on top, abandoned now; the storks had flown to Spain until spring.

And then I was there.

I dropped the bike in the trees away from the road, so it was almost invisible. I walked around the tower, gazing up, shielding my eyes against the sun.

I looked around, but no one seemed to be nearby. A small door was cut into the back wall of the tower, locked with a thick loop of rusty metal, icy in my fingers. Surprisingly, it came away in my hands. Maybe it hadn't been locked in a long time.

I pulled the door open and peered up at an iron stairway circling to the top. It wouldn't be hard to climb, to see the forest and the small paths meandering through the woods.

Closing the door behind me, I pushed a wooden bolt and locked myself inside.

Please let me find him.

The curved stone wall was in front of me,

pockmarked from all the years the tower had stood; the stair railing was so cold I thought my fingers might freeze against it. I pulled off my scarf and wound it around one of my hands. It was an easy climb, the stairway winding gently as it rose toward the top.

Outside, the wind was fierce, the storks' nest larger than it had seemed from below, with sticks hung over the edge of the wall.

I spotted the blue-gray house we'd seen that day, the chestnut tree bare now. From high up, the house and tree were almost like the woodcutter's carved wooden figures.

The woodcutter! Would I ever see him again?

Far beyond that was the bridge over the Rhine. Down below, there was traffic. A line of trucks with the Nazi flag flying in front went by; a motorcycle zigzagged around them. I stood behind the nest, even though I couldn't be seen.

I heard voices, though, blurred in the wind, closer than the road.

Right underneath the tower?

I peered between the branches that lined the storks' nest. Two German soldiers stood there, almost next to the door.

I ducked back, picturing what was happening. I imagined them opening the door, looking up . . .

And I remembered I'd locked it behind me. My hand went to my chest. *Safe, Genevieve, safe.*

I didn't move; I didn't make a sound.

After a moment, I leaned forward again, brushing against the nest, closing my eyes, imagining it toppling, the soldiers looking up.

Stop.

The storks had built it firmly against the wind and against me.

One of the soldiers circled a tree. "Hey, Rudy." Then both of them stared down . . .

At my bicycle lying under the trees.

I imagined the rest as I leaned against the wall: they'd brush it off, wheel it away toward the road; one of them would climb on and begin to pedal, the other back on his motorcycle.

When I looked again, that was exactly what had happened. My bicycle was gone, and I was far away from home. Five miles? Almost six?

It was only then that I looked closer at the storks' nest. A few threads of blue wool were caught there. Threads from Rémy's shirt? Yes.

I pulled at them and they came free.

He'd been here, then, and maybe he would come back. But I couldn't wait. I had to get out of the wind, and down below, in the trees, it would be warmer.

But not safer, I told myself.

twenty-eight

I climbed down the iron steps slowly and pressed my head against the door. Were soldiers outside? Was anyone else nearby?

The door was rock-solid. I couldn't hear anything. I'd have to open it an inch or two. I stood there, my thoughts jumbled. What would I do next? And how would I get back to the farm without a bike?

Cautiously, I pushed back the bolt and opened the door, listening; there were no voices, only the shrill call of a bird. I opened the door farther; I was alone.

And a miracle! My bike was there, leaning against a tree; the rust, the bent spokes, must have sent the Germans away. Who would have wanted that ancient mess?

I did! I was so glad to see it!

I left it there to walk along a narrow path. On either

side, the woods were thick with evergreens and chestnut trees raising their winter arms. Old leaves covered the forest floor.

Where are you, Rémy?

The path opened onto a field. Farther on was the back of the blue-gray house, one of the shutters hanging loose.

Had Rémy walked this path?

I circled the field so I couldn't be seen by anyone inside. My feet were soaked; the blisters, which were almost healed, were beginning to rub against my shoes.

At the house a hoe lay on the ground. The house seemed deserted, looking sad and alone. How different from the house we'd seen that warm summer day when André was still here, when Rémy's family was safe . . .

When Rémy was safe.

I stood in the shelter of the trees, ready to bolt. But the windows were blank and bare, one of the panes broken, so I went closer.

On tiptoes, at one of those windows, I looked into the kitchen. The hearth was filled with gray ashes; nothing lay on the counters.

The door opened easily and I went inside. Without

a fire in the hearth, it seemed colder inside than it had been in the field.

I walked through the hall, seeing a bird's nest spilling out from a chandelier, and glanced up the stairs.

And then I heard it, a whisper of sound. Footsteps on the cellar stairs?

I ran back through the hall, into the kitchen and out the door; I closed it without a sound and dashed around the hoe. Had it been a soldier? Or even the owner of the house?

I'd never get to the trees without being seen. Instead, I turned the corner of the house, leaning against the wall, hidden from the door, catching my breath.

Maybe it had been my imagination: a mouse scurrying across the floor, a bird trapped in the upper hallway.

The door opened as quietly as I had closed it. I heard footsteps, but they were running . . .

Across the field.

I peered around the corner and caught my breath. "Wait! Just wait!"

I stumbled after him. "It's me, Genevieve."

He turned and stopped, his arms out. I ran into him, my arms out too, and we were hugging, laughing. "Only me," I said.

We went back into the house together to sit at the dusty kitchen table, both of us talking at once.

"Your feet clop," he was saying, grinning, and I remembered André saying the same thing when he named Sister.

And I was asking what he'd found to eat.

"The cellar! There was just enough food to stay alive." He shrugged. "The owner must have left quickly. I don't understand why someone else didn't find the jars of vegetables."

I didn't let him finish. We really had no time. I reached out and took his hand, cold from this icy house. "The courier is almost back. Philippe says he'll take you to Switzerland."

He closed his eyes. "So far from Alsace."

"But safe."

Were there tears in his eyes?

"Someone will come for you."

He nodded.

"Oh, Rémy," I said. "Someday, we'll ride bicycles together. We'll..."

He leaned forward, touched my cheek. "I know."

I squeezed his hand, then ran across the field,

paying no attention to the puddles that seeped into my shoes.

I straddled that ancient bike. It was cold and the tires were almost flat again.

I prayed to the Alsatian Saint Odile: *Let me do this.*

twenty-nine

$\mathcal{J}$ slowed down when I reached the village, wanting soldiers to think I was coming from school, or visiting friends.

The bookshop was closed, so I went around the back and knocked. Knocked harder. Kept knocking.

And Philippe didn't come.

Where was he?

I tried the door; it was locked, of course.

Madame Jacques stood at her back window. I went toward her. "Have you seen Monsieur Philippe?"

"I have," she said. "He's delivering books to someone. Come in, wait inside, it's cold." She smiled. "The pâtisserie is closed, but there are éclairs upstairs."

I looked over my shoulder.

"Give him ten minutes or so," she said.

I nodded, glad to go into the warmth, and I hadn't

My mouth was dry enough to ask for a glass of water, and she went past me into the kitchen. "I'll be right back," she said.

I was off the couch, opening the door. I heard her footsteps, but still I took the time to look . . .

To see . . .

Mémé's painting on the wall over her bed!

I closed the door and managed to take a few steps. I didn't make it to the couch, but I was almost there, and turned when she came back with the water.

"Thank you." I made myself take a sip, made myself smile.

Fürst must have given the painting to her.

Why?

To thank her for something? For helping him? For helping the Germans?

I gripped the glass to stop my hands from trembling, and sank down on the couch. I'd never be able to eat the éclair.

And then I realized. Where had the eggs come from? The chocolate? The flour?

"Could I . . . ," I began.

She was sitting across from me. "Too bad Claude isn't here. He thinks you're special."

tasted anything as sweet as éclairs in a long time. I followed her upstairs, into her small living room. "Sit
Genevieve. I'll bring in dessert."

She went into the kitchen and called back. "Yo
need a book from Philippe?"

I opened my mouth to tell her I'd found Rémy, b
then I stopped. "Yes."

I heard the clatter of plates, and my mouth watered
hadn't eaten since breakfast. She brought the éclairs in, co
ered in chocolate icing, forks and napkins on the plate. F
she was shivering. "It's a little cold in here." She pointed
the door at one end of the room. "I need a sweater."

I didn't wait. I took the first bite of éclair; it mel
in my mouth.

She opened the door halfway; her bed was cove
with a patterned blue quilt. And over the bed, I co
see the edge of a narrow frame.

How familiar it looked.

I put down my fork.

I thought of Philippe and the gray sweater. Ma
I'd been mistaken about it being André's, but I ha
know if I was mistaken about this.

Madame Jacques came out of the bedroom, clo
the door behind her, a sweater over her shoulders.

I nodded. "Would it be all right if I took the éclair with me? I need to see if Philippe is back—for the book. And then I have to go home to my grandmother's."

"Of course. Need another napkin?"

I shook my head. "I'm fine." I headed for the stairs, looking back, trying to smile.

I thought of something, and stopped. "Could I ask you? What's your first name?"

"Ah," she said. "It's Suzanne."

"I thought that's what it was." And then I caught myself. "I guess Mémé told me."

I flew down the steps and out the back door. Suzanne.

The one who'd betrayed Rémy and his family?

Maybe the one who'd betrayed my father.

Suzanne the tattletale.

The door was unlocked. I burst inside.

Philippe shrugged out of his coat; he threw his woolen hat on the table, then raised his eyebrows.

I couldn't talk. I didn't know where to begin. I held up my hand.

And then it all spilled out: one word tumbling after another. *The blue-gray house. Rémy there. Waiting. I can show you. Éclairs upstairs. Eggs. Flour. Sugar. From*

Fürst? The painting. Two girls. Mémé. Enormous bows. Over her bed. Over Suzanne's bed. Yes, Fürst!

I couldn't breathe, but I'd said it all, and Philippe understood. I could see that.

His hand was on my shoulder, guiding me into a chair. "You saved Albert's life," he said. "Now we know about Suzanne. We could use more like you." He stood over me, smiling. "The American."

"Yes." My voice was strangled.

He went to the small stove and put on a pot of water. *Coffee without coffee.*

"It will end," Philippe said, putting the cup of water in front of me. "Before that, we'll set everything straight. You can count on it. And someday you'll go home. You deserve it."

Home.

Someday.

If only . . .

I sat drinking the water, so hot it almost burned my tongue. I'd never tasted anything so good.

thirty

Mémé met me at the door. "I thought you'd never come." She took my cold hands in hers. "I've been waiting . . ."

"So much to tell you."

Mémé put her finger to her lip. "Furst has been upstairs for hours," she said. "He has a headache. He thinks you've been nursing your feet in bed all day."

My feet. Boiling water. How long ago that seemed.

Sitting in the kitchen, I told her everything, whispering, my head close to hers, even though Fürst could never hear us from upstairs.

"All these years," Mémé said when I was finished.

I wasn't sure if she was talking about Suzanne, or my father, or even the Germans. But I was too tired to think about it anymore.

I didn't even undress. I pulled off my shoes and went

to bed even though it was early. Tomorrow I'd go back to school as if nothing had happened. And Philippe, or someone, would use the map I'd drawn to find Rémy.

I closed my eyes, but thoughts of my father were in my head. I had a father who was grieving when his picture was taken. Now, I knew who'd probably betrayed him, and the rest of the village would know it eventually.

Her father would have been proud of her.

Hours later, I felt the light coming from the window on my face, a slim lemon drop of sun coming up over the field, and the sound of Fürst's motorcycle pulling away on the gravel path. I fell asleep again, dreaming that I heard voices in the kitchen.

But at last, I awoke. It was time for school. Time to act as if nothing had happened for all those days, except that I had burned my feet.

Mémé put a small chunk of bread in front of me. I knew it would taste like sawdust. Everyone was doing that now, sprinkling bits of sawdust into the batter so there'd be more to eat. "Put a slice of cheese on top and it will improve the flavor," she said.

I looked at her carefully. Was she crying? "What is it?"

She swiped at her eyes. "Dust. Nothing." She pulled

out the chair across from me. "There's something I want to tell you." Her hands were stretched out.

She unwrapped the bandage around her finger, looked down at her ring, then pulled it off. "You have been a gift, Genevieve."

"I disrupted your house, your life, and all I wanted to do was help."

She took my hand and put the worn ring in my palm.

I looked down at it, a slim gold band, her wedding ring. "Why?" Shocked, I ran my fingers over it. "I can't—"

"There is no one but you." She shook her head. "No, that's not the way I want to say it. I want to give you something of mine. You've brought Gérard back to me with everything you've done. And someday, when I'm gone . . ."

"Don't say that," I said fiercely.

"I don't mean now." She smiled. "You'll understand soon."

She went to the cabinet and took out a thin chain. "Wear it around your neck. It will remind you of me and Victor, your grandfather." She ran her fingers over it. "We always knew each other, always loved each other.

One half of this farm belonged to my parents, the other half to his. When we were married, it was ours. We'd run through the field, sit on the stone wall, so happy."

She sighed. "He'd always had trouble with his heart, and one day, just after Gérard was born, he died, coming downstairs for breakfast."

She shook her head and threaded the ring into the chain; then I reached for my coat.

"Wear the blue sweater too," she said. "It's cold."

I nodded.

"Oh, something else," she said. "You must stop at Philippe's on the way to school."

"I'm a little late, I think."

"Never mind." Her voice was stern. "You must go there first."

I held up my hand. "All right." I reached forward, pulled her to me and whispered, "It's the best gift I've ever had, Miel. I do love you."

"I'll remember that always." She patted my shoulder. I left the house and ran along the path toward Katrin's, but she had gone ahead.

It really was late.

I reached the village and saw Philippe in the doorway, beckoning to me.

I shook my head. And I was crying too.

"I had gone alone," he said. "Spying on the garrison, looking for information, and someone saw me in the shadows. I ran through the alley, out into the fields, as they fired after me."

Listening, I couldn't move. I could hardly breathe.

"Shooting me. I lay there bleeding, just as your father had. The two of them came out of the trees, into the line of fire, and pulled me, unable to move, back to where I was hidden. If you could have seen Élise, her hair wild around her face, her face filthy, and your father. Such a wonderful boy."

A boy! I wiped at my eyes.

He smiled, patted my shoulder. "Ah, Genevieve, the memories. But wait, there's a package. Give it to the courier when you see him."

"How will I know who he is?"

He waved his hand. "I've described you to him. He'll be waiting for you." He handed me a box the size of a book, tied with string, and walked to the back of the shop. "A last thing."

I looked up at him.

"Upstairs in my apartment is a small pile of books,

"School," I said. "I have to—"

"Not today."

I glanced toward the road, toward the pâtisserie.

"Come inside, and I'll tell you what we need." He lumbered ahead of me as I followed him inside. "You'll go to the tower and wait for the courier," he said. "You'll help him find the house."

"It's on the road," I said. "Straight past the tower. He won't be able to miss it."

He looked up at the stopped clock. "Ah, American, you have to do this. You'll take my bike and leave it behind the tower."

Philippe was right. I had to do it for Rémy. It was my last chance to say good-bye to him. I nodded. "Yes."

He didn't smile, but there was something in his face; I couldn't imagine what it was. "I want to tell you . . . ," he began. "Such a long time ago. But because you are so like the two of them, your grandmother and your father, I wanted you to know that no one was braver, that no two were ever dearer to me."

Philippe. Tears in his eyes!

"You saved my father, Mémé told me that."

"Ah yes, but she didn't tell you that they saved me as well?"

hidden deep in a closet. American books with your name."

"With my name?"

"They wait for you there until ..."

"But how ..."

"Albert found them just as the war began and knew they might be dangerous for you. We couldn't bring ourselves to destroy them even though they'd been rain-soaked."

He peered outside to be sure no one was there. "Go." He pointed to his bicycle.

I straddled it and dropped the box in the basket on the handlebars. Head down, I cycled along the alley, passing the boarded-up pharmacy, out onto the road, away from the village and on my way to the tower.

thirty-one

$\mathcal{I}t$ was a sunny morning with the promise of spring, and Philippe's bicycle was much better than mine.

I raised one hand to finger Mémé's ring on the chain around my neck, feeling its warmth. *If only the Germans were gone. If only I weren't hungry.*

But I was glad for Rémy. In hours he'd be on his way to Switzerland, where there was no war, where he wouldn't have to hide, to look over his shoulder and worry. He'd be with his mother and sister.

Halfway to the tower, a long convoy of trucks began to fill the road. I veered to one side, bumping along under the trees, and waited for the motors to pass. A motorcycle threaded its way around the trucks, and I saw the driver look up.

I held my breath.

He saw me and came toward me.

I was trapped; the trees in back of me were thick and I'd never get the bike through them.

No time to run.

And the box was in the basket in front of me.

What was in it? How could I explain?

"*Fraülein!*" He stopped and gave me the Hitler salute. I looked down at the patches of melting snow, the dark soil.

"What are you doing here?" he asked.

"Going to my aunt's house. Bringing her..."

He looked at the box.

I couldn't say food. He might take it. "Bringing her...," I began again. "A book. From my grandmother. An old book."

He stared at me for what seemed to be forever. "You're lying," he said. "You're skipping school for the day. Food in the box?" He flicked his finger at it.

I acted as if I were trying not to smile, as if I really might be skipping school, enjoying a day in the woods.

"I used to do that," he said. "Long ago."

Then he was gone, and the convoy as well.

And I was all right.

I sped along the road, watching the sun rise higher. The courier was waiting. And Rémy.

The tower was in front of me. I pedaled around the side, leaned the bicycle against the stone wall and stood there with the package under my arm.

I saw the courier, carrying a small suitcase. His back was toward me; he was tall, his dark hair curly . . .

"I'm here." My voice was so choked I wondered if he could hear me. "André!"

He turned and I held out the box. "I think I have your sweater."

And then I was crying, not small tears but huge sobs, as André came toward me and wrapped his arms around me. "You're going home, Gen."

Aunt Marie. The whistle of the train coming into the Higbie Avenue station at night. Oh, home.

I raised my hands in the air. "How?" And then I saw he was wearing a German uniform.

I stepped back.

"Stolen," he said. "You and Rémy will be my prisoners as we take the train toward Switzerland. We'll walk the rest of the way. There are friends who'll help. Remember the restaurants where I worked. They haven't forgotten me."

I kept shaking my head. "You'll be caught."

He pulled me closer. "I never went home, Gen. I've

been here all this time, bringing people out, because a man named Albert taught me the way."

Herr Albert.

"And you left your sweater . . ."

"Yes."

And then we were laughing, because it was probably the only time in his life he'd left something. He always knew what he was doing. I was the Flyaway Girl, not André.

"I've heard about you and what you've done," he said, his voice catching. Holding hands, we made our way along the small path through the woods to the blue-gray house and to Rémy.

"But Mémé. She'll wonder . . ."

"She knows," he said. "Someone went to her early this morning and asked . . ."

The ring! Oh, Mémé!

We smiled at each other.

Going home.

thirty-two

The three of us sat in the dingy kitchen of the blue-gray house, a torn map spread out on the table.

André traced the route with one finger.

"Strasbourg," he said, "then Colmar. Going south all the time. I have papers for the three of us. It will take weeks, but sometimes we'll be able to sleep in friendly houses, sometimes eat at friendly tables."

I couldn't stop looking at him. He'd grown taller, thinner, and there was the shadow of a beard on his chin.

My brother.

He grinned at Rémy. "The suitcase. Clean clothes."

We waited while Rémy washed himself under a pump in the sink and went into another room to change. We talked, not about Alsace, not about the war. We remembered ice cream sodas at Krisch's, Jones Beach in the summer and stickball on 185th Street outside our house.

I said our father's name, Gérard. We had a father who would have loved us. He did love us. And maybe André was old enough to remember him, to know that.

But there was no time. Rémy was ready.

And so were we.

We walked through the woods, listening to water dripping from tree branches, watching birds fly overhead, going south too.

We stopped dozens of times, to drink from a jug slung around André's shoulder, the sounds of trucks and motorcycles on the road just feet away from us.

I'd be going home to Springfield Gardens, where neighbors could be trusted, where Resistance fighters were far away, where no one had ever heard of a German soldier named Fürst.

I looked at the Vosges Mountains rising up in the west, pictured the village square, the school, the farm, Katrin, Louis, the cat . . .

And Mémé.

Mémé, who knew I was going home, who'd given me her ring so I'd always have it.

Then Philippe: *You saved Albert's life.*

I stopped, leaning against a tree, the bark thick and damp against my hands.

André turned. "What is it?"

"It's nothing."

But it was something. It was everything.

Mémé would have to plant in the field alone, to be in the farmhouse alone, to explain to Fürst that I was at a cousin's or had run away like Louis.

Gérard's mother.

My grandmother.

I began to walk again, stumbled and caught myself.

"Gen?" André asked.

Philippe's voice in my head. *We could use more like you.*

I shook my head and reached between the buttons of my coat to feel the nubby warmth of the blue sweater.

My Americans would come someday. They'd fight their way across France, and then Alsace, to push the Germans back across the Rhine.

Would I be sitting on a stool at Krisch's ice cream parlor, spooning up a hot fudge sundae?

I glanced at Rémy, who was trudging along. "Wait," I said. "Just for a minute. Let's say good-bye here."

He looked surprised. "We still have a long way to go."

"A long way," I echoed. I put my arms around him. "I'll never forget..." I couldn't finish.

He put his hand on my cheek.

I knew he couldn't talk either.

thirty-three

I stepped back. "André?"

We hadn't seen each other in so long, but still he knew what I was thinking. "You don't have to do this, Gen. We'll get you to Switzerland, and then England, and..." He didn't say the word *home*. He waited, his hand gripping my shoulder.

"Mémé," I said. "Philippe. And you, still here."

He leaned over to hold me for a moment. "The Americans will come," he said.

"I'll be waiting for them." I touched his cheek, ran my hand over Rémy's arm and turned back.

"Take Philippe's bicycle," André said.

"What are you doing, Genevieve?" Rémy asked.

"Going back," I said, over my shoulder, trying to smile.

"Flyaway Girl," André called after me.

And Rémy's voice. "No one like her."

I darted through the trees, along the narrow path, my coat snagging on evergreen branches, going toward the tower. The bicycle lay where I'd left it, the metal bars cold and muddy. I wiped them off, and then I was on my way back to the farm.

A freezing rain began, with stinging pellets of ice that quickly settled into a feathery snow.

I'd been so close to going home to America!

What would Mémé say when she saw me? I pictured her in the kitchen, thin as a rail, turning as I opened the door, my boots dripping snow.

Would she be glad to see me? I had to smile. No, her bony hands would go to her mouth. "What have you done this time, Genevieve?"

But I knew her now, loved her now.

I'd go toward her . . .

So I wasn't thinking. I never saw the truck until the horn blasted. The tires screeched as it slid away from me, hitting the rear of the bike.

I was thrown forward into the trees, hitting my head, but up in an instant, leaving the bike, its back wheel twisted, and running, my legs churning, dodging evergreens.

The soldiers were out of the truck, shouting at me, but I didn't stop. I glanced over my shoulder, but I couldn't see more than a foot in back of me.

And they couldn't see me either.

I sank down behind a bare chestnut tree, listening. After a while, I heard the motor start up and the truck pull away.

Still, I waited a long time, taking in huge breaths of the cold air, shivering, before I stumbled over the ruined bike. What would Philippe say? I'd have to leave it.

I'd have to walk.

How far?

It didn't make any difference. Even if it took forever, I was going back to the farm, back to Mémé, back to do whatever I could do for the Resistance.

I sang in an off-key warbling voice under my breath. French songs. American songs. And then . . .

A sound I hadn't heard in a long time.

The clopping of a horse's feet, the rattling of an old cart! I peered through the snow. An old man, wearing a beret, held the reins.

A beret. Amazing. Risking six months in prison.

I caught my breath. It was one of the men from the village, Katrin's grandfather.

I didn't think. I didn't have to think! I ran toward him, slid toward him through the slush, calling.

He pulled up on the reins, turned, and I climbed up on the wooden plank next to him. "Please," I said, "a ride."

He looked across at me, his sparse beard covered with snow. "Katrin's friend, is it? What are you doing out in this weather?"

I opened my mouth, ready to tell him all that had happened. Then I did think. "I was looking for a friend. Martine," I said, instantly making up the name. "I didn't know how far. And then I was lost . . ." I went on, a long story about the woods, and that I'd have to try again in the spring.

Did he believe me? It wasn't a very good story. I asked him, "And you?"

His story was rambling. Even more unbelievable than mine. I leaned back in the wagon, smiling to myself. Who knew what he'd really been doing?

I closed my eyes, feeling the rocking of the cart. What a long day it had been. And André, here all this time, until the end of the war, just as I was. Not safe, but then none of us were.

I must have slept. I awoke to feel the old man shaking my shoulder. "You're home," he said.

I looked across at the farm, the white field, the stone house, dark with the blackout curtains. Mémé's house. My father's house.

"I can't thank you enough," I said, noticing that the beret was hidden away now.

We grinned at each other. We both knew we had secrets!

I climbed off the cart, and then I was running up the gravel path, banging on the locked door, Louis barking. I couldn't wait now. Banging, as I saw Mémé peer out the window!

Oh no! I saw her mouth the words.

She'd be furious. Why not? She was Mémé.

But the door opened, and she pulled me toward her, one hand reaching up to smooth my wet hair. "Ah, Genevieve," she said. "How is it that I knew you'd come?"

We stood there for long moments, Louis at my feet, the cat looking up at me from under the table. I shrugged out of my snowy coat to let it drop on the floor.

Mémé didn't even sigh. I looked into the hallway at the picture of my father. "I'm here," I whispered.

1944

thirty-four

It was December again. The sixth Christmas I'd been here. Another long year was behind us. Early in the morning, I went out to the woods, clumping through the thick snow, and cut down a small tree.

Inside, I hung the carved figures on the tree, with the kitchen full of the scent of pine. Mémé watched, so frail now that she spent most of her days knitting on the bench next to the hearth.

I wasn't the same girl who'd turned back from the train station so long ago. I had no time to lose things, to drop books on the counter, socks on the floor. I was up early, to bed late, or sometimes not to bed all night. Besides school and managing to make meals from almost nothing, I worked for Philippe.

I knew now why Rémy loved farming. To work in the field, the soil under my fingers, watching the seedlings that Mémé and I had nurtured grow, was a wonderful feeling. Still, our harvest had been sparse, without potato eyes to plant and only a few seeds for carrots and beans.

I'd learned to be careful of Mémé; I'd slide an extra spoonful of broth into her bowl; I thought she did the same for me.

But we had the radio too!

In June, we'd heard what I'd been waiting for, praying for! The Americans had landed in Normandy.

"Oh, Mémé," I'd said, almost forgetting to whisper. And then I realized. "What will the Germans do to me? I'm American, after all."

She'd put her hand over my mouth gently. "You have a French passport. You chose Alsace. It's not a worry."

I had to believe her. But it would take time before the Americans fought their way toward us, liberating towns as they went, freeing Paris, and then on to Alsace. A long time before I heard those beloved American voices!

Someday, I told myself as I entered Philippe's shop on Christmas Eve.

"I have books for you today," he said, speaking in German as soldiers lounged around his counter.

"I love to read," I told him. "You know that."

"That's why there are two! Good German books."

It would be another night without sleep! Two more people in hiding would spend at least one night in our attic space, before I led them to André in the woods!

"What about Rémy?" I always asked when we were alone, and Philippe would shrug. "He's not in Switzerland. He's in the heart of France working for the Maquis. The Resistance."

Ah, Rémy, stay alive.

But there was one thing I did that year, one thing, maybe for Gérard, maybe for myself. I crouched in that freezing space upstairs, empty that night, running my hands over his initials, and carved my own initials, *G.M.,* under his, as I talked to him. "I'll never call you Gérard again; I'll never think *my father.* You are *mon père.* You are Papa. I belong to you and you belong to me!"

SOMEDAY

thirty-five

That winter was the coldest I could remember, with fierce ice storms and drifting snow. We had no coal left. Mémé and I wore sweaters over sweaters, coats over coats. But the news was exciting. Everywhere people were whispering: *The Americans are coming. They've reached Colmar. The Germans are putting up a fight, but they're retreating, inch by inch.*

And then Fürst was gone, this time forever! And even though our heads were covered with scarves, we heard the guns, the artillery fire.

And one terrible day, we spent in the cellar. But at last there was silence. My war was over. All of it! Mémé and I hugged. Philippe and I hugged. Over!

The animals seemed to sense our joy. Tiger spent time in my lap, and Louis, old now, sat next to Mémé, tail thumping, as she rubbed his ears.

Days later, I went down the path with Katrin, walking slowly, remembering we were eighteen now. Katrin held a sheaf of papers in her hand. "It's time for me to write."

"All about the war," I said as American soldiers came along the road.

"Hey, beautiful," one of them called, and stopped.

"I'm a New Yorker!" I said back, the American words lovely on my tongue.

He looked surprised. I wondered if he believed me.

"Springfield Gardens, Long Island Rail Road, Empire State Building, Jones Beach," I said.

He had to keep going, but he smiled over his shoulder!

I waited for André. I waited for Rémy.

Albert was back, with books under his arm. And even though we waited, hoping, the woodcutter and Rémy's father didn't return; they would never return.

When travel began again, I knew Aunt Marie would come for a long visit. But my place was here with Mémé, to hang her painting in her bedroom, to farm and harvest. And sometime later, I'd go to New York, to visit my beloved Springfield Gardens.

But there was the sound of the horse and cart

coming up the gravel path. André was coming home, bringing Sister back where she belonged!

I ran to meet them, with Louis at my feet, and André held out a red parasol. "For you, Gen!"

How long ago it was that he'd promised me that parasol!

I helped Mémé to the cart, and we smiled as we drove around the village square and the old men in their berets waved.

I thought of Aunt Marie, as I had so many times. *Sometimes people surprise you:* Philippe, and Albert, and Madame Jacques, who had disappeared somewhere . . .

And Mémé.

I couldn't be sorry I'd come to Alsace. I'd never have loved her, never have known Papa.

Philippe was outside now, his hand raised. "Well done, Americans," he called after us.

Later I'd go back to the bookshop for my books. But then André stopped the cart.

Coming down the road . . .

Yes, walking toward us, arms out . . .

I was out of the cart, and we held each other, Rémy twirling me in his arms. "I've been waiting for you," I said.

"It's *someday*," he said as we walked back to the cart together.

I thought of all the things I wanted to tell him. Most of all that I was staying there, that we'd farm together.

Someday!

But he knew that, of course he did.

Acknowledgments

Heartfelt thanks to Kathy Bohlman and Joan Jansen for their research, to Debbie St. Thomas for suggesting I speak with Marie Kozak, and to Marie for her memories of Alsace.

The Trumbull Connecticut Public Library is home to me; the librarians are warm and knowledgeable. I'm more than grateful to Walter Dembowski, who found two books written in 1915 that were immeasurably helpful in studying the history of Alsace and that even gave me the klapperstein!

It would take pages to thank my editor, Mary Cash! Her thoughts and advice are always tremendously helpful. I thank Terry Borzumato for her support over the years, and Barbara Perris for her careful copyediting. Special thanks to Becca Standlander for the beautiful artwork and to Kerry Martin for the wonderful art direction and design.

When I was young, I longed for a big family, and now I have it. I especially want to mention our newest member, Haylee Elizabeth, who calls me Mimi.

Nothing would be possible without my husband, Jim, my best friend. I think of my son Jimmy with every word I write, his love for books, for family, the joy he gave me and others.

George Nicholson bought my first book at Viking and became my agent. He was a source of advice and encouragement for my writing life. I miss him every day.

Dispatches from the Sporting Life

MORDECAI RICHLER

Foreword by Noah Richler

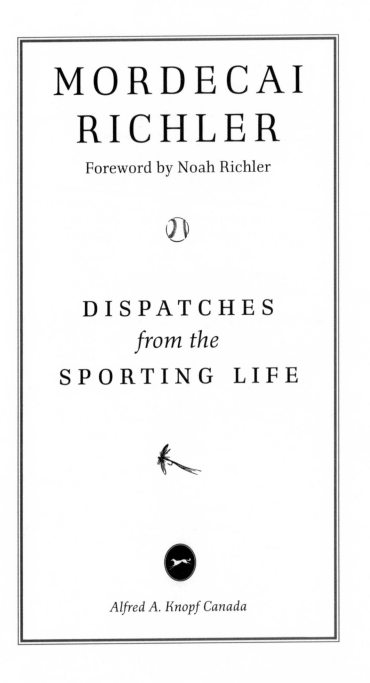

DISPATCHES
from the
SPORTING LIFE

Alfred A. Knopf Canada

PUBLISHED BY ALFRED A. KNOPF CANADA

Copyright © 2002 Mordecai Richler Productions Limited
Foreword © 2002 Noah Richler

All rights reserved under International and Pan-American
Copyright Conventions. Published in 2002 by
Alfred A. Knopf Canada, a division of Random House
of Canada Limited, Toronto, and simultaneously in the
United States by The Lyons Press. Distributed by Random
House of Canada Limited, Toronto.

Knopf Canada and colophon are trademarks.

**National Library of Canada Cataloguing in
Publication Data**

Richler, Mordecai, 1931–2001.
Dispatches from the sporting life

ISBN 0-676-97477-5

I. Title.

GV707.R527 2002   C814'.54   C2001-903525-X

Pages 292 to 295 constitute a continuation of
the copyright page.

First Edition

www.randomhouse.ca

Text design: CS Richardson

Printed and bound in the United States of America

2 4 6 8 9 7 5 3 1

Contents

Dispatches from the Sporting Life

Foreword

NOAH RICHLER

I n 1972, my father brought his family back to Canada after nearly twenty years in England. I learned in no time that his preferred place on Saturday nights from September to May was on the living room couch, watching *Hockey Night in Canada*.

We returned to Canada in the country's prime time, you might say. The Canadian dollar was on par with the American (a detail that matters, when it comes to international leagues), and though Pierre Trudeau and René Lévesque were sparring from their federal and provincial prime ministers' offices, the Péquistes had not yet driven a stake through Montreal's cosmopolitan heart. Montreal was a city on top of the world, rich with memories and history, but an *avenir* too. There was no question, in my father's mind, that it was the only city in Canada where he could possibly live: the most sophisti-cated—which meant, for him, the best restaurants, the most critical and interesting politics and, at the Forum, the chance to watch the Montreal Canadiens—the Habs—playing before the most knowledgeable and demanding hockey crowd in North America.

Twelve years old, I received swift instruction in matters Canadian. My father's love of sports, I quickly saw, was entirely wrapped up in the urban landscape of his childhood: the cold-water flats of Montreal's Jewish ghetto, east of Park and north of Pine, bounded to one side by the well-to-do French Canadians of Outremont and on the other by the francophone working class of the Plateau. Baseball at Delorimier Downs and hockey at the Forum were what Montreal Jews and French Canadians had in common. During the summer, Pa showed me what the bleachers were at Jarry Park, and introduced me to baseball's ritual of the seventh-inning stretch. Then, that September, we watched an overweight Team Canada, fresh off the links, face off against Russia, an opponent the NHL's professionals famously failed to take seriously. It fast became the most extraordinary international hockey series Canada has ever played. The Cold War still on, the Red Army was what the West feared then, but in Canada we held them in awe for a different reason: soldiers who played crisp, mesmerizing, "amateur" hockey—full-time. All Canadians of my generation can hum the grand Soviet anthem as a consequence. We feel a kinship there. We know where we were when Paul Henderson scored, saving face for Canada, and we remember the shock we felt when, after Team Canada scored the first goal of the series in Montreal, the Russians stormed back to win the game 7–3.

I was watching the game with my father that evening, all the family in the living room, Pa's enthrallment palpable. After that series ended, my father took me to the Forum to see the Canadiens, who beat Minnesota 3–0 in an early season NHL game. I was thrilled to be with him, of course, in the building that I knew meant so much to him, but we'd been spoiled by the match with the Soviets: the hockey was somnambulant by comparison.

The Canadiens, at the time, were on their way to becoming the winningest franchise in professional sports, no mean achievement. By the end of the decade, they'd have won more Stanley Cups than the Yankees had World Series, or Liverpool FC had carried football trophies back to Merseyside. They were unquestionably the best—and they belonged to us. Quebeckers many of them, Canadians certainly. The Habs of the 1970s went on to establish themselves as the second most powerful dynasty in the team's history, losing perhaps eight to ten games a season—a couple of them from sheer boredom. The first, setting the bar for my father, had won five Stanley Cups in a row from 1956 to 1960. That was the team Pa got to call *Nos Glorieux*. The Canadiens, for his generation and mine, were a thrilling, easy team to support.

My father the fan, however, was also something of a fatalist, inclined to moments of deep foreboding. The team down one or, just occasionally, two goals at the end of the first period, he'd pronounce on their sloppiness from his uncontested position on the couch: "We're in trouble now," he'd say—before, more often than not, the Canadiens dug themselves out of it. It was, I suppose, the mark of the writer in him, someone who did not expect things to go swimmingly for long.

Come the late eighties, after yet more league expansion, after the owners' and the players' greed turned the game into a television spectacle, the play stopping every few minutes for another commercial break, my father lost interest in hockey. He stopped going to games because—he would never have imagined it—he was often bored at the rink. Pa frowned every time a new Canadiens team, its meagre talent stretched too thin, would dump the puck forward and race on in. This was not the game he grew up with, and by the nineties he'd given up on it entirely.

By then, a string of Péquiste victories had taken its toll, and the dollar was in freefall. Trudeau was no longer a figure in public life, and a huge number of anglophone Montrealers had left the province—though not my father, stubbornly. The Canadiens had been relegated to a shameful box of an arena built by the Molsons, their indifferent last Canadian proprietors; the Expos had been languishing in the horrid Olympic Stadium for more than two decades, playing to the smallest attendances in the National League.

Too many Montreal institutions gone.

Pa's sports were not, as games are for so many fans these days, vessels for statistics or of contrived corporate competition—a city's glory purchased by some conglomerate churning money at the gate. Nor was the game, as Pa writes, the place for "intellectual gibberish"—a tableau for some eclectic, European, Umberto Eco–like reduction of philosophical life. It was, instead, a very real matter. It was about getting ahead, about making your way in the world—as a Canadian. No, we can be more specific than that: as a Montrealer, of the non-WASP kind, during the time that city was original and great.

Pa was serious in his allegiances: hockey in winter, and baseball in summer. Snooker, year-round, was something he could relax to—playing, or watching the sport on television, after his working day was done. Fishing, a pastime he undertook later in life, was, I suspect, a pursuit that had more to do with a feeling of having arrived—as well as his love of the Canadian outdoors, an attribute of my father's writing that is often underestimated. It's there in *Barney's Version*, and in the *a mari usque ad mare* romp of *Solomon Gursky Was Here*—and, of course, in Duddy Kravitz's dream of purchasing all the properties bordering a Laurentian lake. The love of sports had, most of all, to do with home. In all those years in London, cricket, soccer, rugby—they just didn't figure. Hockey and baseball were part of the patrimony in ways those sports could never be. What the journalism offered, those forays into Gordie Howe's garage or to a bodybuilding convention, was the chance to get away from the typewriter and drop in on lives other than his own. One of the unusual complaints my father would sometimes make is that his literary success had come too soon. He'd not had to work in an office or hold down a factory job to get by, so he'd lost out on the material those experiences might have supplied him. The sports assignments helped satisfy that necessary, writer's curiosity.

Morning in the Richler house, before my father set to work: a hard-boiled egg rolls in a puddle of steaming water on the chopping board. "I made you breakfast," he tells my younger brother, Jacob, his fishing companion of choice (that's him on the cover), who's used to this routine. Pa prepares my mother's loving tray—hot black coffee with the froth still riding on it, a glass of orange juice freshly squeezed, and my mother's seaweed and garlic pills—and carries it to the bedroom at the back of the apartment. No one else goes there, unless summoned. In a moment he's back at the table, for sliced tomatoes and toast, and a look at the sports section of the Montreal *Gazette*.

"Here," he says, handing one of his five children the Business or the Classified pages—*chortle, chortle*—"you want a piece of the paper?" Then it's off to the loo to catch up on the Expos or the NHL.

"Richard Nixon," he says, "always read the sports pages first."

Hockey was his Canadian writer's trump card, my father capable of using sports as a vehicle for just about anything—as a way of applauding the virtuosity of Frank Augustyn, the *premier danseur* son of a steel worker from Hamilton, or, in *St. Urbain's Horseman*, Jake Hersh's fantasy of a life of greater moral rectitude. Try this passage, for instance, imagined as only a Montreal lad could, the reverie of someone who, as a boy, watched the likes of black Jackie Robinson play for the Montreal Royals, the farm team for Branch Rickey's Brooklyn Dodgers. Leo Durocher was the coach:

...even though he went twelve innings in the
series opener the day before yesterday, allowing
only two cheap hits, Leo looks at the loaded
bases, Mantle coming up, their one-run lead, and
he asks Jake to step in again.

Jake says, "On one condition only."

"Name it."

"You've got to tell Branch I want him to give
the Negroes a chance in the big leagues."

Originals, and rogues, in the Nixon vein, were
something else sports had to offer. Iffy characters
who'd made a success of themselves against the odds:
Gordie Howe, "a child of prairie penury," the wild-eyed
Maurice Richard, or the Jewish baseball player Kermit
Kitman, "one of ours," a scholar who later went into
the shmatte trade. And let's not forget Don Cherry, an
affectionate target of my father's pen. Once the Boston
Bruins coach, now a television commentator, he is
known in Canada not least for his outrageous, over-
the-top plaid suits—and, in my father's words, for having been hockey's patriotic xenophobe, forever railing
against "chickenshit foreign commies taking away
hockey jobs that rightfully belong to our own slash-
and-grab Canadian thugs." These European players, in
Cherry's view, insisted on wearing masks, protecting
their teeth and otherwise dragging down the game's
fine traditions. My father later suggested that Cherry
should be Canada's next governor general, as his flam-
boyant dress sense would satisfy the demands of the
office, and appeal to jocks and homosexuals alike.
"What do you expect the guy to say," said Cherry,
clearly miffed, "I mean, with a name like *Mordecai?*"

Looking over these essays, I wondered why, as a boy, I'd never asked my father if he could skate—even as he praised his great friend Jack Clayton, the English director of *Room at the Top* (with whom he worked on the screenplay of John Braine's novel, which won an Oscar) for being good on skates. I found the answer in these pages: he couldn't afford a pair—though it's also true that observing, and not playing, is the writer's game. Amazing, that I never asked him.

So Pa would be off to the bleachers at Delorimier Downs, to take in a ball game with the Montreal Royals—or, more often than not, to the poolrooms of Park Avenue. Pa, as I knew him, was a man who bought himself few treats. (One Christmas he was given a bottle of the twelve-year-old Macallan, his favourite brand of Scotch, by each of the children—we couldn't think of anything else he would like more, and he was delighted). There was a motorboat for the country house on the lake in the Eastern Townships, the place where he preferred to write, and when the childrens' educations had all been paid for, he bought himself a snooker table, a throwback to his youth. Ma housed it in a beautiful, airy, cedar-and-glass addition on a terrace overlooking the water—and in winter, the frozen lake. An old chisel that my father's father had used is pinned to one wall of the snooker room. On it are written, in yellow chalk, the words "Moses Isaac Richler—*No Success!*" On Boxing Day, we'd host a tournament, Pa inviting Sweetpea and his other local drinking pals, Eastern Townships descendants of United Empire Loyalists who'd been not much transformed as characters in *Solomon Gursky Was Here*. Ma would cook up a pot of her wonderful chili, safely removed from the boozy action, various of her children and their friends joining the day-long party, playing, at $20 each, for a pot of maybe $200 or $300.

The Richler kids didn't do very well. No success, I'm afraid, letting their father down—*in public*. Pa would usually make it to the final rounds, and sometimes my oldest brother, Daniel, did, but I fared badly year in, year out. Pa, seeking to improve our play, taught the kids a couple of hustling tricks: how to distract your opponent by standing behind the pocket he is aiming at, tossing the cue from hand to hand as a Catskills entertainer might a microphone, subtly putting off his aim. A bit of cheating, I gathered, is acceptable in sports—as long as you are not caught, that is. The lesson was not so much that crime pays (which it probably did, for a couple of his poolroom pals), but that you need to be vigilant if you're going to play a good game. As Max Kravitz writes to Duddy—but affectionately, note—"Remember, the world is full of shits." Or, as Jake Hersh is told by his father, Izzy, in *St. Urbain's Horseman*, "You want me to be proud? Earn a living. Stand on your own two feet." That was the kind of advice he liked to give.

For my pa, sports were also about escape. When I was in my early teens, I remember—I think we were watching some old Pathé Joe Louis newsreel, or could it have been a James Cagney movie?—he told me that boxing and baseball were easy ways out of the ghetto, for blacks and Jews especially. It is interesting to me that Pa writes of the NHL athletes of his day that they were "the progeny of miners and rail-

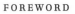

way shop workers and welders," and that in the summer they were "driving beer trucks or working on
construction sites" to get by. If it's an idea that is
repeated, in subtle variations, it's because it is one of
the most important ones. My father was a ghetto
boy. He did not forget where he came from. (That
was a favourite bit of his writer's advice.)

For these reasons, he did not care much for modern players, earning big bucks yet unwilling to go
into the corners. By and large, they were athletes
schooled by hectoring parents on covered rinks at
5:00 a.m., and not on some frozen backyard or
river. They did not appeal much to the storyteller
in him. In their smart Gucci suits, with PR flacks
to stand between them and the kind of clumsy—but
poetic—Ring Lardner utterances he so enjoyed,
they struck him as men without character, too
specifically trained. Wayne Gretzky, I suppose, put
to work by his father, Walt, from an early age, was
the beginning of that sea-change. Pa preferred the
struggle: the striving Pete Rose, grittily singling his
way into the record books, every hit a determined
grunt; the heroic obduracy of Jackie Robinson, enduring the abuse ordered on him deliberately
by Branch Rickey, who was readying his brilliant
shortstop to break the colour barrier in baseball's
National League. Or, consider it, the unknowing cer-
tainty of young Gordie Howe: "pre-paring for what
he knew lay ahead, he sat at the kitchen table night
after night, practising his autograph"—and long
after that, amazingly, at the age of fifty-two, playing on the same line as his children, Mark and Marty.
It interests me, as his son, that Pa quotes—

unmockingly—this poem of the third Howe boy, Murray, a pre-med student.

> So you eat, and you sleep.
> So you walk, and you run.
> So you touch, and you hear.
> You lead, and you follow.
> You mate with the chosen.
> But do you live?

These were stories about talent, determination, and the hunger for a new and better life—a bit of fame, fortune, prowess—but they are also about choosing.

Pa found his own unlikely way out, though he never did leave his beloved Montreal behind. Not in all those years in Britain, perusing the hockey listings in the *Herald Tribune*—or, in the sanctity of his loft office, conjuring up the subtext of a crazy expats' ball game in London's Regent's Park (that chapter from *St. Urbain's Horseman* is included here). He never did stray far from home, eventually, in 1972, coming back to it all, to the seat of it—because he felt he was drying up as writer, he told Ma. (He liked to quote V. S. Naipaul, who'd said of his own writer's relationship with Englishmen that "I don't know what they do when they go home at night"—an explanation for the family's move from Britain that Ma did not easily accept.) That summer, he took the kids to see the Expos in Jarry Park frequently. And come winter, he told his friend the longtime Montreal *Gazette* sports columnist, Dink Carroll, who'd supply us with a pair of his Forum press tickets from time to time, that I was a fleet defenceman.

I think he *wanted* that to be true, and I remember having to keep up the pretence for many years, until Dink died.

Then, in June 1998, my father telephoned me from Montreal—I was living in London at the time—and told me that he was going into hospital, the Montreal General, to have a cancerous kidney removed. I flew to Montreal, knowing remarkably little about operations and hospitals, thank God, and spent the nights there in his small, gloomy, dilapidated room. (So much of his Montreal felt diminished then.) We rented a television set so that I could watch the World Cup and Pa, I'd expected, the hockey playoffs. Except that he was not interested. He was on morphine—hell for a mind like his—and other thoughts were racing through his unfettered consciousness. It must have been the surgical masks of the doctors who'd leaned over him on the operating table, stemming an unexpected loss of blood, that provided his delirium with a thread of crazy reason. "No!" said Pa, bolt upright, that great head of thick hair a standing tussle, when, a few days after the operation, a nurse tried to put an oxygen mask on his face to help him through his recovery. "No. I won't—*it's an anti-Semitic machine*." Even the French-Canadian doctors laughed at that. Then, the queue of doctors and nurses abating for a while, Pa would drift in and out of sleep and the topics that were his lifetime's concerns: Canadian politics, Israel and Palestine—and hockey.

"Noah?"

"Yes, Pa?"

"Where did the U.S. make the speech recognizing Israel? Was it in San Francisco?"

"I think so, Pa, in May 1948, wasn't it? Harry
Truman sent a cable."

"Oh dear, oh dear. Who would have thought it
would all end so badly?"

"It's not over yet, Pa."

What does he mean, I wonder. Israel? Himself?
Pa lifts his arm, as if it were a stranger's, looking at
the intravenous feed indignantly. Then he rolls onto
his side and lets out a big sigh.

"What are we going to do in this country?
Canada's in such a mess. Did you get to the Knesset?
Did you get to the meeting of the men with masks?"

"No, Pa. What meeting was that?"

"That Don Cherry—ha ha!—great guy."

And, before giving in to sleep again, he says, "But
can you imagine, *hockey in June*."

Three years later, Pa went into hospital again, and
this time he died. The family, according to his
wishes, buried him in Montreal's Mount Royal ceme-
tery, in a grave on Rose Hill, overlooking his boyhood home on St. Urbain Street. (The "ghetto" is a
much more affluent community now.) We put this
notice in the paper.

> Mordecai Richler died from complications
> related to kidney cancer early Tuesday morning
> at the Montreal General Hospital. He will be
> sorely missed by Florence, his beloved wife of
> forty years; his five devoted children, Daniel,
> Noah, Emma, Martha and Jacob; their loved

ones, Jill, Sarah, Nigel and Leanne; and the
young grandchildren, Maximillian, Poppy and
Simone. A private funeral will be held today in
Montreal. A public memorial will take place in
the autumn. The family asks that donations be
made to the Canadian Cancer Society, Centrâide,
Médecins sans Frontières (or, say, the Montreal
Canadiens, a true lost cause).

The month before, the Canadiens, who'd missed
the playoffs for the second year in a row, were sold
to an American businessman from Colorado. He
promised not to move the team south, but the
Expos, it soon became apparent, were likely heading
that way. I'm glad Pa did not witness this. It was the
end of an era—but not unthinkable. Quite the opposite, in fact.

Love you, Pa.

I

An Incompleat
Angler's Journal

September 13, 1988. Wednesday. Montreal's Mirabel airport. Before boarding our preferred carrier, British Airways, I loiter close by the insurance vending machine, making sure no shifty-eyed bastard, seeing off his beloved wife, is covering her for two million bucks and then rushing off to embrace his bimbo—"It's done, baby." Pretending to tie my shoelaces, I listen to unattended carry-on baggage that might go tick-tick-tick. Then, composing my soul, gulping down just one more cognac, I allow my wife to drag me to the plane. Florence and I are bound for a short stay in London and then on to the Scottish Highlands and the islands of Shetland and Orkney, where, in fulfillment of a long-cherished dream, I will fish for salar, the leaper.

Salmon.

The first known image of salmon, discovered by a French archaeologist, was carved into a reindeer bone, circa 12,000 B.C. It was Julius Caesar and his men, invaders of Western Europe, who dubbed it salar, the leaper. William the Conqueror and his barons savoured it and so did that swindler John Cabot, when he first sailed to North America in 1497. The first book in English on salmon, published in 1481, *The Gentleman's Recreation, The Boke of St. Alban's*—though possibly a compilation of earlier books on angling—is credited to Dame Juliana Berners, prioress of the Sopwell Nunnery. She went after the fish required for her Friday table with a rod cut from ash and line made from the hair of the horse's tail. Then, in 1653, there came the essential book for fishermen, *The Compleat Angler, or the Contemplative Man's Recreation: Being a Discourse of Fish & Fishing Not Unworthy of the Perusal of Most Anglers,* by Izaak Walton:

> The salmon is accounted the King of fresh-water fish, and is ever bred in rivers relating to the sea, yet so high or far from it as admits no tincture of salt, or brackishness; he is said to breed or cast his spawn in most rivers, in the month of August: some say that then they dig a hole or grave in a safe place in the gravel, and there place their eggs or spawn, after the melter has done his natural office, and then hide it most cunningly, and cover it over with gravel and stones; and then leave it to their Creator's protection, who by a gentle heat, which he infuses into that cold element, makes it brood and beget life in the spawn, and to become Samlets in the Spring next following.

Thrusting Izzy's book aside, I begin to dream about silvery sea-bright salmon rolling in the ripples of the Spey River. Casting with my usual panache, I catch plenty before we've even climbed to 33,000 feet, some 32,994 feet too high for London. Following two lap-of-luxury nights at the Ritz, tainted for me only because my wife insisted it would be bad form for me to practice casting in the lobby, we are driven to Euston station by a couple who are old friends: "Remember," he said, "we're expecting you for dinner the night of your return."

"Should I order a standing roast beef from Harrod's?" she asks.

"Nonsense," I say. "I'll be bringing fresh salmon."

Then we board the overnight train to the Highlands and the fabled Spey, the fastest-flowing river in Europe, thick with salmon, according to legend. Once established on my narrow bunk, I turn to *Orkney & Shetland,* by Eric Linklater, wherein I read of a dizzying succession of Norse conquerors:

> But Sigurd, when he got his Earldom…made
> an alliance with Thorstein the Red, son of Olaf
> the White…and that famous woman Aud the
> Deep-Minded who…was the daughter of Katil
> Flatnose…

On arrival in Aviemore, we're met by a tourist-office flack who drives us over winding country lanes, peasants lurking in the fields of ferns alongside, to Tulchan Lodge, a veritable stone mini-castle, complete with turret, that immediately evokes my boyhood home. The butler who tippled. The saucy second-floor maid. My nanny, a treasure. On the other hand, that delightful lodge, rising in the Tulchan and Cromdale hills above the Spey River, is set in a rolling wooded parkland of no less than twenty-three thousand acres, admittedly a tad larger than my boyhood backyard. Tulchan was built in 1906, an Edwardian fishing and hunting lodge, the private property of one George McCordquodale, Esq., and did not become an *albergo* until 1976. Handsomely appointed, with oak-panelled drawing and billiards rooms, the lodge can accommodate no more than twenty-four guests in its twelve double bedrooms. A room will set you back $200 a night, but that includes breakfast, afternoon tea, and a four-course dinner, and the fare is first-rate. There are additional charges, however, for deerstalking, shooting grouse, or fishing. A rod, along with the services of a gillie, costs $170 a day. The lodge commands Tulchan Water, eight miles long, with four beats, considered to be the most productive on the Spey, but before we have even unpacked I am told:

1. This season the fishing had been the worst in twenty-five years, with only 17 salmon taken in July, whereas the usual catch was 165 or more.
2. Water temperature in July was in the seventies, intolerable for salmon.
3. The wind is up.
4. The water is too low.

Yes, yes, but I do not put much stock in these gloomy reports, because Mordecai the Deep-Minded, son of Moses the Bald, has been salmon fishing before on some of the best rivers of Quebec and New Brunswick (the Cascapédia, the Restigouche, the Miramichi) and is familiar with the perverse tradition peculiar to salmon camps everywhere. The head guide, greeting newcomers, always complains that the water is too high or too low, and you should have been here last week when horny thirty-pound salmon had to be restrained from leaping into the arms of anglers, never mind taking a fly.

In the drawing room, Joseph, the menacingly obsequious wine steward (a Pole who had put in thirteen years as a butler), seems to have wandered in off the set of an old-time Hammer horror film; he stoops to kiss my wife's hand and then asks if we fancy wine with our lunch.

"A bottle of Puligny-Montrachet."

"An excellent choice," Joseph oozes, dentures gleaming.

Late in the afternoon a middle-aged American couple arrives, Joseph greeting the lady with a ritual kiss of the hand. "Would you care for wine with your dinner?" he asks.

"People are so nice in this neck of the woods," the lady says.

"Red or white?" her husband asks her.

"It's all the same, isn't it, dear?"

Husband, consulting the price list, chooses a bottle of Frascati.

"An excellent choice," Joseph responds, beaming.

Greeted at breakfast by a rowdy group of grouse shooters out of Yorkshire, drinking Champagne, dressed in elegant tweed jackets and plus fours. "You're not going after salmon this late in the season?"

"I'm afraid so."

"You're Canadian, did you say?"

"Yes."

"Oh."

There are no keys for our bedroom doors, but the Fly and Tackle Room is securely locked. Seemingly, the guests can trust each other, but the Tulchan management knows that when it comes to fishing flies, anglers are a notoriously thieving lot.

The head gillie, wearing a deerstalker cap, outfits me with hip boots and a fifteen-foot, two-handed rod, traditional in Scotland. At home, we use a ten-foot rod, a one-hander, so I will have to make a considerable adjustment. I am driven down to a beat on the Spey, where I am astonished to see manicured lawns, picnic tables, and a fishing "shack" that would rent for $8,000 a summer in the Hamptons. In Canada, of course, we fish in rough country, bush country, blackflies and mosquitoes the unhappy rule. Within a couple of hours I can manage, but have hardly mastered, the two-handed rod and the tricksy Spey double-cast, all to no avail. The only salmon left in the river in mid-September are black salmon, that is to say, derelict scrawny fish that have loitered in the Spey for years and have learned to eschew any fly thrown over their heads.

Come noon, on Canadian rivers, I would not be surprised to see a moose or a black bear wandering down to the water's edge. But in the Highlands, at the stroke of twelve o'clock, an appropriately attired waiter is sent down from the lodge with a much-needed bottle of single-malt Scotch, white wine, and a baffling hot lunch: pasta served with a baked potato. Then, casting into a stiff wind, I spend another miserable two hours on the beat without raising a fish.

The odious Joseph is lying in wait in the drawing room with his *carte de vin.* "We'll have a bottle of Château Margaux tonight," I say, after consulting my wife.

"Very good, sir."

"Wait. Tell me, Joseph, do you think that's an excellent choice?"

"But, of course, sir."

The American couple drifts in from their afternoon stroll. "I'd like a gin and tonic, please," the lady says.

"Tanqueray?" Joseph asks.

"I don't understand," she replies, appealing to her husband.

"It's their accent," he assures her. "My wife would like a GIN AND TONIC!"

The grouse shooters are back. Those self-satisfied bastards, preceded by an army of beaters from a neighbouring estate, have taken fourteen birds. I retreat to our room just in time to field a phone call from our friends in London.

"Well, we've ordered the wine, but naturally we're counting on you for the yummy salmon."

Shit. Switching on the bedside radio, I tune in on a convention of the Scottish Nationalist Party. The speaker proclaims, "The Soviet Union treats its ethnic minorities better than England does the Scots," and harvests wild applause.

The Highlands Tourist Office, determined to dispel a nasty myth, has issued a pamphlet that claims, "We have wet weather and dry weather, but no bad weather." All the same, I waken to windowpane-rattling wind. Driving rain. But I'm out on the river immediately after breakfast, casting to no point until my arm throbs and cursing the Highlands Tourist Office for assuring me that mid-September was vintage time on the Spey.

Compensations. Today we have been invited to lunch at the Macallan distillery, some ten miles from Tulchan Lodge, on the Spey side in the lee of the Grampian Mountains. Kingsley Amis, who certainly ought to know, has pronounced Macallan "about the most delicious malt ever," and I am inclined to agree, especially as we are being poured the eighteen-year-old stuff. In fact, by the time lunch is ready I have such an agreeable buzz on that I'm even willing to forgive our host for serving us locally caught salmon.

Chatting with the amiable W. C. H. Phillips, managing director of Macallan, I get some notion of just how much a productive stretch of the Spey is actually worth. In 1954, Phillips tells us, Macallan was offered a two-mile section of the river for $10,000 but, following a directors' meeting, declined the deal. Then, four years ago, the two-mile stretch of the Spey came up for sale again. Macallan bid

$765,000 for *one-third* of it, and that offer was promptly declined as insultingly inadequate.

Following a quick breakfast, we say goodbye to our impeccable hosts at the first-class Tulchan Lodge, unaware that we have eaten our last good meal in Scotland. Weather conditions being what they are, our flight to Shetland, via Orkney, is delayed for two hours. The airline clerk is amused when I double-check that our luggage is tagged for the right island. "If you're going to Shetland," he says cheerily, "all you'll need is an umbrella."

Bouncing high over the North Sea, I calm myself by trying once more to tackle the history of our ulti-mate destination, Orkney, this time digging into a real page-turner, *Orkneyinga Saga,* the history of the earls of Orkney from the ninth century to the thir-teenth, translated from the Icelandic by Hermann Palsson and Paul Edwards: "Earl Thorfinn had five sons, one called Arnfinn, the next Havard the Fecund, the third Hlodvir, the fourth Ljot, and the fifth Skuli. Ragnhild Eirik's-Daughter plotted the death of her husband Arnfinn at Murkle in Caithness, then married his brother Havard the Fecund...."

On first sight, Shetland is absolutely haunting. Not a tree to be seen anywhere. Bare, gaunt hills, rock bursting like bone through the thin topsoil. Seemingly endless rolling fields of rich, dark peat, the fuel cut and stacked to dry here and there. Sheep foraging everywhere. And above, intruding helicopters ferrying workers to and from the North Sea oil rigs. Our taxi driver is quick to point out that nobody speaks Gaelic here or would be caught wearing a kilt. The Shetlanders, honouring their Viking heritage, seem to identify more closely with Iceland and Norway (Bergen is accessible by overnight ferry from Lerwick) than they do with Scotland.

As we proceed in the wind and rain through the narrow streets of bleak, grey stone Lerwick, I can't help observing that fishing equipment is being offered at 25 percent off everywhere, a depressing indication that the season is over. I also note that on the island God gave to Calvin, it is illegal to take a salmon or a sea trout on a Sunday.

Finally we reach our hotel, the Shetland, overlooking the harbour but within walking distance of the city centre, especially given favourable tailwinds. Considering the hotel's grim, fortresslike exterior, I wonder whether we're expected to register or if we'll simply be fingerprinted and led to our cell. Inside, it is dark and reeks of damp and of cleaning fluid. Once out for a stroll, however, leaning into the wind, we are overwhelmed by the natural friendliness of the islanders, strangers greeting us warmly everywhere.

Dinner at the Shetland hotel proves inedible. Slabs of fish cemented inside artificially coloured bread crumbs. Potatoes rock-hard and raw through the middle. Slushy green peas. Our host, the hotel manager or warden, tells us that Russian and other Eastern bloc freighters regularly put in at the harbour and that the crews are allowed to wander freely through the port town. Me, I put this down to a clever KGB plot. Once the commie seamen have had a taste of beautiful downtown Lerwick, perhaps their first and only glimpse of the freedom-loving West, they can't wait to sail home to the fleshpots of Leningrad or Gdansk.

Mind you, Shetland (population twenty-three thousand) is well worth a visit. First settled by Neolithic farmers some five thousand years ago, it is uncommonly rich in both fascinating archaeological sites and, for once, truly breathtaking views from the top of jagged cliffs that soar hundreds of feet above the pelting sea. At one point—Mavis Grind—the highway crosses a chicken neck of land, the Atlantic visible on one side and the North Sea on the other.

The prime archaeological site is Jarlshof, hard by Sumburgh airport. Jarlshof, which takes its name from Sir Walter Scott's novel *The Pirate,* leads the amazed visitor from Stone Age settlement, through Bronze, to Iron Age. "Some eighty years ago," Eric Linklater wrote in *Orkney & Shetland,* first published in 1965 and deservedly reprinted many times since, "the ruin of a medieval house stood on a grassy mound beside a small shallow bay. Great gales eroded the mound, and revealed stone walls. The proprietor, John Bruce of Sumburgh, began to excavate, and excavation was continued, at intervals, until quite recently. Oldest of the buildings uncovered was the remains of a Stone Age hut...."

It is possible, at Jarlshof, to walk through Bronze Age shelter and smithy, circa 2000 B.C., into an overlapping Iron Age village, its shelters connected by winding stone-walled passages, right into a broch. A broch, I should point out, is a prehistoric structure peculiar to Shetland and Orkney and the adjacent

Scottish mainland. It is a round stone tower, a considerable engineering feat, with small chambers for human habitation inside.

Jarlshof, once but two days' fair sail from Norway, was settled by the Norse (charmingly described as "recent occupiers" on a plaque I saw in Lerwick) in the ninth century, their rule lasting until 1471, when Scotland annexed the islands.

My gillie, actually a young baker, arrives shortly before noon, having been up most of the night baking scones, which, in my experience of the islands, serve better as projectiles than pastries. A cheerful lad, he has a wool cap pierced by innumerable badges, testimony to his prowess as a trout fisherman. He's a champ, actually, winner of many a competition on Orkney and on Shetland. We set out through lashing wind and rain for Loch Benston, a half-hour drive. En route we pass a couple of bays where salmon is farmed. These tame salmon, he tells me, are a menace. Idiot fish. Breaking free of their restraining pens by the thousands from time to time, without the redeeming memory of a river that spawned them, they have no notion of which way to swim. The fear is that infiltrating a school of wild salmon, the farm fish could contaminate the wild ones. Something else. "The pellets they're fed," the gillie tells me, "contain a pink dye; otherwise the flesh of the farmed salmon would be a sickly white and not fit for market."

Sooner or later, salar, the leaper, will have to be

declared an endangered species. With the benefit of
sonar, commercial fishermen have solved the mystery of where the salmon gather in the winter, under
the Arctic ice, and now net them by the thousands of
tons, heedless of the fact that if the fish don't return
in sufficient numbers to the rivers that spawned
them there will soon be hardly any left. Another
threat to the Atlantic salmon is that wrongheaded
environmentalists, demonstrating in Europe, have
seen to it that there is no more hunting of the
cutesy-poo seal cubs on the Newfoundland ice.
Consequently, the seal herd, its appetite for salmon
prodigious, has increased beyond reason, and fewer
and fewer of the fish return to spawn in Canada's
once-rich network of maritime rivers.

I find casting into the wind of Loch Benston all
but impossible, my leader knotting again and again,
my fly shooting back to nick me in the face more
than once. After an embarrassing two hours of shivering out there on the loch (during which time—ho,
ho, ho—my champion gillie also fails to get a trout to
rise), I say I've had quite enough and suggest we row
to shore.

"Och," the gillie says, "it's a dour loch, but
bonny."

Once dried out back in the Shetland hotel, I hire
a car and my wife and I drive to the Booth, the
island's oldest pub, established in 1698 in St. Magnus
Bay and by the look of it not renovated once since
then. Following my third large single malt, I tell
Florence that if our friends call from London tonight
to say I was out.

"What if you don't catch anything tomorrow?"

"There's still Orkney."

We agree to cut our stay in Shetland by a day and leave for Orkney the next morning.

Out over the North Sea again, I turn once again to the spellbinding *Orkneyinga Saga,* totally absorbed in the hijinks of Oddi the Little, Thorkel Hook-Eye, and Havard the Fecund.

Orkney is only a twenty-five-minute flight, albeit bouncy enough, but also a world away from gaunt Shetland. Even as our plane skitters into the airport, we can see trees, grassy meadows, cultivated fields, cattle. Our taxi driver, once he has heard where we've been, says, "Och, but they're a thieving lot." Then he asks, "Have you come for the fishing?"

"Yes, indeed."

"The water's too high."

We drive through Kirkwall, a refreshingly cheerful-looking town, handsome as well, dominated by the St. Magnus Cathedral, and then on to the Merkister Hotel, a proper fishing lodge, on Harray Loch.

"You're a day early," Angus MacDonald, our ebullient host, says.

"We got time off for good behaviour."

Following a couple of heart attacks seven years ago, the portly Angus MacDonald, an accomplished fisherman himself, chucked his Aberdeen heating business and bought the foundering Merkister, which he and his wife, Elma, have revived with such flair that it is now considered one of the finest

angling hotels in Scotland. Incidentally, $325 is the
weekly rate for room and board.

Angus points out the fish scale in the entrance
hall, underneath which rests a full basket of trout
caught earlier in the day, and then leads me into the
bar. Now that I'm down to my last fishing hole,
salmon is out. Our London friends would have to settle for a bonny basket of trout.

Affable fishermen, still flushed from their day on
the wind-whipped loch, make me instantly welcome: Walter, Sandy, John. "Do you abide in New
York?" Sandy asks.

"No, Montreal."

"Then you wouldn't be familiar with the Loch
Harray roll cast."

"Sorry, no."

"Or the double roll cast."

"He'll catch on soon enough tomorrow morning," Angus says.

Out again in a boat in the punishing wind and rain,
with Angus and a young gillie, I manage the Loch
Harray roll cast one try out of the three. Once, I actually get a trout to rise but fail to set the hook quickly
enough and lose it, and that is that.

Like Shetland, Orkney is rich in archaeological
sites, the most famous being Skara Brae, the ruins of
prehistoric dwellings, and Maes Howe, a prime
example of the Neolithic chambered tomb. Also not
to be missed is the Ring of Brodgar, a circle of standing stones reminiscent of Stonehenge. In fact,

Orkney, first settled in the fourth millennium B.C., boasts so many archaeological sites that farmers, striking one, commonly plow it over before the hordes from Historic Buildings and Monuments descend on them, roping off valuable arable land.

Skara Brae, settled for some six hundred years, from 3100 B.C. to 2500 B.C., is made up of a compelling cluster of six self-contained dwellings, complete with hearth and stone beds, joined by passages. The dwellings were once buried under a heap of ash and midden, which preserved them. The tomb of Maes Howe, probably dating from before 2700 B.C., is an astonishing feat of construction, its largest stones weighing some thirty tons. We were preceded to the site by early souvenir hunters, medieval yuppies, Crusaders, or Vikings, who wintered in Orkney in 1150 and pilfered whatever treasures were to be found in the tomb.

Chilled to the bone on our return to the Merkister, Florence and I repair to the bar.

"There's a nasty storm coming in," Angus says. "I hope you weren't counting on fishing tomorrow morning."

"Naw," I say. "Water's too high anyway."

The windowpanes are rattling again. Gale-force winds. Heavy rain. Florence and I decide to cut our stay short and escape to London this afternoon, if possible. I linger in the hall as she consults the manager's wife, asking for the airline's phone number.

"Did you mean the office in Kirkwall?"

"Yes, please."

"Did you forget it was Sunday?"

"Oh."

"But everything's closed. There's nobody at the airport. There are no flights on Sunday."

Happily, as it turns out, this enables us to visit both Stromness and Kirkwall.

Stromness, which once supplied three-quarters of the Hudson's Bay Company employees in Canada, was of particular interest to me. It was here, in 1845, that Sir John Franklin put in for fresh water at Login's Well before setting out again with a complement of 134 officers and men on two stout three-masted ships, the *Erebus* and the *Terror,* bound for the Polar Seas in quest of the northwest village of substantial stone houses squished together on narrow, twisting cobblestone streets.

Kirkwall is worth a visit if only because of the incredibly beautiful St. Magnus Cathedral, with its red-and-yellow sandstone-brick exterior. St. Magnus, surely one of the most imposing medieval cathedrals in Scotland, is dedicated to the martyred Magnus Erlendsson. Founded in 1137, it took all of three centuries to complete, which accounts for its mélange of styles—Romanesque, Transitional, and Gothic.

Back at the Merkister, we are joined for a farewell dinner by Josh Gournley, director of tourism for Orkney, and it is from him that I learn the probable origin of the Super Bowl. I speak of the Men's Ba', a game played twice annually in Kirkwall, on Christmas and on New Year's Day, between the "Uppies" and the "Doonies." The two sides, made up of most of the able-bodied young men in town, confront each other on Kirk Green, where the Ba' is thrown up in the air. In a contest that has been known to last seven hours, it is then up to the Doonies, pushing and shoving, to deliver the Ba' to the top of the town or to the Uppies to manoeuvre the ball into a harbour splashdown. According to Gournley, who used to compete, many a private score is settled with the elbows during the struggle. "Then," he said, "when you've reached your early thirties like me, and believe you're too old for the contest, you put on your best suit and join the spectators on the sidelines, but before you know it you're back in there, pushing and shoving with all your might, emerging bruised, with your suit torn, most likely."

The airport. Aberdeen. Making sure that I'm not being observed, I purchase two sides of smoked salmon in a shop, comforting myself with some wise words from Mascall's *Booke of Fishing with Hook and Line,* published in 1590: "The Salmon is a gentle fish, but he is cumbrous to take; for commonly he is in deep places of great rivers, and commonly in the middlest of the rivers." Yes, but not in mid-September, damn it.

August 1991

2

Jews in Sports

I. The Encyclopedia of Jews in Sports

Good news. The bar mitzvah gift book has come of age. In my time, we had to make do with Paul de Kruif's inspirational medical books or a year's subscription to the *National Geographic* magazine. Since then, but too late for me, a spill of treasuries has become available: of Jewish Thought, of Jewish Wisdom, of Jewish Humour. Now, after many years of research, filling "a glaring void in the long record of Jewish achievement," comes *The Encyclopedia of Jews in Sports* by Bernard Postal, Jesse Silver, and Roy Silver, "the first all-inclusive volume to tell the complete story of Jews in professional and amateur sports all over the world, from Biblical times to Sandy Koufax's no-hitter in September."

The compendium comes lavishly recommended. "It is," Mel Allen writes on the jacket flap, "a noteworthy contribution to mankind's ever-growing quest for knowledge"; while Senator Abraham Ribicoff, former secretary of health, education and welfare, writes in a foreword, "Interest in sports among Jews—as among all Americans—has intensified as opportunities for leisure activities have increased." Continuing in the same thoughtful, controversial vein, he adds, "For sports are a healthy part of American life, and Jews are involving themselves fully in all aspects of American life."

The encyclopedia should first of all be judged by its own exacting standards. If I am not guilty of misunderstanding editors Postal, Silver, and Silver, they compiled it not to turn a buck in the non-book trade, but for two altogether admirable reasons: that Jews might be made more aware of their sports heritage and to dispel "one of the oldest myths about the Jew...the curious belief that he was a physical coward and a stranger to athletics," or, as Senator Ribicoff puts it, that he is "nimble in the head, perhaps, but not too nimble with the feet." On this test alone, the encyclopedia fails. It will, I fear, make trouble for *us* with *them*. It's dynamite! Rotten with proof of Jewish duplicity and athletic ineptitude.

Until I read the encyclopedia, for instance, I had no idea that Mushy Callaghan (world junior welterweight champion, 1926–30) was really born Vincente Morris Schneer, and I wonder if this will also be a revelation to his Irish-Catholic fans. Neither did I suspect that anybody called Al McCoy (world middleweight champion, 1914–17) answered more properly to the name Al Rudolph, and was actually the son of a kosher butcher who had changed his name because his parents objected to his boxing activities.

Then consider these far from untypical baseball entries:

COHEN, HYMAN "HY." Pitcher, b. Jan. 29, 1931, in
Brooklyn, N.Y. Played for Chicago Cubs in
1955. Total Games: 7. Pitching record: 0-0.
Right-hander.

HERTZ, STEVE ALLAN. Infielder, b. Feb. 26, 1945, in
Dayton, Ohio. Played for Houston in 1964. Total
Games: 5. Batting Average: 000.

Is this the stuff the Jewish Hall of Fame is made of?
Doesn't it suggest that in order to fill only 526 pages
with Jewish athletic "Achievement" Messrs. Postal,
Silver, and Silver were driven to scraping the bottom
of the barrel, so to speak? Still worse. Put this volume in the hands of an anti-Semitic sportsman and
can't you just hear him say, "Nimble in the feet? Ho
ho! Among them 0–0 pitchers and nothing hitters
count as *athletes.*"

Orthodox Jews will also be distressed by certain
entries in the encyclopedia. Was it necessary, for
example, to include Cardinal, Conrad Ceth, a
pitcher with a 0–1 record, when he is only half
Jewish? Or the playboy pitcher Belinsky, Robert
"Bo," just because he is the son of a Jewish mother?
This is more than a purist's racial quibble. Such
entries could lead, if this volume is the first of a
series, to the inclusion of, say, Elizabeth Taylor in a
compilation of Jewish Playmates from Biblical
Times to Today.

Of course there is another possibility. Half-
Jewish players of dubious achievement were
included in the book because the editors are not
only racialists, but cunning ones at that, and what

they intended by listing Belinsky and Cardinal was an oblique but penetrating comment on the capabilities of the issue of mixed marriages.

Something else. You and I might be pleased in our hearts to know that the first man to take money for playing baseball, the first real pro, was a Jew, Lipman E. "Lip" Pike, whose name appeared in a box score for the first time only one week after his bar mitzvah in 1864, but anti-Semites could easily make something unfortunate out of this information. Neither was I proud to discover that, according to a Talmudic scholar at the Jewish Theological Seminary of America, Jews—as early as the second century C.E.—had a special prayer for horse players; and that the bettor was advised to "take this [prayer] tablet and bury it in the ground of the hippodrome where you want to win."

There are some regrettable omissions. While Joe Reichler earns an entry because he is a baseball writer and Allan Roth, resident statistician with the Dodgers, is also included, there is no mention anywhere of Mailer, Norman, who has reported memorably on boxing for *Esquire*. Neither could I find the names of Malamud, Bernard, author of a baseball novel, or Schulberg, Budd, who has written a novel about boxing. Does this suggest an anti-intellectual bias on the part of Messrs. Postal, Silver, and Silver?

This is not to say that *The Encyclopedia of Jews in Sports* is entirely without merit. The three-page ice hockey section pleased me enormously if only because it included my favourite Jewish defence-man, one-time National League player, the astute

Larry Zeidel. An issue of *Jewish Press,* a New York publication, once carried the following Canadian report: "ONLY JEW IN PRO HOCKEY PLAYS A ROUGH GAME." "Larry Zeidal," the story began, "owns a scar for every one of the 20 years he marauded through organized hockey. 'When you're the only Jew in this bloody game,' he said, 'you have to prove you can take the rough stuff more than the average player.'" The story went on to say that Zeidal, in contrast to his teammates, read *Barron's Business Weekly* between periods, perhaps taking "Lip" Pike as his inspiration. Pike, the encyclopedia notes, played baseball at a time when other players were usually gamblers and drunkards. "However, Pike was an exception. Throughout his career contemporary journals commented on his sobriety, intelligence, wit, and industry."

Finally, if the encyclopedia fails, on balance, to rectify the oldest myth about the Jew—that he is "a stranger to athletics"—it must be allowed that this is a pioneering work and a step in the right direction. Let us hope that Messrs. Postal, Silver, and Silver, thus encouraged, will now take on other foul anti-Semitic myths, for instance, that Jews don't drink or practice homosexuality widely enough. I, for one, look forward to an encyclopedia (for delinquent bar mitzvah boys, perhaps) on Jewish Drunks, High School Dropouts, and Thugs from Noah to Today. I would also like to see a compilation of Famous Jewish Homosexuals, Professional and Amateur, Throughout History.

II. Koufax the Incomparable

Within many a once-promising, now suddenly command-generation Jewish writer, there is a major league ball player waiting to leap out; and come Sunday mornings in summer, from the playing fields of East Hampton to the Bois de Boulogne to Hyde Park, you can see them, heedless of tender discs and protruding bellies, out in the fresh air together, playing ball. We were all raised on baseball. While today there do not seem to be that many Jewish major league stars about, when I was a kid there were plenty we could identify with: Sid Gordon and Al Rosen and of course Hank Greenberg. Even in Montreal we had, for a time, one of our own in the outfield, Kermit Kitman. Kitman, alas, was all field and no hit and never graduated from the Royals to the parent Dodgers, but it was once our schoolboy delight to lie in wait for him over the clubhouse at Saturday afternoon games and shout, "Hey, Kermit, you *pipickhead,* you think it's right for you to strike out on *Shabbes?*"

Baseball was never a bowl of cherries for the Jewish player. *The Encyclopedia of Jews in Sports* observes that while the initial ball player to accept money for playing was a Jew, Lipman E. Pike, there were few known Jewish players. *The Sporting News,* in 1902, wrote of one player, "His name was Cohen and he assumed the name of Kane when he became a semi-professional, because he fancied that there was a popular and professional prejudice against Hebrews as ball players." Other major leaguers were more militantly Jewish. Barney Pelty, for instance, who pitched for the St. Louis Browns from 1903 to 1912, seemingly did not object to being known as "The Yiddish Curver." Still, the number of our players in any era has been small, possibly because, as Norm Sherry, once a catcher with the Dodgers, has said, "Many boys find opposition at home when they want to go out for a ball-playing career." Despite opposition at home or in the game, the Jew, as the *Encyclopedia* happily notes, has won virtually every honour in baseball. If there remains a Jewish Problem in the game today, it hinges on the Rosh Hashanah–Yom Kippur syndrome, for the truth we all have to live with is that much as the Reform temple has done to lighten our traditional Jewish burdens, the rush for the pennant and Rosh Hashanah, the World Series and Yom Kippur, still sometimes conflict.

Should a nice Jewish boy play ball on the High Holidays? Historical evidence is inconclusive. Harry Eisenstadt, once a pitcher for the Dodgers, was in uniform but not scheduled to pitch on Rosh Hashanah 1935, but when the Giants began to hurt his team he was called into the game and his first pitch was hit for a grand-slam home run. And yet— and yet—one year earlier, Hank Greenberg, with the Tigers close to their first pennant since 1909, played on Rosh Hashanah and hit two home runs. Greenberg went to *shul* on Yom Kippur, alas, and the Tigers lost. The whole country, rabbis and fans at odds, was involved in the controversy, and Edgar Guest was sufficiently inspired to write a poem, the last verse of which reads:

Come Yom Kippur—holy fast day
world-wide over to the Jew—
And Hank Greenberg to his teaching
and the old tradition true
Spent the day among his people
and
he didn't come to play.
Said Murphy to Mulrooney "We
shall lose the game today!
We shall miss him in the infield
and
shall miss him at the bat,
But he's true to his religion—
and
I honour him for that!"

Honour him, yes, but it is possible that Greenberg, at that time the only Jew in the Hall of Fame, was also tragically inhibited by his Jewish heritage. I'm thinking of 1938, when he had hit fifty-eight home runs, two short of Babe Ruth's record, but with five games to play, failed to hit another one out of the park. Failed... or just possibly held back, because Greenberg just possibly understood that if he shattered the Babe's record, seemingly inviolate, it would be considered pushy of him and, given the climate of the times, not be such a good thing for the Jews.

Greenberg, in any event, paved the way for today's outstanding Jewish player, the incomparable Sandy Koufax. So sensitive is the Dodgers' front office to Koufax's religious feelings that Walter Alston, the Dodgers' manager, who was once severely criticized for scheduling him to play on Yom Kippur, is now reported to keep a Jewish calendar on his desk.

Koufax, who has just published his autobiography, is not only the best Jewish hurler in history, he may well be the greatest pitcher of all time, regardless of race, colour, or creed. His fastball, Bob Feller has said, "is just as good as mine," and Casey Stengel was once moved to comment, "If that young fella was running for office in Israel, they'd have a whole new government over there...." Koufax has won the National League's Most Valuable Player Award, the Cy Young Award as the outstanding major league pitcher of the year, and the Hickok Pro Athlete of the Year Award. He has pitched four no-hit games, more than any other major league pitcher. He holds the major league record for both the most shutouts and the most strikeouts in one season and also the major league record for the number of seasons in which he has struck out more than three hundred batters. He has tied the major league record for most strikeouts in a nine-inning game, and also tied World Series records. I could go on and on, but a nagging question persists. This, you'd think, was enough. Koufax, at least, has proved himself. He is accepted. But is he?

Anti-Semitism takes many subtle shapes, and the deprecating story one reads again and again, most memorably recorded in *Time,* is that Sandy Koufax is actually something of an intellectual. He doesn't mix. Though he is the highest-paid player in the history of the game, improving enormously on Lipman E. Pike's $20 a week, he considers himself above it. Fresco Thompson, a Dodger vice-president, is quoted as saying, "What kind of a line is he drawing anyway—between himself and the world, between himself and the team?" Another report quotes Koufax himself as saying, "The last thing that entered my mind was becoming a professional athlete. Some kids dream of being a ball player. I wanted to be an architect. In fact, I didn't like baseball. I didn't think I'd ever like it." And the infamous *Time* story relates that when Koufax was asked how he felt after winning the last game in the 1965 World Series, he said, "I'm just glad it's over and I don't have to do this again for four whole months."

In *Koufax,* which the pitcher wrote with the dubious relief help of one Ed Linn, he denies the accuracy of most of these stories. In fact, looked at one way, Koufax's autobiography can be seen as a sad effort at self-vindication, a forced attempt to prove once and for all that he is the same as anybody else. Possibly Koufax protests too much. "I have nothing against myths," he begins, "but there is one myth that has been building through the years that I would just as soon bury without any particular honours: the myth of Sandy Koufax, the anti-athlete." He goes on to state flatly that he is no "dreamy intellectual" lured out of college by a big bonus, which he has since regretted, and as if to underline this point, he immediately lapses into regular-guy English. "Look, if I could act that good I'd have signed with 20th Century–Fox instead of Brooklyn...." Koufax protests that though he is supposed to read Aldous Huxley and Thomas Wolfe and listen to Beethoven, Bach, and Mendelssohn, if anybody dropped in at his place they would more likely find him listening to a show tune or a Sinatra album. All the same, he does own up to a hi-fi. "I wish," he writes, "my reading tastes were classier, but they happen to run to the bestseller list and the book-club selections," which strikes this reader as something of an evasion. Which book clubs, Sandy? Literary Guild or Readers' Subscription?

Koufax insists the only thing he was good at in school was athletics (he captained the basketball team that won the National Jewish Welfare Board hoop tournament in 1951–52) and denies, to quote *Time* again, that he is an anti-athlete "who suffers so little from pride that he does not even possess a photograph of himself." If you walk into his room, Koufax writes, "you are overwhelmed by a huge, immodest action painting," by which he means a picture that shows him in four successive positions of delivery. Furthermore, he denies that "I'm mightily concerned about projecting a sparkling all-American image," and yet it seems to me this book has no other purpose. Examined on any other level it is a very bush-league performance, thin, cliché-ridden, and slapped together with obnoxiously clever chapter headings such as, "Where the Games Were," "*La Dolce Vita* of Vero Beach," "Suddenly That Summer," and "California, Here We—Ooops—Come." A chapter called "The Year of the Finger," I should hasten to add in this time of Olympia and Grove Press books, actually deals with Koufax's near tragic circulatory troubles, his suspected case of Raynaud's syndrome.

Projecting an all-American image or not, Koufax hasn't one unkind or, come to think of it, perceptive, word to say about the game or any of his teammates. Anecdotes with a built-in twinkle about this player or

that unfailingly end with "That's John [Roseboro],"
or "That's Lou [Johnson]," and one of his weightiest
observations runs "Life is odd," which, *pace* Fresco
Thompson, is not enough to imply alienation.

Still true to the all-American image, Koufax
writes, nicely understating the case, that though
there are few automobiles he couldn't afford today,
nothing has given him more joy than the maroon
Rollfast bicycle his grandparents gave him for his
tenth birthday when he was just another Rockville
Center kid. "An automobile is only a means of transportation. A bike to a ten-year-old boy is a magic
carpet and a status symbol and a gift of love." Self-
conscious, perhaps, about his towering salary, which
he clearly deserves, considering what a draw he is at
the gate, he claims that most of the players were for
him and Drysdale during their 1966 holdout. "The
players felt—I hope—that the more we got paid, the
more they would get paid in the future," which may
be stretching a point some.

Koufax was not an instant success in baseball. He
was, to begin with, an inordinately wild pitcher, and
the record for his 1955 rookie year was 2–2. The following year he won two more games, but lost four,
and even in 1960 his record was only 8–13. Koufax
didn't arrive until 1961, with an 18–13 record, and
though some accounts tell of his dissatisfaction with
the earlier years and even report a bitter run-in with
the Dodgers' general manager, Buzzy Bavasi—
because Koufax felt he was not getting sufficient

work—he understandably soft-pedals the story in his autobiography. Koufax is also soft on Alston, who, according to other sources, doubted that the pitcher would ever make it.

If Koufax came into his own in 1961—becoming a pitcher, he writes, as distinct from a thrower—then his transmogrification goes some way to belie the all-American image; in fact there is something in the story that will undoubtedly appeal to anti-Semites who favour the Jewish-conspiracy theory of history. Koufax, according to his own account, was helped most by two other Jews on the team, Allan Roth, the resident statistician, and Norm Sherry, a catcher. The turning point, Koufax writes, came during spring training, at an exhibition game, when Sherry told him, "Don't try to throw hard, because when you force your fastball you're always high with it. Just this once, try it my way...."

"I had heard it all before," Koufax writes. "Only, for once, it wasn't blahblahblah. For once I was rather convinced...." Koufax pitched Sherry's way and ended up with a seven-inning no-hitter and went on from there to superstardom. The unasked question is, Would Norm Sherry have done as much for Don Drysdale?

III. Postscript

"Koufax the Incomparable" appeared in *Commentary*, November 1966, and led to a heated correspondence:

MARSHALL ADESMAN, BROOKLYN, N.Y., WROTE:

As a professional athlete in the highest sense of the word, Hank Greenberg would never have purposely failed to tie or break Ruth's record. The material gain he could have realized by attaining this goal would have been matched only by the great prestige and glory that naturally come along with the magical figure of sixty home runs. Greenberg failed only because the pressure, magnified tenfold by the press, weighed too heavily on his shoulders. Very rarely is one able to hit the ball into the seats when he is seeking to do so. Home runs come from natural strokes of the bat, and Greenberg's stroke in those last five games was anything but natural. The pitchers, also, were not giving the Detroit slugger anything too good to hit, not wishing to have the dubious honour of surrendering number sixty. In short, it was the pressure that made Greenberg's bat too heavy, not the political atmosphere. Perhaps Mr. Richler should check his facts before his next article on the National Pastime.

SAMUEL HEFT, LONG BEACH, N.Y., WROTE:
I am stunned by ... some startling statements made by Mordecai Richler....

Even to hint at the possibility that the Hall of Fame baseball player Hank Greenberg "held back" in his efforts to break Babe Ruth's home run record, for any reason, is shocking. To state that Greenberg considered it would be "pushy" of him to do so, is almost too silly for comment. I shudder to think of a player in the Hall of Fame being accused of not giving his all....

Richler states that "many boys found opposition

at home" when they went out for sports. This is understandable. Our parents were not sports-minded, because of their European sufferings.... I'm sure our people didn't get many opportunities to play ball in the *shtetl,* while running away from pogroms.

I disagree that there is a Jewish problem in baseball today. If Walter Alston keeps a Jewish calendar on his desk... it is because he is a good administrator and needs this reminder in his scheduling of pitchers' rotations, and not because of "sensitivity."

So far as playing baseball on the Jewish holidays goes, and yelling *pipickhead* at Kermit, this is not a baseball problem. I see with my own eyes too many Jews of all denominations mowing lawns, shopping, and doing numerous other chores on the *Shabbes....*

Mr. Richler's article may do serious harm in the struggle against discrimination.... Maybe, according to Richler, even Kermit Kitman might have been a good hitter, but he was afraid the Montreal non-Jewish population would think he was "pushy."

E. KINTISCH, ALEXANDRIA, VIRGINIA, WROTE:
...Richler very obviously doesn't think much of Koufax. Then why did he bother reading the Koufax book, or writing about it?...

JEROME HOLTZMAN, *CHICAGO SUN-TIMES,* CHICAGO, ILL., WROTE:
I am but one of approximately two to three dozen Jewish baseball writers—writers from big-city newspapers—who cover major league baseball teams from the beginning of spring training through the World Series—and as such should inform your

readers that Mordecai Richler was off base quite a few times in his "Koufax the Incomparable."

Richler indicates that Hank Greenberg was "tragically inhibited by his Jewish heritage" and thus held back and hit fifty-eight home runs instead of breaking Babe Ruth's record of sixty because the breaking of such a record "... would be considered pushy of him ... and not a good thing for the Jews." Balderdash! Greenberg didn't hit sixty because pitchers stopped giving him anything good to hit at—probably because he was Jewish, and probably also because no pitcher wants to be remembered for throwing historic home-run balls. We must assume also that the pressure was a factor, as it always is; what also hurt was that a season-ending doubleheader (in Cleveland) had to be moved to a bigger ballpark with a longer left field, and that the second game wasn't played to a nine-inning finish. . . .

I agree that the *Time* magazine cover story on Koufax was distorted, but to accuse *Time* of anti-Semitism is presumptuous. *Time* has erred on plenty of other sports cover stories, as have many of the other slicks. The image of Koufax as an intellectual (which he is not) was featured, I suspect, because it made "a good angle" and probably because a *Time* stringer spotted a bookshelf. Moreover, that Koufax likes his privacy isn't unusual. Many star players, Feller, Musial, Williams *et al.,* roomed alone in their later years and did their best to avoid the mob.

Author Richler is looking too hard, also, when he emphasizes that Koufax, in his autobiography, points out that he was helped most by two other

Jews...Sherry, a catcher, advised Koufax not to throw hard, advice I'm sure Sherry has given to dozens and dozens of Gentile pitchers, and advice which previously had been given to Koufax by Gentile coaches. Sherry simply happened to mention this at precisely the right moment, before a meaningless exhibition game, and when Koufax was...eager to listen....

As for Allan Roth, he was a statistician with the Dodgers, the only full-time statistician employed by a big league club. Roth borders on genius in this field. It was his job to keep and translate his findings to the Dodger players and the Dodger management. Whatever information Roth gave Koufax (and I don't know what this was), I'm sure was part of the routine. Richler's attitude is disgusting if he thinks that Roth would favour Koufax because both are Jews. In effect, Richler is saying that Roth would withhold significant statistics from Gentiles such as Drysdale, Newcombe, or Podres.

I agree that from a so-called Jewish standpoint, the Koufax book is disappointing, and I agree with Richler that Koufax protesteth too much in emphasizing that he is not anti-athlete. It is unfortunate that Koufax didn't control his anger, not only at the *Time* story but at several minor pieces that preceded it. In his book, Koufax tells us almost nothing about his Jewishness; that he is Jewish is mentioned almost in passing. But he doesn't owe us any detailed explanations. As a baseball book, and as a text in pitching, I found it excellent.

I should think that *Commentary,* in this rare instance when it did touch on sports, could have done better than offer the long-distance musings of a novelist....

AVRAM M. DUCOVNY, NEW YORK CITY, WRITES:

I am shocked that Mr. Richler in his treatise on Curve Balls: Are They Good or Bad for the Jews? overlooked Willie Davis's three errors in one inning behind Koufax in the 1966 World Series—which was one of the most flagrant acts of Negro anti-Semitism since the panic of 1908.

He does get somewhere in pointing out the Jewish-conspiracy angle in the Norm Sherry–Koufax cabal; however, he does not really go deep enough. What of Norm's brother Larry—also a Dodger pitcher at the time—stopped from the advice that made a super start because of piddling sibling rivalry? There's one for Bill Stern!

And yea, verily, let us weep for the likes of Don Drysdale—disenfranchised WASP—alone in a sea of Gentile coaches whose knowledge of baseball never had the benefit of the secret indoctrination into the *Protocols of the Elders of Swat.* By the way, what is that resident genius, Norm Sherry, doing today? Have I somehow missed his name among the current great pitching coaches of baseball?

And finally, finally, the true story of the whispered Greenberg caper, wherein he was visited by representatives of the Anti-Defamation League, the American Jewish Committee and Congress, and the many, many Friends of the Hebrew University, who said unto him: "Hershel, thou shalt not Swat; whither Ruth goest, thou goest not."

I am looking forward with great anticipation to

Mr. Richler's exposure of Mike Epstein (the self-labelled "super-Jew" rookie of the Baltimore Orioles) who all "insiders" know is a robot created at a secret plant in the Negev and shipped to Baltimore for obvious chauvinistic reasons.

FINALLY, THAT VERY GOOD WRITER DAN WAKEFIELD WROTE A MOST AMUSING LETTER THAT BEGAN:

I greatly enjoyed Mordecai Richler's significant comments on Sandy Koufax, and the profound questions he raised about the role of Jews in American sports. Certainly much research still needs to be done in this area, and I hope that some of the provocative points raised by Richler will be picked up and followed through by our social scientists, many of whom are capable of turning, say, a called strike into a three-volume study of discrimination in the subculture of American athletics.

I REPLIED:

The crucial question is, Did Hank Greenberg hold back (possibly for our sake), or was the pressure too much for him? Mr. Adesman, obviously a worldly man, suggests that Greenberg couldn't have held back, because of "the material gain he could have realized" by hitting sixty home runs. This, it seems to me, is gratuitously attributing coarse motives to an outstanding Jewish sportsman.

Mr. Heft is stunned by my flattering notion that Greenberg might have placed the greater Jewish good above mere athletic records and goes on to nibble at a theory of Jewish anti-gamesmanship based on our parents' "running away from pogroms." This theory, clearly unattractive if developed to its logical big league conclusion, would surely have resulted in a more noteworthy Jewish record on the base paths. Mr. Heft is also of the opinion that if Walter Alston keeps a Jewish calendar on his desk, it is because he is a good administrator. Yom Kippur, Mr. Heft, comes but once a year, and surely Alston doesn't require a calendar to remind him of one date. If Koufax had also been unwilling to take his turn on the mound on Tishah-b'Ab or required, say, a *chometz*-free resin bag for the Passover week, then Alston would have had a case. As things stand, the calendar must be reckoned ostentatious.

About Kermit Kitman: I'm afraid his poor hitting had no racial origins, but was a failure all his own, regardless of race, colour, or creed. His superb fielding, however, was another matter: a clear case of the overcompensating Jew. Briefly put, Kitman was a notorious *chapper*—a grabber, that is to say, any fly ball hit into the outfield had to be *his* fly ball, if you know what I mean.

Mr. Kintisch errs. I admire Koufax enormously and shall miss him sorely this season. He was undoubtedly the greatest pitcher of our time, and yet—and yet—now that he has retired so young, is it possible that carping anti-Semites have already begun the whispering campaign: great, yes, but *sickly*. Without the staying power of Warren Spahn. An unnatural athlete.

Jerome Holtzman, a dazzling intellectual asset to the sports department of the *Chicago Sun-Times,* raises darker questions. Greenberg, he says, would never have held back. He "didn't hit sixty because pitchers stopped giving him anything good to hit at—*probably because he was Jewish....*" Now there's something nasty even I didn't think of: the possibility that Bob Feller, Red Ruffing, and others threw big-oted anti-Semitic curveballs at Hank Greenberg while a later generation of American League pitch-ers fed Roger Maris pro-Gentile pitches.... Next season I would implore Holtzman and other Jewish baseball writers to keep a sharp eye on the racial nature of pitches thrown to (or God forbid, even at) Mike Epstein.

As for *Time,* if it is not anti-Semitic, then it is cer-tainly Machiavellian; otherwise, why second-best Juan Marichal on a cover last summer when Koufax was also available? Either as a back of the hand to Jewish achievement or as a shameful, possibly Jewish-motivated, attempt to apply the famous *Time* cover jinx to the one Gentile who might have won more games than Koufax.

Messrs. Ducovny and Wakefield are another mat-ter. They think I would joke about Jews in sport, which strikes me as presumptuous.

Mr. Ducovny cunningly introduces Willie Davis's three errors behind Koufax in one inning and imme-diately claims this was a case of Negro anti-Semitism. Not necessarily. It depends on whether Davis dropped the three fly balls in his character as a Negro or in his office as an outfielder. Me, I'm keep-ing an open mind on the incident.

On the other hand, Mr. Wakefield is right when he says there is much more research to be done about Jews in sport. Not only Jews, but other minority and out-groups. Allan Roth, *pace* Jerome

Holtzman, may border on genius in his field, but though it may seem to some fans that baseball is already stifled with statistics, these are only statistics of a certain kind, safe statistics. It has been left to me to establish, haphazardly I admit, the absorbing statistic that homosexuals in both major leagues prefer playing third base over all other positions. As a group, they hit better in night games and are more adroit at trapping line drives than catching flies. They do not, as the prejudiced would have it, tend to be showboats. They are a group with a gripe. A valid gripe. Treated as equals on the field, cheered on by teammates when they hit a homer, they tend to be shunned in the showers. On road trips, they have trouble finding roomies.

Finally, since I wrote my article, so unexpectedly controversial, world events have overtaken journalism.

1. Sandy Koufax has retired.
2. Ronald Reagan has been elected governor of California.
3. Tommy Davis has been traded to the Mets.
4. Maury Wills has been given, it would seem, to Pittsburgh.

I'm not saying that Ronald Reagan, who in the unhappy past has been obliged to play second-best man again and again for Jewish producers, has been harbouring resentments...or is behind the incomparable Koufax's departure from California. I'm not saying that image-conscious Governor Reagan, mindful of right-wing support, was against being photographed shaking hands with Captain Maury Wills on opening day. I'm also not saying that after Willie Davis dropped the three flies, Mr. O'Malley turned to one of his minions and said, "Davis belongs with the Mets." Furthermore, I'm not saying that the aforementioned front-office minion could not tell one Davis from another.... Just remember, as they said in the sports pages of my boyhood, that you read it here first.

1968

3

A Real Canadian
Success Story

"You'll find this is a good story for you,"
he said. "A real Canadian success
story."

The party at the other end of the line was Ben
Weider, president of the International Federation of
Body Builders, who was sponsoring the Official
Combination Contests to Select Mr. America and Mr.
Universe at the Monument National Theatre, in
Montreal, in 1960. The competition, according to
advance publicity, was going to be the "Greatest
Physical Culture Contest ever organized anyplace in
the World!"

"I've been to eighty-four countries in the last six
years," Weider told me, "including Red China. But
I'm not a communist, you know."

Weider was a man of many offices. He was, with his
brother Joe, the Trainer of Champions, with outlets
in cities as far-flung as Tokyo, Rio de Janeiro, and
Vienna. He was president and director of Weider
Food Supplements (makers of Super Protein 90 and

Energex) and the Weider Barbell Company, and managing editor of *Mr. America* and *Muscle Builder,* among other magazines. He was the author of such books as MANGEZ BIEN *et restez svelte* and JEUNE *toute sa vie*. In one of his many inspirational articles, "The Man Who Began Again," he wrote, "True sportsmen always cheer for the underdog...for the guy who has come up from down under—the hard way," and that's certainly how Ben Weider had risen to eminence as manufacturer, publisher, author, editor, world traveller, and number-one purveyor of muscle-building equipment and correspondence courses in North America.

Weider was only thirty-six years old. His brother Joe, who ran the American end of their various enterprises out of Union City, New Jersey, was thirty-nine. They had both been brought up in Montreal's St. Urbain Street area during the thirties. Skinny, underdeveloped boys, they first took to body development as a form of self-improvement. Then, in 1939, they began to write and publish a mimeographed magazine that would tell others how they could become he-men. To begin with, the magazine had a circulation of five hundred copies. Enthusiasts started to write in to ask where they could get the necessary equipment to train themselves. And so, from their modest offices on Colonial Street, the Weiders began to supply the desired equipment and correspondence courses until, Ben Weider said, they became the acknowledged leaders in the field. *Muscle Builder* and *Mr. America,* no longer mimeographed, now appeared monthly in ten languages with, Weider claimed, a total circulation of a million copies.

In May 1960, Ben Weider moved into his own

building on Bates Road, from which he overlooked his widespread empire in the comfort of a most luxurious office. For inspiration, perhaps, there hung behind Weider's desk a painting of a resolute Napoleon, sword drawn, mounted atop a bucking stallion. It was here, amid trophies, diplomas, and the odd bottle of Quick-Wate (Say Goodbye to Skinny Weakness), that we had our first chat.

"Why don't you send me a chapter from your next novel," Weider offered, "and we could shove it into *Muscle Builder* or *Mr. America.* It ought to win you a lot of new readers."

Yes, possibly. But, alas, I had to let on, I had never been considered A BIG HITTER by the muscle-building set.

Weider looked at me severely.

Later, once I had read some of his correspondence courses, I realized that he had probably spotted my inferiority complex. I was not thinking BIG, *positive* thoughts. "DON'T BE ENVIOUS OF SOMEONE ELSE'S SUCCESS," brother Joe advised people who felt inferior. "MAYBE SOMEONE ELSE ENVIES YOU! They are bald... *you have a head full of hair.* They are fat... *you are building a he-man body.*"

Weider was a soft-spoken, courteous, ever-smiling man ("YOUR TEETH," Joe wrote, "ARE THE JEWELS OF YOUR FACE") with a high-pitched voice. A conservative dresser, he had surely grasped, just as Joe advised in BE POPULAR, SELF-CONFIDENT, AND A HE-MAN, that it was necessary to MAKE YOUR FIRST IMPRESSION A GOOD ONE! Why? Because, as Joe said, *your packaging is your appearance.* Another thing was that Ben had chosen his hairstyle wisely. *It fitted his face!* He was not the sort of birdbrain Joe complained about who wore his hair in, say, a Flat-Top Crew Cut, just because "it's what everybody else is wearing now."

Weider, married in 1959, had recently become a father. His boy, he told me, weighed ten pounds eleven ounces at birth. *He was also twenty-three inches long!*

"CONGRATULATIONS!!!" I said, grasping his hand *firmly.* And, even as we parted, I made a note to remember his name, for... "people like to be called by name.... You can make yourself a real *somebody* by being known as the *one* man who never forgets names."

At home, I had time to read only one of Weider's correspondence lessons before going to bed. My choice was *Secrets of a Healthy Sex Life.*

Choosing the right girl, brother Joe wrote, was vitally important. "*Is she sports-minded?*" he asks. "Would she frown on you having your own home gym? DOES SHE LIKE WORKING OUT WITH YOU?"

Weider also suggested that young couples should pray together, use a good deodorant and positive thinking, and keep their weight *normalized.* He offered sensible advice to young husbands. "Wear clean pyjamas each night... and be sure that you have a variety of patterns in pyjamas. You would not expect her to retire in a torn nightgown with cold cream daubed over her face... hence you should make yourself as attractive as she."

All in all, *Secrets* gave me plenty of food for thought. It seemed a good idea to absorb its message before plunging into other, more advanced lessons, like *How to Get the Most Out of People,* although this particular pamphlet looked most intriguing. The illustration on the cover showed an assured, smiling young man grasping piles of dollar bills, coins, and money bags. I was keen to learn from him how to use people, but one BIG, *positive* thought was enough for one day. So, putting the lessons aside, I turned to *Muscle Builder.* There I read that Chuck Sipes, a recent Mr. America champion, had built his TERRIFIC muscles by using the Weider Concentration Principle.

A couple of days later I met Sipes at the Mount Royal Studio, where he had come to train for the approaching contest.

"Been in weightlifting a long time?" I asked.

"Yeah."

"Like it?"

"Yeah."

"Enjoying your stay in Montreal?"

"Yeah."

Sipes managed a gym in Sacramento, California. He told me that when he started lifting weights eight years ago he had been just another puny guy of some 165 pounds, but now he weighed in at 204. I wished him luck in the contest and went on to chat with Mr. Ireland, Mr. Bombay, and Mr. Hercules of India, all fine fellows. But the man who made the greatest impression on me was Mr. Scotland Sr., otherwise known as R. G. Smith, of the electricity board in Edinburgh. Smith, who was to become my friend, had come to Montreal both to visit his children and to enter the contest—not that he had the slightest chance of winning. Smith was fifty-four years old. He had begun to practice body building at forty-seven.

The body builders' exhibition was held on Eaton's

fourth floor on the Friday night before the contest. There was a good turnout. Some three to four hundred people, I'd say. An associate of Weider's introduced me to Dr. Frederick Tilney, who had flown in from Florida to be one of the contest judges. "Dr. Tilney," the man said, "has seven degrees."

The doctor, a sturdily built man in his mid-sixties, looked surprisingly young for his years.

"Can you tell me," I asked, "at what colleges you got your degrees?"

"What's the difference what college? A college is a college. Some college graduates end up digging ditches. It's what you make of yourself that counts in this world."

"What exactly do you do, Doctor?"

"Oh, I lecture on health and success and that sort of stuff."

Suddenly Ben Weider was upon us. "Sorry to interrupt your interview," he said, "but the show must go on."

A young French-Canadian body builder mounted the platform to introduce Dr. Tilney. "The doctor," he said, "has travelled all over the world and is one of the most famous editors and writers in it."

"Well, then," Dr. Tilney said, "I'm sure all you washed-out, weak, worn-out, suffering, sickly men want to renew your youth and delay that trip to the underground bungalow."

A body builder came out and struck a classic pose.

Dr. Tilney beamed at us. "We have assembled here some of the finest examples of manhood in the world. We are building a new race of muscular marvels, greater than the Greek gods. We're doing it scientifically."

Mr. Ireland assumed a heroic pose.

"You too," Dr. Tilney told us, "can develop a physique like Bill Cook's and overcome constipation, hernia, hardening of the arteries, diarrhea, heart disease, tuberculosis, rheumatism, and so forth."

We were introduced to Ed Theriault and his eight-year-old son, who demonstrated the Weider Chest Expander.

"This man here," the doctor said, "is the strongest short man in the world. He can do it—so can you! And look at this boy here. Isn't he sensational? Body building is one of the finest means of overcoming delinquency. If the kid's in the gym he's not in the poolroom. Why, I'm sure none of you want your boy to grow up a skinny runt—puny! You want him to be a real Weider he-man!"

Some other men came out to demonstrate weight lifting.

"And just look at the fine equipment, Weider equipment," the doctor said. "Guaranteed to last a lifetime. No parts to break. Isn't it something? And I have news for you. Eaton's is going to make this beautiful equipment available to you on their wonderful convenient time-payment plan. Isn't that something?"

Ben Weider applauded.

"You men out there," the doctor said, "want to have the bodies the Creator meant you to have, don't you?"

Mr. Scotland Sr. asked if he could say a few words.

"Sure."

"I just wanted to tell you," he said, "that I'm glad to be in your city, it's a wonderful opportunity, and I think body building is marvellous."

"Isn't that sensational?" Dr. Tilney said.

Chuck Sipes, the former Mr. America, came out and bent some enormous nails. He asked for a hot-water bottle and blew it up and exploded it just like a child's balloon.

"He's demonstrating wonderful lung power," Dr. Tilney said.

Chuck said he'd like to tear a telephone book for us.

"You'll notice," the doctor said, "that he's starting on the real tough end, the bound end of the book."

Chuck pulled, he grimaced, he grunted, he pulled again.

"A lot of you folks have heard body builders are musclebound. Well, you just watch Chuck here demonstrate..."

Chuck couldn't tear the book. He apologized, explaining that his hands were still greasy from having rubbed so much olive oil on his chest before posing for us.

"See you on Sunday at the Monument National," Dr. Tilney said.

The crowd began to disperse. I went home to study Weider's magazines and correspondence courses and to read up on Dr. Tilney, in anticipation of the grand contest on Sunday.

The pinups and articles in *Muscle Builder* and *Mr. America* appear between advertisements for Weider equipment. In one advertisement in *Muscle Builder,* Weider offers his readers $50 worth of personality courses FREE—with each order for $21.98 worth of equipment. Otherwise, his booklets sold for $1 each. They included *How to Make Women Like You, How to Develop Leadership Qualities,* and *Sex Education for the Body Builder.* "WHAT YOU DARE TO DREAM," one booklet advised, "DARE TO DO."

All the personality-course booklets were signed "Joe Weider, Trainer of Champions," but Dr. Tilney assured me that he was the actual author. The doctor, who had been in the health business for fifty years, also claimed that he had written the original Charles Atlas courses in the twenties and, to his regret, sold them outright for $1,000.

Tilney was a doctor of philosophy, divinity, natural law, naturopathy, chiropractic, and food science. I am indebted to Armin Mitto-Sampson of Trinidad for this information. Mitto-Sampson, author of *Meet...Dr. Frederick Tilney,* writes, "He stands like a Colossus, a God-propelled Titan, floodlighting the cosmos with his inspirational thunderbolts. He has zoomed up the voltage of more downtrodden souls than most all the Teachers, Adepts, Masters and Leaders of Men put together.... Most of Dr. Tilney's articles are stunners—torrid capsules.... His word-arrows are the language of TRUTH, not the piffle of intellectual witch-doctors.... At his lectures truth-starved souls gulp his gems, eager to utilize the Jewels of his Thoughts."

The next time I saw the doctor it was backstage at the Monument National Theatre on the day of the Mr. Universe and Mr. America contests, and all around me body builders were busy rubbing olive oil on each other's back and chest, posing for photographers, and trying out difficult postures before a full-length mirror. Ben Weider flitted anxiously from group to group, like a bad-tempered schoolmarm on scholarship day. I spotted my friend Mr. Scotland Sr. standing alone. He was, like so many of the body builders in the contest, an unusually short man. "If you ask me," he said, "it's going to be Mr. Guadeloupe and Mr. France. They can't be beat."

Joe Weider, who had flown in from Union City for the contest, wore a dark suit, a conservative tie, and a pleated dress shirt. A romantic drawing of him appeared in almost all Weider advertisements and bottle labels. The drawing showed Joe with enormous arms folded over a massive bare chest, his expression manly, commanding, but of course it could give no indication that in real life he also suffered from a nervous twitch.

"You all get into a circle now," Joe ordered the bashful contestants. *"Did you hear what I said?"* And he began to strut around them like a ringmaster. Meanwhile, Ben, followed everywhere by a sad, nearsighted photographer, grabbed Mr. Guadeloupe. "Take my picture with him." Briefly, Ben smiled. "Got it?"

The photographer nodded.

"Where in the hell's Mr. France?"

I took a seat in the orchestra pit with the judges and noted that the contest had attracted a full house. Ben Weider welcomed us on behalf of the IFBB. The master of ceremonies came out and told us, "I will announce each contestant as Mr. So-and-so from here-here in English and French. Then I'll tell you his weight, height, and measurements of chest and biceps. That's biceps," he said, grinning, "not bisex.

I will also tell you where each contestant has flown in from for the contest."

The boys began to appear onstage. The former Mr. Eastern Canada Jr., Mr. Calcutta, the Most Muscular Man from the Middle Atlantic, Mr. Hercules Jr., Mr. Montreal, Mr. Northern Quebec, and Mr. Muscle Beach. One by one they stepped under the spotlight, assumed a series of virile poses, and showed some spectacular muscle control. The last activity includes throwing the shoulder blades astonishingly far apart, jerking breast muscles, raising shoulder humps, and revolving yet other muscles.

During the intermission, between the Mr. America and Mr. Universe contests, the activity backstage was frenetic, what with cameramen competing to get shots of the likely winners. Ben Weider, here, there, and everywhere, attempted to gather his body builders into a corner. "Now listen to this! Will you come here and listen, please!"

Slowly the contestants gathered around.

"There will be no more gum chewing or muscle control. And I'm not kidding, guys. Anybody who does chew gum or do muscle-control stunts onstage will lose points."

I was, I must say, taken aback by Weider's behaviour. Only the other day I had read, in *How to Develop Leadership Qualities,* "*Avoid shouting* . . . BE FIRM—BUT DON'T BULLY. The most commanding people I've met were the gentlest and the kindest. Only the weak individual becomes a bully." But this, I felt, was not the right time for reproaches.

The second half of the program, the Mr. Universe contest, moved along more quickly than the first, and after the lads had done their bit Ben Weider summoned them into a corner once more. "Okay, we're soon going to announce the results. Now listen, you guys, *will you listen, please.* EVERYBODY'S GOING TO GET A MEDAL. But you have to be ready to go on as soon as your name is called. *Understand?* Be ready when your name is called. And just don't come crying to me afterwards and say you didn't get your medal. *Because you won't get your medal afterwards.*"

Before the results were announced, Weider, once more composed and soft-spoken, came onstage to present an award to Dr. Tilney for his tremendous contribution to the cause of body building. "The doc," he said, "is a real okay fella."

Then, one by one, the contestants' names were called, and, just as Weider had promised, there were medals for everybody. Mr. Guadeloupe and Mr. France both won bigger trophies than the rest, but the grand prize of all, Mr. Universe, went to Chuck Sipes. He burst into tears.

Then it was off to the City Hall in the rain for the official reception. Dr. Tilney and the other judges had already arrived by the time I got there. Heaps of sandwiches and glasses of fruit juice were laid out on a long table. Finally, the boys began to turn up. And after a short delay, Ben Weider rushed into the hall, carrying diplomas in both arms. Tony Lanza, one of the judges, went to summon the mayor.

Sarto Fournier, then mayor of Montreal, told us how much he admired body builders. "I have been told," he said, "that you boys have come from twenty different countries."

Weider summoned his photographer to take

pictures of himself with the mayor. Shuffling through diplomas, he began to call the boys forward. "And this," Weider said to the mayor, "is the young man who won the Most Muscular Man in America Award. *He's a fine French-Canadian boy,* Your Worship."

The mayor grasped the boy's hand and smiled. Photographers drew nearer. Weider, also smiling, stepped between the mayor and the boy, thrusting his wife into the picture as well.

"And this, sir, is Bill Cook, MR. IRELAND!"

Cook wore a green jacket.

"I can see," the mayor said, with a twinkle in his eye, "that you are Irish."

Weider shook with laughter.

Then, as more and more boys came forward to collect diplomas, the mayor glanced anxiously at his watch. Weider began to speed things up. "The mayor," Weider said, "has taken off valuable time from his work to greet us here. Well, I think everybody will agree he's a jolly good fellow."

As Ben Weider and his wife, brother Joe, and Chuck Sipes gathered around, the mayor got out his Golden Book. Everybody smiled for the sad, nearsighted photographer. "No, *no,* NO," Weider protested. "I want my wife to sign the Golden Book too."

1984

4

With the Trail Smoke Eaters in Stockholm

In 1963 the world ice hockey championships were not only held in Stockholm but, for the third time, the Swedes were the incumbent champions and the team to beat. Other threatening contenders were the Czechs and the Russians, and the team everyone had come to see humiliated was our own peppery but far from incomparable Trail Smoke Eaters.

"No nations can form ties of friendship without there being personal contact between the peoples. In these respects sports builds on principles of long standing," Helge Berglund, president of the Swedish Hockey Association, wrote warmly in the world hockey tournament's 1963 program. Berglund's bubbly letter of greeting continued, "I do hope the ice hockey players will feel at home here and that you will take advantage of your leisure to study Swedish culture and Swedish life. Welcome to our country."

Yes, indeed; but on the day I arrived in Stockholm a poster advertising a sports magazine on kiosks everywhere announced "THE CANADIANS WANT TO SEE BLOOD." Only a few days later a headline in the *Toronto Daily Star* read "UGLY ROW IN SWEDEN OVER OUR HOCKEY TEAM."

I checked into the Hotel Continental, a well-lit teak-ridden place where well on a hundred other reporters, radio and television men, referees, a hockey priest, and a contingent of twenty-seven Russians were staying and immediately sought out Jim Proudfoot of the *Toronto Daily Star*. Proudfoot had just returned from a cocktail party at the Canadian embassy. "What did the players have to say?" I asked.

"The players weren't invited."

The next morning things began to sizzle. On Saturday night, according to the most colourful Swedish newspapers, a substitute player with the Canadian team, Russ Kowalchuk, tried to smuggle a girl into his room and was knocked senseless by an outraged hall porter. Kowalchuk, enthusiastically described as a "star" in one Swedish newspaper and "a philandering hoodlum" in another, was not flattered: he denied that there had been a girl involved in the incident and claimed he had been flattened by a sneak punch.

Two things worried me about this essentially commonplace story. While it seemed credible that a hotel porter might be shocked if a hockey player tried to sneak a stuffed rabbit into the elevator, it did seem absurd that he would be shaken to his roots if a man, invited by Helge Berglund to study Swedish life, tried to take a girl to his room. And if the Canadians were such a rough-and-ready lot, if they were determined to crush Swedish bones in Friday night's game, wasn't it deflating that one of their defencemen could be knocked out by a mere porter? More important, mightn't it even hurt the gate?

The Trail Smoke Eaters, as well as the Czech, Russian, and American players, were staying at the Malmen—not, to put it mildly, the most elegant of hotels, a feeling, I might add, obviously shared by the amateur hockey officials associated with the Smoke Eaters, which group sagaciously put up at the much more commodious Grand Hotel.

When I finally got to the Malmen at noon on Sunday, I found the sidewalk outside all but impassable. Kids clutching autograph books, older boys in black leather jackets, and fetching girls who didn't look as if they'd need much encouragement to come in out of the cold, jostled each other by the entrance. An American player emerged from the hotel and was quickly engulfed by a group of autograph-hungry kids. "Shove off," he said, leading with his elbows; and if the kids (who, incidentally, learn to speak three languages at school) didn't grasp the colloquialism immediately, then the player's message, I must say, was implicit in his tone. The kids scattered. The American player, however, stopped a little farther down the street for three girls and signed his name for them. I knew he *could* sign too, for, unlike the amateurs of other nations, he was neither a reinstated pro, army officer, or sports equipment manufacturer but a bona fide student. Possibly, he could sign *very well.*

In the lobby of the Malmen, Bobby Kromm, the truculent coach of the Smoke Eaters, was shouting at a Swedish journalist. Other players, reporters, camp followers, cops, *agents provocateurs,* and strong-armed hotel staff milled about, seemingly bored. Outside, kids with their noses flattened against the windows tried to attract the attention of the players who slouched in leather chairs. Suddenly the Russian team, off to a game, emerged from the elevators, already in playing uniforms and carrying sticks. A Canadian journalist whispered to me, "Don't they look sinister?" As a matter of fact, if you over-looked the absence of facial stitches, they closely resembled the many Canadians of Ukrainian origin who play in the National Hockey League.

Bobby Kromm and his assistant manager, Don Freer, were also off to the game, but they agreed to meet me at eight o'clock.

When I returned to the Malmen that evening, I saw a car parked by the entrance, three girls waiting in the backseat. Kids, also hoping to attract the play-ers' attention, were banging coins against the lobby windows. The players ignored them, sucking on matchsticks. Kromm, Freer, and I went into the dining room, and while I ordered a cognac I was grat-ified to see that the reputedly terrifying Smoke Eaters, those behemoths who struck fear into the hearts of both Swedish mothers and Russian defencemen, stuck to coffee and pie.

Kromm, assuming our elderly waiter could under-stand English, barked his order at him and was some-what put out—in fact, he complained in a voice trained to carry out to centre ice—when the waiter got his order wrong. The waiter began to mutter. "You see," Kromm said, "they just don't like Canadians here."

I nodded sympathetically.

"Why do they serve us pork chops, *cold* pork chops, *for breakfast?*"

"If you don't like it here, why don't you check out and move right into another hotel?"

This wasn't possible, Kromm explained. Their stay at the Malmen was prepaid. It had been arranged by John Ahearne, European president of the International Ice Hockey Federation, who, as it turned out, also ran a travel agency. "If they'd treat us good here," Kromm said, "we'd treat them good."

Freer explained that the Smoke Eaters had nothing against the Swedes, but they felt the press had used them badly.

"They called me a slum," Kromm said. "Am I a slum?"

"No. But what," I asked, "is your big complaint here?"

Bobby Kromm pondered briefly. "We've got nothing to do at night. Why couldn't they give us a Ping-Pong table?"

Were these men the terror of Stockholm? On the contrary. It seemed to me they would have delighted the heart of any YMCA athletic director. Freer told me proudly that nine of the twenty-one players on the team had been born and raised in Trail and that ten of them worked for the CM and S.

"What does that stand for?" I asked.

"I dunno," he said.

It stands for Consolidated Mining and Smelting, and Bobby Kromm is employed as a glassblower by the company. All of them would be compensated for lost pay.

Kromm said, "We can't step out of the hotel without feeling like monkeys in a cage. People point you out on the streets and laugh."

"It might help if you didn't wear those blazing red coats everywhere."

"We haven't any other coats."

I asked Kromm why European players didn't go in for body checking.

"They condone it," he said, "that's why."

I must have looked baffled.

"They condone it. Don't you understand?"

I did, once I remembered that when Kromm had been asked by another reporter for his version of the girl-in-the-lobby incident, he had said, "Okay, I'll give you my impersonation of it."

Kromm and Freer were clear about one thing. "We'd never come back here again."

Jackie McLeod, the only player on the team with National Hockey League experience, didn't want to come back again either. I asked him if he had, as reported, been wakened by hostile telephone calls. He had been wakened, he said, but the calls weren't hostile. "Just guys in nightclubs wanting us to come out and have a drink with them."

While Canadian and Swedish journalists were outraged by Kowalchuk's misadventures, the men representing international news agencies found the tournament dull and Stockholm a subzero and most expensive bore. Late every night the weary reporters, many of whom had sat through three hockey games a day in a cold arena, gathered in the makeshift press club at the Hotel Continental. Genuine melancholy usually set in at 2:00 a.m.

"If only we could get one of the Russian players to defect."

"You crazy? To work for a lousy smelting factory in Trail? Those guys have it really good, you know."

The lowest paid of all the amateurs were the Americans, who were given $20 spending money for the entire European tour; and the best off, individually, was undoubtedly the Swedish star, Tumba Johansson. Tumba, a $10-a-game amateur, had turned down a Boston Bruins contract offer but not, I feel, because he was intent on keeping his status pure. A national hero, Tumba earns a reputed $40,000 a year through a hockey equipment manufacturer. First night on the ice not many Swedish players wore helmets. "Don't worry," a local reporter said, "they'll be wearing their helmets for Tumba on Wednesday. Wednesday they're on TV."

It was most exhilarating to be a Canadian in Stockholm. Everywhere else I've been in Europe I've generally had to explain where and what Canada was, that I was neither quite an American nor really a colonial. But in Sweden there was no need to fumble or apologize. Canadians are known, widely known, and widely disliked. It gave me a charge, this—a real charge—as if I actually came from a country important enough to be feared.

The affable Helge Berglund claims there are more than a hundred thousand active players and about seven thousand hockey teams in Sweden. How fitting, he reflects, that the Johanneshov *isstadion* should be the scene of the world champion-ship competition. "The stadium's fame as the Mecca of ice hockey," he continues in his own bouncy style, "is once more sustained."

My trouble was I couldn't get into Mecca.

"You say that you have just come from London for the *Maclean's*," the official said warily, "but how do I know you are not a...chancer?"

With the help of the Canadian embassy, I was able to establish that I was an honest reporter.

"I could tell you were not a chancer," the official said, smiling now. "A man doesn't flow all the way from London just for a free ticket."

"You're very perceptive," I said.

"They think here I am a fool that I do everybody favours—even the Russians. But if I now go to Moscow, they do me a favour and if I come to London," he said menacingly, "you are happy to do me a favour too."

Inside the *isstadion,* the Finns were playing the West Germans. A sloppy, lacklustre affair. Very little body contact. If a Finn and a West German collided, they didn't exactly say excuse me; neither did any of them come on in rough National Hockey League style.

I returned the same night, Monday, to watch the Smoke Eaters play the exhausted, dispirited Ameri-cans. Down four goals to begin with, the Canadians easily rallied to win 10–4. The game, a dull one, was not altogether uninstructive. I had been placed in the press section and in the seats below me agitated agency men, reporters from Associated Press, United Press International, Canadian Press, and other news organizations, sat with pads on their knees and telephones clapped to their ears. There was a scramble around the American nets and a goal was scored.

"Um, it looked like number 10 to me," one of the agency men ventured.

"No, no—it was number 6."

"Are you sure?"

"Absolutely."

"I'm with Harry," the man from another agency said. "I think it was number 10."

A troubled pause.

"Maybe we ought to wait for the official scorer?"

"Tell you what, as long as we all agree it was number 10—"

"Done."

All at once, the agency men began to talk urgently into their telephones.

"...and the Smoke Eaters add yet another tally. The second counter of the series for..."

The next game I saw—Canada vs. Czechoslovakia—was what the sporting writers of my Montreal boyhood used to call the big one, a four pointer. Whoever lost this one was unlikely to emerge world champion. Sensing the excitement, maybe even hoping for a show of violence, some fifteen thousand people turned up for the match. Most of them were obliged to stand for the entire game, maybe two hours.

This was an exciting contest, the lead seesawing back and forth throughout. The Czech amateurs are not only better paid than ours but play with infinitely more elegance. Superb stickhandlers and accurate passers, they skated circles around the Smoke Eaters, overlooking only one thing: in order to score frequently, it is necessary to shoot on the nets. While the Czechs seemed loath to part with the puck, the more primitive Canadians couldn't get rid of it quickly enough. Their approach was to wind up and belt the puck in the general direction of the Czech zone, all five players digging in after it.

The spectators—except for one hoarse and lonely voice that seemed to come from the farthest reaches of Helge Berglund's Mecca—delighted in every Canadian pratfall. From time to time, the isolated Canadian supporter called out in a mournful voice, "Come on, Canada."

The Czechs had a built-in cheering section behind their bench. Each time one of their players put stick and puck together, a banner was unfurled and at least a hundred chunky broad-shouldered men began to leap up and down and shout something that sounded like "Umpa-Umpa-Czechoslovakia!"

Whenever a Czech player scored, their bench would empty, everybody spilling out on the ice to embrace, leap in the air, and shout joyously. The Canadian team, made of cooler stuff, would confine their scoring celebration to players already out on the ice. With admirable unselfconsciousness, I thought, the boys would skate up and down poking each other on the behind with their hockey sticks.

The game, incidentally, ended in a 4–4 tie.

The Canadians wanted to see blood, the posters said. Hoodlums, one newspaper said. The red jackets go hunting at night, another claimed. George Gross, the Toronto *Telegram*'s outraged reporter, wrote, "Anti-Canadian feeling is so strong here it has become impossible to wear a maple leaf on your lapel without being branded ruffian, hooligan and—since yesterday—sex maniac."

A man, that is to say, a Canadian man, couldn't help walking taller in such a heady atmosphere, absorbing some of the fabled Smoke Eaters' virility by osmosis. But I must confess that no window shutters were drawn as I walked down the streets. Mothers did not lock up their daughters. I was not called ruffian, hooligan, or anything even mildly deprecating. Possibly, the trouble was I wore no maple leaf in my lapel.

Anyway, in the end everything worked out fine. On Tuesday morning Russ Kowalchuk's virtue shone with its radiance restored. Earlier, Art Potter, the politically astute president of the Canadian Amateur Hockey Association, had confided to a Canadian reporter, "These are cold war tactics to demoralize the Canadian team. They always stab us in the back here." But now even he was satisfied. Witnesses swore there was no girl in the lobby. The Malmen Hotel apologized. Russ Kowalchuk, after all, was a nice clean-living Canadian boy. In the late watches of the night, he did not lust after Swedish girls, but possibly, like Bobby Kromm and Don Freer, yearned for nothing more depraved than a Ping-Pong table. A McIntosh apple, maybe.

Finally, the Smoke Eaters did not behave badly in Stockholm. They were misunderstood. They also finished fourth.

1968

5

Safari

A week before our scheduled departure for
Kenya in 1982, excitement ruled our home.
After all, we were soon to abandon wintry
Montreal for the fabled Aberdare Salient, Lake
Baringo in the Great Rift Valley, and the Masai Mara
Game Reserve. Lions, leopards, elephants, zebras,
antelopes, and gazelles. Florence and I took to
studying Ker and Downey Tented Safari brochures in
bed. Our insect-proof tents, we were assured, would
include bedside lamps, washbasins, and adjoining
shower and toilet tents. African crew would do our
laundry overnight, except for women's lingerie, a
task they took to be humiliating. Our group was to
consist of three couples. All old friends, all new to
Africa. Remember, a thrilling covering letter
enjoined us, to bring two pairs of sunglasses. "It's
one thing to drop them from a Land Rover; another,
in murky, crocodile-infested waters."

A week before we left, my arm rendered leaden
by a cholera shot, I repaired to my favourite downtown bar. How about one for the road, a crony asked.
"Certainly," I replied. *"But first,"* I added in a voice

calculated to boom across the bar, "*I must take my malaria pill.*"

We landed in Nairobi (fifty-five hundred feet above sea level, population 135,000) early in the morning, flying overnight from London. A testing time, this, for at the Jomo Kenyatta Airport we were to meet the two guides with whom we would trek through the reserves for the next eleven days. If the chemistry weren't right, we all agreed, the trip could be a washout. Happily, our apprehensions were for nothing. David Mead, forty-three, and Alan Binks, thirty-eight, turned out to be affable, cultured fellows, both of them fluent in Swahili. Truly good companions.

Mead, a Sandhurst graduate, had been in Africa since 1968, a professional white hunter until it was ruled illegal in 1977. Binks, a naturalist and photographer, immigrated to Africa in 1967 and was now a Kenyan citizen. "In England," he said, "the horizon meant the next garden hedge. Here, the space is immense." But, he allowed, there were problems in Kenya. "We have no oil, no natural resources. Just coffee, tea, and tourism."

The Norfolk, where we were to stay overnight, is possibly the most legendary hotel in East Africa, built in 1904 by Maj. C. G. R. Ringer. Its guest list since then would seem to include just about everybody accounted for in *Burke's Peerage,* as well as Teddy Roosevelt and his son Kermit, Isak Dinesen (Karen Blixen), author of the classic *Out of Africa,* Winston Churchill, and, of course, Mr. Hemingway. Abraham Brock, who arrived from South Africa in 1903, when the lands of the Great Rift Valley were proposed as a projected colony for Jewish settlement—a new Canaan that was just not to be—bought the hotel in 1927. It was now part of the Brock chain, which included Treetops, the Lake Baringo Club, and seven other hotels and lodges. Brock was reported to have played a crucial role in the celebrated Israeli raid on Entebbe airport, in 1976, which liberated Israeli captives who had been on a plane hijacked by the PLO. It was said that he was the one who negotiated refuelling rights in Kenya for the Israeli special forces, en route to Uganda.

There was no need, incidentally, to fret about safari suits. Once installed at the Norfolk, we hurried over to Colpro, a shop on Kimathi Street run by enterprising Indians, where we were equipped with the appropriate cotton safari suits, very reasonably priced, and altered within a couple of hours.

The churning streets of downtown Nairobi teem with persistent hawkers of ugly, factory-made souvenirs. Shoeshine boys lie in wait everywhere. Possibly the only place where you can safely buy authentic indigenous jewellery and artifacts is at the government-run African Heritage, a handsome shop. We paused there so that Florence could select some things for our children. Her modest purchases in hand, she was boorishly thrust aside from the cash-register counter by burly American secret service men, as then vice-president George Bush laid out his collection of spears and shields and masks. The elegant black woman clerk toted up the items and handed Bush a considerable bill. "I'm the vice-president of the United States," said Bush. "Don't I get a discount?"

"No, you don't," she replied.

From African Heritage, it was only a short stroll to the famous Thorn Tree Bar at the New Stanley Hotel, an obligatory stop, even if you pass on the impala stew. Ensconced on the terrace, I asked a settler at a neighbouring table about the abortive air-force-led coup of last August 1. "What, in fact, happened to the air force?"

"They were, um, disbanded."

"Do you mean...liquidated?"

"Quite."

Kenya, independent since 1963, is a one-party state with a population of some fifteen million, maybe fifty thousand of them white. The autocratic successor to the great Jomo Kenyatta, President Daniel arap Moi was staunchly supported by the local press in 1982. On November 13, the page-one headline in the *Daily Nation* proclaimed, "THUGS IN POLLS RACE, SAYS MOI":

"Some political *majambazi* [thugs] have joined the race for the Nakuru North parliamentary seat," President Moi said yesterday.

The President said this when he conducted a harambee funds drive at Ol Kalou, Nyandarua District, Central Province. A total of about Sh. 3.5 million was collected.

President Moi, who spoke in Kiswahili, said he did not mind anybody being elected. But he urged the electorate to vote in a Nyayo man.

He said he did not take pleasure in detaining anybody and added that some political *majambazi* had rushed to enter the race in Nakuru North street.

He also asked the electorate not to elect
wakora [hooligans]. He said he was not interested in any group and warned people not to
blame him if things went wrong.

A story on page four noted that bargain hunter
George Bush might cut short his African tour to fly to
Moscow for the funeral of President Leonid Brezhnev,
whose death had been announced the day before.
And, on page seven, there was an interesting letter to
the editor from George Wanyoike of Nairobi:

> During the recent Commonwealth Games in
> Brisbane, Australia, I noticed that while all coun-
> tries fielded national teams, the United Kingdom
> fielded hers on tribal lines.
>
> There were tribal teams from England,
> Scotland, Wales and Northern Ireland. What
> should we expect next time: Eskimos and
> Quebecan Canadians being fielded as separate
> teams or Luos, Kikiyus and Kalenjins being
> fielded as separate teams? This should be dis-
> couraged.

A Moi supporter, Raphael Obwori Khalumba,
surfaced in the letters column of Nairobi's *True Love
with Trust* magazine:

> I congratulate President Moi, the government
> and the Kenya Army, GSU and Police for sup-
> pressing the insurgence by the KAF rebels on
> August 1, 1982. The episode shall remain a dark
> and unforgettable mark in the Kenya history. The

perpetrators of the attempted coup should be hunted down and punished severely. If it were not for our loyal forces, we don't know what shape Kenya would have assumed by now.

God is with the government of Kenya. There is no leadership as dedicated as that of our beloved President Daniel arap Moi in the whole of Africa. God bless Moi, our country Kenya, the armed forces, and all the people of Kenya.

Back at the Norfolk my telephone rang and rang, but each time I picked it up the line was dead. I finally took my problem to the clerk at the front desk.

"You go back to your room," he said, "and the operator will ring you."

"But it's no use, don't you see? The line is dead. I can't get a dial tone."

"You go back. Operator will ring you."

I did. She did. The line was dead. I returned to the front desk.

"Your telephone doesn't work," said the desk clerk. "It will be fixed."

"Thank you. When?"

"We must get an engineer from the post office."

"When will that be?"

"Unfortunately, he just left. He will return, if he has a car."

A couple of hours later I confronted the front-desk clerk yet again.

"If the engineer comes," he said, "your phone will certainly be fixed."

"What if he doesn't come?"

"We like to think he will."

We all went to dinner at Alan Bobbé's Bistro, reputedly the best restaurant in East Africa. I didn't try the parrot's eye, a specialty, but I can certainly vouch for the smoked sailfish, the truly giant shrimp from the Indian Ocean, and the king crab.

Early the next morning, we set out with our guides in two Toyota Land Cruisers. The eight Africans who would lay out our luxurious camp in the Aberdare Salient, some one hundred miles north of Nairobi, had moved on ahead of us. In theory you are supposed to keep to the left-hand side of the road in Kenya, but in practice you drive on either side, wherever the potholes are fewest. Again and again we passed *mantatus,* astonishingly overcrowded little makeshift buses run by private entrepreneurs. There were pathetic shantytowns, slapped together out of waste tin and battered crates. Pineapple and coffee plantations. Long, lean, languid Africans tending to papyrus stands by the dusty roadside. Men cutting building bricks out of rock in a roadside quarry, women stooping over tiny vegetable plots, more men ambling along the road, carrying pangas. Indeed, wherever we drove there were people out walking, infinitely patient, the women sometimes carrying black parasols, more often knitting, as they passed, the men in tribal attire, stopping to wave, the children reaching out for candies. And then there were the magnificent flame trees in flower. Fever trees looming over muddy streams. The small whistling thorn, umbrella trees, and the spectacular euphorbia, or candelabra, trees. Finally, at 1:00 p.m., we arrived at the gates of Aberdare National Park, some sixty-five hundred feet above sea level:

> Visitors enter this national park entirely at their own risk. Please exercise care and keep a safe distance from any dangerous animals. They have the right of way.

Immediately beyond the gates was our first wild beast, a warthog, seemingly bemused, willing to pose for pictures. It was a hefty specimen, say two hundred pounds, with an enormous wart-filled face and two sets of menacing tusks, the lower with a razor-sharp cutting edge. Soon we would discover these hogs are ubiquitous in the Aberdare as well as the Masai Mara, constantly on the trot, followed by their mates and troops of piglets. If animals drank booze, the barrel-chested warthog would be a beer belter. A hard hat. Ugly yet somehow endearing. The giraffes, on the other hand, which Isak Dinesen described as "rare, long-stemmed, speckled, gigantic flowers," would certainly affect pince-nez and sip Dom Perignon.

We were hardly into the forested salient when David Mead said, "There were elephants through here, maybe in the last hour." And round a bend in the track there they were, seven of them, munching punishingly prickly thorn-tree branches. Elephants, wrote Isak Dinesen, "travelling through the dense native forest...pacing along as if they had an appointment at the end of the world." Later we would come upon a herd of them, frolicking in a muddy waterhole. Sometimes, however, they were not so sweet-tempered, alertly extending their huge floppy ears, raising their trunks to trumpet at us. "They are perfectly capable," Binks informed us jauntily, "of stomping on a car, flattening everybody in it." Then he told us about the time a hippo, grazing in the evening, had espied a foolish woman with a camera poised between him and his waterhole, cutting off his retreat. He promptly chomped her to bits. "Of course, I think at least one tourist should be scarfed a year. It adds a certain spice to the safari, don't you think?"

We reached camp, exhilarated, and settled into a delicious lunch. Actually, the best food we would eat in Kenya would be prepared right in camp, our miracle-making chef baking bread and cooking roasts, equipped with nothing more than two metal ammunition cases laid out on a carefully tended bed of hot charcoal.

In the afternoon we caught sight of our first bunch of black-and-white colobus monkeys, squealing as they squirted from tree to tree. Wherever the baboons gathered, two or maybe three of them stood on the high ground to guard against predators. Herds of large black Cape buffalo, their curled horns massive, scowled at us from every open glade. These weighty buffalo, dripping animosity, seemed already cast in bronze.

Here and there in the salient there were large,

peculiar craters. "Oh, those," said Mead. "This was once Mau Mau country. They hid out here, living off the land, their only protection against the cold the animal skins that were glued to their backs. The British scatter-bombed the area, hoping to flush them out. All they did was create havoc for the wildlife."

The densely forested, hilly, dark green Aberdare was filled with breathtaking surprises. Around one rising bend in the road at twilight we came upon our first leopard—liquid, muscular grace—fondly nuzzling the head of a long-dead antelope. Probably not his own kill, Mead explained, because a leopard promptly removes his kill to a high fork in a convenient tree, where he can ravage it at ease, proof against thieving lions and hyenas. Reacting to our presence, the leopard sprang free of the dead antelope, glared at us, and then, even more disturbed by a sudden burst of thunder, retreated into the bush. Not quickly, but with considerable grace.

In the evening, less than twenty-four hours on the land but already old Africa hands, our safari suits gratifyingly mud-caked, we gathered round a fire, prompting Mead to tell us tales of his hunting exploits. A reticent man, he made light of a serious injury he had suffered when a wounded Cape buffalo got his horns into him, "tossing me like I was a piece of paper." There are no stuffed animal heads or horns or tusks mounted in Mead's home on the outskirts of Nairobi. In fact, he made it abundantly clear that he had never gone in for wanton destruction, only very selective killing. If animals were to survive on the reserves for another generation, he felt, sentiment wouldn't do it; it had to be made plain to Kenyans that the animals were a natural resource, a rare economic asset. They brought in tourists. Foreign currency. "The truth is," he said, "I much prefer this kind of safari to hunting."

The next morning we came across a dead buffalo lying in a shallow stream. Probably a lion kill. And then, tracking vultures circling high over a distant hill, we set off in pursuit and discovered an even more malodorous buffalo corpse being devoured by those fierce, ugly birds, a blight of them squabbling over their putrescent spoils.

In the afternoon, en route to Jonathan Leakey's Island Camp, on Lake Baringo, we made a pit stop at the Aberdare Country Club, a grand old colonial mansion, commanding an achingly beautiful view of what had once been a white settler's coffee plantation. Mead told us, "Most of them had to sell. The estates, some of which ran to forty thousand acres, were broken up. But, really, they had little to complain about. They came here worth nothing and sold their farms for half a million quid or better in '63. I think they were jolly lucky."

Bumping over dusty roads through an everchanging, always-spectacular landscape, we had soon crossed into the Rift Valley country, hot and humid, the dun-coloured hills, seemingly moth-eaten, yielding to soaring purplish walls on both sides. Hard by the Menenga Crater, we drove past President Moi's enormous estate. Here, in the president's very own tribal district, the road, not surprisingly, was actually paved. Finally we took a motorboat across the crocodile-infested waters of Lake Baringo to Leakey's Island Camp, remembering not to drop our sunglasses. The camp, overlooking the lake, is hewn right out of the cliffside, embedded with cacti and desert roses and acacias. Something of a South Seas oasis in the middle of the Rift country. Our double tents, tucked into the cliffside with integrated flush toilets and showers, were certainly commodious, but the food was mediocre. In a land where the fresh pineapple is truly succulent, we were served tinned pineapple juice for breakfast. But never mind; birdwatching the next morning was simply marvellous. I had never seen such a gaudy, splendiferous display. Suffice it to say that there are around fifteen hundred different species of birds in Kenya, almost as many as in all of North America.

In the morning we quit the Island Camp for nearby Lake Bogoria, pausing en route to marvel over the termite heaps that loomed everywhere, some of them twenty feet high, representing fifty years of labour. And then there were the gorgeous elands, the largest antelopes on earth, with their splendid corkscrew horns. Dr. Chris Hillman, of Nairobi University, writes: "The eland is the most common animal in bushman rock paintings. Louis Leakey reckoned it was second only to the giraffes, over the whole of Africa, for the frequency of depiction in prehistoric paintings and rock engravings." And as we approached the shores of Lake Bogoria itself, there was an endless swirling slash of pink, soon to be revealed as flocks of flamingos, thousands of them.

From Lake Bogoria, we scooted across the country to the Masai Mara, where we would camp for five days. Giraffes. Waterbucks. Herds of roaming elephants. Wildebeests. Prides of lions. Cheetahs. Leopards. Hippos. Crocodiles. Hyenas. Jackals. Baboons. But, above all, herds of exquisite antelopes and gazelles: impalas, topis, Thomson's gazelle, and Grant's gazelle. Gazelles, gazelles, breaking into a trot and, if alarmed, literally flying across the flat open country.

At first sight, the Masai Mara, its horizon endless, seems the most enchanting of pastoral scenes. All those grazing animals. This, you might think, is how things were in the Garden of Eden. But, on closer examination, it is most certainly not a peaceable kingdom. Put plainly, it's a meat rack—those exquisitely frolicking antelopes and gazelles being coolly eyed by the predators on the plain, none more obscene than the loping, slope-shouldered hyena, constantly on the prowl. In the morning, these vile creatures are everywhere, their pelts greasy and bellies bloated.

One evening—a scene right out of hell, this—we came upon a pack of thirty-three hyenas, hooting and cackling as they fed on a freshly dead hippo. Finding the hippo hide an impediment—although hyenas have the strongest jaws of any animal on the plain—they had eaten their way in through the softer anus, emerging again and again with dripping chunks of meat or gut, thrusting the scavenging jackals aside. The lion may be king of the animals, but, Mead assured me, he had seen a swift pack of hyenas move a lion off its kill more than once. Still, the lions are feared. One morning we caught two cheetahs gorging themselves on a wildebeest, eating hastily, constantly alert for lions that could rob them of their feast. But the lions are not invincible. Another time we came upon two lions on the hunt, attacking a herd of Cape buffalo. Eight of the buffalo formed a line, lowering their heads and charging, driving off the lions.

At twilight we watched the gazelles and antelopes cavort, a sight I never tired of, but, come morning, their skulls and rib cages would be strewn across the plain, being picked clean by vultures.

Our camp, neatly tucked into a stand of shade trees, was actually a corner that a bunch of baboons called home. Perched high and quarrelsome in the trees, they did not take kindly to our intrusion, pissing on our tents and pelting them with sticks at night. This, however, was not the only thing to disturb our sleep. After dark there came the shrieking of birds. Hooting hyenas on the prowl. Lions coughing. Once we wakened to find an elephant feeding on a thorn tree only six feet behind our tent.

After we turned in, zipping up our tents, a guard patrolled the camp all night, panga at the ready. He was there to protect not so much us but rather the kitchen tent from hungering hyenas, capable of biting right through a frying pan.

Weeks after our safari was done, I continued at home to awaken at 3:00 a.m. to afterimages of Africa. A Masai tribesman, his robes brilliantly coloured, his spear in hand, strolling casually toward us across the open plain. A leopard springing out of its cave and darting into the night. Adolescent topis at play, locking horns, testing themselves. Lions lazing in the sun or padding in a slow line through the tall grass. Elephants gathering their vulnerable young into the centre of their circle. And the giraffes, elegant beyond compare, always out there on the far horizon, looming over the trees.

Go, go, before it's gone. Before the rough tracks of the Masai Mara are paved and hamburger havens and pizza parlours spring up and the Masai herdsman who approaches across the plain has his ears plugged into a Walkman. Or is talking into a cellular phone.

February 1983

6

You Know Me, Ring

When I was a boy in Montreal, during the Second World War, my parents feared Adolf Hitler and his seemingly invulnerable panzers beyond all things, but my old bunch, somewhat more savvy, was in far greater terror of Mr. Branch Rickey. Let me explain. In those days our hearts belonged to the late, great Montreal Royals of the old International League. In 1939, the Royals signed a contract with Mr. Rickey—the baseball intellectual who built the legendary Brooklyn teams—making the club the Dodgers' number-one farm team. Five years later, our club was sold outright to the Dodgers. This meant that come the dog days of August, the imperial Mr. Rickey could descend on our colony and harvest its best players to bolster the Dodgers' perennial pennant drive. Gone, gone were Duke Snider, Jackie Robinson, Roy Campanella, Ralph Branca, Don Newcombe, and Carl Furillo just when we needed them most. My romance with baseball, still unrequited, goes back that far.

Since then, of course, there have been many changes in the game, some of them heartening but most of them diminishing. Among the most heart-ening changes I naturally count the coming of major league baseball in the shape of those sud-denly traditional bridesmaids, our very own Expos, to Montreal in 1969. Mind you, if once we lost our most gifted players to the majors, now that we are in the biggies ourselves we can't even sign them. Take young Pete Incaviglia, for instance. He was the Expos' number-one college-draft choice in 1985, but, obviously having majored in geography rather than haute cuisine, he didn't want to come this far north. He was lost to the balmier climes of Texas, where in early July he was hitting .266, with thir-teen home runs and forty-two RBIs (and I hope suf-fering heartburn on a daily diet of greasy ribs and twice-warmed-over chili).

As I am a supporter of Band-Aid, Oxfam, and food stamps, willing to join hands or rub noses across America any day, rain or shine, I am also relieved that the hardworking players (ruining their knees on artificial turf, risking skin cancer in the afternoon sun out there in stadiums as yet undomed) are now earning decent beer money. But I do some-times worry about the owners' generosity, making instant millionaires of many a .250 hitter or a pitcher with a bloated ERA. "It isn't really the stars who are expensive," the late Bill Veeck once said, "it's the high price of mediocrity."

One of the most depressing changes in the game has been the advent of the insufferably cute team mascot. Montreal's very own Youppi, for instance, has led me to reconsider my hitherto impeccable stand on capital punishment. I preferred it when the game was played out on the grass in the afternoon sun rather than on a carpet in glorified hangars.

Happily, there is a constant. Baseball's clichés remain largely unchanged through the years. The mop-up pitcher with a 2–12 record will still complain, "If only they give me a chance to start, I know I can help this team." Similarly, the utility infielder, batting .198, can be counted on to protest, "I know I'm a .300 hitter, but they've got to play me every day." The manager, enduring a ten-game losing streak, is absolutely required to point out, "It's a long season," and if his team is going to be sacrificed to Dwight Gooden that very night, he will assuredly remind the fans, "The way I look at it, he gets into his trousers one leg at a time, just like the rest of us." Of course, we can assume everybody between those white lines will give 110 percent, damn it, but the player who wins the MVP award this autumn is bound to kick the dirt and say, "I'm willing to trade in any individual awards for a World Series ring," just as Peter Rose, Esq., will come clean at last when he retires in 2001, saying, "Individual stats never meant anything to me."

Stats.

If there is anything really new in the game it is the sudden and sometimes bewildering proliferation of stats, which now go beyond the traditional BA, HR, SO and RBI to include such recherché items as RRF (runs responsible for), SA (slugging average), hits made during LIP (late-inning pressure), on grass or artificial turf, with two out, or fewer than two out, after a tiff with the wife or a night out on the town, etc., etc. I have resisted reading the new baseball mavens, however brilliant, because my fear has been that they might diminish my joy in the game even as earlier intellectuals—Edmund Wilson being a case in point—arguably ruined vaudeville by analyzing it too closely. But Messrs. Seymour Siwoff, Steve Hirdt, and Peter Hirdt, compilers of *The 1986 Elias Baseball Analyst*—a volume that comes highly recommended by that fine baseball writer Thomas Boswell—have certainly stitched together a compendium of considerable value to the armchair manager or, come to think of it, the real managers. It helps, however, if you are not so much a fan as an addict and absolutely need to know that Dave Winfield's career home-run percentage when facing left-handed pitchers is 5.36.

Bill James, the acknowledged pioneer in the field, has published two books this season: *The Bill James Baseball Abstract 1986* and *The Bill James Historical Abstract*. This master of Sabermetrics (the systematic, scientific study of baseball-related questions) turns out to be not only illuminating but also considerably charming and honest. "Hi," he writes in his 1986 abstract,

> I'm Bill James. Let's assume that you're standing
> in your local bookstore flipping through the
> pages and trying to decide whether to buy this
> book or save the money for a down payment
> on a pair of nylon underpants for grandpa's
> birthday.... In this year's book, I looked into
> questions like whether artificial turf shortens a
> player's career... what the *de facto* standards for
> the Hall of Fame are... what a player's chances
> are of getting 3,000 hits.... If you enjoy thinking

about questions like these, and you have a certain amount of patience with statistical information that relates to them, then you'll enjoy this
book; if you're not interested, you won't.

His *Historical Abstract,* grand fun for browsing, rich in
wacky asides, deserves a place on that small shelf
reserved for essential baseball books such as Joseph
L. Reichler's *Baseball Encyclopedia,* sixth edition,
revised in 1985; Jim Brosnan's *Long Season;* Roger
Kahn's *Boys of Summer;* Jim Bouton's *Ball Four;* Roger
Angell's *Late Innings: A Baseball Companion;* and Red
Smith's anthology of favourite sports stories, *Press
Box,* which includes John Updike's wonderful piece
on Ted Williams's last game at Fenway Park, "Hub
Fans Bid Kid Adieu."

Of course, the best baseball book ever, published as long ago as 1916 but still fresh and acute, is
Ring Lardner's *You Know Me Al,* available again from
Vintage Books, with an introduction by my col-
league Wilfrid Sheed. *You Know Me Al,* a novel written in the form of letters home by Jack Keefe, a
busher who catches on in the majors his second
time out, was enormously appreciated by as
unlikely a reader as Virginia Woolf. "With extraordinary ease and aptitude," she wrote, "with the quick-
est strokes, the surest touch, the sharpest insight,
[Lardner] lets Jack Keefe the baseball player cut out
his own outline, fill in his own depths, until the figure of the foolish, boastful, innocent athlete lives
before us." Lardner, Mrs. Woolf concluded, had
talents of a remarkable order. Yes, indeed. He could
be funny, very funny, but he also, as his son John

once noted, carried a sharp knife. Astonishingly, *You Know Me Al,* Lardner's first novel, was originally written as a serial for the *Saturday Evening Post,* with the last installments earning Lardner 1,250 bucks. If the unassuming Lardner wrote it with an eye on the rent money rather than on posterity, there is no doubt that the upshot was an American classic. Lardner was an original, a writer with an impeccable ear and an enviable gift for clean prose. He was Mark Twain's legitimate heir, perhaps, and an important influence on Hemingway and Fitzgerald. And so I also urge you to read Lardner's *Haircut and Other Stories,* which includes another superb baseball story, "Alibi Ike." Here's a short paragraph from that story:

> "He's got the world beat," says Carey to Jack and I. "I've knew lots o' guys that had an alibi for every mistake they made; I've heard pitchers say that the ball slipped when somebody cracked one off'n 'em; I've heard infielders complain of a sore arm after heavin' one into the stand, and I've saw outfielders tooken sick with a dizzy spell when they've misjudged a fly ball. But this baby can't even go to bed without apologizin', and I bet he excuses himself to the razor when he gets ready to shave."

In fact, you can't go wrong reading just about anything Lardner wrote. But don't take my word for it—you can look it up in H. L. Mencken. "Lardner," he wrote, "knows more about the management of the short story than all of its professors." I'm not going to say any more, because as Ring Lardner Jr. once wrote of his father, "He thought all prefaces (and most literary criticism) were nonsense."

September 1986

7

Writers and Sports

In an otherwise generous review of my most recent novel, *Barney's Version,* that appeared in the London *Spectator,* Francis King had one caveat. Noting the sharpness of protagonist Barney Panofsky's intelligence and the breadth of his culture, he doubted that he could also be a sports nut. "Would such a man, obsessed with ice hockey, be able to pronounce with such authority on topics as diverse as the descriptive passages in the novels of P. D. James, *Pygmalion* as play, musical and film, the pornography published by Maurice Girodias's Olympia Press and Dr. Johnson's *The Vanity of Human Wishes?*—rather strains credulity."

But North American literary men in general, and the Jewish writers among them in particular, have always been obsessed by sports, an enthusiasm we acquired as kids and have carried with us into middle age and beyond, adjudging it far more enjoyable than lots of other baggage we still lug around. Arguably, we settled for writing, a sissy's game, because we couldn't pitch a curve ball, catch, deke, score a touchdown, or "float like a butterfly and sting like a bee." Never mind manage a 147 clearance on a snooker table.

George Plimpton, acting out our fantasies, did get to pitch in Yankee Stadium, while a bona fide intellectual, Robert Silvers, editor of *The New York Review of Books,* marked a scorecard in the stands. Plimpton next trained with the Detroit Lions and wrote engaging books about both his experiences. He also wanted to try his hand at tending the nets of the Detroit Red Wings, but, he told me, he was refused permission by the coach who warned him, "The puck is mindless." And, he might have added, can come zinging in on a goalie at a hundred miles per hour.

Norman Mailer got to spar with both Archie Moore and José Torres. And, in perhaps the most famous boxing match in literary history, Morley Callaghan fought Ernest Hemingway in a Paris gym in the twenties, Scott Fitzgerald acting as timekeeper. In his memoir, *That Summer in Paris,* Callaghan claimed that he had famously knocked Hemingway down only after Papa had both startled and insulted him by spitting in his face. The embarrassed Hemingway, on the other hand, accused the duplicitous Fitzgerald of allowing the round to go beyond three minutes, or there would have been no knockdown. He also complained that Callaghan, in search of publicity, had passed on news of Hemingway's humiliation to a New York newspaper gossip columnist, but Callaghan denied the story.

Sport weighs heavily on the American literary man's psyche. Back in the seventies, when I once met Irwin Shaw for drinks in the Polo Lounge, in Beverly Hills, he was still touchy about being patronized by the Jewish literary mafia, the *Commentary* intelligentsia rating him far below the trinity of Bellow, Malamud, and Roth. "They could never forgive me for being such a good football player," he said.

North American men of letters, incidentally, are not the only literary sports nutters. Albert Camus, for one, liked to brag about his prowess on the soccer pitch. However, if we are sports obsessed, at least we don't attempt to dignify our boyish enthusiasms with intellectual gibberish. Were you aware, for instance, that the soccer ball is a symbol of sainthood? Or that goalkeepers are patriarchal figures with roots deep in the culture of European Christendom? Such, in any event, were the conclusions reached by Günter Gebauer, professor of philosophy at the Institute of Sport in Berlin, speaking at Cité Philo, a month-long philosophy festival that took place late in 2000 at Lens, near Lille in northern France. Ruminating on the meaning of the soccer ball, Herr Gebauer said, "It is mistreated in the most vile fashion... but it returns to your feet and is cherished and loved. This is like the saint who is thrown out of town and comes back to conquer people's hearts."

He also had some original thoughts on the goal and goalkeeper. "They are bound up with intrinsically European values, where our house is our castle and the source of pride and honour. We guard it against intrusion, just as a goalkeeper guards his goal. Scoring is like penetrating into a stranger's house, burning his belongings or raping his wife and daughter."

Then, as no conference of European intellectuals would be complete without its anti-American dig, he added, "In the U.S. the attachment to notions of honour and pride are far less strong, which no doubt explains why there is no goal or goalkeeper in their version of football."

Never mind that the American corruption of soccer does include a goal or touchdown line, coveted by rapists, but what about ice hockey?

My all-time favourite hockey goalie, Gump Worsley, also a philosopher of sorts, once tended the nets for the hapless New York Rangers.

"Which team gives you the most trouble?" a reporter once asked.

"The Rangers," he said.

Another professor of philosophy at Cité Philo, Jean-Michel Salanskis, ventured that soccer was not for the, um, mentally disadvantaged. "Wherever you go in the world," he said, "people talk about soccer in terms of theories. There is the theory of the play-maker, the theory of the counter-attack, the theory of the three-man defence and so on." Such capacity for abstract thought, he suggested, made every fan a potential philosopher.

Obviously he had never been to a British soccer match, the riot police and ambulances in atten-dance, the philosophers in the stands, many of them with shaven heads, heaving bananas at the black players, pissing against the nearest wall or even where they sat, an intimidating puddle once forming immediately below.

It was sport that first enabled me, as a child, to grasp that the adult world was suspect. Tainted by lies and betrayals. This insight came about when I discovered that our home baseball team, the Triple A Montreal Royals, which I was enjoined to cheer for, was in fact made up of strangers, hired hands, most of them American Southerners who were long gone once the season was over and had never been tested by a punishing Montreal winter. Only during the darkest days of the Second World War when deprivation was the unhappy rule, coffee and sugar and gasoline all rationed, American comic books temporarily unavailable, one-armed Pete Gray toiling in the Toronto Maple Leafs outfield—only then did French-Canadian players off the local sandlots briefly play for the Royals: Stan Bréard at *arrêt-court,* Roland Galdu at *troisième bu,* and Jean-Pierre Roy as *lanceur.* A few years later my bunch could root for a Jewish player, outfielder Kermit Kitman, who eventually married a Montreal girl and settled here, ending up in the schmata trade. Lead-off hitter for the Royals, only twenty-two years old, but a college boy, rare in baseball in those days, he was paid somewhat better than most: $650 monthly for six months of the year, a bonanza enriched by $13 a day meal money on the road. Kitman told me, "As a Jewish boy, I could eat on that money and maybe even save a little in those days. The Gentile players had enough left over for beer and cigarettes." If the Royals went all the way, winning the Little World Series, he would earn another $1,800.

My disenchantment with the baseball Royals, counterfeit hometowners, didn't matter as soon as I discovered that I could give my unqualified love to the Montreal Canadiens, *Nos Glorieux,* then a team unique in sport because most of its star performers were Quebeckers born and bred, many of whom had to drive beer trucks or take construction jobs in summer in order to make ends meet. I speak of the incomparable Richard brothers, Maurice and Henri; goalie Jacques Plante, who knitted between periods; and Doug Harvey, universally acknowledged as the outstanding defenceman of his time, who never was paid more than $15,000 a season, and in his last boozy days earned his beer money sharpening skates in his brother's sports shop, for kids who had no idea who he was.

Then as now I turn to the sports pages first in my morning newspaper, unlike Frederick Exley, who would begin by reading the book review and entertainment sections: "Finally I turned to the sports sections. Even then I did not begin reading about the Giants. I was like a child who, having been given a box of chocolates, eats the jellies and nuts first and saves the creamy caramels till last. I read about the golf in Scotland, surf-boarding in Oahu, football as Harvard imagines it played, and deep-sea fishing in Mexico. Only then did I turn to the Giants...."

In the forties radio was our primary source of sports news. Saturday nights we usually tuned in to the overexcited Foster Hewitt on *Hockey Night in Canada.* Like millions of others on the night of June 18, 1941, we huddled round our RCA Victor radio to listen to the broadcast from the Polo Grounds in New York, as former light heavyweight champion Billy Conn took on the great Joe Louis. The Brown Bomber, patronizingly described again and again as "a credit to his people," also qualified as a Jewish hero ever since he had redeemed our people by knocking out Max Schmelling in their second meeting. Conn, a clever boxer, was ahead on points after twelve rounds, but in the thirteenth he foolishly stood toe to toe with Louis, intent on flattening him. Instead, Louis knocked him out at 2:52 of the thirteenth.

My heart went out, however grudgingly, to the Brooklyn Dodgers, if only because so many of their players had served their apprenticeship with our Montreal Royals. One autumn afternoon I joined a concerned knot of fans outside Jack and Moe's barbershop, on the corner of Park Avenue and Laurier, to listen to the radio broadcast of the infamous 1941 World Series game, wherein catcher Mickey Owen dropped that third strike, enabling the dreaded Yankees to trample the jinxed Dodgers yet again.

When we were St. Urbain Street urchins, Hank Greenberg, the Detroit Tigers' first baseman, was our hero. Proof positive that not all Jews were necessarily short, good at chess, but unable to swing a bat.

Numbering high among my most cherished sports memories is the night in the sixties, in New York, when Ted Solataroff, my writer chum, took me to the Polo Grounds to watch Sandy Koufax pitch a two-hitter. He went nine innings, of course, but those were the days when a starter was expected to go nine, or at least eight, rather than to be hugged by his teammates if he managed six, to be followed on the mound by a succession of multimillionaire holders and closers.

Although I spent some twenty years in England, I could never, unlike our children, who were brought up there, acquire a taste for soccer or cricket. So I can appreciate that most Englishmen of my acquaintance have no interest in ice hockey and consider baseball a bore. "Isn't that the game," I have been asked more than once, "that grown men play in their pyjamas?"

The absurdity of sport in general, American football in particular, to people who weren't brought up on our games was once illuminated for me by the Canadian writer and broadcaster Peter Gzowski. Gzowski, a frequent traveller to the Arctic, told me that as far as the Inuit were concerned, football was funnier than any sitcom available on TV. They would gather round a set in Inuvik falling about with laughter at the sight of the players in their outlandish gear, especially savouring the spectacle of them testing their armour on the sidelines, banging into each other like caribou in heat.

American literary guys tend not only to be obsessed by sport, but many have also written with distinction about games. George Plimpton, already mentioned, has hardly ever written about anything else. A baseball game between yeshiva students and goy boys was crucial to Chaim Potok's novel *The Chosen*. Bernard Malamud and Philip Roth have both had their tickets punched with baseball novels: *The Natural* and *Our Gang*. Saul Bellow has yet to oblige, but in his most recent novel, *Ravelstein*, the imposing intellectual protagonist is also a sports nut, an avid fan of both the Chicago Cubs and the Chicago basketball Bulls. At the risk of appearing pushy, I will also include my own modest contribution here: a long set-piece in my novel *St. Urbain's Horseman* about a baseball game

played by blacklisted expatriate American filmmakers on Hampstead Heath in the sixties.

Robert Coover contributed one of the most
original baseball novels I know of, *Mr. Waugh's
Universal Baseball League.* But the classic baseball
novel, first published in 1916 and happily still in
print, as fresh and acute as ever, is Ring Lardner's
You Know Me Al.

Boxing, above all, has attracted the attention of
literary men in England as well as America. Dr.
Johnson, Swift, Pope, and Hazlitt have all had their
considerable say. In America Jack London, James
Farrell, Nelson Algren, John O'Hara, Hemingway,
Irwin Shaw, Budd Shulberg, Norman Mailer, and
Wilfrid Sheed have all written about the sport. So
have W. C. Heinz and Ted Hoagland, and of course
there is Leonard Gardner's wonderful novel *Fat City.*
Not only guys have pronounced on what Pierce Egan
dubbed "the sweet science," but also Joyce Carol
Oates. Her erudite *On Boxing* must be the only book
about the game that refers, *en passant,* to Petronius,
Thorstein Veblen, Santayana, Yeats, Beckett,
Ionesco, Emily Dickinson, and both William and
Henry James, among others. Joyce Carol Oates was
introduced to boxing in the early fifties when her
father first took her to a Golden Gloves tournament
in Buffalo, New York. Happily, in her original, if somewhat eccentric, take on the game she does pay tribute, as is only proper, to the great Pierce Egan, who
published his classic *Boxiana: Sketches of Ancient and
Modern Pugilism,* acknowledging that his prose was as
wittily nuanced as that of Defoe, Swift, and Pope.
However, she finds herself "uneasily alone" in being

scornful of A. J. Liebling, a journalist whose boxing writing I cherish. She dislikes Liebling "for his relentless jokey, condescending, and occasionally racist attitude toward his subject." Perhaps because it was originally published in *The New Yorker* in the early fifties, *The Sweet Science: Boxing and Boxiana—a Ringside View* is a peculiarly self-conscious assemblage of pieces, arch, broad in humour, rather like a situation comedy in which boxers are "characters" depicted for our amusement. Liebling is even uncertain about such champions as Louis, Marciano, and Robinson—should one revere or mock? And he is pitiless when writing about "Hurricane" Jackson, a black boxer cruelly called an animal, an "it," because of his poor boxing skills and what Liebling considers his mental inferiority.

Obviously Ms. Oates does not consider this to be the case with Mike Tyson, with whom she spent considerable time. Astonishingly, she adjudges Tyson "clearly thoughtful, intelligent, introspective; yet at the same time—or nearly the same time—he is a 'killer' in the ring...one of the most warmly affectionate persons, yet at the same time—or nearly—a machine for hitting 'sledgehammer' blows."

Be that as it may, Joyce Carol Oates won me over with a fetching analogy: "The artist senses some kinship, however oblique and one-sided, with the professional boxer in this matter of training. This fanatic subordination of the self in terms of a wished-for destiny. One might compare the time-bound public spectacle of the boxing match (which could be as brief as an ignominious forty-five seconds—the record for a title fight!) with the publication of a writer's book. That which is 'public' is but the final stage in a protracted, arduous, grueling, and frequently despairing period of preparation."

And this, she ventures, may be one of the reasons for the habitual attraction of serious writers to boxing.

John Updike, that readiest of writers, has pronounced adoringly about golf both in incidental pieces and his Rabbit Angstrom novels. "Like a religion," he wrote in *Is There Life After Golf?*, "a game seeks to codify and lighten life. Played earnestly enough (spectatorship being merely a degenerate form of playing), a game can gather to itself awesome dimensions of subtlety and transcendental significance. Consult George Steiner's hymn to the fathomless wonder of chess, or Roger Angell's startlingly intense meditations upon the time-stopping, mathematical beauty of baseball. Some sports, surely, are more religious than others; ice hockey, fervent though its devotees, retains a dross of brutal messiness...."

In common, I should have thought, with Islam, Christianity, and Judaism. Or conversely, hockey is just the ticket for sports agnostics like me.

Over the years, unable to act out my fantasies like George Plimpton, I have, all the same, on assignment for various magazines, been able to accompany the Montreal Canadiens on a road trip, shooting the breeze with Guy Lafleur and playing poker with Toe Blake and others on the coaching staff. I have also got to hang out with Pete Rose and Johnny Bench in Cincinnati, and I once spent some time with the Edmonton Oilers when Wayne Gretzky was still with them. Gretzky, his immense skills undeniable, has to be one of the most boring men I ever met. To come clean, neither was the far more appealing snooker sensation Stephen Hendry the wittiest of luncheon companions, but, to be fair, I doubt that Gore Vidal ever scored a maximum.

8

Gretzky in Eighty-five

Nineteen eighty-five. Edmonton. One day in March, at Barry T's Roadhouse out there on tacky 104th Street—wedged between welding shops and cinder block strip joints and used car lots—the city's amiable sportswriting fraternity gathered for its annual award luncheon. The writers were going to present Wayne Gretzky with their Sports Professional of the Year Award again. "I'll bet he tells us it means more to him than the Stanley Cup," one of the writers said.

"Or the Hart."

"Or his contract with General Mills. What do you think that's worth, eh?"

Bill Tuele, director of public relations for the Oilers, joined our table. "Does flying really scare Gretzky that much?" I asked.

"Nah. It doesn't scare him *that* much," Tuele said. "It's just that if we go bumpety-bump, he staggers off the plane with his shirt drenched."

Gretzky, who was running late, finally drifted into Barry T's. A curiously bland twenty-four-year-old in a grey flannel suit, he graciously accepted his plaque. "Anytime you win an award, it's a thrill," he said. "With so many great athletes in Edmonton, I'm very honoured to win this." Then, his duty done, he retreated to a booth to eat lunch. And in Western Canada, where civility is the rule, he was not immediately besieged by reporters with notebooks or tape recorders. They left him alone with his overdone roast beef and curling, soggy french fries.

There had been a game the night before, the slumping Edmonton Oilers ending a five-game losing streak at home, edging the Detroit Red Wings 7–6, only their second victory in their last eight outings. Even so, they were still leading the league. Gretzky, juggling his crammed schedule, had fitted me in for an interview at the Northlands Coliseum at 9:00 a.m. Increasingly caught up in the business world, he told me he had recently read *Iacocca* and was now into *Citizen Hughes.* Though he enjoyed watching television soap operas and had once appeared on *The Young and the Restless* himself, he never bothered with fiction. "I like to read fact," he said. "I'm so busy, I haven't got the time to read stories that aren't real."

After the interview, there was a team practice, and following the sportswriters' lunch, he was scheduled to shoot a television commercial, and then there was a dinner he was obliged to attend. The next night, there was a game with Buffalo. It would be the seventieth for the Oilers in the regular NHL schedule but the seventy-second for Gretzky, who had played in eight Canada Cup games immediately before the NHL season. There were a further ten games to come in the regular season and, as it turned out, another eighteen in the playoffs before the Oilers would skate to their second consecutive Stanley Cup.

But at the time, Gretzky, understandably, was in a defensive mood, aware that another undeniably talented club, the Boston Bruins, led by Bobby Orr and Phil Esposito, had promised better than they had paid, faltering more than once in the playoffs. "We've already been compared to the great Boston team of the early seventies, which won only two cups but they still say should have won four," Gretzky said.

I asked Gretzky if he didn't consider the regular NHL schedule, which more than one wag has put down as the longest exhibition season in sport, to be insufferably long and meaningless. After all, it ran to 840 games, from September to April, and when it was over only five of the then twenty-one teams had been cut from what knowledgeable fans appreciated as the real season—the Stanley Cup playoffs. "Well," he said, "this city's not like New York, where there are lots of things to do. In Edmonton in February, we're the only attraction."

When I asked Peter Pocklington, the owner of the Oilers, about the seemingly endless season, he protested, "We're the only show in town. Coming to see Gretzky is like going to watch Pavarotti or Nureyev. What else are you going to do in Edmonton in the middle of the winter? How many beers can you drink?"

The capital of Alberta is a city you come from, not a place to visit, unless you have relatives there or an interest in an oil well nearby. On first glance, and even on third, it seems not so much a city as a jumble of a used-building lot, where the spare office towers and box-shaped apartment buildings and cinder-block motels discarded in the construction of real cities have been abandoned to waste away in the cruel prairie winter.

If Canada were not a country, however fragmented, but instead a house, Vancouver would be the solarium-cum-playroom, an afterthought of affluence; Toronto, the counting room, where money makes for the most glee; Montreal, the salon; and Edmonton, the boiler room. There is hardly a tree to be seen downtown, nothing to delight the eye on Jasper Avenue. On thirty-below-zero nights, grim religious zealots loom on street corners, speaking in tongues, and intrepid hookers in mini-skirts rap on the windows of cars that have stopped for traffic. There isn't a first-class restaurant anywhere in town. For all that, Edmontonians are a truly admirable lot. They have not only endured great hardships in the past but also continue to suffer an abominable climate as well as isolation from the cities of light. And to some degree, like other Westerners, they thrive on resentments against the grasping, self-satisfied East, which has exploited their natural resources for years, taking their oil and gas at cut prices to subsidize inefficient Ontario and Quebec industries.

Insults, injuries.

For as long as Edmontonians can remember, the biggies were elsewhere. Though they had contributed many fine hockey players to the game, they could only hear about their feats on radio or later see them on television. Hockey was *their* game, damn it, *their* national sport, but New York, Chicago, Detroit, and Boston were in the NHL long before the league's governors adjudged Edmonton not so much worthy as potentially profitable. But in 1984, Canada's hockey shrines were either in decline, as was then the case in Montreal, or in total disrepute, as in Toronto. In those glory days, if Easterners wanted to see the best player in the game more than twice a season, if they wanted to catch a dynasty in the making, why, then, they had to pack their fat coats and fur-lined boots and head for Edmonton, home of the Stanley Cup champions and the Great Gretzky himself.

In March 1984, Gretzky the commodity was soaring to new heights of fame and fortune; Gretzky the most famous player ever was struggling, justifiably fatigued.

In a five-week period, Gretzky had been on the cover of *Sporting News,* two Canadian hockey magazines, and *Sports Illustrated* (for the fifth time), and he had shared a *Time* cover with Larry Bird of the Boston Celtics. He had tested his scoring skills against no less a goalie than George Plimpton, and he had been the subject of an article in the *Saturday Evening Post* and an interview in *Playboy.* He had, Gretzky told me, been criticized for submitting to the *Playboy* interview, accused of endorsing pornography. But as he put it, "You can't please everybody." Actually, the engaging truth is that his interview with *Playboy* was a triumph of small-town Canadian rectitude over that magazine's appetite for salacious detail.

PLAYBOY: How many women have been in your life?

GRETZKY: Vickie Moss was my first girlfriend. I never dated anyone else.

PLAYBOY: Do you have *any* vices?

GRETZKY: Oh, yeah, I'm human. I do have a bad habit of swearing on ice. I forget that there are people around the rink. It's a problem. I hope I'm heading in a direction where I can correct it, but I don't know if I will be able to.

Gretzky was what athletes are supposed to be, but seldom are—McIntosh-apple wholesome, dedicated, an inspirational model for young fans. He was an anachronism, rooted in an age when a date wasn't a disco, then your place or mine, but rather a movie, then maybe a banana split at the corner soda fountain. He had owned a Ferrari for four years but had never had a speeding ticket. He still phoned home to Brantford, Ontario, to report to his father three times a week. He struck me as nice, very nice, but incapable of genuine wit or irreverence, like, say, Tug McGraw. What he did tell me, his manner appropriately solemn, was that he felt it was his responsibility never to refuse to sign an autograph: "For that person, that kid, it could be the greatest thing that ever happened to him."

Gretzky worked hard, incredibly hard, both for the charities he supported and for himself. He was boffo sales stuff. The hockey stick he endorsed, Titan, leaped from twelfth to first place in sales in thirty-six months. Gretzky also pitched for Canon cameras, Nike sportswear, General Mills Pro Stars cereal, Mattel toys, Travellers Insurance, and American Express. These endorsements were handled by Michael Barnett of CorpSport International out of handsomely appointed offices in an old converted Edmonton mansion. There was a large portrait of Gretzky in action on a wall in the reception room as well as the essential LeRoy Neiman, and a placard with a quotation from Ralph Waldo Emerson: "Make the most of yourself, for that is all there is of you."

CorpSport International represented other athletes, but for the past four years Gretzky, who then earned an estimated $1 million annually in endorsements—about the same as his salary—had been the major preoccupation of its thirty-four-year-old president. Barnett, a former minor league hockey player himself, was in daily contact with Gretzky's lawyer as well as the firm that handled his investments. "Though Wayne listens to all his advisers," Barnett said, "he makes his own business and investment decisions. We get some three dozen personal appearance requests for him a month, but he will only speak for charities. Pro Stars cereal advertises the Wayne Gretzky Fan Club on four million boxes. It costs seven bucks a year to be a member, and for that you get four annual Wayne Gretzky newsletters as well as this set of photographs.

"There have been seven unauthorized biographies," Barnett continued. "Wayne gets between two to five thousand fan letters a month. Vickie Moss's mother handles that for him."

Mattel has marketed a Wayne Gretzky doll ("For avid fans, his out-of-town uniform, jogging suit, and tuxedo are also available"), which has led to cracks about the need for a Dave Semenko doll to beat up any kid who roughs up the Gretzky doll.

Late at night, even as he talked business with Barnett, Gretzky autographed colour photographs of himself. Mattel supplied the photographs, which included its logo, but Gretzky, according to Barnett, paid the postal charges, about $2,000 monthly. Barnett also pointed out that since the Oilers took their first Stanley Cup on May 19, 1984, Gretzky had only six weeks off the ice before joining the Canada Cup training camp, playing in that series, and then moving directly into the NHL season.

And in March, things weren't going well. Gretzky was playing without his usual intensity. I asked saucy, streetwise Glen Sather, president, general manager, and coach of the Oilers, if he was guilty of overplaying Gretzky. "Wayne," he said, "plays something like twenty-two minutes a game. He thrives on work. The more ice time he gets, the better he is."

Yet Gretzky hadn't had a two-goal game since February 19 or scored a hat trick for two months. He would, however, finish the 1984–85 season with 208 points (73 goals, 135 assists). This marked the third time he had scored more than 200 points in his six seasons in the NHL. A truly remarkable feat, this, when you consider that no previous player in league history had managed it even once.

Records.

The Official Edmonton Oilers 1984–85 Guide lists a modest three records under the heading, "NHL Individual Records Held or Co-Held by Edmonton Oilers (excluding Wayne Gretzky)," and there follows a stunning full page of Wayne Gretzky's contribution to the NHL records. Paraphrasing the guide, here are Gretzky's statistics:

"No. 99, centre: height, 6'0"; weight, 170 lbs.; born, Brantford, Ontario, Jan. 26, 1961; shoots, left. He is not the fastest or the most graceful skater in hockey; neither does he boast the hardest shot. But he now holds 38 NHL records."

Of course, he would, as was his habit, set or tie even more records in the 1985 playoffs, as well as win the Conn Smythe Trophy for most valuable player in that series. But back in March 1984 all I asked him was, did he feel a hundred-goal season was possible?

"Sure, it's possible," Gretzky said. "Somebody will do it. The year I got ninety-two, everything went my way." But he had begun to feel the pressure. "Yesterday you got two goals in a game, tomorrow the fans want three." He has said he would like to retire at the age of thirty, after fifteen years in hockey. "When Lafleur retired, it made me open my eyes," he said.

Lafleur, who quit suddenly in 1984 (temporarily, as it would turn out) at the age of thirty-three after four mediocre years, had scored sixty goals in his best season, 1977–78. "I wasn't surprised he retired," Gretzky said. "You wake up, you're no longer in the top-ten scorers, you think, 'Oh, my God,' and you begin to press. When Lafleur was in his prime, it was a much rougher league, but slower. We get hit, but not as much as in the late seventies."

Danny Gare, the Red Wing veteran who had played against Gretzky the night before, told me, "They don't run against him like they did on Lafleur."

Acknowledging Gretzky's enormous talent, he added that it had been more exciting to watch Lafleur. Well, yes, so it was. And come to think of it, the same could be said of Bobby Orr.

When either Lafleur or Orr was on the ice, you never took your eyes off him, never mind the puck. Orr could literally establish the pace of a game, speeding it up or slowing it down at will. Lafleur couldn't do that. He was—in Ken Dryden's felicitous phrase—the last of the river-hockey players, who had learned the game outdoors instead of in a rink, a solitary type, often lost in a reverie on ice all his own. Gretzky was something else again. Sometimes you didn't even realize he was out there, watching as he whirled, until he emerged out of nowhere, finding open ice, and accelerated to score. Other times, working out of a seemingly impossible angle in a corner, he could lay a feathery pass right on the stick of whoever had skated into the slot, a teammate startled to find the puck at his feet against all odds.

It's not true that they don't run on him. The hit men seek him here, they seek him there, but like the Scarlet Pimpernel they can't board him anywhere: he's too elusive. Gretzky can fit through a keyhole. Watching him out there, I often felt that he was made of plasticine. I've seen him stretch his arms a seeming two feet more because that's what was required to retrieve a puck. Conversely, putting a shift on a defenceman, cruising very low on ice, he seemed to shrink to whatever size was necessary to pass. He is incomparably dangerous behind the opposition's net and unequalled at making a puck squirt free from a crowd.

If, to begin with, Gretzky had a fault, it was his tendency to whine. For a while, all an opposing player had to do was skate past Gretzky thinking negative thoughts for number 99 to fall to the ice, seemingly mortally wounded, his eyes turned imploringly to the referee. In Edmonton, this had earned him a pejorative nickname: "The Wayner."

In June, Gretzky won the Hart Memorial Trophy, the league's most valuable player award, for the sixth straight time, this in a year in which he had already won his fifth consecutive Art Ross Trophy, for the NHL's leading point scorer during the regular season. One hundred and eighteen years after Confederation, the only thing out of Canada more famous than Gretzky was the cold front.

For a hockey player, it should be noted, this was a grand accomplishment, for, as a rule in 1985, NHL stars had to cope with a difficult paradox. Celebrated at home, they could, much to their chagrin, usually pass anonymously south of the forty-ninth parallel. Not so Gretzky. But for all his fame, he remained something of an enigma, a young man charged with contradictions. Ostensibly modest beyond compare, he had taken to talking about himself in the third person. Speaking of the endless hours he clocked on his backyard skating rink as a child, he said: "It wasn't a sacrifice. That's what Wayne Gretzky wanted to do." Discussing possible commercial endorsements, he allowed, "The thing to look for is...is there a future in it for Wayne Gretzky?"

Seemingly self-composed, he didn't fly on airplanes easily. Obviously, there was a lot of inner tension bottled up in Gretzky, and at thirty thousand feet it began to leak. In 1981, trying to beat his fear of flying, he tried a hypnotherapist, but it worked only briefly. Come 1984 he flew with pilots in the cockpit as often as possible, which helped only some, because they had to send him back into the cabin once they began landing procedures, and Gretzky had been known to sit there, unable to look, holding his head in his hands.

As I sifted through the Gretzky file, it appeared that just about every reply he had ever given in an interview was calculated to oblige. Again and again, his answers were not only boringly proper but tainted by what W. H. Auden once condemned as the rehearsed response. Under all the superficial sweetness, however, I suspected there was a small residue of bitterness. This, in remembrance of a boy deprived of a normal childhood, driven to compete on ice with boys four to six years his senior from the age of six.

Gretzky, for example, unfailingly went out of his way to pay obeisance to his father, his mentor. Walter Gretzky, a thwarted hockey player himself, a man who was mired in Junior B for five years, was still working as a telephone repair man in 1984. In his brash memoir, *Gretzky,* written with Jim Taylor, he gloated, "Wayne learned to skate and Walter Gretzky built a hockey star." He had Wayne, at the age of four, out in the backyard skating rink well into the dark evening hours, learning to crisscross between pylons made of Javex bleach containers.

Walter Gretzky wrote, "You can just see them think-ing, 'Boy, did he push those kids! That's a hockey father for you!' Actually, it was the most natural thing in the world." But in an epilogue to the book, Wayne, recalling that he had been shipped to Toronto to further his hockey career when he was barely a teenager, noted, "There's no way my son is leaving home at fourteen." At fourteen, he added, he thought Toronto was the greatest thing in the world, "but if there was one thing I could do over again, I'd like to be able to say I lived at home until I was eigh-teen or nineteen."

Wayne was only eleven years old when he began to set all manner of amazing records in minor league hockey, even as he would later astound the NHL. But in 1984, even as Gretzky was arguably the best player the game had ever known, a much-needed publicity bonanza for the NHL in the United States, he was also, ironically, a menace to the game.

Imagine, if you will, a baseball outfielder, not yet in his prime, who hits .400 or better every season as a matter of course and you have some notion of Gretzky's hockey stature. Furthermore, since Gretzky's sophomore year in the NHL, there had been no contest for the Art Ross Trophy. Gretzky is so far superior to any other forward, regularly win-ning the point-scoring title by a previously unheard of fifty or sixty points, that he inadvertently makes the other star players appear sadly inadequate. And while the other players tend to tell you, tight-lipped, that "Gretz is the greatest...he has all the moves and then some," I don't think they really like him, any more than Salieri did the young Mozart.

Peter Gzowski, in one of the very few intelligent books ever written about hockey, *The Game of Their Lives,* ventures, "Often the difference between what Wayne Gretzky does with the puck and what less accomplished players would have done with it is simply a *pause,* as if, as time freezes, he is enjoying an extra handful of milliseconds." Gzowski goes on to cite experiments done with athletes by a neurologist at McMaster University in Hamilton, Ontario. Based on this and other research, he suggested that Gretzky, like other superstars (say, Ted Williams or Bjorn Borg), benefited from motor neurons that fired faster than those of mere mortals. Or, put more simply, time slowed down for him. Gretzky also profited from an uncanny ability to react quickly to everybody's position on the ice. "What separates him from his peers in the end," Gzowski writes, "the quality that has led him to the very point of the pyramid, may well have nothing to do with physical characteristics at all, but instead be a manner of perception, not so much of what he sees—he does not have exceptional vision—but of *how* he sees it and absorbs it."

As Gretzky often emerged out of nowhere to score, so did Peter Pocklington, the owner of the Oilers. The son of a London, Ontario, insurance agent, he parlayed a Ford dealership, acquired at the age of twenty-three, some choice real estate, and a meat-packing firm into a fabled fortune, even by western oil-patch standards. Pocklington got into hockey, he said, because he wanted to be recognized on the streets. In 1984, he not only owned the most talented team in the NHL, a club that boasted such players as Paul Coffey and Mark Messier, but he also had Gretzky tied to a personal-services contract that made him one of the world's highest-paid indentured labourers. It was said to be worth $21 million and to extend until 1999.

In 1981, Pocklington's assets were estimated to be worth $1.4 billion, but the recession got to him, and his holdings by 1984 had reportedly shrunk to a mere $150 to $200 million. Gone, gone, was the $9 million worth of art, the private Learjet, and the Rolls-Royce. I asked Pocklington about the rumours, rampant at the time, that—such were his financial difficulties—he might be offering his legendary chattel to the nefarious Americans, say Detroit or New York. Looking me in the eye, he denied it adamantly. "There's nothing to it," he said. "You can imagine what they would do to me here if I sold Wayne. It's almost a sacred trust."

September 1985

9

From Satchel,
through Hank Greenberg,
to El Divino Loco

ome spring, I turn hungrily to the sports pages first every morning to ponder the baseball scores, held in the thrall of overgrown boys whose notion of humour is to slip an exploding device into a cigar, drench a phone receiver with shaving cream, or line the inside of a teammate's hat with shoe polish. But, to be fair, a certain corrosive wit is not unknown among some ball players. Asked if he threw spitters, Hall of Fame pitcher Lefty Gomez replied, "Not intentionally, but I sweat easy." Invited to comment on whether he favoured grass over AstroTurf, relief pitcher Tug McGraw said, "I don't know. I never smoked AstroTurf." On another occasion, a reporter asked McGraw how he intended to budget his latest salary increase. "Ninety percent I'll spend on good times, women, and Irish whisky," he said. "The other 10 percent I'll probably waste." Then the immortal Leroy "Satchel" Paige once said, "Don't look back. Something might be gaining on you."

Satchel Paige, one of the greatest pitchers the game has ever known, was shamefully confined to the Negro leagues in his prime. Only in 1948, when he was forty-two years old, did he finally get a chance to compete in the majors, signed by Bill Veeck to play for the Cleveland Indians. Paige helped the Indians to win a World Series in 1949, went on to pitch for the St. Louis Browns for a couple of years, and then dropped out of sight.

The film director Robert Parrish once told me a story about Paige that he then included in his memoir, *Hollywood Doesn't Live Here Anymore.* In the early fifties, Parrish was shooting a western in Mexico, *The Wonderful Country,* in which Robert Mitchum was playing the lead. Mitchum suggested that they get Satchel to play a black sergeant in the U.S. Tenth Cavalry.

"Where can we find him?" Parrish asked.

"Why don't you call Bill Veeck?"

Parrish called Veeck and learned that Paige was now with the Miami Marlins in the Southern Association, but he didn't think that Parrish could contact him because he was in jail on a misdemeanour charge and the judge, who was a baseball fan, would let him out only on the days he was to pitch. Parrish called the judge.

"Well," said the judge, "I think we can work it out. Leroy has a sore arm and has lost his last four games. I'll let him out if you'll guarantee he doesn't touch a baseball until he comes back to Miami."

Paige arrived in Durango, Mexico, a week later, accompanied by a beautiful teenage black girl whom he introduced as Susan. Parrish knew he had a daughter and assumed that's who she was. "Paige... stayed with us for six weeks," wrote Parrish in his memoir, "and when it was time to send him back to Miami, Mitchum and I took him to the airport. Susan boarded the small commuter plane, and Mitchum, Paige, and I stood on the tarmac... and after a while, Mitchum asked a question that had been bothering both of us since Paige arrived. "Is Susan your daughter?" he asked.

"No," said Paige. "She's my daughter's nurse."

There was a pause and then Mitchum finally said, "But your daughter's not here."

Paige looked at Mitchum and smiled. "How about that?" he said. Then he turned and boarded the plane, still smiling.

The late Hank Greenberg wrote in his autobiography, *Hank Greenberg: The Story of My Life,* of John King, a legendary left-handed slugger who hit .380 in the Texas League but never made it to the bigs because he couldn't cope with southpaw pitching. Once, according to Greenberg, King came out of a restaurant and saw a beggar with a tin cup: "King slipped a quarter into the cup. As he turned around, he saw the beggar pull the quarter out of the cup with his left hand and John went back and grabbed the coin out of his hand, and said, 'No left-handed son of a bitch is going to get any of my money.'"

If my devotion to baseball is an occasional embarrassment to me, I blame it on being a Montrealer. We put up with plenty here. Going into the 1989 season of dubious promise, for instance, Claude Brochu, president of Les Expos and a former Seagrams marketing maven, pronounced that the year would be successful if fans would just increase their consumption and spend $7.25 per game on soggy hot dogs and lukewarm beer rather than the measly $5.50 they grudgingly parted with the previous season. Baseball, once a game of inches, was now a business of pennies. Hank Greenberg's father, a prescient man, understood this as early as 1929, when Hank signed his first pro contract.

"Pop," Hank said, "are you against baseball as a career?"

His father nodded.

"The Tigers offered nine thousand dollars."

His father whistled softly. "Nine thousand dollars," he said. "You mean they would give you that kind of money just to go out and play baseball?"

"That's right."

"And they'll let you finish college first?"

"Yes."

"I thought baseball was a game," his father said, "but it's a business—apparently a very good business. Take the money."

My problem with Montreal baseball is compounded by the fact that in a climate where we are fortunate to reap seven weeks of summer, maybe six, the game is played on a zippered carpet in a concrete container that resembles nothing so much as an outsize toilet bowl—a toilet bowl the cost of which would humble even a Pentagon procurement agent. The ugly Olympic Stadium, more properly known in

Montreal as the Big Owe, cost $650 million to build in 1976, *more than the combined cost of all the domed stadiums constructed in North America up to that time.* And this price doesn't include the parking facilities, which set taxpayers back another $70 million. Nor did it take into account the so-called retractable roof, finally put in place in 1988, its reported cost another $80 million. A roof that retracted only erratically come 1989 and already leaked in several places.

Despite these local difficulties, I am not only addicted to the game but also to books that celebrate it: say, George V. Higgins's *Progress of the Seasons: Forty Years of Baseball in Our Town,* composed in praise of those who came closest to the sun, playing in Boston's Fenway Park. Baseball, writes Higgins, differs from football and basketball in that it is "a game played by generally normal-sized men whose proportions approximate those of the majority of onlookers, and whose feats are therefore plausibly imagined by the spectator as his own acts and deeds."

There is a lot in that, certainly, but also an exception to the rule, the towering six-foot-four Hank Greenberg, who first came up with the Detroit Tigers in 1930 and before he was done, in 1947, had hit 331 home runs in a career that was interrupted by four years of military service in the Second World War. Greenberg, whose lifetime batting average was .313, was twice named MVP. He drove in 1,276 runs and remains tied with Lou Gehrig for highest average of runs batted in per game with .920, or nearly one RBI a game for his career. He is also one of only two Jewish players in the Hall of Fame, the other being Sandy Koufax.

Ira Berkow, who did an admirable job of editing and amending *Hank Greenberg,* an autobiography that remained unfinished when Greenberg died of cancer in 1986, notes that Greenberg's onetime teammate Birdie Tebbetts recalled, "There was nobody in the history of the game who took more abuse than Greenberg, unless it was Jackie Robinson." But Greenberg, a man of immense dignity, refused to either anglicize his name or flaunt his Jewishness. Instead, he put up with the taunts, though on one occasion he did walk over to the Yankee dugout, which was riding him hard, and challenge everybody on the team.

The racial slurs that Jewish players once heard in the majors were not always devoid of wit. Andy Cohen, a New York Giants infielder who came up to the bigs before Greenberg, tells about one Texas League game in 1925. "I made a good catch and the fans gave me a pretty big hand. Then I heard one guy yell out, 'Just like the rest of the Jews. Take everything they can get their hands on.'"

Even more famous, of course, was the end of the 1938 season, when Greenberg hit fifty-eight home runs, two under Babe Ruth's record, with five games left to play. When he was unable to hit another homer, a lot was made of the story that pitchers had thrown him anti-Semitic fastballs, racist sliders, and Jew-baiting curves, but Greenberg would have none of it. "Some people still have it fixed in their minds," he writes, "that the reason I didn't break Ruth's record was because I was Jewish, that the ball players did everything they could to stop me. That's pure baloney. The fact is quite the opposite: So far as I could tell, the players were mostly rooting for me, aside from the pitchers."

Walter Matthau told Berkow that when he was growing up on the Lower East Side of Manhattan, his idol was Hank Greenberg: "Greenberg for me put a stop to the perpetuation of the myth at the time that all Jews wound up as cutters or pants pressers. Or, if they were lucky, salesmen in the garment centre."

Years later Matthau joined the Beverly Hills Tennis Club only because Hank Greenberg was then a member.

"For thirty years," said Matthau, "I told a story which I read in the newspapers about Hank Greenberg at a port of embarkation during the Second World War. The story had it that there was a soldier who had had a little too much to drink, and he was weaving around all the soldiers sitting there. He was quite a big fella. And he said in a very loud voice, 'Anybody here named Goldberg or Ginsburg? I'll kick the livin' daylights out of him.' Or words to that effect. Hank had been sitting on his helmet, and he stood up and said, 'My name is Greenberg, soldier.' The soldier looked at him from head to foot and said, 'Well, I said nothin' about Greenberg, I said Goldberg or Ginsburg.' I told this to Hank when I met him at the club. He said it never happened. I told him I didn't care to hear that. I was going to continue to tell that story because I liked it. He said, 'Okay, whatever you say, Walter.'"

The most original and quirky baseball book I have read in ages, *El Béisbol: Travels through the Pan-American Pastime,* by John Krich, is an antic tour through far fields, where Fan Appreciation Day is *El Día de Los Fanáticos,* the Day of the Fanatics; pitchers must beware of a *robador de bases;* and Roberto Clemente is still worshipped above all. *El Béisbol* abounds in vivid set pieces, among them a game Krich attended in Puerto Rico with Vic Power, a slugger with the Cleveland Indians in the late fifties, and Rubén Gomez, a.k.a. *El Divino Loco* (the Divine Crazy), who pitched for the Giants in the first game they played after their move to San Francisco. "Oh, baby," Power told Krich. "My biggest salary in the major leagues was thirty-eight thousand dollars. Now the average Puerto Rican kid wants that for a signing bonus. The kid's mama, she knows too much!"

July 1989

10

Eddie Quinn

On July 28, 1939, the following item appeared in the Montreal *Gazette:*

FORUM WRESTLING
TO RESUME AUGUST 8

At a meeting of the Montreal Athletic Commission, yesterday morning, Eddie Quinn, of Boston, was granted a matchmaker's licence as representative of the Forum in succession to Jack Ganson.... [Quinn] was given permission to go ahead with the arrangements for his first big show on August 8.... Yvon Robert, formerly recognized locally as heavyweight champion, will appear in the inaugural program....

Apparently Quinn intends to have no traffic with the "noble experiment" which was Ganson's swan song locally; that of a return to straight, scientific wrestling. Quinn stands solidly behind rip-roaring rassling with all the frills. He is not even daunted by the plethora of "champions" that infest the mat landscape.... Referring to

Ganson's attempt to take the fun out of wrestling, Quinn said, "The public will not fall for that
pink-tea stuff."

Quinn, who used to drive a taxi in Brookline,
Massachusetts, never looked back. In 1960 he not
only promoted all the wrestling matches at the
Montreal Forum, but, as he said, "I got most of
Canada, Boston, thirty percent of St. Louis, and fifty
percent of Chicago. Things have gone pretty fast in
the last twenty years."

So fast, in fact, that Quinn was netting as much
as a quarter of a million dollars a year for his activities. He had made wrestling the number-two spectator sport in Quebec.

Quinn, who necessarily travelled a good deal,
was a difficult man to catch up with. His offices,
Canadian Athletic Promotions, were in the Forum.
The first time I dropped in, there were two men
seated in the outer office: Larry Moquin and somebody called Benny. Moquin, who books the wrestlers
for Quinn, used to be a famous performer himself.
He was a semi-pro football player when Quinn discovered him. Benny, a greying, curly-haired man-of-
all-jobs, reminded me of the horseplayers I used to
know as a kid around the roaring Main.

Moquin and Benny were playing gin rummy, $10
bills changing hands often. The phone rang a couple
of times, and Moquin, his tone belligerent, said,
"He's gone fishing. Yeah." Once Benny answered the
phone, held it, and looked quizzically at Moquin.
"For God's sake," Moquin said, "he's gone fishing."

Actually, I was waiting for one of Quinn's publicity

men, Norman Olson, to show up. The first thing Olson said to me after he came in was "Are you here to knock us?"

I told him no.

Olson, in his early thirties, was a fat, swarthy man with a little black moustache. "Eddie isn't here," he said.

"He's gone fishing," I said.

Olson laughed. "Aw, Eddie's in the pool. He's in the pool all day. On the phone. His phone bills come to $2,000 a month."

Quinn lived in the town of Mount Royal, one of Montreal's more affluent suburbs. His swimming pool, he would later tell me, held 38,500 gallons of water and cost him $12,000. Olson got him on the line and all at once the office jumped to life. Everybody wanted to talk to Eddie, who had just flown in from Chicago. "How's the Irishman?" Olson asked with a nervous little laugh. There was a pause. "Sure," Olson said, intimidated. "I'll fix it."

Dan Parker, then the *New York Daily Mirror*'s sports editor, had made a sarcastic remark in his column about Quinn's having one world champion wrestler in Montreal, another in St. Louis, and a third in Chicago.

"Parker doesn't like Eddie," Olson said. "There's more to wrestling than meets the eye. We've got all kinds of people coming here. I know one psychiatrist who never misses a match. All day people tell him nutty things. At night he comes here. It relaxes him." Olson believed that wrestling, like golf, had great therapeutic value. "The immigrants come here," he said, "because it makes them feel good inside to see the Anglo Saxon, the blond guy, get it. The French like it too, you know. It's a release for them." He felt that TV had given the sport a big boost. One-hour shows in Detroit and Chicago, he said, outdrew other sports. Before TV, Killer Kowalski and Yukon Eric drew only $1,500 at the gate in Chicago, but after three months of appearing on studio shows with a small invited audience, the same two performers drew $56,000.

Quinn, Olson predicted, would begin to run studio shows out of Montreal as soon as his contract with the CBC ended. "These days," he said, giving the TV set an affectionate slap, "you've just got to come to terms with the one-eyed monster. But it's killed the night-clubs, you know. Today only the walkers will bring them in." Walkers, he explained, were girls who took their clothes off on stage, slipped into them again, and then drank with the customers on commission. "I could tell you a lot about this town," he said.

Olson gave me a couple of wrestling magazines, tickets for the next show, and promised to arrange meetings for me with Killer Kowalski and Eddie Quinn. "Eddie's a wonderful guy," he said. "He's got a wonderful sense of humour."

In the outer office Benny and Moquin were still playing gin rummy. Moquin was losing.

"You'll like Kowalski," Olson said. "A lovable guy."

Before going to the match the next night I read up on the sport in *Wrestling Revue* and *Wrestling News*. The former, a most spirited quarterly, featured biographies of top performers, action pictures, and an especially informative department called "Rumours versus Facts," wherein I learned that 640-pound Haystack Calhoun does *not* suffer from a glandular disorder (he's a big boy, that's all), and that Skull Murphy does *not* rub a special kind of animal grease over his hairless head so that opponents cannot hold him in a headlock (in Skull's own words, "I use ordinary Johnson's baby oil on my head. I find it helps to prevent irritation from rubbing on the dirty canvas"). However, Princess Zelina, slave girl of the hated Sheik, *does* come from a royal family in Lebanon (her old man, living in penurious exile in London, hopes to regain his throne before long). In *Wrestling News,* which is actually a section of *Boxing Illustrated,* I was taken with a defence of girl midget wrestlers by Buddy Lee. In a truculent piece titled "Don't Sell These Girls Short," Lee assured his readers that those "pint-sized pachyderms, Baby Cheryl, a real toughie for one so tiny, and Little Darling Dagmar, 'the Marilyn Monroe of the Maulin' Midgets,' are a couple of sweet kids, happy with their work."

Both magazines rated Killer Kowalski as number three among the world's wrestlers. This was especially gratifying to me as the following night I was to see the Killer battle "Nature Boy" Buddy Rogers for the world championship and an $18,000 winner-take-all purse.

There were, I'd say, only about four thousand fans at the Forum for the occasion. Many of the older men still wore their working clothes. The teenagers, however, favoured black leather jackets, their names implanted with steel studs on the back. The most engaging of the preliminary performers was Tiger Tomasso, an uncouth villain who not only eye-gouged and kicked below the belt but also bit into his opponent's shoulder when aroused.

Before the main bout, a precautionary net was

tied around the ring. This was necessary because Kowalski, a strapping six feet seven, is, all the same, a most bashful performer, given to fleeing the ring when the going gets rough. Not only that. Struck the slightest blow, he tends to whine and even plead for mercy from his opponent. Even so, the wily Pole made short work of the golden-haired Nature Boy and won the coveted championship belt. This was a popular win with all us non–Anglo Saxons.

The next afternoon, back in the modest offices of Canadian Athletic Promotions, Kowalski told me, "I indulge in lots of histrionics in the ring. I shout, I snarl, I jump up and down like a madman. Am I mad? I earn more than $50,000 a year."

Kowalski told me that he used to work on the Ford assembly line in Windsor for $50 a week. He was paid more than that for his first wrestling match in Detroit and quickly realized that he was in the wrong business. A top performer in 1960, Kowalski wrestled three times a week, usually for a percentage of the gate, and lived with his brother and sister-in-law in a house he had recently bought in Montreal. He was thirty-three years old and expected to be able to go on wrestling until he reached his mid-forties. Meanwhile, against that retirement day, Kowalski had been investing his money in securities.

"I've built up a personality," he said, "a product, and that's what I sell. Ted Williams is no different. Why do you think he spat at the crowd that day? It's showmanship. Everything is showmanship today. Richard Nixon has his act and I have mine." Kowalski bent over and showed me a scar on his head. "Last week in Chicago," he said, "after I'd won a match, my opponent hit me over the head with a chair. You think he wanted to hurt me? He wanted to make an impression, that's all."

Norman Olson, who had joined us earlier, now began to stir anxiously. "You're forgetting that wrestling takes a lot of natural ability," he said.

"Sure," Kowalski said.

"You've got to keep in shape."

"The most dangerous thing," Kowalski said, "are those crazy kids. They come to the matches with clothespin guns and sometimes they shoot rusty nails at us. Once one got embedded in my side." Kowalski also pointed out that young performers, taking part in their first big match, are also a threat. "They're so nervous," he said, "they might do something wrong."

I asked Kowalski if there was any animosity among wrestlers.

"No," he said.

"Tell him about the night here when you ripped off Yukon Eric's ear," Olson said gleefully.

"Well," Kowalski said, "one of my specialties is to climb up on the ropes and jump up and down on my opponent. One night Eric slipped aside, trying to avoid me, and I landed on his ear, ripping it off. He was very upset and he fled to his dressing room. Before long the dressing room was full of reporters and relatives and fans. Finally Eric looked up and asked for his ear. He'd forgotten it in the ring. The referee had picked it up, put it in his pocket, and by this time was showing it to all his friends at the other end of the Forum. When they got it back from him it was too late to sew it on again."

A few days later Olson arranged for me to have

lunch with Eddie Quinn in the Kon-Tiki Room in the Mount Royal Hotel. Quinn was already there when I arrived, seated with one of his referees and Olson. He wore rings on both hands—one was an enormous signet and the other was diamond encrusted. A chunky man with an expressive if hardbitten face, he spoke out of the corner of his mouth, just the way promoters did in the movies. "There's nothing left," he said, "but death and taxes. They belt you here, they belt you there. I just go on to keep people working. The government takes all the money, you know." He turned to the referee. "I dropped ten thousand this morning," he said.

"You're used to it."

"That doesn't mean I like it."

"Eddie's got a wonderful sense of humour," Olson said.

"You're too fat, Norman. Hey, where's your broad?" Quinn asked the referee. Then, turning to me, he added, "We're waiting for a French chantoosie."

"She's at the hairdresser's upstairs."

"Well, go get her. We want to eat."

The referee hurried off. "Hey, what's your name?" Quinn asked me. "Norman here says to call you Moe for short but not for long."

"Norman's too fat."

Quinn laughed and slapped my knee. The referee returned with the girl. "Meet the Freedom Fighter," Quinn said. "She was Miss Europe. She worked with Chevalier. She can't sing, either."

The referee shook with laughter.

"Say hello to Mr. Richler," Quinn said to the girl. "Hey, waiter. Another round of the same." The waiter handed Quinn a menu. "How do you order this stuff?" Quinn asked, and then he made some loud, unintelligible noises that were supposed to sound like Chinese. The Chinese waiter smiled thinly. "Just bring us lots of everything," Quinn said, and then he turned to me. "You like this food? Looks like it's been through a sawmill. Hey, waiter, if you don't know what to get us, just call the health board and ask them to recommend something."

"Eddie's a natural-born kibitzer," Olson said.

I asked Quinn about Yvon Robert, the most popular performer ever to wrestle in Quebec. "Around here," Quinn said, "it used to be the pope, Robert, and Maurice Richard. In that order."

"Robert was great," Olson said.

Quinn, who had a phenomenal memory for facts, told me the exact date, place, and take of his most successful bouts. In 1959, he drew ten thousand people to the Forum with a novel attraction, boxer versus wrestler. Former world heavyweight champion "Jersey" Joe Walcott took on Buddy Rogers, the Nature Boy. Rogers dived for the canvas immediately and seldom rose higher than a low crouch. In the first round Walcott nailed the wrestler with a hard right and seemed to have him nearly out, but in the third Rogers got Walcott's legs and Walcott quit.

Quinn's biggest gates came from the three Yvon Robert matches against Gorgeous George. George's gimmicks included long curly hair that he had dyed blond and a female valet who used to spray the ring with perfume before the wrestler himself deigned to appear. Religious leaders objected to the gorgeous one's effeminate antics and brought pressure to bear on the Montreal police. As a consequence, George never wrestled in the Forum again.

I asked Quinn about midget wrestlers. "The crowd loves 'em," he said.

The girl who had sung with Chevalier produced some photos of herself and handed them around. She explained that she had to take the photos to a theatrical agency round the corner and asked Quinn if he would accompany her.

"Delivering pictures is Benny's department," Quinn said. He seized a linen napkin, wrote a phone number on it with a ballpoint pen, and handed it to the girl. "Call Benny," he said. "Hey, waiter"—Quinn made some more Chinese-like sounds—"the bill." He didn't look at the amount. Turning to me, he said, "Shall I sign it Eddie Quinn, the Men's Room?"

I smiled.

"We must meet again and talk," he said. "Come to my pool one day. Norman will fix it."

"Sure thing," Norman said.

On the way out we ran into the French chantoosie. She told Quinn she owed the bellboy a dime for the phone call. "Here, kid," Quinn said, and he handed the boy a dollar.

"Couldn't we walk there?" the girl asked Quinn once more.

"Walking is Benny's department. I only walk as far as elevators."

A couple of nights later I went to another wrestling match, this time at the small Mont St. Louis Gym. There wasn't much of a crowd, but those who did turn up were fierce. There were several fistfights. A fan attempted to break a folding chair over Killer

Kowalski's back. On the whole, though, this was an evening of indifferent performances. Obviously, wrestlers, like actors, need a big, responsive audience. Only Tiger Tomasso, a dedicated performer, put on a good exhibition: spitting, eye-gouging, biting.

I was lucky enough to meet the Tiger a week later.

I had asked Olson if, once the wrestlers started to travel on the summer circuit, I could drive with one of them to Trois-Rivières. Olson arranged for Ovile Asselin, a former Mr. Canada, to take me out. Asselin picked me up at four in the afternoon and we drove to a road junction, outside of town, where we were to meet another wrestler, Don Lewin. While we were waiting, two other cars, both Cadillacs, pulled up and out stepped Tiger Tomasso, Eddie Auger, Maurice Lapointe, and three other wrestlers who were on the card that night. I immediately went up to chat with the Tiger.

Tomasso told me he used to be a deskman in a hotel in Hamilton. All the wrestlers used to stay there, and he began to work out with them. Finally, he went into the game. "What are you doing here?" he asked.

I was writing an article, I explained, as two pretty girls in shorts strolled past.

"That's the only kind of article I'm interested in," Tomasso said.

Eventually Lewin, a surly ex-marine, arrived, and he, Asselin, and I drove off together. Lewin, a suspicious type, wouldn't talk much in my presence. He had performed in Buffalo the previous night and had been driving all day to make the date in Trois-Rivières. He was, understandably, extremely tired. And unfriendly. On arrival, he made it clear that I would have to find another lift back to Montreal.

There was only a thin crowd at the seedy little arena in the city, and Lewin, excusably, pulled his opponent out of the ring after five minutes of lacklustre wrestling and held him there long enough to be disqualified. Larry Moquin arranged for me to be driven home by a young French Canadian who had taken part in a tag-team match earlier in the evening. His side, the villainous one, had lost.

The wrestler had taken a bad fall, and on the drive back to Montreal he kept rubbing his back. "Tomorrow," he said wearily, "I have to go to Hull. I'm working there."

"Don't you guys ever take time off?" I asked.

He explained that you had to be available when a promoter wanted you; otherwise, you were considered unreliable. "It's a dangerous profession," he said. "My insides are all shaken up. You take your life in your hands each time you step in the ring." He had wrestled for a long time in Florida, where a Puerto Rican fan had once knifed him. "But that's a good territory. They liked me there. The worst was the West." Once, he said, he had driven 450 miles each way to make matches in two western cities. Four wrestlers, taking turns at the wheel, had managed the trip there and back within a day. "The worst things are canvas burns. They're extremely painful and we all get them. Sometimes they last a week, other times a month." Suppressing a yawn, he added, "I used to sell cars. I could always go back to that. I like meeting the public."

November 1960

II

Cheap Skates

I n the distant future, after I die before my time, a promising 120-year-old writer, my seminal novel unfinished, I can anticipate my youngest son saying to his son, "I'll tell you what your grandfather was like. Wonderful, truly wonderful, except for Wednesday and Saturday nights from October to May."

"What happened then?"

"There were hockey games on TV, and if I dared to tiptoe into the living room to inform him, say, I've just won a scholarship to Harvard, or I'm getting married tomorrow, or, 'Hey, congratulations! My wife just gave birth—you're a grandfather,' he would glare at me and say, 'Not now, you fool. We can discuss such trivialities between periods.'"

My wife will have another story to tell.

"On New Year's Eve 1975, when all the other ladies were preparing to go out to dinner parties or dances, dressed in their finest gowns, he took me to the Forum, where I could eat lukewarm hot dogs and watch the Canadiens play the Russians."

The quality of play isn't what it once was; the endless regular season is meaningless. After 840 games, only five of the twenty-one teams in the NHL have been eliminated from the playoffs. I know, I know. But once that first puck is dropped, I'm married to my TV set. Come game time, if one of my daughters is foolish enough to protest that *Hamlet,* with Olivier, is playing on another channel, I will point out, justifiably, that I know how *Hamlet* comes out but not how the Montreal Canadiens will fare tonight against the fabled New Jersey Devils.

In the fall, professional sports schedules overlapping as they do, I watched football, a baseball playoff, and a hockey game all in the same day.

Bliss.

Speaking of baseball, Canadian paranoia, never far from the surface, suffered a vintage eruption even as the skies turned wintry, the trees went black and bare, and we were adjusting to the coming hockey season. In a bar where I drink, nobody was surprised when the Toronto Blue Jays lost the first game of their crucial end-of-the-season series with the Yankees. Instead, there was much wagging of knowledgeable heads. "Of course, the Jays are not going to make it," I was told. "If they did, can you imagine what a disaster it would be for NBC-TV? The fix is in."

As we all know, the Blue Jays did take their division title but choked in the playoffs they were favoured to win. Mind you, by failing to appear in and perhaps win a World Series, they did avoid a possible international incident. Obviously had the Blue Jays won the World Series, calls of congratulations to the dugout would have come from both President Reagan and Prime Minister Mulroney. Which one would manager Bobby Cox have put on hold?

Another problem: Even had the Blue Jays won, after the shouting had died down it would still not have counted as much as it once did to bring home our true Holy Grail, the Stanley Cup. It would only mean that Toronto's hired hands out of California and Florida had beat somebody else's mercenaries out of the same sunbelt states. Once, however, it was different, certainly in the grand game of hockey. Once, if the Canadiens won a Stanley Cup, something of a habit in the old days, the players who had turned the trick were either from Montreal or Thurso or Trois-Rivières or Chicoutimi, which is to say they were Quebeckers like the rest of us. They were *our* team, unlike the players, however splendid, who performed for other dynasties, say the Yankees or the Reds, but were not really of New York or Cincinnati, Pete Rose being the happy exception to that rule.

Once hockey was ours, its nuances an enigma to most Americans and just about everybody British. When Canadians ran into each other in New York or London, cities rumoured to have other things going for them, we could talk about hockey, our joy, our secret idiom, excluding sniffy superior foreigners, much as my parents used to lapse into Yiddish on a bus when they didn't want *them* to know what they were going on about.

Now all that has changed. Though most Americans are still without puck sense, something red-blooded Canadians are born with, they do support fourteen of the twenty-one teams in the NHL. Where once the Canadiens, as well as lesser teams here, used to comb the northern bush and mining towns for raw talent, today they scout Sweden and Finland, they tempt adolescent Czechs to defect, and—above all—they cover the American colleges. Having watched a number of skilful but timorous Swedes on NHL ice, a sportswriting friend of mine has observed, "I now understand how come Sweden was neutral in the Second World War." But young Americans do not avoid the corners; they are doing very well indeed here, six of them now regulars on the Montreal Canadiens. They are a new hockey breed—young men who have seen cutlery before, know how to dial long distance, and are capable of saying more to a young lady than "How much?"

As if that weren't enough of an intrusion, we are now being asked to suffer an American carpetbagger. That notorious amateur professional, George Plimpton, has had the audacity to surface with a book about our game, *Open Net.* Picking up this necessarily offensive trifle, I recalled the hero of Walker Percy's memorable novel *The Moviegoer.* Only after a Hollywood company had filmed his hometown did it actually seem real to him. Would Plimpton, I wondered, having exhausted the possibilities of baseball, football, golf, and hockey—coming to our game in desperate middle age, as it were—make hockey real or would his cultural imperialist gesture be redeemed (for me, at any rate) by a plethora of boners, proving Plimpton out of his league at last?

There are, it grieves me to report, no boners in Plimpton's presumptuous study. If it is not the most knowledgeable book I have ever read about the game, it is certainly one of the most engaging. It is so intelligent, charged with such enthusiasm, such fun to read, that I can even forgive Plimpton, who is a fellow *GQ* contributing writer, for revealing in his final chapter that he once actually addressed the "Junior Achievers" of Edmonton. This, I should explain, is a group of prairie brats so unspeakably pushy as to sell stocks in their little companies and busy themselves with bottom lines and profit margins at an age when they could have been doing much more socially useful things, such as shoplifting or looking up dirty words in the dictionary. However, the trip did afford the intrepid Plimpton an opportunity to go into the nets against the Great Gretzky. Mind you, by this time Plimpton was an experienced net minder, certainly as literate as Ken Dryden, if not quite so adroit between the pipes.

The core of Plimpton's entertaining book deals with the post-Orr-and-Esposito Boston Bruins, a team that allowed him to mind the nets occasionally at their training camp. Why, they even let him risk life and limb in an exhibition game against the Philadelphia Flyers, or Broad Street Bullies, as they were then known, an aggregation of thumpers and slashers and goons that included Gary Dornhoefer and Bobby Clarke and Dave "the Hammer" Schultz. Plimpton's account of his net-minding stint in this game and the teasing in the Boston locker room that led up to it is rendered with considerable panache.

I am especially grateful to Plimpton for his portrait of Don Cherry, who was then coach of the Bruins. Cherry, whom I had long ago dismissed as insufferably brash, is revealed as a likable and astute observer of the game. He was particularly good on the days when he had to play for the notorious Eddie Shore, a former hockey great, in minor league Springfield. Shore, Cherry confirms, "was the stingiest guy you ever heard of. To keep the light bills down, we had our practices in the semi-darkness.... When it was payroll time, you never knew quite what was going to happen. If the payroll was too high for the week he'd simply fine guys for poor play... though maybe the guy hadn't been on the ice for a month!" Shore, Cherry quotes, also had "these strange ideas about sex and especially sex and the athlete. Once, when the team was going terrible, he called a meeting for all the players and their wives, and in this little steamy locker room, with the jockstraps hanging from the pegs, he proceeded to tell the wives they were allowing their husbands too much sex. It was affecting their play. 'Now you just cut that stuff out!' he yelled at them."

Plimpton soon discovers that goaltenders, who contend with pucks zooming in on them at one hundred miles per hour, are a special breed. The immensely talented Glenn Hall was regularly sick before each game as well as between periods. Jacques Plante, a Canadiens great, once commented on the indignity of allowing an easy shot to slip past. "Imagine yourself sitting in an office and you make an error of some kind—call it an error of judgment or a mistake over the phone. All of a sudden, behind you, a bright red light goes on, the walls collapse and there are eighteen thousand people shouting and jeering at you, calling you an imbecile and an idiot and a bum and throwing things at you, including garbage."

While a player is with a team, the camaraderie is intense—there is nothing else like it—but retiring is hard, very hard. "You see your teammates every day," former Bruin John Wensink explained, "and then when it's over, it's over. You never see them again. You wonder why so-and-so who was your friend, and you roomed with him on the road trips, wouldn't give a call when he comes through town. You could sit around and tell stories. Have a beer. He could come to your house and see your children.... But they don't call. They never call. You wonder. You wonder. After you leave, there is no contact with anyone. It hurts. It makes you feel like you're a gust in the wind."

According to Don Cherry, "the only club which has any concern about this is, as you might expect, Montreal. The Canadiens. In the Forum they have a room set aside for their old-timers. It's down the corridor; the old players can go in there with their wives and sit around...."

George Plimpton's *Open Net* belongs up there on that still unfortunately small shelf of literate hockey books, alongside the best of them.

I am grateful, as I am sure Plimpton is too, that he survived his ordeal without ever taking a puck in the groin, "ringing the berries," as they say. The pain, one goalie warned him, is like "taking your top lip and folding it back over your head," a thrill professionals contend with each time out.

January 1986

12

Maxie

A s usual, early one morning in August, I climbed upstairs to my studio in our dacha on the shores of Lake Memphremagog, tea tray in hand, and sat down at my long plank table, ready to begin work. I could no longer make out the cigarillo burns and tea stains on the table, because it was now buried end to end in snooker books by various hands, newspaper clippings, photocopies, computer printouts, stacks of *Snooker Scene,* and tournament programs and press releases. I just had time to flick on the power on my electric typewriter when the phone rang. It was an old Laurier poolroom chum who was still driving a taxi at the age of seventy-three. Last time I had run into him, outside that singularly ugly warehouse, the Molson Centre, where the Canadiens now play hockey of a sort, he was trying to flog tickets for that evening's game. "So," he said, "you became a writer and I became a scalper, and we're both *alter kockers* now." We exchanged phone numbers. I promised to meet him for lunch one day, but I had never called. Now he was on the phone at 7:15 a.m.

"Have you seen this morning's *Gazette*?" he asked.

"Not yet."

"Maxie Berger died."

"How old was he?" I asked, because this information is of increasing interest to me.

"Eighty-three. I want you to write something nice about him. He was a good fighter. A *mensch* too."

"I'll call you soon, Abe, and we'll have that lunch."

"Yeah, sure."

H. L. Mencken once wrote, "I hate all sports as rabidly as a person who likes sports hates common sense."

George Bernard Shaw was also disdainful: "It is a noteworthy fact that kicking and beating have played so considerable a part in the habits of which necessity have imposed on mankind in past ages that the only way of preventing civilized men from kicking and beating their wives is to organize games in which they can kick and beat balls." Or each other.

Back in the days when I used to hang out in poolrooms, boxers were greatly admired by my bunch, some of whom could rattle off the names of the top ten in each division, as listed in Nat Fleischer's *Ring* magazine. I had hoped to qualify for the Golden Gloves but had been taken out in a qualifying three-rounder; my ambition then was not a Booker Prize or a perch on the *New York Times* bestseller list but a Friday night main bout in Madison Square Garden, sponsored on radio by Gillette razor blades ("Look sharp! Feel sharp! Be sharp!").

At the time, I believed snooker to be a game

played only by working-class hooligans like us. I was unaware that Montreal's most elite men's clubs (the Mount Royal, the Mount Stephen) boasted oak-panelled rooms with nifty antique tables. All right, that was naive of me. But I thought then, and still do, that no sport comes without its class or racial baggage.

Where I come from, hockey and baseball appealed to every class and faith, distinctions limited only to where fans could afford to sit. Since then, however, we have suffered the National Hockey League's ostensibly mindless expansion into the American sunbelt, a move actually informed by a subtext seldom mentioned. The owners hope to eventually acquire fan support by offering rednecks the only team sport left that is just about 100 percent white.

In the thirties and forties we counted football, golf, and tennis as strictly WASP as sliced white bread. We associated football with universities fastidious enough to have Jewish quotas, and golf and tennis with country clubs and resorts that wouldn't tolerate any Jews whatsoever. A down-and-dirty sport like boxing, on the other hand, belonged to tough kids out of Italian, black, Polish, Irish, and Jewish mean streets. Jack Solomons, one of ours, was the promoter with heft in London, and Joe "Yussel the Muscle" Jacobs called the shots in New York, where the great and near-great trained in Lou Stillman's gym. And welterweight champ Barney Ross, the son of a Talmudic scholar, gave us bragging rights.

In those days boxing-beat hacks in Toronto had not yet been muzzled by political correctness. Describing a 1934 fight, one of them wrote: "For once, the Gentile barracking brigade will have to choose between the lesser of 'two evils,' when Sammy Luftspring and Dave Yack, a pair of Hebes, battle for supremacy at Frank Tenute's Elm Grove show at the Mutual Street Arena on Monday night." Not much later Lou Marsh, of the *Toronto Daily Star,* got to cover what was, as he put it, "an honest-to-Henry grudge fight between a Celt and a son of Moses." Sammy Luftspring vs. Chick McCarthy. The good news was this promising "slugfest" had attracted an all-Canada record attendance of 6,000, "of which 5,795 talked turkey to the box office staff." Luftspring won a unanimous decision, but not before, wrote Marsh, "McCarthy opened the final round with a right-hander that made the aggressive little Jew boy lean like the Tower of Pisa."

A couple of days after Maxie Berger died in August 2000, both the Toronto *Globe and Mail* and *National Post* ran obituaries, noting that Maxie had briefly been world junior welterweight champion. Lacking the earlier verve of the *Star,* the tame *National Post* headline ran:

BOXER WAS LOVED
IN THE BRONX,
A STAR IN QUEBEC
Fought Five World Champions
He dressed well
and was popular
with women

In common with other newspapers, the *National Post* featured a silly photograph of Maxie, obviously retrieved from an ancient Canadian Press file. It harked back to the days when newspaper photographers in a hurry could always be counted on to honour their own code of clichés. Photographing a novelist, they had him hold his latest book to his chest. Snapping two politicians shaking hands, they enjoined them not to look at each other but to smile menacingly sincerely into the camera. Dispatched to shoot a photograph of a real estate developer who was launching a hospital building campaign with a $25,000 donation, they got the donor and recipient to pose together, both clutching a four-foot-long copy of the cheque. I used to drink with one of those photographers when I was a teenager writing for the long-defunct Montreal *Herald,* filing for two cents a line. Late one afternoon he told me that he had been paid fifty bucks by Nat Sugarman, who was running for alderman again in our district, to attend his debate with Herb Feingold, who also coveted a job that came with advance real estate information that could be worth plenty. "Now listen to me," said Sugarman, "you don't load that fucking camera with film because I'm not paying for that. But every time I hold up my pencil like this. Watch me, see, I'm now holding up my pencil. Every time I do that, you leap out of your chair to go flash flash flash. But whatever that shit Feingold says, you never take his picture. Got it? Good."

The incongruous photograph of Maxie showed him assuming his ring stance, leading with his left. But he is standing in the corner of a room, wearing an open-necked sports shirt and trousers belted high, addressing a blank wall. His swept-back hair suggests it was brilliantined or he had just got out of a shower.

"Clean up good, Maxie, for Christ's sake. You know how long it is since they took your picture for the papers?"

Cauliflower ears. Soft dim eyes. Scarred eyebrows. Pulpy nose. Swollen knuckles. And no wonder. Over the wasting years, the New York mob had fed Maxie to Fritzie Zivic, Beau Jack, and the great Sugar Ray Robinson, among others. Maxie took on Sugar Ray in Madison Square Garden in 1942, knocked to the canvas twice before the referee stopped the fight. Maxie had wanted to continue, but the referee had shouted at him, "Do you want to get killed?"

The son of immigrants out of a Polish *shtetl*, Maxie had an education limited to elementary school, after which he went to work as a grocery delivery boy. He learned to box at the YMHA, on Mount Royal, which was then in the heart of the city's working-class Jewish quarter. He won a silver medal in the British Empire Games in the 1930s before turning pro, fighting out of the Bronx. Married four times, on his retirement he returned to Montreal and opened a custom-made shirt business, where the smart guys could acquire those ghastly white-on-white shirts, inevitably worn with initialled cufflinks, and what we used to call a one-button-roll sports jacket with outsize padded shoulders.

I first encountered Maxie in the forties in the Laurentians, our minor league Catskills, at the Castle des Monts Hotel in Ste Agathe. A seething Maxie came roaring out of the hotel pursued by a hollering wife. When we shot *The Apprenticeship of Duddy Kravitz* in 1974, I made sure there was a small part for Maxie. The *National Post* obituary writer noted that Maxie was "like a character in a Studs Terkel novel," but Terkel never wrote a novel. The obviously nice man who had written Maxie's obit also had it that "he became a stockbroker in the early 1960s, profiting from the 1960s stock market boom." Actually, he served as a factotum for a brokerage house. In those days he would occasionally turn up in the Montreal Press Club, then in the Mount Royal Hotel, and I would chat with him there, an uncommonly gentle man who had taken too many punches to the head in close to a hundred fights. He was out of it for the last ten years of his life, a sufferer from dementia.

R.I.P., Maxie.

September 2000

13

Paper Lion

atching Luis Miguel Dominguin fight in Valencia in 1951, I suddenly saw a scrawny boy, two rows down, leap from his seat, vault the *barrera,* broomstick and sack in hand, and make it clear onto the sands of the bull ring, stamping his foot for the bull to charge. Around me people were cheering or laughing warmly, but I remember watching the boy, my heart hammering, until attendants hustled him off. I did not yet know that these boys, called *espontaneos,* were commonplace. A week later, in Paris, a friend showed me a new French Communist Party publication, a *Life*-size picture magazine lampoon about America. On the first page there was a photograph of Harry Truman, then president, looking bumpkinish as he waved a shoe aloft at an American shoe convention. Opposite, Al Capone smiled darkly behind a cigar, and there was a quote from him endorsing capitalism. The best system, Capone said. On the following page, clinching the case for bestiality, there was a full-page spread of a behemoth of a football player: crouching, the eyes mean, the mouth snarling, arms hanging ape-like.

This, the caption said, was a typical American university student.

I toss in these two memories, seemingly unrelated, because at the bullfight in Valencia it did not occur to me that a gifted reporter, mulling over just such a bit of adolescent daring, as George Plimpton once did, could develop it into two unusual sports books: *Out of My League,* published in 1962, and now *Paper Lion.* And then I have always shared what I take to be the French Communist Party line on American football. I am, I should hastily add, not so much a fellow traveller as a committed sports fan. Living in England for more than twelve years, I follow the baseball and ice hockey results conscientiously in the Paris *Herald,* but football, even after reading Plimpton's uncommonly good *Paper Lion,* is still alien to me. Possibly my prejudice against football, like just about everything else, breaks down to race and class. On our street, a working-class street, we wanted to be boxers or, failing that, baseball pitchers. Bonus boys. Speaking for myself, I got so far as to train for the Golden Gloves when I unfortunately came up against a schoolmate called Manny, who was already fighting professionally, working in preliminaries under an alias in small towns. Manny had the unnerving habit of blowing his nose on his glove before swatting me. I still insist he didn't knock me out. Revolted, I fainted. In Montreal we had the example of Maxie Berger, who fought in the Garden and once went the distance with Ike Williams; and we also had our one and only Ziggy "The Fireball" Freed, who would have been a star with the Athletics had Connie Mack not been such a lousy anti-Semite.

Ziggy was actually signed by a scout at the age of eighteen and was sent out for seasoning with a Class D team in the Carolinas. He lasted only a season. "You think they'd give a Jewish boy a chance to pitch out there?" he asked. "Sure, in the ninth inning, with the bases loaded and none out, with their home-run hitter coming up to the plate, the manager would shout, Okay, Ziggy, it's your ball game now."

Football, however, was always remote. A middle-class WASP's game. I still associate it with hip flasks, raccoon coats, and loud boring McGill alumni making damn fools of themselves in downtown Montreal. I also have a problem with the players, the boors of my university days. Of James Thurber's university days too, if you remember Bolenciecwcz, the Ohio State University tackle, in *My Life and Hard Times*. "In order to be eligible to play," Thurber wrote, "it was necessary for him to keep up on his studies, a very difficult matter, for while he was no dumber than an ox he was not any smarter." Bassum, the economics professor, asks the star tackle to name a means of transportation ("Just any means of transportation. That is, any medium, agency, or method of getting from one place to another"), but this he is unable to do. "Toot-toot-toot," the professor says. "Choo-choo-choo." Finally, Bolenciecwcz comes up with train, thereby qualifying for the Illinois game.

I've been to pro games, and I can't help feeling that there is something fundamentally unsportsman-like about men, mostly oversize to begin with, strapping themselves into all that outlandish equipment and wearing cages to protect their faces, all for a game's sake. It's brutish. In the epilogue to *Paper*

Lion, Plimpton writes, "Detroit had a bad season my year. The team finished fourth in its division.... Injuries hurt their chances. Eleven of the first-line players were knocked out of the line-up with injuries, most of them on the defensive team. Joe Schmidt and Carl Brettschneider of the linebackers were crippled, and so were Yale Lary and Night Train Lane. Gary Lowe ruptured his achilles tendon...."

If I have already made it abundantly clear that football isn't exactly my game, then I must say that George Plimpton's *Paper Lion* is at once a more satisfying and complex book than *Out of My League,* wherein the writer unwinds the sometimes nightmarish story of how he came to pitch to an all-star lineup of National and American League players in the Yankee Stadium, the team with the most hits picking up $1,000.

Plimpton got *Sports Illustrated* to put up the pot. It was his notion, he told the editor, that he would pitch "not as a hotshot—that'd be a different story— but as a guy who's average, really, a sort of Mr. Everybody, the sort who thinks he's a fair athlete...." If it worked out, he hoped to go on to play tennis with Pancho Gonzalez, box with Archie Moore, play golf with Snead or Hogan, and so forth.

The writing in *Out of My League* is fresh and observant, but it suffers from spinning out a one-day adventure into a book. It is original, there is much to admire, but I think it would have read better as a shorter piece, like John Updike's splendid account of Ted Williams's last day with the Boston Red Sox. Ultimately, the most compelling thing about *Out of My League* is what I can only call the author's chutzpah, his actually going through with it, imposing himself on the players and the unsuspecting crowd at the Yankee Stadium. Many of the players were indifferent, others were cold. With Plimpton floundering on the mound, Mantle yawns ostentatiously. But then we never really worry about the author's pitching performance per se as we do, say, about Jim Brosnan's good and bad days in *The Long Season.* Plimpton's professional pride, unlike Brosnan's, could never be truly involved. Neither is his livelihood.

We also do not fret about how Plimpton will stack up on the field as the Detroit Lions' last-string quarterback, but from the moment he begins haphazard practice, whacking a football into an armchair in his apartment, until he is finally allowed to call five plays in an intersquad scrimmage at Pontiac, Plimpton holds us with the force of sheer good writing. His account of his stay with the Lions makes for a most enjoyable, likable book. If he was, predictably, a disaster on the field, I can think of no other non-fiction book that evokes more successfully the special taste and feeling of a game and the men who play it.

To begin with, Plimpton had trouble getting a team to allow him to work out with them, let alone take part in an actual game. Red Hickey, coach of the Western Conference All-Stars, said, "Did I hear you right? You—with no experience—want to train and then *play*—in the Pro-Bowl game?"

The New York Giants wouldn't have him and neither would the Jets. Fortunately George Wilson, the earthy coach of the Detroit Lions, was amused by the idea and invited Plimpton to camp. From the moment of his arrival, Plimpton reveals a necessarily good and receptive nature and an enviable eye for detail. Of course, he's got a lot going for him. Even a run-through of some of the names on the Detroit roster has a distinctive tang to it: Milton Plum, Yale Lary, Nick Pietrosante, Dick LeBeau, Scooter McLean . . . as well as a linesman, nicknamed the Mad Creeper, who was, Plimpton writes, a near pathological case. "No one knows who the Mad Creeper was. . . . His habit was to creep along the corridors late at night, three or four in the morning, sneak into someone's room, lean over his bed and throttle him hard and briefly, just closing his hands around the fellow's throat and then skittering off down the corridor, listening to the gasping behind him."

The trade idiom is rich. Night Train Lane speaks of his "captainship," tells how you get "a great communion to get to the Hall of Fame," and teases Plimpton about the unstoppable Roger Brown the night before the intersquad scrimmage. "Jawge, you set to find if Roger's going to *disjoin* you? I mean in Pontiac you are goin' to have expectation in this whole question—he's goin' be at you shufflin' and breathin' *hard*."

Paper Lion is very rewarding on superfans and hangers-on, including a tailor who has become a touchstone to the rookies. Before the rookies know whether they've made the squad, the tailor, who has the ear of the coaches, may come to measure them for a team blazer. Conversely, he may pass them by. Plimpton seems to catch exactly the tension between rookie and veteran, the competition for jobs; the night of the team out-offs; and the nerves that build up before a game, even an exhibition game. Originally, Plimpton had hoped to pass for just another rookie, but Wayne Walker, a regular, had read *Out of My League.* This killed Plimpton's ready-made (and libellous) excuse for his own ineptitude, the bare-faced lie that he had once been good enough to play ball with a semi-pro Canadian team, the Newfoundland Newfs. Canadian pro football, let me point out at once, gives gainful employment to many an American journeyman player, as long as he is able to adjust to a slight difference in rules, such as the need to say excuse me before tackling. Then, just as we came through for the United States during prohibition, the year Plimpton was maligning us in Detroit, my permissive country was able to take on several first-line NFL players who had been suspended for gambling. Neither is the Canadian game without its glories. Only a few years ago our Super Bowl, the Grey Cup game, had to be called in the third quarter because of fog. It was no longer necessary to conceal the ball. Players couldn't find each other and fans couldn't see the field. A moment in sports history, I think, that rivals the 1951 boat race, when Oxford sank.

Before Plimpton left to join the Lions, a friend in New York, who had once played for the Washington Redskins, warned him about the stupidity of ball players and told him to expect juvenile behaviour. The barracks room humour of the camp (water pistols, jock straps) does seem more than a bit over-hearty at times, but Plimpton makes a convincing case for similar lapses among supposedly loftier groups, such as *New Yorker* staff writers; and I must admit that I found the fright masks funny. Working off tensions, the players would, it seems, some nights don masks made of thin pliable rubber—vampire heads, Frankenstein monsters—and sneak up on a sleeping teammate to startle him.

Curiously, it is not until page 300 of *Paper Lion* that Plimpton goes into the question of salaries and bonuses and then only fleetingly, almost as though talk about money embarrasses him. But as Red Smith has written again and again, there is no question that the name of the game is money, and that these are men being paid to play a boys' game. One needn't be a football fan to know about the $400,000 paid to Joe Namath for signing with the New York Jets, the bigger bonuses that have been handed out to others since, and the $15,000 earned by each of the Green Bay Packers for a day's work against the Kansas City Chiefs. At the risk of sounding old-fashioned, I'd say it goes against the grain. This sort of reward *is* socially unbalanced. I would have liked to know more about the money in the game and what the players felt about it. Without asking for a grey sociological work rather than the lively journal Plimpton has given us, I still could have done with decidedly more information about the economics of the football business and the profits involved.

Sports, obviously, is a bloody big business, a growth industry, as they say, with the National Hockey League expanding to twelve teams next season, new professional basketball and soccer leagues promised, and the purses offered on the PGA circuit the highest ever. If the profit to be made from sports is immense, just possibly immorally high, then club owners differ from the tycoons in other industries by asking for our hearts as well as our money. We are entreated to trust them with our boyish admiration and enthusiasm, with what we retain of the old school holler, at an age when we are more immediately concerned with falling hair, mortgages, and choosing schools for the kids.

Professional sports, though I am still addicted to them, have begun to alienate me in yet another way. It was George Plimpton's notion that as a sort of Mr. Everybody, a Central Park quarterback, a Sunday pitcher, he would try his hand at baseball, football, and other sports. James Thurber, he told the editor of *Sports Illustrated,* once wrote that the majority of American males put themselves to sleep by striking out the batting order of the New York Yankees. Yes, but if at one time Plimpton's idea of testing himself, seeing how well he could do in pro company, seemed a feasible, even charming, conceit, I fear it is considerably less so today. If once athletes were really rather like us, only more beautifully made, better conditioned, more gifted, suddenly too many of them are not like us at all. All at once basketball players tend to be seven feet tall and football players weigh three hundred pounds. Then football, rather more than most sports, has come to suffer from overspecialization, with different teams for offence and defence. In contrast it would seem that soccer players, all of them ninety-minute men, must be far more resourceful. They are certainly more elegant and recognizably human to watch, trotting out onto the field in jersey and shorts, unarmed, so to speak.

Finally, George Plimpton's *Paper Lion* joins a growing body of first-rate writing about sports: one thinks immediately of Norman Mailer on the fights, Updike, and Mark Harris. Nevertheless, I have a reservation. Much as I enjoyed Plimpton's book, I can't help feeling guilty, like having been to a movie on a fine summer's afternoon. An earlier generation of American writers had to test themselves not against Bart Starr and Archie Moore but the Spanish Civil War and the Moscow trials. In Europe, Isaac Babel, looking for a change, rode with the Red Cavalry. George Orwell went to Wigan Pier and then Catalonia. Arthur Koestler came out of Spain with his *Spanish Testament.* This is not meant to be an attack on Plimpton, but all of us, Plimpton's generation and mine. One day, I fear, we will be put down as a trivial, peripheral bunch. Crazy about bad old movies, nostalgic for comic books. Our gods don't fail. At worst, they grow infirm. They suffer pinched nerves, like Paul Hornung. Or arthritic arms, like Sandy Koufax.

1968

14

Gordie

C learly, he came from good stock. Interviewed on television in 1979, his eighty-seven-year-old father was asked, "How do you feel?"

"I feel fine."

"At what time in life does a man lose his sexual desires?"

"You'll have to ask somebody older than I am."

His son was only five when he acquired his first pair of skates. He repeated the third grade, more intent on his wrist shot than reading, developing it out there in the subzero wheat fields, shooting frozen horse buns against the barn door. When he was a mere fourteen-year-old, working in summer on a Saskatoon construction site with his father's crew, both his strength and determination were already celebrated. He could pick up ninety-pound cement bags in either hand, heaving them easily. Preparing for what he knew lay ahead, he sat at the kitchen table night after night, practising his autograph.

Gordie Howe was born in Floral, Saskatchewan, in 1928, a child of prairie penury, and his hockey career spanned thirty-two seasons in five decades. The stuff of legend.

Gordie.

For as long as I have been a hockey fan, Mr. Elbows has been out there, skating, his stride seemingly effortless. The big guy with the ginger-ale-bottle shoulders. I didn't always admire him. But as he grew older and hockey players apparently younger, many of them younger than my oldest son, he became an especial pleasure. My God, only three years older than me, and still out there chasing pucks. For middle-aged Canadians, there was hope. In a world of constant and often bewildering change, there was one shining certitude. Come October, the man for whom time had stopped would be out there, not taking dirt from anybody.

Gordie, Gordie, the old fart's champion.

Gordie Howe's amazing career is festooned with records, illuminated by anecdote. Looked at properly, within the third-grade repeater there was a hockey pedagogue longing to leap out.

Item: In 1963, when the traditionally stylish but corner-shy Montreal Canadiens brought up a young behemoth, John Ferguson, from the minors to police the traffic, he had the audacity, his first time over the boards, to go into a corner with Mr. Elbows. He yanked off his gloves, foolishly threatening to mix it up with Howe.

"In this league, son," Howe cautioned him, "we don't really fight. All we do is tug each other's sweater."

"Certainly, Mr. Howe," the rookie said.

But no sooner did he drop his fists than the old educator creamed him.

Toe Blake, another Canadien who played against Howe, once said, "He was primarily a defensive player when he started, and he'd take your ankles off if you stood in front of their net."

That was in 1946, when eighteen-year-old Gordie, in his first season with the Detroit Red Wings, scored all of seven goals and fifteen assists. Thirty-four years later, Steve Shutt, who wasn't even born in 1946, reported a different problem in playing against the now silvery-haired legend. "Sure we give him room out there. If you take him into the boards, the crowd boos, but they also boo if you let him get around you."

Which is to say, there were the glory years (more of them than any other athlete in a major sport can count) and the last sad ceremonial season, when even the fifty-two-year-old grandfather allowed that he had become poetry in slow motion. But still a fierce advocate for his two hockey-playing sons, Marty and Mark.

"Playing on the same line as your sons," Maurice Richard once observed, "that's really something."

When I finally caught up with Howe, I asked him if, considering his own abilities, it might have been kinder to encourage his sons to do anything but play hockey.

"Well, once somebody said to Marty, 'Hey, kid, you're not as good as your father.' 'Who is?' he replied."

Consider the records, familiar but formidable.

Until Wayne Gretzky came along, Gordie Howe had scored the most assists (1,383) and, of course, played in the most games (2,186). He won the National Hockey League scoring title six times and was named the most valuable player (MVP) six times in the NHL and once in the World Hockey Association. He had scored more goals than anybody (975—801 of them in the NHL). His hundredth goal, incidentally, was scored on February 17, 1951, against Gerry McNeil of Montreal as the Red Wings beat the Canadiens 2–1 on Maurice Richard Night. Obloquy. And a feat charged with significance for those of us who cut our hockey teeth debating who was really *numero uno,* Gordie Howe or the other number 9, Maurice "Rocket" Richard of the Montreal Canadiens.

Out West, where the clapboard main street, adrift in snow, often consisted of no more than a legion hall, a curling club, a Chinese restaurant, and a beer parlour, the men in their peaked caps and lumberjack shirts—deprived of an NHL team themselves, dependent on CBC-Radio's *Hockey Night in Canada* for the big Saturday-night game—rooted for Gordie. One of their own, shoving it to the condescending East. Gordie, educating the fancy-pants frogs with his elbows. Giving them pause, making them throw snow up in the corners. But in Montreal, elegant Montreal, we valued élan (that is to say, Richard) above all. For durable Gordie, it appeared the game was a job in which he had undoubtedly learned to excel, but the exploding Rocket, whether he appreciated it or not, was an artist. Moving in over the blue line, he was incomparable. "What I remember most about the Rocket were his eyes," goalie Glenn Hall once said. "When he came flying toward you with the puck on his stick, his eyes were all lit up, flashing and gleaming like a pinball machine. It was terrifying."

Seven years older than Howe, Richard played eighteen seasons, retiring in 1960. Astonishingly, he never won a scoring championship, coming second to Howe twice and failing two more times by a maddening point. He was voted MVP only once. But Maurice Richard was the first player to score fifty goals in fifty games. That was in the 1944–45 season, in the old six-team league, when anybody netting twenty goals was considered a star. Toe Blake, once a linemate of the Rocket and a partisan to this day, maintains, "There's only one thing that counts in this game and that's the Stanley Cup. How many did Jack Adams win with Gordie and how many did we take with the Rocket?"

The answer to that one is that Detroit took four cups with Gordie and the Canadiens won eight propelled by the Rocket. However, Richard's supporting cast included, at one time or another, Elmer Lach, Blake, Richard's brother Henri, Jean Beliveau, Boom Boom Geoffrion, Dickie Moore, Doug Harvey, Butch Bouchard, and Jacques Plante. Howe had Sid Abel and Terrible Ted Lindsay playing alongside him, and there was also Alex Delvecchio. He was backed up by Red Kelly on defence, either Glenn Hall or Terry Sawchuk in the nets, and, for the rest, mostly a number of journeymen. Even so, the Red Wings, led by Gordie Howe, finished first in regular-season play seven times in a row, from 1949 to 1955.

They beat the Canadiens in the 1954 Stanley Cup final and again in 1955, although that year the issue was clouded, a seething Richard having been suspended for the series.

"Gordie Howe is the best hockey player I have ever seen," Beliveau has said. Even Maurice Richard allows, "He was a far better all-round player than I was."

Yes, certainly, but there's a kicker. A big one.

The Rocket's younger brother, former Canadiens centre Henri Richard, has said, "There is no doubt that Gordie was better than Maurice. But build two rinks across from one another. Then put Gordie in one and Maurice in the other, and see which one would be filled."

Unlike the Rocket, Bobby Hull, Bobby Orr, and Guy Lafleur, Howe always lacked one dimension. He couldn't lift fans out of their seats, hearts thumping, charged with expectation, merely by taking a pass and streaking down the ice. The most capable all-round player the game may have known was possibly deficient in only one thing—star quality. But my oh my, he certainly could get things done. In the one-time rivalry between Detroit and Montreal, two games linger in the mind—but first a few words from Mr. Elbows himself on just how bright that rivalry burned during those halcyon years.

"Hockey's different today, isn't it? The animosity is gone. *I mean, we didn't play golf with referees and linesmen.* Why, in the old days with the Red Wings, I remember once we and the Canadiens were travelling to a game in Detroit on the same train. We were starving, but their car was between ours and the diner, and there was no way we were going to walk through there. We waited until the train stopped in London and we walked around the Canadiens' car to eat."

Going into a game in Detroit against the Canadiens, on October 27, 1963, Howe had 543 goals, one short of the retired Rocket's then record of 544. The aroused Canadiens, determined not to allow Howe to score a landmark goal against them, designated Henri Richard his brother's recordkeeper, setting his line against Howe's again and again. But in the third period Howe, who had failed to score in three previous games, made his second shot of the night a good one. He deflected a goalmouth pass past Gump Worsley to tie the record. Howe, then thirty-five, did not score again for two weeks, until the Canadiens came to town once more. Again they put everything into stopping Howe. But in the second period, *with Montreal on the power play,* Detroit's Billy McNeil sailed down the ice with the puck, Howe trailing. As they swept in on the Canadiens' net, Howe took the puck and flipped a fifteen-foot shot past Charlie Hodge, breaking the Rocket's record, one he would later improve on by 127 NHL goals.

Item: In 1960, there was a reporter sufficiently brash to ask Howe when he planned to retire. Blinking, as is his habit, he replied, "I don't want to retire, because you stay retired for an awfully long time."

Twenty years later, on June 4, 1980, Howe stepped up to the podium at the Hartford Hilton and reluctantly announced his retirement. "I think I have another half year in me, but it's always nice to keep something in reserve." The one record he was terribly proud of, he added, "is the longevity record."

Thirty-two years.

And just possibly we were unfair to him for most of those years. True, he eventually became an institution. Certainly he won all the glittering prizes. But true veneration always eluded Howe. Even in his glory days he generated more respect, sometimes even grudging at that, than real excitement. Outside of the West, where he ruled supreme, he was generally regarded as the ultimate pro (say, like his good friend of the Detroit years, Tiger outfielder Al Kaline), but not a player possessed. Like the Rocket.

In good writing, Hemingway once ventured, only the tip of the iceberg shows. Put another way, authentic art doesn't advertise. Possibly that was the trouble with Gordie on ice. During his vintage years, you seldom noticed the flash of elbows, only the debris they left behind. He never seemed *that* fast, but somehow he got there first. He didn't wind up to shoot, like so many of today's golfers, but next time the goalie dared to peek, the puck was behind him.

With hindsight, I'm prepared to allow that Gordie may not only have been a better all-round player than the Rocket but maybe the more complete artist as well. The problem could have been the fans, myself included, who not only wanted art to be done but wanted to see it being done. We also required it to look hard, not all just in a day's work.

A career of such magnitude as Gordie Howe's has certain natural perimeters, obligatory tales that demand to be repeated here. The signing. The injury that all but killed him in his fourth season. The rivalry with the Rocket, already dealt with. The disenchantment with Detroit. Born-again Gordie, playing the WHA with his two sons. The return to the NHL with the Hartford Whalers. The last ceremonial season, culminating in his final goal.

History is riddled with might-have-beens. Caesar, anticipating unfavourable winds, could have remained in bed on March 15. That most disgruntled of stringers, Karl Marx, might have gone from contributor to editor of the *New York Tribune.* Bobby Thomson could have struck out. Similarly, Gordie Howe might have been a New York Ranger. When he was fifteen, he was invited to the Rangers' try-out camp in Winnipeg, but they intended to ship him to Regina, and he didn't sign because he knew nobody from Saskatoon who would be playing there. The Red Wings wanted him to join their team in Windsor, Ontario. "They told me there would be carloads of kids I knew, so I signed. I didn't want to be alone."

The following season, the Red Wings handed Gordie a $500 bonus and a $1,700 salary to play with their Omaha farm club. ("Twenty-two hundred dollars," Gordie said. "I earn that much per diem now.") A year later he was with the Red Wings, signed for a starting salary of $6,000. "After we signed him," coach Jack Adams said, "he left the office. Later, when I went into the hall, he was still there, looking glum. 'All right, Gordie, what's bothering you?'

" 'Well, you promised me a Red Wing jacket, but I don't have it yet.' "

He got the jacket, he scored a goal in his first game with the Red Wings, and he was soon playing three-, even four-minute shifts on right wing. A fast, effortless skater with a wrist shot said to travel at 110 miles per hour. Then, in a 1950 playoff game against the Toronto Maple Leafs, Howe collided with Leaf captain Teeder Kennedy and fell unconscious to the ice. Howe was rushed to a hospital for emergency surgery. "In the hospital," Sid Abel recalled, "they opened up Gordie's skull to relieve the pressure on his brain and the blood shot to the ceiling like a geyser."

The injury left Howe with a permanent facial tic, and on his return the following season, his teammates dubbed him "Blinky," a nickname that stuck. Other injuries, over the years, have called for some four hundred stitches, mostly in his face. Howe can no longer count how many times his nose has been broken. There also have been broken ribs, a broken wrist, a detached retina, and operations on both knees. He retires with seven fewer teeth than he started with.

The glory years with Detroit came to an end in 1971, Howe hanging up his skates after twenty-five seasons. Once a contender, the team had gone sour. Howe's arthritic wrist meant that he was playing with constant pain. Hockey, he let it be known, was no longer fun. But, alas, the position he took in the Red Wings' front office ("a pasture job," his wife, Colleen, said) proved frustrating, even though it was his first $100,000 job. "They paid me to sit in that office, but they didn't give me anything to do."

After two years of retirement, the then forty-five-year-old Howe bounced back. In 1973, he found true happiness, realizing what he said was a lifelong dream, a chance to play with two of his sons for the Houston Aeros of the WHA. The dream was sweetened by a $1 million contract, which called for Howe to play for one season followed by three in management. Furthermore, nineteen-year-old Marty and eighteen-year-old Mark were signed for a reputed $400,000 each for four years. A package put together by the formidable Colleen, business manager of the Howe family enterprises.

Howe led the Aeros to the WHA championship; he scored one hundred points and was named the league's most valuable player. Mark was voted rookie of the year. A third son, Murray, later shunned hockey to enter pre-med school at the University of Michigan. Murray, who was twenty years old in 1980, also wrote poetry:

> So you eat, and you sleep.
> So you walk, and you run.
> So you touch, and you hear.
> You lead, and you follow.
> You mate with the chosen.
> But do you live?

Gordie went on to play three more seasons with the Aeros and two with the Whalers, finishing his WHA career with 174 goals and 334 assists. With the demise of that league and the acceptance of the Whalers by the NHL in 1979, Howe decided to play one more year so that the father-and-sons combination could make it into the NHL record books.

It almost didn't happen, what with Marty being sent down to Springfield. But they finally did play together on March 9 in Boston. And then, three nights later, out there in Detroit, *his* Detroit, Gordie finally got to take a shift in the NHL on a line with his two sons, Marty moving up from his natural position on defence. "After that game, Gordie could have just walked off," Colleen said. "'I've done all I've ever wanted,' he told me."

I caught up with Gordie toward the end of the 1980 season, on March 22, when the Whalers came to the Montreal Forum for their last regular-season appearance. Before the game, Gordie Howe jokes abounded among the younger writers in the press box. Scanning the Hartford lineup, noting the presence of Bobby Hull and Dave Keon, both then in their forties, one wag ventured, "If only they'd put them together on the ice with Howe, we could call it the Geritol Line."

Another said, "When is he going to stop embarrassing himself out there and announce his retirement?"

"If he's that bad," a Hartford writer cut in, "why do they allow him so much room out there?"

"Because nobody wants to go into the record books as the kid who crippled old Gordie."

Going into the game, Hartford's seventy-second of the season, Howe had fourteen goals and twenty-three assists, and there he sat on the bench, one of only six Whalers without a helmet.

There were lots of empty seats in the Forum. It was not the usual Saturday-night crowd. Many a season ticket holder had yielded his coveted seat in the reds to a country cousin, a secretary, or an unlucky nephew. Kids were everywhere. Howe, who had scored his eight-hundredth goal a long twenty-three days earlier, jumped over the boards for his first shift at 1:27 of the first period, the Forum erupting in sentimental cheers. He did not come on again for another five minutes, this time joining a Hartford power play. Howe took to the ice again with four and a half minutes left in the period, kicking the puck to Jordy Douglas from behind the Montreal net, earning an assist on Douglas's goal. Not the only listless forward out there, often trailing the play, pacing himself, but his passing still notably crisp, right on target each time, Howe came out six more times in the second period. On his very first shift in the first period, he had thrown a check at Réjean Houle, sending him flying. Hello, hello, I'm still here. But his second time out, Howe drew a tripping penalty, and the Canadiens scored on their power play. The game, a clinker, ended in a 5–5 tie.

In the locker room, microphones were thrust at a weary Gordie. He was confronted by notebooks. Somebody asked, "Do you plan to retire at the end of the season, Gordie?"

"Not that fucking question again," Gordie replied.

So somebody else said, "No, certainly not. But could you tell me what your plans are for next year?"

Gordie grinned, appreciative.

A little more than two weeks later, on April 8, the Whalers were back, it having been ordained that these upstarts would be fed to the Canadiens in their first NHL playoff series. This time the Canadiens, in no mood to fiddle, beat the Whalers 6–1. Howe, who didn't play until the first period was seven minutes old, took his first shift alongside his son Mark. He appeared only twice more in the first period, but in the second he came on again, filling in for the injured Blaine Stoughton on the Whalers' big line. He was ineffectual, on for two goals against and hardly touching the puck during a Hartford power play. Consequently, in the third period, he was allowed but four brief shifts. There must have been some satisfaction for him, however, in the fact that Mark Howe was easily the best Whaler on ice, scoring the goal that cost Dennis Herron his shutout.

The next night, with Montreal leading 8–3 midway in the third period, the only thing the crowd was still waiting for finally happened. Gordie Howe flipped in a backhander. It was his sixty-eighth NHL playoff goal— but his first in a decade. It wasn't a pretty goal. Nor did it matter much. It was slipped in there by a fifty-two-year-old grandfather who had scored his first NHL goal in Toronto thirty-four years earlier when the Boston Red Sox left-fielder Carl Yastrzemski was only seven years old, pot was something you cooked the stew in, and Ronald Reagan was just another actor. "Hartford goal by Gordie Howe," Michel Lacroix announced over the PA system. "Assist, Mark Howe." The crowd gave Gordie a standing ovation.

Later, in the Whalers' dressing room, coach Don Blackburn was asked what his team might do differently in Hartford for the third game. "Show up," he said.

Though the Whalers played their best hockey of the series in the next game, they lost in overtime. In the dressing room, everybody wanted to know if this had been Gordie's last game. "I haven't made up my mind about when I'm going to retire yet," he said.

But earlier, in the press box, a Hartford reporter had assured everybody that this was a night in hockey history: April 11, 1980, Gordie Howe's last game. He said Whaler director of hockey operations Jack Kelley had told him as much. "They've got a kid they want to bring up. Gordie's holding him back. The problem is they don't know what to do with him. I mean, shit, you can't have Gordie Howe running the goddamn gift shop."

The triumphant Canadiens stayed overnight in Hartford, and I joined their poker game: Claude Mouton, Claude Ruel, the trainers, the team doctor, Floyd "Busher" Curry, Toe Blake. "Jack Adams always used him too much during the regular season," Toe said, "so he had nothing left when the playoffs came round."

"Do you think he was really a dirtier player than most?" I asked.

"Well, you saw the big guy yesterday. What did he tell you?"

"He said his elbows never put anybody in the hospital, but he was there five times."

Suddenly everybody was laughing at me. Speak to Donnie Marshall, they said. Or John Ferguson. Or, still better, ask Lou Fontinato.

When Donnie Marshall was with the Rangers, he

was asked what it was like to play against Howe. In reply, he lifted his shirt to reveal a foot-long angry welt across his rib cage. "Second period," he said.

One night, when then Winnipeg general manager John Ferguson was still playing with the Canadiens, a frustrated Howe stuck the blade of his stick into his mouth and hooked his tongue for nine stitches.

But Howe's most notorious altercation was with Ranger defenceman Lou Fontinato in Madison Square Garden in 1959. Frank Udvari, who was the referee, recalled, "The puck had gone into the corner. Howe had collided with Eddie Shack behind the net and lost his balance. He was just getting to his feet when here's Fontinato at my elbow, trying to get at him.

" 'I want him,' he said.

" 'Leave him alone, use your head,' I said.

" 'I want him.'

" 'Be my guest.' "

Fontinato charged. Shedding his gloves, Howe seized Fontinato's jersey at the neck and drove his right fist into his face. "Never in my life had I heard anything like it, except maybe the sound of some-body chopping wood," Udvari said. "*Thwack!* And all of a sudden Louie's breathing out of his cheekbone."

Howe broke Fontinato's nose, fractured his cheekbone, and knocked out several teeth. Plastic surgeons had to reconstruct his face.

The afternoon before what was to be Howe's last game, I had taken a taxi to his house in the suburbs of Hartford. "You can't be a pauper living out here," the driver said. "I'll bet he's got racehorses and everything. There's only money out here."

Appropriately enough, the venerable Howe, hockey's very own King Arthur, lived down a secluded side road in a town called Glastonbury. Outside the large house, set on fifteen acres of land, a sign read Howe's Corner. Inside, a secretary ushered me through the office of Howe Enterprises, a burgeoning concern that held personal-service contracts with Anheuser-Busch, Chrysler, and Colonial Bank. A bespectacled, wary Howe was waiting for me in the sun-filled living room. Prominently displayed on the coffee table was an enormous volume of Ben Shahn reproductions.

"I had no idea," I said, impressed, "that you were an admirer of Ben Shahn."

"Oh, that. The book. I spoke at a dinner. They presented it to me."

After all his years in the United States, Howe remained a Canadian citizen. "I can pay my taxes here and all the other good things, but I can't vote." He was one of nine children, he added, and the family was now spread out like manure. "It would be nice to get together again without having to go to another funeral."

Sitting with Howe, our dialogue stilted, not really getting anywhere, I remembered how A. J. Liebling was once sent a batch of how-to-write books for review by a literary editor and promptly bounced them back with a curt note: "The only way to write is well and how you do it is your own damn business." Without being able to put it so succinctly, Howe possibly felt the same way about hockey. Furthermore, over the years, he had also heard all the questions and now greeted them with a flick of the conversational elbow. But for the record, Howe adjudged today's hockey talent bigger and better than ever. Wayne Gretzky reminded him of Sid Abel. "He's sneaky clever—the puck always seems to be coming back to him. Lafleur is something else. He stays on for two shifts. I don't mind that, but he doesn't even breathe heavy." Sawchuk was the best goalie he ever saw, and he never knew a line to compare with Boston's Kraut Line: Milt Schmidt, Woody Dumart, Bobby Bauer. Howe was still bitter about how his years in Detroit came to an end with that meaningless front-office job. "Hell, you've been on the ice for twenty-five years, there's little else you learn. I was a pro at seventeen. Colleen used to answer my fan mail for me—I didn't have the words. Now it's better for the kids. They get their basic twelve years of school and then pick a college."

Determined to surface with fresh questions, I asked when he planned to retire.

"I can't say just yet exactly when I'm going to retire, but I'm the one who will make that decision."

The next morning, in the Whalers' offices, Jack Kelley asked me, "Did he say that?"

"Yes."

"He's retiring at the end of the season."

Almost two months later, on June 4, Howe made it official. "It's not easy to retire," he told reporters. "No one teaches you how. I found that out when I tried it the first time. I'm not a quitter. But I will now quit the game of hockey."

Howe had kept everybody waiting for half an hour after the scheduled start of his 10:00 a.m. press conference. "As it got close to ten-thirty I had the funny suspicion that he had changed his mind again," Kelley said.

But this time Howe left no doubt in anybody's mind. "My last retirement was an unhappy one, because I knew I still had some years in me. This is a happy one, because I know it's time."

An ice age had come to an end.

"They ought to bottle Gordie Howe's sweat," King Clancy of the Maple Leafs once said. "It would make a great liniment to rub on hockey players."

Yes, certainly. But I remember my afternoon at Howe's Corner with a certain sadness. He knew what was coming, and before I left he insisted that I scan the awards mounted on a hall wall. The Victors Award. The American Academy of Achievement Golden Plate Award. The American Captain of Achievement Award. "I played in all eighty games this year, and I got my fifteenth goal in the last game of the season. Last year I suffered from dizzy spells. My doctor wanted me to quit. But I was determined to play with my boys in the NHL. I don't think I have the temperament for coaching. I tried it a couple of times and I got so excited, watching the play, that I forgot all about the line changes."

That afternoon only one thing seemed to animate him. The large Amway flow chart that hung from a stand, dominating the living room. Gordie Howe— one of the greatest players the game had ever known, a Canadian institution at last—Blinky, the third-grade repeater who had become a millionaire—now distributed health-care items, cosmetics, jewellery, and gardening materials for Amway.

Offering me a lift back to my hotel in Hartford, Howe led me into his garage. There were cartons, cartons, everywhere, ready for delivery. Cosmetics. Gardening materials. It looked like the back room of a prairie general store.

"I understand you write novels," Howe said.

"Yes."

"There must be a very good market for them. You see them on racks in all the supermarkets now."

"Right. Tell me, Gordie, do you deliver this stuff yourself?"

"You can earn a lot of money with Amway," he said, "working out of your own home."

Say it ain't so, Gordie.

November 1980

15

Pete Rose

C rouching over home plate in Riverfront
Stadium one night in September 1984, claim-
ing it in that aggressive manner he has made
his own, he couldn't be confused with one of your
latter-day California-bred players: flaxen-haired, fea-
tures finely chiselled, the manner of a man who in
the off season might be doing a guest spot on *Dynasty*
or finishing a Merrill Lynch trainee course. Endlessly
striving Pete Rose, home at last, at bat for the
15,099th time in his major league life, was a throwback to an earlier age. If he didn't exist, Ring Lardner
might have invented him. If he hadn't been capable of
playing ball, then surely the alternative would have
been shifting beer cases or working on a construction site. He hit a line drive. A single. "If he had the
natural ability of a Johnny Bench," said one of the
sportswriters, "he would have had to pack it in long
ago. But he never had natural ability. It's all hustle."

Going into the new season, the legendary Rose,
player-manager for the Cincinnati Reds, was only 94
hits shy of the game's ultimate statistic: Ty Cobb's
record of 4,191 career hits. "All the reporters do is

ask me about it," Rose complained by rote. "All I do is answer them. It would be great for baseball if I got it, but I'm not going to jump off a bridge if I don't." But later, his eyes hot, his manner disconcertingly boyish considering his age, he added, "It took Ty Cobb twenty-four seasons. I'm going to do it in twenty-three."

But sour baseball rabbis waiting in the tall grass would certainly howl that Rose had already had 1,982 more times at bat than Cobb and, furthermore, that Cobb's career batting average was .367, whereas Rose's stood at .305. Rose was forty-three years old in 1984, his long-pursued grail within tantalizing sight. He allowed that he now found it harder to overcome injuries, but also insisted, "Medical people tell me I have the body of a thirty-year-old. I know I've got the brain of a fifteen-year-old. You got both, you can play baseball."

Rose, a shrewd judge of his own quotes, watched for my reaction. I asked him if he had any other interests. "Say, politics."

"When Reagan was coming here for a campaign rally he called me from Air Force One; he wanted me to introduce him. I can't do that. Maybe 51 percent of the people are for Reagan, 49 percent against him. I introduce him, 49 percent of the fans don't like me. So Johnny Bench introduces him, he doesn't have to worry about being booed anymore. On the podium, Reagan tells them he called me. They made it seem I was sorry I couldn't be there."

In 1984, Rose played for the Expos until August 15. He started out in left field, but less than two weeks into the season his elbow went bad on him. Rose, who could no longer throw more than one hundred feet, was shifted to first base. Then, on July 26, the foundering Expos traded for another first baseman, Dan Driessen of the Reds, because Rose was hitting only .259. So the man who had been three times the National League batting champion, with National League and World Series MVP awards to his credit, and who had connected for two hundred hits a season ten times, was benched by a second-division club.

Rose, who had come off an embarrassing .245 season with Philadelphia in 1983, reduced to an aging sideshow for hire, might have gone to Seattle but opted for the Expos. "They brought me there to teach them how to win," he said, "but I never played for a team that took losing so easy. Gary Carter ran that team. He's okay as long as he goes two for four; otherwise, he doesn't work the pitchers. He's always saying, 'I did this, did you see me do that?' I told him, 'Hey there, kid, I played with Johnny Bench.'"Later Rose, wearing his manager's hat, would say that if the Expos ever wanted to trade Carter, he would be glad to have him. But the Mets got him.

Before I caught up with Rose, my first afternoon in Cincinnati, I met with his agent, Reuven Katz, in a hotel bar. Johnny Bench joined us. "Being a player-manager," he said, "would be awkward for anybody but Pete. When I first came up, he took me under his wing. He always wanted me to hit .300. I told him, 'You hit .300, I'll drive you in.' Nobody else will ever get four thousand hits."

In 1978, Bob Trumpy, a sportscaster for WLW radio, had the inspired notion of declaring Pete Rose a national monument. "He represented the work ethic here," Trumpy said. "He's a role model. Cincinnati belongs to him. He can park his Rolls anywhere, nobody will touch him. He can floor it in one of his Porsches and the cops will look the other way. You can take away all the records, everything, Rose has all the intangibles rolled into one. He's unique. He's an art form, the baseball diamond his canvas. But when he came back here, he had to talk to Bob Howsam for an hour and a half on the phone to convince him that he could still play ball. When he left here the fans called in one after another to say, 'I will never return to Riverfront Stadium as long as Pete Rose is not playing.' And they didn't."

Bob Howsam, the amiable club president and CEO, allowed that since the days of the fabled Big Red Machine, attendance had slipped from 2.5 million a season to 1.4 million. "We're more interested in him as a manager than a player," he said. "We'll have to see how well he does."

The truth is that truly gifted players—Ty Cobb, Rogers Hornsby, Mel Ott, and Frank Robinson among them—have not signed the skies with their acumen as managers, an exception being Frank Chance, who won four pennants for the Cubs. Out of necessity, however, Rose had always looked for an edge as a player. He had the advantage of being an astute as well as an ebullient student of the game. A great judge of talent, according to Johnny Bench. Yes, but would he find it difficult to be patient with players of lesser ability or hustle? "I don't expect anybody to play like me," Rose said, unabashed, "because they can't, they just can't."

On opening day in Cincinnati, on April 8, 1963, at Crosley Field, popular Don Blasingame was no longer at second base, having been displaced by a brash twenty-one-year-old interloper called Pete Rose. Rose had come up to the Reds a graduate of Macon, Georgia, in the Class A Sally League, where he had been known as "Hollywood," "José Hustle," or "Hotdog." He had signed with the Reds for a $7,000 bonus and scrambled on to win the National League Rookie of the Year Award and, in succeeding seasons, playing in the outfield or at second or third base, just about every trophy on the shelf. In 1975, the year Sparky Anderson's Big Red Machine won a mind-boggling 108 games, Rose led the last real National League dynasty in hits and doubles. Then, in one of the most exciting World Series in living memory, Boston taking the Reds to seven games, Rose hit .370 and was named MVP. Two years later, at the age of thirty-six, he surprised everybody by breaking yet another National League record, hitting safely in forty-four consecutive games. Then came the diminishing years. He was gone, first to Philadelphia for five seasons and then to Montreal, enjoying only one more vintage season, 1979, when he hit .331 for the Phillies.

On August 14, 1984, enduring the humiliation of the Expos' bench, Rose seemed to sniff his magnificent career coming to an end, not with a bang but a whimper. "It looks like I'm not going to get Ty Cobb's record," he told a reporter, "unless something happens."

The next day the fifth-place Reds, their record a dismal 51–70, announced that they had hired Rose as player-manager, and among baseball fans everywhere joy was unconfined.

"PETE COMES HOME," ran the *Cincinnati Enquirer*'s headline. A playing field in Cincinnati is named after Rose. There is also a Pete Rose Drive. Sparky Anderson, who managed Rose for nine years, said, "I told Pete long ago that when he goes to the Hall of Fame he should only take one uniform with him."

A crowd of 35,038 fans, each one awarded an "I Was There" certificate, turned out to hail the prodigal's return on August 17, 1984, and when he stepped up to the plate they remembered when he was young and they were young and there was a Big Red Machine.

Rejoining the Reds had cost Rose a big cut in pay but, he told me, he didn't need the money. Outside of baseball he was earning $1 million a year, maybe more, largely as the representative of a Japanese firm, Mizuno Sporting Goods. He was also a partner in the Precinct, the best steakhouse in town. "You've got to try it," he said. "It's run by a friend of mine, an expert. He was at Yale. Is that where they teach restaurant management?"

At the Precinct, I drank in the upstairs bar with co-owner Jeff Ruby, a graduate of the Cornell Restaurant School. Indicating all the attractive young women milling about, I asked, "Are they groupies?"

"Don't say that," he said. "We've got a mailman, he's only five feet four, he comes in here. He says all these girls are golddiggers, they won't talk to him. 'Hey,' I said to him, a mailman, 'what are you going to get, a better route?' These ballplayers are young and their bodies are in good shape and they've got lots of money." Some nights, Ruby went on to say, he enlisted celebrities to tend bar. "The last time Pete did it, he asked me, 'How much did we take in tonight?' I told him, 'Thirty-eight hundred bucks.' 'And how much,' he asked, 'did you take in the night Johnny Bench was here?' 'Four thousand,' I said. Pete pondered that. 'Johnny had better weather,' he said."

Old teammates, Bench and Rose remained friendly rivals. The more thoughtful Bench retired in 1983 at the age of thirty-five. "If you have to hang in there beyond your time for the applause, if your happiness is in the hands of others, you're in trouble. After you quit, though, there's a long time between Monday and Friday."

I asked him about Rose.

"Once his objective was three thousand hits. Then it was Musial's record. He knows all his own stats. In the early days, remember, he wasn't making money. He wanted to become the first singles hitter to drive that Rolls. Now Cobb's record is basically everything to him. Okay. But nobody wants to see him embarrass himself out there or for the pursuit to become blinding. There's so much respect for him."

Rose, who lived out in Indian Hill, a choice suburb, was outside hosing down his Rolls-Royce when I arrived for a late breakfast with him and his new young wife, a former cheerleader for the Philadelphia Eagles. Carol was expecting a baby within a week. All the same, she had cooked us enormous steaks, with eggs and home fries. Pete showed me around the house, which sat on a five-acre lot. There was a TV satellite dish and a large kidney-shaped swimming pool in the backyard. Inside, there were twelve rooms. Marble floors. Three giant TV screens, one on each floor. A sauna. A Roman-size bath. A trophy room with the lineup card for Rose's first World Series game; the bats he had used in his all-stars games encased in glass; embarrassingly bad oil portraits of Rose standing at the plate in his prime; and a plaque listing his stats during his forty-four-game hitting streak. There was also a mahogany bar in his sunken living room. "And I don't even drink," Rose said.

Rose didn't see himself as a desperately needed attraction for a team that was going nowhere. An aging star without a vehicle. "There is no dynasty-type team in our division," he said. "It's up for grabs."

Nor did he see himself as a man so absorbed in the game that he had possibly sacrificed his family to it: his first wife, of sixteen years, Karolyn, and their two children, Fawn, nineteen, and Petey, fourteen.

He led me through his ritual interview. "Sure I'm divorced—so are 60 percent of American men. So why focus on me?" Yes, Koufax had been the hardest thrower he had ever faced, but Marichal was the best pitcher. Cobb's record, he assured me once more, was not an obsession. Captain Ahab, if I had interviewed him, would have said he didn't give a tinker's damn about white whales—it was the amount of oil he brought home that counted. "If I'm hitting, I'll play. If I'm not hitting good, I won't play. Hey, I don't need the money. I'll play as long as I'm useful."

Accompanying me outside after lunch, Rose looked back at his big house in the hills. "They say you can't live good hitting singles." Then we got into one of his Porsches and drove back into town together. "I can't think of anything I'd rather do in summer than play baseball," he said.

March 1985

16

Kiss the Ump!

P.G. Wodehouse observed some years ago that it is difficult to write anything without offending a special-interest group. Even being irreverent about porcupines can be risky. "Just try it," he wrote, "and see how quickly you find your letter-box full of communications beginning: 'Sir, with reference to your recent tasteless and uncalled-for comments on the porcupine....'" So in compiling this list of complaints about women (not, mark you, that women are to be compared to anything so benign as the porcupine, which raises its quills only when menaced), I do not anticipate that it will endear me to the sisterhood.

My deep concern about the threatening proclivities of some of the new women (especially those who wish to become prizefighters, hockey goalies, or baseball umpires) was heightened on a trip to New York a few years back. At the time, I was startled to see a billboard, sailing over Broadway maybe ten storeys high, that showed a gorgeous woman posing in men's underwear. This was too much. A calculated affront. Me, I wouldn't wear women's underwear in public; what in the hell did they want with mine?

Before outraged feminists address rude, unsigned letters to me, let me make my position clear. I find it astonishing that American women weren't enfranchised at the same time as their dim husbands and that they had to chain themselves to fences and endure forced feedings, among other indignities, in order to win the right to vote. After all, if I am bound to help with the shopping and the washing up, it seems only fair that women should be obliged to share in the embarrassment of having thrust Bush and the Quayle into office, possibly to be followed by the slippery Bill Clinton.

It is the shrillness of some of the more militant feminists that confounds me, but I can remember at least one occasion when I found one of their leaders to be absolutely engaging.

Once, scheduled to appear on a TV talk show in Washington, D.C., I discovered that one of the other guests was a celebrated American feminist. As we waited together in the lounge, she crossed her long, elegant legs. Far from immune to the whisper of silky things, I nevertheless averted my eyes, pretending to be absorbed in my copy of *Organic Gardening,* lest I be accused of appraising her as a sex object. If she wanted to debate Marx's theory of surplus value while we waited, okay, but I wasn't going to give her the satisfaction of looking her up and down, confirming her prejudices. Imagine my surprise, then, when minutes before she was to go on camera, this champion of women's lib opened her Gucci handbag, plucked out a brush and a compact, and proceeded to backcomb her hair and touch up her eyeshadow.

My prejudices against women, such as they are, range from trivial to larger grievances.

It seems to me that every time I get in line at the supermarket checkout, there is a woman immediately ahead of me, her bill coming to $94.87. She doesn't, as most men would, fork over $100, take the change *without counting it,* and repair immediately to the nearest bar. No, no. Instead, she will dig elbow-deep into a voluminous handbag filled with things that go clunk, within the depths of which is a wallet, within which is a change purse to be slowly unzipped and overturned, spilling onto the counter and the floor pennies that have to be toted up three times before they total eighty-seven. Meanwhile, I manfully resist tipping my yogurt over her lacquered helmet of hair, which smells like model-airplane glue. In defence of such an offender, my wife has argued that the woman is possibly oppressed, obliged to account to an overbearing husband for every penny spent. If that's the case, she ought to dump a yogurt over *his* head, *but meanwhile, would she please keep the checkout line moving?*

I seldom go to parties anymore, but when I do, I am often cornered by mature women who tell me how they have had to sacrifice a brilliant career in order to make a home for an unfaithful husband and ungrateful children. Nonsense. More often than not, it is clear that the only alternative career available to them is to serve behind the counter at McDonald's or possibly do something even less useful, such as become a sociologist or a professor of English Lit 101. Mind you, I would not go as far as Marike de Klerk, the wife of South Africa's prime minister, who recently told a church audience, "We are not important. We are here to serve, to heal wounds and to give love.... If the woman inspires the man to be good, he is good. We want [men]...to look after us."

Obviously, women do have legitimate complaints. I am a staunch supporter of the Equal Rights Amendment. I am prochoice, though troubled by some of its implications. But I am not prepared to fight for the right of women to drive steamrollers, serve with impunity on submarines, interview inarticulate naked athletes in stinky locker rooms, box, play hockey with the guys, or umpire baseball games.

Item: Last year, *Maclean's,* the Canadian magazine, published the following report.

> Thérèse Robitaille made boxing history last
> week in Sydney, N.S., when she beat Jenny
> Reid in the first sanctioned amateur women's
> match ever held. After three rounds, Robitaille,
> 26, a freelance sign-language interpreter in
> Fredericton, earned a unanimous decision
> over Reid, 28, a Kingston, Ont., lawyer. Said
> the elated winner after the fight: "It felt great
> to be in a real fight." Added Reid, whose lobbying
> led to the historic Canadian bout: "We certainly
> showed people we could do it."

Since then, also in Canada, the very pretty nineteen-year-old Manon Rhéaume made hockey history, becoming the first woman ever to play in an official game for a Canadian major junior team. Ms. Rhéaume entered the nets of the Trois-Rivières Draveurs in a home game against the Granby Bisons at 12:28 of the second period, welcomed by a standing ovation from more than two thousand fans at the Trois-Rivières Colisée. She allowed three goals on thirteen shots before being obliged to leave the ice in the third period, after being struck in the mask by a puck. And then she needed three stitches to close a gash over her right eye.

And now along comes an ill-written, foulmouthed memoir of sorts, *You've Got to Have Balls to Make It in This League: My Life as an Umpire,* by Pam Postema and Gene Wojciechowski. "It's hard enough to make your way as a young umpire through minor-league baseball," the blurb writer has it. "It's harder still when you've been kissed by a player at home plate, had a bra pulled out of your shirt by The Chicken, found messages in your underwear from amorous managers...."

Ms. Postema, who drives a Federal Express truck these days, worked as a minor league ump from 1977 through 1989, pronouncing in more than two thousand games, without ever being invited to perform in the bigs. This, so far as she was concerned, was a clear case of sexual discrimination, the guilty male chauvinist pig being Dick Butler, assistant to the president of the American League, who was, and remains, in her opinion, a hypocrite. On the other hand, since Ms. Postema admits she is no bookworm, possibly she's unaware of the dictum "Many are called, but few are chosen."

In any event, before her career was aborted, Ms. Postema did get to eject some future multi-millionaires from games in the minors, among them Messrs. Strawberry, Gwynn, Canseco, Mitchell, Clark, Bonilla, and Johnson. "I saw them when they were scared and a little unsure of themselves," she writes. "Just like me."

Far from "little me," however. For when the misguided Ms. Postema, the daughter of an Ohio vegetable farmer, gave up pulling onions for a hundred bucks a week to register in the Al Somers Umpire School, she was five eight and tipping the scales at 175 pounds. Graduating seventeenth in her class of a hundred, she was offered a job in the Gulf Coast League ($800 a month) and soon moved up to the Florida State League, where Jim Leyland, then managing the Lakeland Tigers, protested to the president of the GCL, "How could you send the girl?"

Next stop for the upwardly mobile Ms. Postema was the Double A Texas League, and in 1983 she graduated to the highest possible rung on the minor league ladder: the Triple A Pacific Coast League. She was now earning $1,900 a month but also suffering indignities. Once, when she called a high pitch a strike, a hooligan in the Vancouver dugout yelled, "That was boob-high!" Another time, a player taunted her with "What's another name for a female umpire?"

The answer: "A call girl."

Putting in time in winter ball in Colombia, she

had to endure the indecent proposals of Carmelo Martinez, who spent much of his time in the batter's box flirting with the ump.

"I love you, honey," he'd say.

Pam would ignore him.

"Mi amor."

The most miserable man in baseball, in Pam's opinion, is Larry Bowa, whom she ran into when he was managing the Las Vegas Stars in the PCL. Following a dispute over the veracity of a call Pam had made, Bowa, never at a loss for words, shouted, "You're a fucking cunt!"

A charge to which Pam responded with the equally witty "You're just a fucking jerk...."

Atlanta Braves manager Chuck Tanner, encountered between the white lines just before the start of an exhibition game, presented Pam with another problem. "Would you like a kiss?" he asked.

Ms. Postema had already been featured on the cover of *Sports Illustrated,* a thirty-three-year-old minor league ump, when she ran into "Mr. Neanderthal himself," pitcher Bob Knepper. Knepper told a reporter that a woman shouldn't be an umpire, a president, or a politician. "I'm not going to condemn her," he said, then went on to warn, "but if God is unhappy with her, she's going to have to deal with that later."

Based on her experience with America's game, Ms. Postema writes: "Nobody ever mentions this, but ballplayers are, for the most part, the crudest, lewdest bunch of assholes ever assembled. And out of necessity, umpires, for the most part, aren't far behind. To an umpire...the word *fuck* becomes an all-purpose weapon: a noun, verb, adjective, and adverb all rolled into one."

Finally, I have no idea whether Ms. Postema was denied a job in the bigs because she was inadequate or as a consequence of sexual prejudice. But I have no doubt, Mr. Wojciechowski's help notwithstanding, that she is a minor league writer. Or, to lapse into the phrase that is her personal favourite, "You're fucking gone!"

June 1992

17

Soul on Ice

C anadians, your nice neighbours to the north, are not merely pseudo-Americans. We *are* different. While fastidious New York beer drinkers, for instance, will continue to insist on a Molson's, Labatt's, or a Moosehead, their modish northern counterparts would much rather be seen nursing a Budweiser or a Miller High Life, now that they are both licensed in Canada.

An even more illuminating example of the difference between us is how we each measure the Russian threat. Americans have become increasingly agitated about missile counts and Soviet incursions into Afghanistan and possibly Central America, but we see that as incidental mischief. Clever diversions. So far as red-blooded Canadians are concerned, the real Russian menace to our manhood comes on ice. It comes in the intimidating shape of their national hockey team.

Try to understand.

Consider, if you will, a hitherto unheard of baseball team coming off the Moscow sandlots to appear in Yankee Stadium, lugging their own equipment, going on to thrash the World Series winner and both all-star teams, year after year after year, and there you have the Canadian dilemma.

Hockey, after all, is our game. *The* game. In Los Angeles, you have to search through the sports section twice before stumbling on reports of last night's games, and in New York, hockey's appeal is largely to hard hats, but in Canada it is something else again. When Conn Smythe ran the Toronto Maple Leaf Gardens, any fan who turned up in the choice seats inappropriately dressed—that is, without jacket and tie—did so at the risk of receiving a hand-delivered note the next morning that threatened to cancel the season tickets. In Montreal, until recently, season tickets were passed on in wills, more highly valued than the family silver.

Until 1972, Canadians were the best hockey players in the world. For once, the major league was right here, in Montreal and Toronto. We walked tall. Then the Russians came. Playing fast, stylish hockey, the sort of game we grew up with, *actually carrying the puck over the blue line,* their short and long passes equally crisp, they have humiliated various NHL combinations in five series since 1972. Given a shot at it, they would likely abscond with the Stanley Cup as well. Our Holy Grail, our manhood, an exhibit in the Kremlin.

Worse news. Three of the leading fifteen scorers in the NHL last season were foreigners—two defectors from Czechoslovakia and a Finn. Players from Sweden are everywhere in the league. The Swedes, paid on both sides during the Second World War, are still intent on keeping the peace at any price. They throw up a lot of snow, avoiding both the corners and the front of the net, where sticks and elbows tend to fly in the thick traffic. But the Czechs are magnificent. Tiger Williams, of the Vancouver Canucks, isn't pleased with the new situation. "We got commies, we got Swedes, we got Indians. I'm the only white people we got."

In recent years, when panhandlers still accepted change, Coke was a pause that refreshed, acid rain had not yet begun to fall, and the Canadians still ruled the rinks, there were two great Montreal teams. The greatest, certainly, was the Canadiens club that won the Stanley Club for the fifth consecutive year in 1959–60: Jean Beliveau, Dickie Moore, Bernie "Boom Boom" Geoffrion, Henri Richard and an aging Maurice "Rocket" Richard up front, Doug Harvey minding the blue line, and Jacques Plante in the nets.

The second great Canadiens team, led by Guy Lafleur, Jacques Lemaire, Guy Lapointe, Yvan Cournoyer, Serge Savard, and Larry Robinson, won its fourth Stanley Cup in a row in 1979. The greedy Canadiens also took the cup in 1970–71, the season the club was joined by a young goalie out of Cornell, Ken Dryden, who made a spectacular debut in the nets against the Boston Bruins, a far from inconsiderable club led by Phil Esposito and the greatest player of our time, Bobby Orr.

Dryden was the Most Valuable Player in the 1971 playoffs and went on to star on the second great Canadiens team. Now he has written a thoughtful, fascinating memoir of his years in hockey, *The Game*. Dryden is especially good in evoking the sounds and smells of the dressing room. "When you like some-one," he writes,

> there is something quite nice in knowing what's
> coming next, in knowing that nothing has
> changed; that when laces are cut, when
> petroleum jelly is smeared on the earpiece of a
> phone, we will all look at Lapointe, and he'll say,
> "Hey, get the right guy"; that when interest rates
> go up and the Dow Jones goes down, Houle will
> complain of inflation and taxes, and if he forgets,
> someone will remind him; that when Lemaire
> giggles and squeals and collapses to the floor,
> someone will say, "There goes Co again"; that
> when Savard has a "hot tip," Houle and Shutt
> will be interested, and if it pays off, Ruel will
> have backed away at the last minute; that before
> a game Lafleur will take out his teeth and grease
> back his hair, oil the blades on his skates, set
> off an alarm clock, smash the table in the centre
> of the room with his stick, then laugh and say,
> "Wake up, *câlisse*"; and that when the room
> goes suddenly quiet, someone will bring
> up Larouche's checking, Risebrough's shot,
> Chartraw's spinouts, Houle's breakaways,
> something, *anything,* to keep the feeling going.
> In a life that changes with the score, this is our
> continuity, our security.

From the beginning, Dryden was an incongru-ous figure on the Canadiens team. Intelligent, artic-ulate, a law school graduate. A man with options. Traditionally, our hockey players were without such possibilities. They came off the farm or out of northern mining towns, rawboned boys with angry red boils on the backs of their necks and no front teeth to call their own. In the old days of the six-team NHL, the players earned so little that they had to work during the summer months. But then, as Dryden observes, came expansion, fat TV contracts, handsomely rewarded players armed with lawyers, tax advisers, agents, and investment consultants.

Even so, until recently, when they began to be drafted out of college hockey, the players remained a largely ill educated bunch, hockey the only thing they knew. Celebrated as heroes in Canada, certainly, but still taken for ruffians in many American cities, only slightly more refined than roller derby players. The sport, as promoted on American TV or portrayed in that funny Paul Newman film *Slapshot,* emphasized the brawls, not the graceful play that raised you out of your seat: Bobby Orr on an end-to-end rush. Guy Lafleur, seemingly emerging out of a daydream, to take a clearing pass from Larry Robinson and literally fly in on the opposition goal.

Out for a quick buck following expansion, new club owners tried to sell the game in the United States on the promise of violence, even hooliganism. They gave us the Broad Street Bullies (the Philadelphia Flyers). It is this misunderstanding of the game, a perception of hockey players as louts, that may explain the largest fault in Ken Dryden's book. A tendency to overcompensate. A showy determination to establish that he is no pug but commendably literate, something of an intellectual, perfectly capable of quoting Brecht here, Naipaul there, and Yeats somewhere else. In the end, however, Dryden gives away the game. He lets in a soft goal. Describing a breakfast scene at home, he writes, "I drink my orange juice and coffee and read the paper. I start with the front page." But, in truth, every dues-paying intellectual *I* know begins with the sports section. The blessed box scores.

Other times Dryden is almost too painfully self-aware, over-earnest, unnecessarily defensive about his high salary and celebrity. Still, he has written a very special hockey book, possibly the best I have ever read. Certainly his affectionate yet realistic portrait of the players is unrivalled in hockey writing. His notion of Guy Lafleur as one of the last players to be weaned on freewheeling, frozen-river hockey, rather than a confined indoor rink, is first-rate. Hockey, Dryden writes, has left the river and will never return. "The river is less a physical space than an *attitude,* a metaphor for unstructured, unorganized time alone. And if the game no longer needs the place, it needs the attitude. It is the rare player like Lafleur who reminds us."

The Game, incidentally, is also enriched by a rare appreciation of what it meant to be an English-speaking Toronto-born player on the Canadiens, a French-Canadian institution. Or, just possibly, once a French-Canadian institution.

In a telling passage, Dryden recalls the emotions that stirred in him as he sat in the Canadiens' dressing room and contemplated the legendary bilingual inscription on the wall:

NOS BRAS MEURTIS VOUS TENDENT
LE FLAMBEAU,
A VOUS TOUJOURS DE LE PORTER BIEN HAUT!
TO YOU FROM FAILING HANDS WE THROW
THE TORCH,
BE YOURS TO HOLD IT HIGH!

From Maurice Richard, through Jean Beliveau, to Guy Lafleur, there had been glory, there was continuity, but today, with Lafleur sadly past his prime, there is nobody to take up the torch. The Montreal Canadiens—once the proudest dynasty in sports, now in sharp decline—are not, as tradition surely demanded, now looking for a marginal Québécois skater for renewal. No sir. They are looking to an aging commie—Vladislav Tretiak, goalie for the Red Army—whom they devoutly hope to sign following the 1984 Olympic Games in Sarajevo.

Ça, alors.

November 1983

18

From Gladu,
through Kitman, to the
Victoire Historique
and After

Pronouncing on Montreal, Casey Stengel once said, "Well, you see they have those polar bears up there and lots of fellows trip over them trying to run the bases and they're never much good anymore except for hockey or hunting deer."

Unfortunately we have no polar bears up here, but kids can usually heave snowballs at the outfielders at the opening game of the season, and should the World Series ever dare venture this far north, it is conceivable that a game could be called because of a blizzard.

Montreal, it must be understood, is a city unlike any other in Canada. Or, more important, the National League. On the average, eight feet of snow is dumped on us each winter, and, whatever the weather, we can usually count on three bank robberies a day. This is the city of wonders that gave you Expo in 1967—the baseball Expos a couple of years later—and in 1976 the Olympic Games. Their legacy, among other amazing artifacts, is a stadium that can seat (or intern, as some have it), fifty-five thousand baseball fans—the monstrous Big Owe, where the Expos have been disporting themselves in summer ever since they moved there from Jarry Park in 1977. For years the Expos' endearing idea of loading the bases was to have two of their runners on second. Hello, hello. Their notion of striking fear into the heart of the opposition was to confront them with muscle, namely one of their pinch-hitting behemoths coming off the bench: group average in 1978, .135.

Major league baseball, like the Olympics and the Big Owe itself, was brought to this long-suffering city through the machinations of our very own Artful Dodger, Mayor Jean Drapeau. Bringing us the Games, the mayor assured Montrealers that it would be as difficult for the Olympics to cost us money as it would be for a man to have a baby. He estimated the total cost of all facilities at $62.2 million, but what with inflation and unfavourable winds, his calculation fell somewhat short of the mark. Counting stationery and long-distance calls, the final tab was $1.2 billion. Never mind. To this day our ebullient mayor doesn't allow that the Games were run at a loss. Rather, as he has put it to the rest of us, there has been a gap between costs and revenue. Furthermore, considering the spiffy facilities we have been left with, it would be churlish of us to complain.

Ah, the Big Owe. The largest, coldest slab of poured concrete in Canada. In a city where we endure seven long months of winter, and spring comes and goes in an afternoon, it is Drapeau's triumph to have provided us with a partially roofed over six-hundred-and-fifty-million-dollar stadium, where the sun seldom shines on the fans. Tim Burke, one of the liveliest sportswriters in town, once said to me, "You know, there are lots of summer afternoons when I feel like taking in a ball game, but I think, hell, who wants to sit out there in the dark."

Shivering in the dark might have been more accurate, watching the boys lose line drives in the seams of the artificial turf.

"The outfield," another friend remarked, "looks like the kind of thing my aunt used to wear."

It's a shame, because the Expos, admittedly major league in name only, at least until recently, came to a town rich in baseball history. To begin with, we were all charged with hope. On April 14, 1969, the 29,184 fans who turned up for the home opener at makeshift Jarry Park were electrified by an announcement over the public-address system. "When the Expos play a doubleheader," we were informed, "the second game will go the full nine innings, not seven."

Those of us old enough to remember baseball's glory days here, the Montreal Royals of the old International League, nodded our heads, impressed. This was the big time, baby. "Montreal," said Warren Giles, president of the National League, "is a growing and vibrant city." Yes, yes. So we hollered and stamped our feet as our champions took the field under the grim gaze of manager Gene Mauch, who had the look of a marine drill sergeant.

The morning after the season's home opener, the big bold front-page headline in the *Montréal-Matin* exclaimed: "30,000 PERSONNES ACCLAMENT LES EXPOS SOUS SOLEIL RADIEUX: ECLATANTE PREMIERE." *La Presse* pronounced the occasion, in which our expansionist Expos humiliated the National League champion St. Louis Cards 8–7, a "VICTOIRE HISTORIQUE."

If that wasn't sufficient glory to sustain us through the long losing streak to come, only four days later one William Hambly Stoneman, a pitcher hitherto noted for nothing so much as mediocrity, a youngster who had deservedly never started a major league game in his life, strode to the mound, adjusted his potent red, white, and blue Expo cap for the nth time, fingered the rosin bag, loosened his shoulders, and, before you could utter *shazam*, reared back and threw a no-hitter against the Philadelphia Phillies. Canada, only two years older than major league baseball, had entered league history like a lion. Never mind that the *habitant* hero of the day, the suddenly incomparable Stoneman, was born in Oak Park, Illinois, and bred at Antonio Junior College in Walnut, California; his hobbies, like those of many a red-blooded *Canadien,* were golf and fishing. Something else. "Stoney" Stoneman's heart was in the right place. On his return from Philadelphia, he revealed to reporters, "I'm especially happy for the town... Montreal, I mean. Now they know we're not up there just to appear on the field. We're going to win ball games."

Jim Fanning, Expo GM at the time, responded munificently. "It is customary to give a no-hit pitcher a new contract or bonus, usually about $1,000," he said. "But Montreal is an unusual city and this is an unusual team. We are giving him a $2,000 raise."

The team was also paying Maury Wills, who had been caught stealing base fifty-two times the year before, more than he ever earned in his halcyon years with Los Angeles or Pittsburgh. "Why," a reporter asked Sam Bronfman's then thirty-seven-year-old son Charles, "did you sink more than a million into the team in the first place?"

"I learned from my father," he replied, "that citizenship means more than paying taxes or writing cheques for charity."

Let's face it, from owner to batboy, no-hit pitcher to bullpen bum, everybody connected with the Expos was...beautiful.

Canada, the prescient Bronfman told reporters in Florida, has a national inferiority complex and will gain status by being major league in baseball. "Nothing is so big league as major league baseball. Mr. Average Citizen of Montreal can now feel just as good as Mr. Average Citizen elsewhere."

Happily for Montreal, the supreme importance of major league baseball was also undoubted by big John McHale, club president and investor, who was formerly with Milwaukee and Detroit. Soon after joining the Expos, McHale was announced as a favoured candidate for the office of commissioner of baseball. He turned down the post rather than abandon Montreal—our Montreal, his investment—but not without first informing the picayune natives that in the United States the job of baseball commissioner was second in importance only to that of the U.S. president. Of such conviction, surely, were future World Series winners made.

To come clean, when I first read that one of the most untiring and tiresome of our city councillors, hand-pumping Gerry Snyder, had cajoled a couple of second-generation multimillionaires, Bronfman and Lorne Webster, into staking a major league ball club, enabling them to make their very own mark, I was exceedingly skeptical. After the grandeur that was Expo, Montreal was enduring the inevitable business slump as well as a sobering morning after of whacking bills to be paid, with the upshot that escalating city property tax had become the highest in the country. Furthermore, French Canada was growing increasingly restive, separatists finally knitted into one respectable political party by the formidable René Lévesque. English-speaking Montreal was beginning to feel the chill. While Ontario burgeoned, its investment plans calling for a 14 percent growth rate, all that went boom in the Montreal stock exchange was a separatist bomb, brokers sliding under the desks faster than Maury Wills ever broke for second base.

If this seemed a dubious climate for an expensive, risky new venture, then cynics, myself *numero uno,* had not counted on the energy of Gerry Snyder and Mayor Drapeau's consummate hunger for glory. Or Charles Bronfman's boyish eagerness and matured money.

Among the supplicants for an NL franchise in 1968 were Milwaukee, Dallas, San Diego, Buffalo, and Montreal. Milwaukee, with a lawsuit pending against the league, was immediately counted out. Dallas, deserving maybe, would have bitten into the Houston Astros' TV pie. The Buffalo ballpark, league officials ordained, was unsuitably located, vulnerable to race riots. From the onset, Montreal was the most cherished of all the cities applying for entry into the NL. After all, the city had a proud (and profit-proven) baseball tradition. Until 1960, it was the home of the Montreal Royals.

An article in the memorable opening-day program of the Expos noted that while the province of Quebec had never been known as a hotbed of major league talent, we had nevertheless produced a few ball players, among them pitchers Claude Raymond and Ron Piché, and that three native sons, Roland Gladu, Jean-Pierre Roy, and Stan Bréard, had once played for another ball club here, the Royals.

Oh, I remember the Royals—yes indeed—and if they played in a Montreal that was not yet growing and vibrant, *pace* Warren Giles, it was certainly a place to be cherished.

Betta Dodd, "the Girl in Cellophane," was stripping at the Gayety, supported by twenty-three Kuddling Kuties. Cantor Moishe Oysher, the Master Singer of His People, was appearing at His Majesty's Theatre. The Johnny Holmes Band, playing at Victoria Hall, featured Oscar Peterson; and a sign in the corner cigar and soda warned Ziggy Halprin, Yossel Hoffman, and me that

LOOSE TALK COSTS LIVES!
Keep It Under
Your
STETSON

I first became aware of the Royals in 1943.

MAY U-BOAT SINKINGS
EXCEED REPLACEMENTS
KING DECORATES 625
CANADIANS ON BIRTHDAY

Many of our older brothers and cousins were serving overseas. Others on the street were delighted to discover they suffered from flat feet or, failing that, arranged to have an eardrum punctured by a specialist in such matters.

R.A.F. HITS HARD AT
COLOGNE AND HAMBURG
2,000 Tons of Bombs
Rain on Rhine City

Even in fabled Westmount, where the very rich were rooted, things weren't the same anymore. H.R., fashion emporium to the privileged, enjoined Westmount to "take another step in further aid of the government's all-out effort to defeat aggression!"

HOLT RENFREW ANNOUNCE THAT
BEGINNING JUNE FIRST NO DELIVERIES OF
MERCHANDISE WILL BE MADE
ON WEDNESDAYS

This forethought will help H.R. to save many gallons of gasoline...and many a tire...for use by the government. Moreover, will it not thrill you to think that the non-delivery of your dress on Wednesday will aid in the delivery of a "block-buster" over the Ruhr...Naples...

Berlin...and many other places of enemy
entrenchment?

Nineteen thirty-nine was not only the date we had
gone to war, it was also the year the management of
the Royals signed the contract with Branch Rickey,
making them the Dodgers' farm team. Before we had
even reached the age of puberty, Ziggy, Yossel, and I
had learned to love with caution. If after the first death
there is no other, an arguable notion, I do remember
that each time one of our heroes abandoned us for
Ebbets Field, it stung us badly. We hated Mr. Rickey
for his voracious appetite. "There has been no mention officially that the Dodgers will be taking Flowers,"
Lloyd MacGowan wrote in the *Star* on a typical day,
"but Rickey was in Buffalo to watch the team yesterday. The Dodgers can't take Flowers without sending
down a flinger, but chances are the replacement for
the burly lefty will hardly be adequate."

The International League, as we knew it in the
forties, its vintage years, was Triple A and composed
of eight teams: Montreal, Toronto, Syracuse, Jersey
City, Newark, Rochester, Baltimore, and Buffalo.
Newark was the number-one farm team of the
Yankees, and Jersey City filled the same office for the
Giants. But organized baseball had actually come to
Montreal in 1898, the Royals then fielding a team in
the old Eastern League, taking the pennant in their
inaugural year. In those days the Royals played in
Atwater Park, which could seat twelve thousand.
From all accounts it was a fine and intimate stadium,
much like Jarry Park. During the twenty-one years
the Royals played in Atwater Park, they offered

Montreal, as sportswriter Marc Thibault once wrote, *"du baseball parfois excitant, plus souvent qu'autrement, assez détestable,"* the problem being the troubled management's need to sell off their most accomplished players for ready cash. Be that as it may, in 1914, long before major league baseball came to Montreal, George Herman Ruth took to the mound in Atwater Park to pitch for the Baltimore Orioles. Two years later the Royals folded, a casualty of the First World War, and another eleven years passed before the team was resuscitated.

It was 1928 when George Tweedy "Miracle Man" Stallings bought the then defunct Syracuse franchise and built Delorimier Downs, a stadium with a capacity of 22,000, at the corner of Ontario and Delorimier Streets. An overflow crowd of 22,500, among them Judge Kenesaw Mountain Landis, was at the opening game. The Royals won, defeating the fearsome Reading Keystones, 7–4. A year later Stallings died. In 1929, the Royals finished fourth. Two years later, Delorimier Downs, like just about everything, was in deep trouble. There were tax arrears and a heavy bank debt to be settled. The original sponsors resigned.

In the autumn of 1931 a new company was formed by a triumvirate that included a man who had made millions in gas stations, the rambunctious, poker-playing J. Charles-Emile Trudeau, father of the prime minister. Another associate of the newly found club, Frank "Shag" Shaughnessy, cunningly introduced the playoff system in 1933, and two years later became the club's general manager. In 1935, fielding a team that included Fresco Thompson, Jimmy Ripple, and Del Bissonnette, the

Royals won their first pennant since 1898. However, they finished poorly in '37 and '38, and the following year Mr. Rickey surfaced, sending in Burleigh Grimes to look after his interests.

Redemption was at hand.

Bruno Betzel came in to manage the team in 1944, the year the nefarious Branch Rickey bought the Royals outright, building it into the most profitable club in all of minor league baseball, its fans loyal but understandably resentful of the head office's appetite, praying that this summer the Dodgers wouldn't falter in the stretch, reaching down for fresh bats and strong arms, just when we needed them most.

The Royals finished first in 1945, and in '46 and '48 they won both the pennant and the Little World Series. They were to win the pennant again in '51 and '52, under Clay Hopper, and the Little World Series in '53, when they were managed by Walter Alston. If memory serves, the Royals fielded their greatest team in 1948, the summer young Duke Snider played here, going to bat seventy-seven times before he was snatched by Mr. Rickey.

Sammy Jethro was here in 1949, and two years later, Junior Gilliam was at third as George Shuba hit twenty home runs. In 1952, our star pitcher was southpaw Tommy Lasorda, the self-styled Bob Feller of the International League. Lasorda pitched his last game for the Royals on July 4, 1960, against Rochester, which seemed to be hitting him at will. Reminiscing recently, Lasorda recalled, "I knew I was in trouble when I saw our manager's foot on the top of the dugout step. If the next guy gets on base, I'm going to be out of there. I turned my back on the hitter and looked up toward the sky. Lord, I said, this is my last game. Get me out of this jam. I make the next pitch and the guy at the plate hits the damnedest line drive you ever saw. Our third baseman, George Risley, gets the tips of his fingers on it but can't hang on. The ball bloops over his hand and our shortstop, Gerry Snyder, grabs it. He fires it to Harry Shewman at second base, who relays it to Jimmy Korada at first. Triple play."

A year later the Royals were dissolved, and in 1971, Delorimier Downs was razed to make way for the Pierre Dupuy School.

On weekday afternoons kids were admitted free into the left-field bleachers, and by the third inning the more intrepid had worked their way down as far as the first-base line. Ziggy, Yossel, and I would sit out there in the sun, cracking peanuts, nudging each other if a ball struck the Miss Sweet Caporal sign hitting the young lady you know where. Another diversion was a porthole in the outfield wall. If a batter hit a ball through it, he was entitled to a two-year supply of Pal Blades.

Sunday afternoons the Royals usually attracted capacity crowds, but come the Little World Series, fans also lined up on the roof of the adjoining Grover Knit-to-Fit Building, and temporary stands were set up and roped off in centre field. Ziggy, who used to sit out there, liked to boast, "If I get hit on the head, it's a ground-rule home run."

In 1945, the Royals acquired one of ours, their first Jewish player, Kermit Kitman, a William and Mary scholarship boy. Our loyalty to the team redoubled. Kitman was a centre fielder. On opening day, a story in *La Presse* declared, *"Trois des meilleurs porte-couleurs de Montréal depuis l'ouverture de la saison ont été ses joueurs de champ: Gladu, Kitman et Yeager. Kitman a exécuté un catch sensationnel encore hier après-midi sur le long coup de Torres à la 8e manche. On les verra tous trois à l'oeuvre cet après-midi contre le Jersey-City lors du programme double de la 'Victoire' au stade de la rue Delorimier."*

In his very first at-bat in that opening game against the Skeeters, Kitman belted a homer, something he would not manage again until August. Alas, in the later innings he also got doubled off second. After the game, when he ventured into a barbershop at the corner of St. Catherine and St. Urbain, a man in another chair studied him intently. "Aren't you Kermit Kitman?" he asked.

"Yeah," he allowed, grinning, remembering his homer.

"You son of a bitch, you got doubled off second. It cost me five hundred bucks."

The lineup for that 1945 team, which was to win the pennant, included Eddie Stevens, 1b; Salty Parker, 2b; Stan Bréard, ss; Stan Powalski, 3b; and Al Todd, c. Jean-Pierre Roy, Honest John Gabbard, and Jack Banta were the pitchers, and the others in the outfield were Red Durrett and Roland Gladu. "If I could hit pitchers like Gladu, I wouldn't be in the needle trade today," Kitman said.

He's an engaging man, a prospering partner in

Leslie Fay Originals, Pretty Talk Fashions, and Fancy That. Fifty-four years old when I talked to him in 1978, somewhat chunky, he tried to take in at least one game in every Expo series and still can remember his own box scores as if it were yesterday. In 1946, he recalled, Dodgers with a certain seniority were released from the armed forces: Furillo, Olmo, Snider. Kitman didn't get to move up, as he had hoped, but was slated for the Royals again. And out there in Daytona, where they trained, a raw young man was seen to knock ball after ball into the wilderness.

"What can you do besides catch, son?" Leo Durocher asked him.

"I can play third base," Gil Hodges said.

There was yet another change in the summer of 1946. After scouting the Negro leagues for more than a year, Mr. Rickey brought the first black player into organized baseball. So that spring the Royals could not train in the regular park in Daytona, which was segregated, but had to work out in Kelly Field instead.

Actually, Jackie Robinson had been signed on October 23, 1945, in the offices of the Royals at Delorimier Downs, club president Hector Racine saying, "Robinson is a good ball player and comes highly recommended by the Brooklyn Dodgers. We paid him a good bonus to sign with our club."

The bonus was $3,500 and Robinson's salary was $600 monthly.

"One afternoon in Daytona," Kitman told me, "I was leadoff hitter and quickly singled. Robinson came up next, laying down a sacrifice bunt and running to first. Stanky, covering the sack, tagged him hard and jock-high. Robinson went down, taking a fist in the balls. He was mad as hell, you could see that, but Rickey had warned him no fights. After the game, when he was resting, Stanky came over to apologize. He had been testing Robinson's temper, under orders from Rickey."

Kitman, a good glove man, was an inadequate hitter. Brooklyn-born, he never got to play there. Following the 1946 season, he was offered a place on the roster of another team in the Dodger farm system but wisely elected to quit the game instead.

The 1946 season opened for the Royals on April 18, with a game in Jersey City. The AP dispatch for that day, printed in the Montreal *Gazette,* ran: "The first man of his race to play in modern organized baseball smashed a three-run homer that carried 333 feet and added three singles to the Royals' winning 14–1 margin over Jersey City. Just to make it a full day's work, Robinson stole two bases, scored four times and batted in three runs. He was also charged with an error."

Robinson's .349 average led International League hitters that year. He hit three home runs, batted in sixty-six runs, stole forty bases, scored 113 runs, and fielded .985 at second base. And, furthermore, Montreal adored him, as no other ball player who has been there before or since. No sooner did Robinson reach first base, on a hit or a walk, than the fans roared with joy and hope, our hearts going out to him as he danced up and down the base path, taunting the opposing pitcher with his astonishing speed.

We won the pennant that year and met the Louisville Colonels, another Dodger farm club, in the

Little World Series. The series opened in Louisville, where Robinson endured a constant run of crude racial insults from the Colonels' dugout and was held to a mere single in two games. Montreal evened the series at home and returned to Delorimier Downs for the seventh and deciding game. "When they won it," Dick Bacon recently wrote, recalling that game in the two-hundredth-anniversary issue of the *Gazette,* "Jackie was accorded an emotional sendoff unseen before or since in this city."

First they serenaded him in true French-Canadian spirit with "*il a gagné ses épaulettes,*" and then clamoured for his reappearance on the field.

When he finally came out for a curtain call, the fans mobbed him. They hugged him, kissed him, cried, cheered, and pulled and tore his uniform while parading him around the infield on their shoulders.

With tears streaming down his face, Robinson finally begged off in order to shower, dress, and catch a plane to the States. But the riot of joy wasn't over yet.

When he emerged from the clubhouse, he had to bull his way through the waiting crowd outside the stadium. The thousands of fans chased him down Ontario Street for several blocks, before he was rescued by a passing motorist and driven to his hotel.

As one Southern reporter from Louisville, Kentucky, was to write afterwards: "It's probably the first time a white mob of rioters ever chased a Negro down the streets in love rather than hate."

That was a long time ago.

I don't know what ever became of Red Durrett. Roland Gladu, who got to start twenty-one games with the old Boston Braves, failed to sign the major league skies with his ability. Robinson died in 1972, and six years later a plaque to his memory was installed in the Big Owe. Jean-Pierre Roy now does the French-language broadcasts for the Expos, and a greying, rotund Duke Snider is also back, doing the colour commentary for the games on CBC-TV.

City councillor Gerry Snyder must be acknowledged as the trigger for major league baseball in Montreal. In December 1967 he put his case to NL President Warren Giles. Sure, Giles said, he would be happy to receive an expansion bid from Montreal, but it would have to be sweetened by a list of backers willing to plunk $10 million U.S. on the table and a guarantee of a domed stadium. Snyder hoped the Autostade, a prefabricated concrete stadium built for Expo, would do temporarily, if it was expanded to accommodate 37,500 fans. But the highly unpopular Autostade wasn't on the subway line, and the parking situation there was nightmarish. Furthermore, the Autostade was right next to an abattoir, which would not be so life-enhancing on a steamy summer afternoon. Nevertheless, the indefatigable Snyder began to pursue backers, all of whom were willing to listen but not pledge. All except Charles Bronfman, whose father did so much to slake the thirst of Americans during Prohibition, the rock on which Mr. Sam founded one of the largest family fortunes in North America. Charles immediately promised he would come in for $1 million. Then Prime Minister Lester Pearson, who had once played semi-pro ball and remained an ardent fan, undertook to write his friend Philip Wrigley, owner of the Chicago Cubs, to solicit support.

There were, as I mentioned earlier, other contenders for the two expansion spots. But Walter O'Malley, one member of the three-man expansion committee, remembered with considerable warmth how much money he had made with the Montreal Royals. Another committee member, Judge Julius Hoffheinz of Houston, had enjoyed himself at Expo. The third member, John Galbraith of Pittsburgh, also liked Montreal's bid. So at a meeting in the Excelsior Hotel in Chicago in April 1968, it was ordained that San Diego would have one franchise and Montreal the other. Back in Snyder's hotel room, Dick Young of the *New York Daily News* suggested, "Call 'em the Expos."

Call 'em whatever you like, but where was the $10 million and where were they going to play ball?

Snyder had promised the National League a domed stadium for the club by 1971, but the city, looking at the estimated cost—between $35 and $45 million—said no. It also said no to tarting up the Autostade for about $7 million. Everybody despaired but Mayor Drapeau. As potential investors faded, he got Bronfman to come in for another $4 million, some say much more, and he drove NL president Giles out to Jarry Park, then a three-thousand-seat junior baseball stadium. The public address announcer let it out that Giles was in the park, and he was given a standing ovation. He left the park with tears in his eyes. "For years right until he died," Snyder has said, "he told me every time we met that this was the greatest thing that had ever happened to him in his life—total strangers giving him a standing ovation."

The federal government, though not moved to tears, came through with a huge tax write-off for multimillionaire Bronfman and the other investors, among them club president John McHale, and on August 14 a dry-eyed Giles returned to Montreal, endorsed the plans for a Jarry Park expanded to accommodate thirty thousand fans, and accepted a $1.1 million down payment on the franchise.

The Expos were born. October 14, 1968, was declared Baseball Day, and the plebs, ten thousand strong, filled the Place des Nations to greet visiting NL dignitaries. Les Grands Ballets Canadiens offered a choreographed version of "Take Me Out to the Ball Game." Warren Giles beamed. Mayor Drapeau, outspoken as always, came right out and declared Montreal to be the greatest city in the world. Later in the day, at the Windsor Hotel, the NL owners got down to the real business. The draft. The rendering, on consideration of $10 million, of thirty bodies to each expansion team, thirty players who, hereafter (unless traded before opening day), would be flesh-and-blood Expos. "It's only a day after [Canadian] Thanksgiving," a sportswriter said, "and we're being offered all the turkey." Not so, another ventured, scrutinizing the list of command-generation players on offer from the league. "We could end up with the all-star team of 1954."

Come morning, Expos were more than a name. We had a team. At once fledgling Expos and senior citizens of baseball. Among them, such reputable performers as Maury Wills, Manny Mota, Don

Clendenon, Mack Jones, Larry Jaster, and Larry Jackson. "We've got to build for the day these guys retire," GM Jim Fanning said—prophetically, as it turned out, for the next day thirty-seven-year-old pitcher Larry Jackson, the team's only established starter, announced his retirement, and the Expos, yet to be rained out on a Sunday, were more than $300,000 out of pocket.

The other players procured at the NL-sponsored bazaar were either young and unknown quantities or too-well-known nonentities. Considering they were largely fire-sale goods, the management was touchingly defensive. "The Expos hope," the official guide said, "Bob Bailey has matured enough to live up to the expectations the Pittsburgh Pirates had for him, when they outbid most of the other major league clubs for his services in 1961." They did not emphasize unduly that for the last two years he had been punishing the ball, as sportswriters say, at a regular .227 clip. A highly esteemed baseball expert, the guide informed us, had said only three years ago of Don Bosch, another Expo acquisition, that "in the field, he can be favourably compared with none other than Willy Mays!" At the plate, alas, he could be compared but to you and me, his average being a far from lusty .171. We were also told that Jim "Mudcat" Grant, who was later to be traded to St. Louis, had won twenty-one games for Minnesota in 1965. However, another look at the record revealed he had won only five in 1967 and six in 1968. This, the guide suggested, is the year Don Shaw, who pitched all of twelve innings with the Mets the year before, might be coming into his own, and, who knew, "a change of scenery might be all the doctor ordered" for Bill Stoneman, who had won none and lost two in the minors in 1968.

Who knew, indeed? Stoneman went on to pitch two no-hitters for the Expos, and even before the season opened I had learned to respect John McHale's sagacity. At the Expos' training camp in Florida, a state where, surely, to be bilingual was to be fluent in English and Yiddish, the management saw to it that all announcements were made in English and French, thereby charming the locals. A month later, New York sportswriters were to delight in outfielders who were also *voltigeurs,* a shortstop introduced as an *arrêt-court,* and pitchers as *lanceurs.*

McHale & Co. also engineered a dazzling trade, surrendering one reputable and two fringe players to Houston for Rusty Staub, a twenty-four-year-old all-star outfielder. "The best ballplayer an expansion team ever had," wrote Larry Merchant in the *New York Post.*

Meanwhile, back in Montreal, we read of such springtime coups still deep in a severe and seemingly endless winter. Many doubted that Jarry Park—the stands still without seats, the field encrusted in ice and snow—would be ready or fit to play on come the April 14 opener. I, for one, anticipated disaster. Something to cherish, like the year Oxford sank in the boat race, or the autumn the Grey Cup game had to be called because of fog, the players unable to find each other or the football.

The Expos trotted onto the field for their first major league game out of town. They opened at Shea Stadium, in New York, on April 8, and before forty-five thousand outraged fans defeated the Mets with rare panache. The ubiquitous Mayor Drapeau threw out the opening ball, and amiable Charles Bronfman sat with his heart thumping as his team, well ahead going into the ninth, wobbled, finally squeaking by, 11–10. Rusty Staub, as advertised, hit a homer. So did rookie Coco Laboy. Larry Merchant wrote in the *New York Post:* "Shed a tear for the Royal Canadian Mounties. Wear a black patch for the separatists of Quebec. A moment of silence please for the seal hunters on Hudson Bay. Send a word of condolence to the Indians.... Apologize to George Chuvalo.... The Montreal Expos are their team and never will they know the joys and agonies of the Amazin' Mets."

For the victors after the game, for team management and well-wishers, dinner in a private dining room at Toots Shor. Broadway. The Big Time. Mayor Drapeau shook any hand proffered and reached for many that weren't. Gerry Snyder scooted from table to table, grinning, never forgetting a name. Charles Bronfman sat quietly at his table. A rich young Montreal celebrant, the owner of a large laundry chain, turned to me, his face glowing, and said, "We will be able to tell our grandchildren we were here."

So, I imagine, did men good and true speak to each other at Agincourt, Waterloo, Normandy, and Iwo Jima. Anyway, the headline on the front page of the next morning's Montreal *Gazette* read:

Look who's in first place!
EXPOS TAKE OPENER

Ted Blackman's exuberant story began, "And 100 years later an upstart team from Canada showed the

Americans how their game of baseball is really played." Never mind that our upstart team from Canada was composed of Americans, too. Glory days are hard come by and chauvinism is ill-becoming. Blackman's story continued: "Well, not quite, but the Montreal Expos certainly avenged those Fenian Raids yesterday when they invaded the national pastime of the United States and swiped their centennial spotlight with an 11–10 victory over the Mets in the historic 1969 National League inaugural."

A week later, after the Expos had won one more and lost four on the road, the team came home, so to speak, heralded by a poem from pitcher Jim "Mudcat" Grant, which began,

> Life is like a game of baseball,
>   and you play it every day.
> It isn't just the breaks you get,
>   but the kind of game you play.

Workers toiled through the night at Jarry Park, hammering in seats and struggling with the soggy field, and, come morning, the sun shone brightly and the temperature soared, settling into a rare summer's day. "EVERYONE BUT EVERYONE WAS OUT THERE, MY DEAR," a *Star* reporter wrote of the team brunch that preceded the game. "The Versailles Room at the Windsor Hotel," the reporter went on to say, "was simply filled to brimming with people who matter...." Among them, the fellow who was in charge of Montreal's Public Water Works, the first dignitary to be introduced. We applauded. We also applauded Quebec premier Jean Jacques Bertrand and, naturally, Mayor

Drapeau. We ate an unspeakable chicken à la king without complaining and bolstered ourselves with Bloody Marys against the mighty St. Louis Cards, who even then awaited the sacrificial Expos at Jarry Park.

Then, in a park filled to capacity, we watched the Expos beat the Cards 8–7, Mack Jones driving in three runs with a homer and becoming an instant hero. Positioned in the choice seats on the first-base line, I recognized many of the plump faces there. Among them were some of the nervy kids who used to skip school with me on weekday afternoons to sit in the left-field bleachers of Delorimier Downs, cheering on the Royals and earning nickels fetching hot dogs for strangers. Gone were the AZA windbreakers, the bubble gum, the scuffed running shoes, the pale wintry faces. These men came bronzed to the ballpark from their Florida condominiums. Now they wore foulards and navy blue blazers with brass buttons, they carried Hudson's Bay blankets in plastic cases for their bejewelled wives and sucked on Monte Cristos, mindful not to spill ashes on their Gucci loafers. Above all, they radiated pleasure in their own accomplishments and the occasion. And why not? This was an event and they were there, inside looking out at last, right on the first-base line. Look at me. "Give it some soul, Mack!" one of them shouted.

I asked the portly man in front of me to remove his hat, a snappy little fedora. "I can't," he protested. "Sinus. Took pills this morning. The sun. I can't."

Jim "Mudcat" Grant's opening-day poem concluded:

> This game will not be easy,
>   there'll be struggle, there'll be strife,
> To make the winning runs,
>   for it's played on the field of life.
> So stand behind your team, son,
>   there'll be many who'll applaud.
> Remember you're the player,
>   and the umpire there is God.

Eleven years passed, managers had come and gone, the Expos abandoning delightful Jarry Park for the chilly Big Owe, before the team won more games than they lost, finishing 95–65; they also carried their divisional title dream into the final game of the season, before they succumbed to Steve Carlton and the Phillies. Over the years the Expos had been caught in some foolish, even demented, trades, but they also put together one of the best organizations in baseball. A farm system that produced Steve Rogers, Scott Sanderson, David Palmer, Bill Gullickson, Tim Wallach, Gary Carter, Tim Raines, Terry Francona, André Dawson, and Ellis Valentine. Ellis, alas, was adjudged *not a good citizen.* A boy playing a boys' game.

Going into the 1980 season, in the most curious addendum to a contract this side of a third-grade report—Addendum No. 4—Ellis, in the absence of a lollipop, was to be paid a $2,000 monthly bonus if he fulfilled the following conditions:

a. general excellence of offensive and defensive play;

> *b.* general effort and practice effort;
>
> *c.* co-operation with management and field leadership;
>
> *d.* good physical condition;
>
> *e.* good citizenship.

In April, May, July, and August, Ellis was good hit, field, and hygiene, winning untold brownies and the $2,000 per, but in June the bad boy went and fractured his cheekbone and his bonus was withheld until the last month of the season, when management decided not to award it, because he had been found wanting in "practice effort" and "good citizenship." Seemingly, if Ellis so much as sneezed or suffered a tummy tumble, he withdrew from the field, saying he would not play unless he could give his best. Furthermore, on September 22, he had to be threatened with suspension unless he returned to Montreal pronto for the examination of a wrist he'd injured in St. Louis. "We didn't give a hoot about the money," said Valentine's agent. "All Ellis wanted was a thank-you from the club. Instead he had to sit through some ninety-minute meetings about why he didn't deserve the bonus. That hurt him."

Still grieving in October, Ellis asked to be traded, a demand he was to repeat in spring training and after. Finally, in 1981, even as Ellis was ailing again, he was sent to the Mets for reliever Jeff Reardon, a minor league outfielder, and a player to be named later. "I love him," John McHale said, "and I hope he does well."

Valentine was exuberant. "That's great," he said. "I hope Shea Stadium will help my legs. Maybe

McHale is trying to make me happy by trading me to a place where there is natural grass."

To which *Gazette* columnist Ted Blackman responded the following morning that he thought Ellis had been playing on grass all along.

When we acquired a franchise of our own in 1969, our cherished Montreal in the majors at last, we congratulated each other, because seemingly things had changed, we were in the biggies now. Increasingly, the engaging Expos brought us joy, a much-needed distraction, pulling in the town's largest and most good-natured crowds. Such was their appeal, in fact, that they attracted some 1,534,564 fans in 1981, the notorious split season when, with only the third-best divisional record overall, the Expos sneaked into the playoffs and damn near the World Series, finally undone by Fernando Valenzuela and a ninth-inning homer by Rick Monday, a hit that still resounds here as tragically as Bobby Thomson's historic blow against the old Brooklyn Dodgers.

Possibly, deep down in the adolescent Expo psyche, players too young to have seen the legendary Triple A Royals still consider themselves the Dodgers' number-one sons. Management may suffer from the same affliction. After all, it was only after the Expos let reliever Mike Marshall go that he went on to win fifteen, and save twenty-one, games for the Dodgers, winning them a pennant and himself a Cy Young award. Manny Mota, the original Expo draft choice, and the first to be traded, went on to play ten very productive years with the same Dodgers. Ron Fairly, in all the years he played here, reportedly drove manager Gene Mauch wild telling him again and again what a grand organization he had sprung from. While Mauch himself, I'm told, always yearned to manage one team more than any other: yes, the Dodgers. After all this time, still Montreal baseball's Big Daddy. Obviously, the Expos' most urgent need is for a pitcher called Oedipus Rex.

Meanwhile, two other problems remain. The signing of free agents. And holding on to players developed by the organization after their talent has matured.

John McHale insists that the Expos have no trouble competing for free agents, the players adore it in Montreal, but though he offered Reggie Jackson $1 million more than the Yankees, Reggie understandably opted for New York, where his chocolate bar would sell considerably better than 1981's Cro-bar named after outfielder–first baseman Warren Cromartie. Don Sutton also balked at playing for his good neighbour to the north.

"Do the players like it here?" I asked pitcher Bill Lee.

"I like it here and I want to stay, but most of the players dislike it intensely. There's the weather problem and the culture shock. The wives don't want to learn French. And then there's the tax situation."

At the gate, the Expos take in Canadian dollars, worth roughly 81 cents American, but they fork out U.S. funds at the pay window, and are also obliged to compensate players for any losses they suffer on double taxation. All the same, the players don't like the headache. Even more to the point, they feel neglected out on the tundra. Until they become contenders, they are seldom seen on the Game of the Week, and unless their relatives in Florida or California catch them on American TV, they have no idea how well their boys are doing in Canada.

The problem of holding on to draft choices who have been developed within the organization, becoming stars, could become prohibitively expensive. Take Gary Carter, for instance, an Orange County boy, long coveted by the Dodgers. Before he condescended to sign a new contract with the Expos for a rumoured $15 million, spread over seven years, he told me, "When I play out there in California all the papers do interviews now. Even my old local paper—the one I used to deliver."

Other players, nourished by the Expos but now on the threshold of stardom—say, young Tim Wallach—may elect to shine under a large media sun. To keep him, come contract-renewal time, the Expos would be required to pay more than any other team could offer, because of intangibles it is simply not within their power to provide. Danny Menendez, director of Expos scouting, told me, "A player, if he becomes a star here, can get maybe $15,000 to $20,000 for an endorsement, but in the States he can earn from $50,000 to a $100,000 for the same thing. It adds up."

So though we have ostensibly leaped from Triple A to the biggies, it could yet prove an illusion. Possibly we are doomed to be a farm club forever. Developing talent for California and New York. Meanwhile, there is hope. Hope of a kind. Next year, or maybe five years from now, the Big Owe will be completed. A retractable roof will be set in place. And in this city of endless winter and short hot summers, it will become possible to watch baseball played under a roof, on artificial turf, in an air-conditioned, maybe even centrally heated, concrete tomb.

Progress.

1984

19

The Fall of the Montreal Canadiens

Nineteen eighty, certainly, was the winter of Montreal's discontent. During the last week of February, our sidewalks were still bare of snow. Unheard of here, bizarre beyond belief. In fact, only a piddling twelve inches of snow (in other years, one blizzard's good blow) had fallen on our stricken city by February 24, the least amount since 1875, when the McGill Observatory first began to monitor the weather here. Knowledgeable Montrealers were shaking their heads. Incredulous, apprehensive. Something was wrong somewhere.

That freaky winter our city had endured good news and bad news—all of it mind-boggling.

The unpredictable Montrealer we leased to the country as prime minister for eleven bumpy years, Pierre Elliott Trudeau, had risen again like Lazarus, having announced his retirement the previous November, only to reconsider and lead the Liberal Party back into power in Ottawa in February. Meanwhile, in Quebec City, where the separatist Parti

Québécois was rooted in provincial office, another Montrealer, that party's cultural ayatollah, Dr. Camille Laurin, had pronounced again, urging French-only announcements at the Forum, hockey's undisputed shrine. Moved to outrage, Montreal *Gazette* sports columnist Tim Burke wrote, "Only minds filled with mischief and vindictiveness could lean on the Forum to strike the language of 25 percent of its fans from its program. It is the kind of mentality dedicated to converting Montreal from a once-great metropolis into a sickly, swollen Trois-Rivières."

Within a couple of days another columnist, Jerry Trudel, countered with equal heat in the pages of *Dimanche-Matin: "Aujourd'hui, Tim Burke me fait rire: il demeure, lui, l'un des nombreux bastions du bigotisme anglo-saxon dans cette mosaique balkanisée qu'on appelle le Canada."* Furthermore, a seething Trudel pointed out that when *"ces bons Canadiens"* were playing in Vancouver, and a stanza of the national anthem was sung in French, the team was greeted by a *"crescendo des poumons."* Resounding boos from the yahoos in the stands.

"Politics and sports don't mix," a slippery Guy Lafleur has insisted more than once, but that embarrassing night many of *ces bons Canadiens* were deeply offended. "Some of the players were so angry," Serge Savard said, "they didn't even want to go out on the ice."

Other nights, other yahoos. At a game in Toronto a separatist-inclined columnist who travels with the team remained resolutely seated in the press gallery when "O Canada" was sung, this time *en anglais*. A security guard, fulminating behind him, promptly jerked him upright by the scruff of the neck. "In *this* city," he advised him, "we stand up for *that* song."

But it was not the eerie absence of snow, Trudeau's second coming, or the continued squabbling between English and French Canadians that profoundly perplexed Montrealers that season, making it a winter of infamy. It was something far more incredible, infinitely more unsettling. In the longest November we could recall, the Montreal Canadiens, our fabled Canadiens, actually managed to lose six games in a row, something that hadn't happened for forty years, not since the season of 1939–40, a year uninformed out-of-towners may remember for other reasons.

A few days after the fall, I ran into Tim Burke in a favoured downtown bar. "The Canadiens," he said, fuming, "are now on a two-game win streak." And then, contemplating his rum and Coke, he added, "Can you imagine even thinking such a thing? A two-game win streak! The *Canadiens!*"

Soon, floating on too many drinks, we were reminiscing about what was by common consent the greatest Canadiens team ever, the club that in 1959–60 won its fifth Stanley Cup in a row. In those days, Tim recalled, glowing, we would quit the Forum after a game as emotionally drained as any of the players were. Such, such was once the quality of the action.

In Montreal, easily the most prescient of hockey towns, everybody you meet these days is down on the game. "There was a time, not so long ago," a sportswriter told me, "when if I walked into the Press Club with two tickets for a game, I was immediately surrounded, I was going to make enemies—everybody wanted them. Now I walk in with two tickets and I can't even find a taker."

The players, they say, are fat, indolent, and overpaid. Frenetic expansion, obviously fed by avarice rather than regard for tradition, has all but ruined a fine institution. The season is horrendously long and the present playoff system an unacceptable joke. Come mid-May the Stanley Cup finals have usually yet to begin. And yet—and yet—Saturday night is still *Hockey Night in Canada.* Diminished or not, *les Canadiens sont là.* And so am I, my eyes fixed on the television set.

The legendary Canadiens.

For as long as I can remember, *le Club de Hockey Canadiens* has always been something unique. Never just another hockey club. To appreciate that properly, what's called for, first of all, is some grasp of my Canadian generation's dilemma.

An earlier generation, not mine, was raised to manhood on a British standard. *The Boy's Own Annual.* "Fear God, Honour the Crown, Shoot Straight, and Keep Clean." But those of us who were kids during the Second World War (flipping the diddle as the battles raged elsewhere) and went on to become teenagers in the late forties were a thoroughly American bunch. We endured Montreal and blackheads, but New York, New York, was our heart's desire. The real world, the big time. We tolerated our own CBC but couldn't wait for Monday night when Cecil B. DeMille presented Hollywood on *Lux Radio*

Theater. We accepted Montreal welterweight Johnny Greco because he actually got to fight Beau Jack and others in Madison Square Garden. He was rated in *Ring.* Later, we also took Morley Callaghan seriously, because we found out he had been to Montparnasse with Hemingway and Fitzgerald, real writers, who hadn't spat on him. We rooted for Deanna Durbin because, after all, she was a Canadian like us, a born flunk; but the star we yearned for and wanted to go the limit with was Lana Turner.

As late as the fifties, Pierre Berton reveals in *Hollywood's Canada,* there was a government-sponsored film group in Ottawa, the Canadian Co-operation Project, composed of grown men who actually compiled an annual list of film mentions of Canada that they had pried out of obdurate Hollywood. Such dialogue gems as, from *Red Skies of Montana,* "We tie in with the authorities north of the border in Canada," or, from *The Tanks Are Coming,* "The Canadians were on our left and although taking a terrific pounding were holding magnificently." In fact, the CCP was so effective that it was even responsible for the occasional dialogue change. Originally a line in *New York Confidential* read: "They caught Louis Engelday in Detroit." But a rare combination of Canadian imagination and muscle altered it to read: "They caught Louis Engelday on his way to Canada."

If, in larger terms, our indigenous culture had always been suspect, most of it not for export, our ball clubs traditionally minor league, and even our prime minister a what's-his-name, we were at least armed with one certitude, and it was that when it came to playing the magnificent game of ice hockey we were, indeed, a people unsurpassed. At least until the nefarious Russians moseyed into town in 1972.

I can remember exactly where I was on VE-Day, on the day John F. Kennedy was shot, and when the first man landed on the moon. If I can't recall what I was doing on the day Stalin died, I do remember that a journalist I know was in the elevator of the *Montreal Star* building the morning after. Ascending, she turned to a neighbour and said, "Stalin died."

The elevator operator overheard. "Oh my God, that's terrible," he said. "Which floor did he work on?"

The point I'm trying to make is that on days that shook the world, or my world, at any rate, I was never on the spot until the night of September 2, 1972, when Team Canada tested our belief in God, the free-enterprise system, and the virility of the Canadian male by taking on the Russians at the Montreal Forum in the first of an eight-game series. A series, Tim Burke wrote in the *Gazette,* that the Canadian public viewed as something of a political Armageddon. Going into the contest we were more than overconfident—with pity our hearts were laden. The pathetic Russian players had to lug their own equipment. Their skates were shoddy. The players themselves had names appropriate to a plumbing firm working out of Winnipeg's North End, but otherwise unpronounceable: Vasiliev, Liapkin, Maltsev, Mikhailov, Kharmalov, Yakushev, and, oh yes, Tretiak. Everybody but John Robertson, then with the *Montreal Star,* predicted that our champions would win all the games handily or, at worst, might drop a game in Russia. A matter of *noblesse oblige.* Robertson called for the U.S.S.R. to win the series six games to two. On the other hand, Alan Eagleson, one of the organizers of the series, ventured, "Anything less than an unblemished sweep of the Russians would bring shame down on the heads of the players and the national pride."

After Ypres, following Dieppe, Team Canada and our very own belated St. Crispin's Day. Brad, Rod, Guy, Yvan, Frank, and Serge, once more unto the breach, once more for Canada and the NHL.

From this day to the ending of the world,
But we in it shall be remember'd;
We few, we happy few, we band of brothers…

We were only thirty seconds into the fray at the Forum when Phil Esposito scored. Some six minutes later, Paul Henderson, taking a pass from Bobby Clarke, scored again. But the final count, as we all know, was Communism 7, Free Enterprise 3. And our players were booed more than once in the Forum, ostensibly for taking cheap shots at the Russians as they flew past but actually for depriving us of one of our most cherished illusions. We already knew that our politicians lied and that our bodies would be betrayed by age, but we had not suspected that our hockey players were anything but the very best. If Team Canada finally won the series, Paul Henderson scoring one of hockey's most dramatic goals at 19:26 of the third period in the last game in Moscow, the moral victory clearly belonged to

Russia. After the series, nothing was ever the same again in Canada. Beer didn't taste as good. The Rockies seemed smaller, the northern lights dimmer. Our last-minute win came more in the nature of a relief than a triumph.

After the storm, a drizzle. Which is to say, the endless NHL season that followed was tainted, revealed as a parochial affair, and the Stanley Cup itself, once our Holy Grail, seemed suddenly a chalice of questionable distinction. So, alas, it remains. For the Russians continue to be the dominant force in real hockey, international hockey, with the Czechs and Swedes not far behind.

But when I was a boy, and the Russians were still learning how to skate, the major league was right here. And furthermore, the most dashing and aesthetically pleasing team to watch, in the old vintage six-team league, was our own unrivalled Montreal Canadiens.

Les Canadiens sont là!

The legend began before my time, on the night of November 29, 1924, with Aurel Joliat, Howie Morenz, and Billy Boucher, the first of many fabled lines. On that night, their first night in the Montreal Forum, the line scored six goals, defeating the Toronto St. Pats, 7–1. "Of course," wrote sports columnist Andy O'Brien, "the line had a lot of ice time because the Canadiens only carried three subs, while Georges Vezina (the Chicoutimi Cucumber) in the goal left back-checking superfluous."

Actually *le Club de Hockey Canadiens* even pre-dates the NHL; it was founded in 1909, eight years before the NHL came along, and won its first Stanley Cup in 1915–16, with Vezina and Newsy Lalonde in the lineup. But the team didn't enter into legend until 1923–24, when Howie Morenz arrived and the Canadiens won the Stanley Cup yet again.

Morenz was our Babe Ruth. Alas, I never saw him play; neither was I present in what must be accounted the most tragic night in hockey, January 28, 1937, when Morenz, in a rush against the Chicago Black Hawks, crashed into the boards and suffered a quadruple leg fracture. He was still in the hospital early in March, complications set in, and the Stratford Streak was no more. His fans, French-Canadian factory workers and railroaders, had once filled the Forum's cheap seats to the overflow, and to this day that part of the Forum is known as the "millionaires' section." "His body," wrote Andy O'Brien, "was laid out at centre ice and the greats of hockey took turns as guards of honour around the bier day and night. Then a sportswriter with the old *Standard,* I arrived at the Forum to find the front doors jammed. I entered by the furnace room and, as I walked toward the Closse Street entry, the stillness made me wonder—was nobody else in the building? But there were fifteen thousand fans, quiet and motionless in a tribute to a man—and hockey—that has never been matched."

Morenz played on three Canadiens Stanley Cup winning teams, but with his passing a drought set in. The Flying Frenchmen, or the Habitants, as they came to be known, a team that has won the Stanley

Cup twenty-two times, more often than any other club, did not claim it again until 1943–44, with the lineup that became a golden part of my childhood: Toe Blake, Elmer Lach, Ray Getliffe, Murph Chamberlain, Phil Watson, Emile "Butch" Bouchard, Glen Harmon, Buddy O'Connor, Gerry Heffernan, Mike McMahon, Leo Lamoureux, Fernand Majeau, Bob Fillion, Bill Durnan, and, above all, Maurice "Rocket" Richard.

To come clean, this was not the greatest of Canadiens teams—that came later—but it remains the one to which I owe the most allegiance.

In 1943–44, cousins and older brothers were overseas, battling through Normandy or Italy, and each day's *Star* brought a casualty list. Others, blessed with a nice little heart murmur, stayed home, making more money than they had ever dreamed of, moving into Outremont. But most of us still lingered on St. Urbain Street, and we seldom got to see a hockey game. Our parents were not disposed to treat us, for the very understandable reason that it wouldn't help us to become doctors. Besides, looked at closely, come playoff time it was always our pea-soups, which is what we used to call French Canadians in those days, against their—that is to say, Toronto's—English-speaking roughnecks. What did it have to do with us? Plenty, plenty. For, much to our parents' dismay, we talked hockey incessantly and played whenever we could. Not on skates, which we also couldn't afford, but out on the streets with proper sticks and a puck or, failing that, a piece of coal. Saturday nights we huddled around the radio, playing blackjack for dimes and nickels, our eyes on the cards, our ears on the score. And the man who scored most often was Maurice Richard, once, memorably, with an opposing defenceman riding his back, and another time, in a playoff game against Toronto, putting the puck in the net five times.

I only got to see the great Richard twice. Saving money earned collecting bills for a neighbourhood butcher on Sunday mornings, my friends and I bought standing-room tickets for the millionaires' section. And then, flinging our winter caps ahead of us, we vaulted barriers, eventually working our way down to ice level. Each time we jumped a barrier, hearts thumping, we tossed our caps ahead of us, because if an officious usher grabbed us by the scruff of the neck, as often happened, we could plead, teary-eyed, that some oaf had tossed our cap down and we were only descending to retrieve it.

Among the younger players on ice with the Rocket during the last years was the consummate artist who would succeed him as the leader of *les Canadiens:* Jean Beliveau.

I was, by this time, rooted in London, and used to make a daily noontime excursion to a Hampstead newspaper shop especially to pick up the *International Herald Tribune,* seeking news of big Jean and his illustrious teammates. Such was their prowess on the power play that they were responsible for a major change in the NHL rulebook. The Canadiens, with the man advantage, could score as many as three goals in their allotted two penalty minutes. Consequently, a new rule was introduced. It allowed the penalized team to return to full strength once a goal had been scored.

I didn't get to see Beliveau play until 1956 and was immediately enthralled. He was not only an elegant, seemingly effortless skater but an uncommonly intelligent playmaker, one of the last to actually carry the disc over the blue line rather than unload before crossing, dumping it mindlessly into a corner for the others to scramble after, leading with their elbows. "I not only worry about him when he's carrying the puck," said Punch Imlach, then coach of the Toronto Maple Leafs, "but about where the fuck he's going once he's given it up." Where he was going was usually the slot, and trying to budge him, as Toronto's Bill Ezinicki once observed, "was like running into the side of an oak tree."

Ah, Beliveau. Soon, whenever I was to fly home from England, I would first contact that most literate of Montreal sportswriters, my friend Dink Carroll, so that my visit might coincide with a Canadiens game, affording me another opportunity to watch big Jean wheel on ice. I was not alone. Far from it. In those halcyon days knowledgeable Montrealers would flock to the Forum to see Beliveau on a Saturday night as others might anticipate the visit of a superb ballet company. Big, handsome Jean was a commanding presence, and as long as he was on the ice, the game couldn't degenerate into Ping-Pong: it was hockey as it was meant to be played.

Beliveau was truly great, and a bargain, even if you take into account that *le Club de Hockey Canadiens* had to buy an entire team to acquire him.

In 1951, Beliveau, already a hockey legend, was playing for the "amateur" Quebec Aces, his salary a then stupendous $20,000 a year. The cunning Canadiens bought the Aces, thereby acquiring the negotiating rights to Beliveau. He received a $20,000 bonus and signed a five-year, $105,000 contract, which was unheard of in those days for a twenty-three-year-old rookie. Beliveau went on to score 507 goals for *les Canadiens.* He made the all-star team nine times, won the Hart Trophy for the most valuable player twice, and led his team to ten Stanley Cups in his eighteen years with the club as a player.

If Beliveau was the leader of the best Canadiens team ever, it's also necessary to say that decadence, as well as grievous loss, characterized those memorable years. Decadence came in the unlikely shape of one of the team's most engaging and effective forwards, Bernie "Boom Boom" Geoffrion, who introduced the slap shot, wherein a player winds up like a golfer to blast the puck in the general direction of the net, sometimes scoring, more often watching the puck ricochet meaninglessly off the glass. Loss, irredeemable loss, came with a change in the draft rules of 1969. Until then, *les Canadiens* had call on Quebec's first two draft choices, but come '69 and expansion, that was no more. In practical terms this meant that Marcel Dionne and Gil Perreault, among others, were lost to Montreal. Sadly, if either of them had a childhood dream it was certainly to play with *le Club de Hockey Canadiens,* but when they skate out on the Forum ice these days, it is as dreaded opponents.

A tradition was compromised in the dubious name of parity for expansion teams. For years, years and years, *les Canadiens* were a team unlike any other in sports. Not only because they were the class of the league—for many years, so were the New York Yankees—but also because they were not made up of hired outsiders but largely of Québécois, boys who had grown up in Montreal or the outlying towns of the province. We could lend them our loyalty without qualification, because they had not merely been hired to represent us on ice—it was their birthright. As boys, Beliveau and I had endured the same blizzards. Like me, Doug Harvey had played softball in an NDG park. Downtown had always meant the same thing to Henri Richard as it had to me. So the change in the draft rules meant that *les Canadiens* were bound to lose a quality that was unique in sport. Happily, however, the time was not yet. Not quite yet.

For one player promising true greatness did slip through the revised draft net. After Morenz, following Richard and Beliveau—Guy Lafleur. Lafleur, born in Thurso, Quebec, in 1951, was, like Beliveau before him, a hockey legend even before he came to *les Canadiens.* In 1970–71, still playing with the Quebec Remparts, a junior team, he scored a record-making 130 goals and graduated to *les Canadiens* under tremendous pressure. Universally acclaimed Beliveau's heir, he was even offered Beliveau's number 4 sweater. "He asked me what he should do," said Beliveau. "I told him if you want number 4, take it. But, in your shoes, I would take another number and make *it* famous."

Lafleur chose number 10, and for his first three years in the league, helmeted years, he was a disappointment. His manner on ice was tentative, uneasy.

Seated on the bench between shifts, he seemed a solitary, almost melancholy figure. Even now, having acquired some of Beliveau's natural grace by osmosis, perhaps, he is far from being a holler man, but then in the winter of 1974 he suddenly bloomed. Not only did Guy score fifty-three goals, but, eschewing his helmet, he was undoubtedly the most dazzling player on ice anywhere that year, leading old-style end-to-end rushes, splitting the defence, carrying the puck as if it were fastened to his stick with elastic, unleashing swift and astonishingly accurate wrist shots, deking one goalie after another and coming back with the play, going into the corners. Once again the Montreal Forum was a place to be, the Saturday-night hockey game an occasion.

Even so, *les Canadiens* failed to win the Stanley Cup in 1975, ignominiously eliminated by Buffalo, an expansion team, in the semifinals. Little Henri Richard, then thirty-nine years old, silvery-haired, the last player who had skated with the vintage Canadiens, kept his stick after the final defeat, a clue that he would be retiring. The end of one era and, it was to be hoped, the beginning of another. Though the *Gazette*'s Tim Burke was far from convinced. After *les Canadiens* went out, seemingly with more golf than hockey on their minds, he sourly observed that the league, and *les Canadiens* in particular, was not what it used to be.

"Most fans apparently feel the same way. They no longer concern themselves about the Canadiens the way they once did."

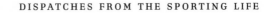

Before brooding at length on reasons and rationalizations for the fall, I should emphasize once more that the Canadiens are a team unlike any other. From Howie Morenz through Richard and Beliveau to Lafleur, they have been a family. This team was not built on haphazard trades, though there have been some, or on the opening of the vaults for upwardly mobile free agents, but largely on the development of local boys who had dreamed of nothing more than wearing that red sweater ever since they first began to play peewee hockey at the age of eight. They are the progeny of dairy farmers and miners and railway shop workers and welders. There is a tradition, there is continuity. Eighty-seven-year-old Frank Selke, who built the original dynasty, still sits brooding in the stands at every game. If the late Dick Irvin, a westerner, was the coach who fine-tuned the team for Mr. Selke, it is now his son, also called Dick, who still travels with the team, working on the television and radio broadcasts. Gilles Tremblay, a star with the team until asthma laid him low in 1969, handles the French-language telecasts. Scotty Bowman was a player in the organization until he fractured his skull, as was Claude Ruel until he lost an eye. Beliveau is still with the team, a vice-president in charge of public relations, a job Guy Lafleur would like to fill one day. Another former player, Floyd "Busher" Curry, acts as road secretary. Former GM Sammy Pollock comes from one end of Montreal, and his successor, the embattled Irving Grundman, from another. Traditionally, following the Stanley Cup parade, the team repairs to Henri Richard's brasserie. "Every year," Richard told me, "I think they will forget—they won't come this time. But win or lose, the boys are here."

However, the man who most personifies continuity on the team today is Toe Blake. Originally a winger on the high-scoring Punch Line—with Elmer Lach and Maurice Richard—in the forties, then the team's most successful coach, at the age of sixty-eight he was still padding up and down hotel lobbies on the road, remembering never to throw his fedora on the bed, which could only bring bad luck; a once-fierce but now mellowing Toe, available to all the players, a consulting vice-president with the team. "But vice-president of what," he says, "they never told me."

Try to understand that in this diminishing city we have survived for years confident that any May the magnificent Canadiens did not bring home the Stanley Cup was an aberration. An affront to the fans. Or just possibly an act of charity. *Pour encourager les autres.*

Yes, yes. But in 1980, in the very Forum where the rafters were festooned end to end with Stanley Cup pennants, our champions, who came back— even after Tim Burke pronounced them dead in 1975—to win the Stanley Cup for four years running, had been humbled by the sadly inept Colorado Rockies and the St. Louis Blues. On the road, they had come up shockingly short against the kind of pickup teams they were expected to toy with: the Edmonton Oilers, the Winnipeg Jets, and the Quebec Nordiques.

Bob Gainey maintained that the rot, such as it was, had set in in 1979. "Looking back, people remember we won the Stanley Cup again, so they think we whistled through another year. But we didn't whistle. We dropped fourteen points on the previous season and twenty goals against. We snuck out with the Cup. We were lucky enough to have the momentum of the previous year to carry us, and that, with the talent and experience, got us by. We ran the tank empty last year and now it's showing up."

Actually, fissures in the dynasty began to appear as early as the summer of 1978, when Molson's Brewery bought the Canadiens from Peter and Edward Bronfman for $20 million. A month later, Sam Pollock, the unequalled dealer and hoarder of draft choices—with the organization for thirty-one years, the last thirteen as GM—took his leave with the Bronfman brothers. Pollock, who built the present dynasty, anointed Irving Grundman as his heir. Grundman had come to hockey and the Forum with the Bronfmans in 1972; he was now appointed executive vice-president and managing director of the Canadiens, that is to say, GM. Coach Scotty Bowman, who believed he was going to get the job, exploded. "The Second World War could have broken out in the Forum and I wouldn't have known a thing about it." An embittered Bowman, who had agreed to a two-year contract with the club a couple of months earlier, let it be known that he had been conned. He never would have signed, he said, had he realized that Pollock was leaving. "I've got my own future to think about," he said. "I don't want to spend the rest of my life behind the bench."

And later on, he would hint darkly that in making Grundman GM, Pollock had ensured his own continuing career with the Bronfman brothers' investment company.

Along came the 1978–79 season. Bowman, a hot-tempered disciplinarian, seemed to let up some, and acute observers of the team noted that once-safe leads now tended to evaporate. Teams lacking the Canadiens' talent made games much closer than they ought to have been. All too often games that should have produced a cozy two points became a tough one point, that is to say, ended in a tie.

Steve Shutt told me, "For the first couple of years here, Scotty was a yeller and a screamer. But it was his team, he built it. Besides, I think everybody needs a good kick in the ass once in a while. Last year, however, when it became obvious Scotty wasn't going to get the GM's job, he didn't want to do anything. He was really, really upset."

In the summer of 1979 the inevitable happened. Bowman, arguably the best coach in hockey, however personally unpopular—Scotty, ferocious leader of the team since 1971, a streetwise Montreal boy himself—walked out of the Forum to become general manager and director of hockey operations for the Buffalo Sabres.

Something else happened that summer. Ken Dryden, five-time winner of the Vezina Trophy, announced that he was retiring from the game to practice law. More bad news. Jacques Lemaire, just possibly the most complete centre in hockey, surprised even his best friends on the team by saying that he had had quite enough of Stanley Cup pressure, thank you very much, and that from now on he would be doing his skating in the more salubrious climate of the Swiss Alps.

Early in September, only days before training

camp was to open, Bernie Geoffrion, a fifty-goal scorer, a regular with the greatest Canadiens team ever, was named coach. "A dream come true," he said, beaming, but on the night of December 13 he was to resign. "I'm sick and tired of them. Guys coming in at two or three in the morning, laughing and joking around. They're not acting like professional athletes. I'm not going to stick around and let everyone in Montreal blame me for what's happening. . . ."

Geoffrion named names, too.

"Larouche walking through the airport, smoking a cigar, acting like we won the Stanley Cup when we'd lost a game. I thought Savard would help me. But he's more interested in his horses. I feel sorry for Robinson. How do you think he feels?"

The players, of course, told a different tale. "He flunked out in New York," Shutt said, "he flunked out in Atlanta. Why would he come here, a town like Montreal, where the fans are so demanding?" Where, as yet another veteran put it, "You've got seventeen thousand assistant coaches and the fans are right behind you, win or tie."

Other players, among them honest Larry Robinson, readily admit they came to camp out of condition. With Scotty gone, they grasped that they would not be scorchingly reprimanded for it. Geoffrion, a new boy, was out to ingratiate himself.

"Geoffrion didn't want to push us," Gainey said, "but we needed it."

So faithful Claude Ruel, a former coach and then assistant to Scotty Bowman, stepped loyally into the breach. But come the Christmas break, the team that had lost only seventeen games in 1978–79 and a mere ten the year before stood at an embarrassing 17–13–6.

Something had happened. Something bad.

Where once the players on the other teams, knees wobbly, skated out on the Forum ice determined not to disgrace themselves, now they leaped brashly over the boards actually looking for two points.

"We are no longer intimidated by all those red sweaters," New York Islander goalie Glenn Resch said.

Canadiens defensive forward Bob Gainey agreed. "When you start to slip, everybody else in the league sees it, the others catch on. Now even the fringe players on the other teams think they can score here."

Since then, everybody's been taking the pulse, few as knowledgeable as Henri Richard. Richard, who played with the team for a record-breaking twenty years and eleven Stanley Cups, feared the dynasty was coming to an end. "They miss the big guy," he told me.

Sam Pollock.

"Nobody ever saw Sam," the left-winger Steve Shutt said. "I noticed him in the dressing room maybe two or three times in five years. But you always knew he was out there somewhere. Watching."

Watching, yes, but sometimes to inadvertent comic effect.

"Sam," Doug Risebrough told me, "was very impressed with how scientific football coaching had become, and so for a while he tried to adapt their methods to our game. He would wander the highest reaches of the Forum, searching out patterns of play, and if he detected something he would quickly radio Busher Curry, who would be pacing the gangway, a plug in his ear. No sooner would the Busher get Sam's message than he would rush up to Bowman with the words of wisdom. Once, when we were leading the Bruins here, 3–2, with a couple of minutes to go, Sam, watching above, got on the radio to the Busher, who immediately rushed to the bench with the message for Scotty, which Scotty passed on to us. The message was 'Sam says don't let them score on you.'"

The rap against fifty-year-old Irving Grundman, Pollock's successor, is that he is not a hockey man, he lacks fraternity credentials, but neither did he inherit the team with his daddy's portfolio. The taciturn, driving Grundman is a butcher's boy, and when he was a kid he was up at 5:00 a.m. to pluck chickens in his father's shop on the Main. He became a city councillor and went on to build a bowling empire, hooking up with the Bronfman brothers, who shrewdly took him to the Forum with them. "When I came here eight years ago it wasn't with the intention of having Sam's job. But once I got here I took a crash course with him. Five hours a day every day. He recommended me for the job. Now I'm in a no-win situation. If things go well, I did it with Sam's team. If not, it's my fault. However, we've already won one Stanley Cup, so I'm ahead of the game."

It was also Grundman, obviously a quick learner, who engineered the trade—or theft, some say—that did so much to enable the troubled Canadiens to hang in there in 1980. He sent Pat Hughes and Rob Holland to Pittsburgh for goalie Doug Herron. The season before, the fans, in their innocence, were demanding more ice time for backup goalie Michel

Larocque. In 1980 the same fans were grateful that Herron was number one.

Still, Dryden was missed. Bob Gainey felt that it was his retirement that had hurt the team most. "The other teams are overjoyed. They look down the ice and he isn't standing there anymore."

Red Fisher, sports editor of the *Gazette,* who travelled with the Canadiens for twenty-five years, allowed that Dryden used to let in soft goals if the team was ahead 5–1, "But if they were down 1–0 on the road, he was the big guy. He kept them in there until they found their legs."

Others insisted that the most sorely missed player was Jacques Lemaire. Lemaire, hanging back there, brows knitted, scowling, as Lafleur and Shutt swirled around the nets. Certainly he would be missed in May. Lemaire, the leading scorer in the 1979 playoffs, accounted for eleven goals and twelve assists in sixteen games. But the biggest adjustment the team had to make in 1980, according to Larry Robinson, was the loss of Scotty Bowman. Bowman was feared, maybe even hated, by most of the players, but he got the best out of them. "With Scotty gone, the fear and motivation is gone. He's a great hockey man. He made us work hard. You never knew what to expect."

Something else. In 1980, as all the players were quick to point out, the team had endured an unseemly number of injuries, and for the first time in recent memory, there was nobody down there in Halifax threatening to crack the lineup. The bench was thin.

Another consideration was that the one superlative defence hadn't been playing up to par. "In the first half," Shutt allowed ruefully, "Savard and Lapointe couldn't have made Junior A."

"We can't do it all with one line," Shutt said, and the other lines were simply not scoring.

But then, on New Year's Eve, there was a miracle at the Forum. Playing fire-wagon hockey, buzzing around the nets like the Canadiens of cherished memory, a revived team put on a dazzling display, beating the Red Army 4–2 in a so-called exhibition game. Many a fan, his faith in mankind restored, was saying the Canadiens, awake at last, would not lose another game during the rest of the season. Look out, Flyers. Boston, beware. *Les Canadiens sont là.*

On New Year's Day, rotund Claude Ruel, mistaken for a buffoon by some, announced, "The past is dead. They are playing a little harder now, with more enthusiasm and pep."

Alas, the past was prologue. The following night *les Glorieux* ventured into Pittsburgh and lost again. They continued to play erratically, but with rather more success than in the first half, before Lafleur sounded off early in February. Some players, he said, were less interested in playing hockey than in drawing their salary. "It's reached a point where some of them don't want to play because they have a little headache. What do you expect a guy like Ruel to do then?" Lafleur also felt that some of the bigger players, say six-foot-six Gilles Lupien, were not doing enough hitting. "I know a number of players who are satisfied with thirty goals, while they could easily score fifty. But they don't because they say then the public and the boss would be more demanding."

By this time I had caught up with the Canadiens myself, determined to stay with them for six games, come to scrutinize the troubled club firsthand; and what follows is in the nature of a concerned fan's journal.

February 7, the Forum, Canadiens 4, Rockies 3.

Good news. Savard and Lapointe, coming off injuries, are back together in the lineup for the first time in a month. Bad news. Back and stumbling. Savard, racehorse owner and proprietor of a suburban newspaper, is wearing a helmet for the first time this season. And Lapointe, as everybody knows, is having marital problems. The first period is largely smash-and-grab, the sort of play that is giving hockey a bad name, but, at the period's end, the Canadiens lead 3–2. A disgruntled journalist, rising from his seat in the press gallery, observes, "Will you look at that. I mean, they're playing the Colorado Rockies. The most compelling man on the team is their coach." Don Cherry.

In the second period, the Canadiens stumble badly. From Doug Harvey to Gilles Lupien, I note, is not so much a fall as a suicidal leap. Lupien treats the puck as somebody else might being caught with another man's wife. No sooner does it connect with his stick than he shoots it blindly out of his zone, as often as not onto a waiting Colorado blade. Lafleur scores twice. Mario Tremblay once, his first goal in ten games.

February 9, the Forum, Canucks 4, Canadiens 3.

"Look at those menacing black uniforms!" somebody in the press box exclaims as Vancouver skates out on the ice.

"Yeah, but that's all they've got."

Tonight it's enough to beat the disorganized Canadiens, their play distressingly tentative. Once more the team squanders a two-goal lead, characteristically provided by Lafleur and Shutt, and stumbles through a punk second period. Lapointe separates his shoulder once more and will be out again, possibly for another month. "He has to be thinking about something else out there," a reporter observes sadly.

The unnecessary loss is a bummer flying into Boston for a Sunday-night game. On our chartered flight, the subdued players sip their beer morosely. I sit with Doug Risebrough, a scrapper on ice, who turns out to be most engaging. "That game was given to them," he says. "A lot of nights what's missing with us is the concentration. It's just not there."

As we check into the hotel in Boston, after 1:00 a.m., three garishly made up hookers, their smiles menacing, are fluttering around the registration desk, eager to begin negotiations.

"How would they know when we're coming in?" I ask one of the writers.

"They're always in touch with the sports desk. They ring me all the time in Montreal to find out when a team is flying in and where they will be staying."

When Frank Mahovlich was still with the Canadiens, one of his teammates connected with a groupie in a hotel lobby, but unfortunately he was slated to share a room with still another player. Instead, he got Mahovlich, who had a room to himself, to switch with him. Settling in with his girl, the player dialled room service. "I want two rye and ginger ale. Room 408. Mr. Mav'lich."

"How do you spell that, sir?"

"M, A—M, A, V—no, no—M, A, H—H, V—oh, fuck it. Never mind."

In the morning, I meet Bob Gainey for breakfast.

"We don't seem to want to do it this year," he says, "or have the ability to do it all the time." He invokes the Cincinnati Reds. "You can hold on to it for so long, then it slips away. But we still have the potential," he concludes wistfully.

Toe Blake is in the lobby, mingling with the players. It's been a long haul for Toe, working in the mines in summer in Falconbridge when he was playing with the Punch Line, and then coaching the greatest Canadiens team ever, its total payroll $300,000. A long way from there to here. Now travelling with today's *Glorieux,* disco-smart in their Carin jackets, ostentatious fur coats, suede boots; a team representing a total payroll estimated at $3 million. "When I was playing in this league," Toe says, "I worried about my job. Even the stars worried. If you went sour for five games, maybe even a couple, down you went, but now…" Today's average player, he acknowledges, is a better skater, but he misses the passing and the play-making of the vintage NHL years. In that feathery voice of his, Toe laments that even on the power play, forwards tend to shoot the puck into the corners, rather than carrying it over the blue line. "If I were still coaching I'd bring back puck handling. I wouldn't want them to throw the puck away. Look at the Russians. They're skating all the time. That's their secret." Neither is Toe an admirer of the slap shot. "Dick Irvin used to say it doesn't matter how hard you hit that glass or the boards, the light won't go on."

The team bus is due to leave for the Garden at five o'clock, but come four Lafleur is pacing the lobby, enclosed in a space all his own. Doug Herron, whose wife gave birth to a baby girl the day before, will be in the nets. "I know I'm ready," he says. "But sometimes you've got it, sometimes not."

February 10, Boston Garden, Canadiens 3, Bruins 2.

In the first period, the surging Bruins outshoot the Canadiens 8–4, and the difference is Herron, who makes some spiffy stops. Fifteen long minutes pass before Montreal has its first shot on the Boston nets. A goal. Engblom. Trooping out of the press gallery, everybody agrees that if not for Herron we could easily be down three goals. Like Dryden, he is keeping them in there.

In the second period, Boston outshoots Montreal again, 12–8, scoring twice. Both goals come on two-on-ones. Savard is caught up the ice on one, Robinson on another. An overworked Robinson is not making many end-to-end rushes this season. He can't. Poor Robinson is playing forty minutes a game, maybe more, and seems to be out on the ice every time I look down. "Last season," Toe says, "Larry wouldn't be out there for more than a minute, maybe a minute and a half, and then in would come Savard and Lapointe, but now..."

Finally, the Canadiens surface with what was once their traditionally big third period. Napier, who some observers thought would help us forget Cournoyer, ties the game with his first goal since December 23. Then Lafleur sets up Larouche for the winning goal with a pass from the corner that I can only call magical.

On the chartered jet back to Montreal, the players are in high spirits, a smiling Lafleur drifting down the aisle, serving beer. These are a classy bunch of athletes, not the sort to goose stewardesses or embarrass other guests in hotels. The French- and English-speaking players mingle easily; they don't drift off into separate groups.

February 14, the Forum, Canadiens 5, Nordiques 1.

Suddenly, the others are scoring. Mondou, Jarvis, even Chartraw. And of course Lafleur is there, with a goal and two assists.

"What you are really seeing," a bemused French-Canadian sportswriter tells me, "is a battle between two breweries." Molson's owns the Canadiens; Labatt's, the Quebec City Nordiques. "Loyalties are split in the province for the first time," he adds, "and we will have to wait and see which brewery improves their beer sales most."

A couple of days after the game, Ruel announces he will wait until the season is over before deciding whether to continue coaching. "The decision is mine," he says.

The players are fond of Ruel but not intimidated by him. This is now a matriarchal society, Ruel fussing fondly over his charges rather than threatening them. But he remains a joke to some of the writers. At a practice, coaching the team on two-on-ones, he bellows at the lone defenceman, "Each guy take a man."

During his previous short-lived stint as coach, Ruel was standing behind the Canadiens' bench in the Boston Garden when a brawl broke out among the fans. Clearing the aisle behind the bench, enthusiastic cops shifted Ruel out with all the troublemakers. "I de coach!" he shouted back at them unavailingly. "I de coach!"

Now that so many Europeans were playing in the NHL, a writer asked Ruel why he didn't scout the Swedes and the Czechs during the off season. "Nutting," he shot back, "would make me cross the Athletic Ocean."

February 16, the Forum, Canadiens 8, Penguins 1.

One of the season's rare laughers. Mondou scores twice and so does Lafleur, now only a point behind Marcel Dionne in the race for the scoring championship. It is Lafleur's 399th goal.

It is announced in the dressing room that our charter will not be taking off tonight as expected. Instead, we will be leaving for Buffalo at ten-thirty tomorrow morning.

At the airport, Sunday morning, everybody is reading *Dimanche-Matin,* wherein Maurice Richard, who ought to know about such things, observes in his column, *"A lui seul, Guy Lafleur vaut le prix d'entrée."*

Ten forty-five. Still no plane. "Hey," one of the players asks, "do you think Scotty's behind this?"

"Damn right."

This will be the team's first trip to Buffalo. In two earlier games against the Sabres, both in Montreal, Scotty has failed to appear behind the bench. Montreal won the first meeting 6–3, but was routed the second time out, 7–2. "Is there anything personal against Scotty in this game?" I ask.

"Aw, he won't be wearing blades," Robinson replies.

I catch up with Scotty in the somewhat frenetic

Buffalo dressing room just before the game, and we retreat to his adjoining office.

"I have no axe to grind with anybody, except Sam," he says. "Sam duped me. Sure, I was offered what they called the GM's job for the year following this one, but I would have had to serve on a five-man committee. I wouldn't have had the right to make trades. Would Sam have taken the job under those terms? I have nothing against Grundman, but Sam looked after himself. Well, that's the name of the game." He sneaks a glance at his wristwatch. "Last summer, at the individual awards dinner, not one Montreal player mentioned me. They miss Dryden, you know. He was a great goalie. He very rarely had two bad games in a row. Well, *we're* second overall, you know."

February 17, Buffalo Memorial Auditorium, Canadiens 2, Sabres 2.

Bowman is not behind the bench, but he was carrying a walkie-talkie in the dressing room, so I suspect he is in direct touch with Roger Neilson. Surprisingly, Larocque is in the Montreal nets. It turns out to be a boring, defensive game, possibly a dress rehearsal for the playoffs, scoreless going into the third period. In the third, both teams collect a couple of goals, but Lafleur fails to earn a point and now trails Dionne by three.

In Landover, Maryland, a couple of nights later, the Canadiens were defeated 3–1 by the Washington Caps, the latter's first victory over Montreal in thirty-four games. Once more Lafleur, still looking for his four hundredth goal, failed to earn a point. The next morning it was reported that he had bruised his knee, and would be out for another game. But a few days later, after Lafleur had missed his third game in a row, the club allowed that he was suffering from a contusion of the knee, along with stretched ligaments. He wouldn't be in the lineup for at least another week, but there would definitely be no surgery, trainer Yvon Belanger said.

"I hate to think where we'd be without Lafleur," Toe Blake had conceded earlier. "Maybe even worse off than the Leafs. He's one of the all-time greats. Bobby Orr was the best for ten years, the best I've ever seen, in fact, but after Guy has played for ten years, I might just change my mind."

Lafleur, who was then earning a rumoured $350,000 a year with the Canadiens, told me that he could easily get $1 million elsewhere. Possibly in New York. "Why don't you leave, then?" I asked.

"A friend once told me, better to be a king in your own country than a valet somewhere else."

The next season was the shortest ever for a suddenly vulnerable, clearly perplexed Lafleur, who missed twenty-eight games and, for the first time in seven years, failed to challenge for the scoring championship or to net the magical fifty goals. Poor Guy. Essentially a private man, in 1981 he also became the stuff of gossip columnists and public scolds. Beset by marital conundrums, as well as highly publicized income tax troubles, the once seemingly indestructible player was out of action nine times, either ill or injured. Coming off his last injury—a minor one, a charley horse—he was, according to reports, exhilarated by his best practice of the season, and then he was obliged to endure yet another round of bargaining with obdurate income tax officials. Depressed, he met new teammate Robert Picard for dinner at Thursday's, a singles bar on Montreal's modish Crescent Street. They had a few drinks and wine with dinner, which Guy followed with a couple of Amarettos. Afterwards, they repaired to Le Saga, a disco bar, to meet another friend for a nightcap. Lafleur left at 2:00 a.m., alone, in his Cadillac.

"Don't drive," Picard pleaded, reaching for his car keys. But Lafleur insisted, with some heat, that he was just fine.

Maybe fifteen minutes later, out on the highway, Lafleur fell asleep at the wheel. His car plowed through sixty feet of fence and a light standard. A metal plate shattered the car's window, trapping him between the door and the steering wheel. The light standard, a veritable spear now, sliced his ear. An inch or two more to the right, and he would have been impaled.

An off-duty Mountie, who just happened to be driving past, promptly removed Lafleur from the wrecked Cadillac and rushed him to the hospital, where he underwent surgery to his ear but was otherwise pronounced healthy. On balance, he was lucky to escape with his life. Very lucky. But he was never the same player again, losing speed and showing his vintage form only in increasingly rare bursts.

The same was true of the Montreal Canadiens.

In 1980, they were eliminated by the Minnesota

North Stars in the second round of the playoffs.

In 1981, they went down to the Edmonton Oilers, losing three games in a row.

In 1982, they were humiliated in the first playoff round by the Québec Nordiques, and in 1983, they were knocked out in the first round, yet again.

General manager Irving Grundman was fired.

Coach Bob Berry was also fired and then rehired by Serge Savard, the newly appointed general manager.

Morenz. Richard. Beliveau. Lafleur.

The Montreal Canadiens, a proud dynasty now in sharp decline, are not, as tradition surely demanded, counting on a magical Québécois skater to renew their dominance of the league. Somebody now playing out there in Thurso or Trois-Rivières or Chicoutimi. No, sir. Today *le Club de Hockey Canadiens* is looking to an aging commie—Vladislav Tretiak, goalie for the Red Army—whom they devoutly hope to sign following the 1984 Olympic Games in Sarajevo.

Ça, alors.

1984

Playing Ball on Hampstead Heath

An Excerpt from *St. Urbain's Horseman*

Summer.

Drifting through Soho in the early evening, Jake stopped at the Nosh Bar for a sustaining salt beef sandwich. He had only managed one squirting mouthful and a glance at the unit trust quotations in the *Standard* (S&P Capital was steady, but Pan Australian had dipped again) when he was distracted by a bulging-bellied American in a Dacron suit. The American's wife, unsuccessfully shoe-horned into a mini-skirt, clutched a *London A to Z* to her bosom. The American opened a fat credit-card-filled wallet, briefly exposing an international medical passport which listed his blood type; he extracted a pound note and slapped it into the waiter's hand. "I suppose," he said, winking, "I get twenty-four shillings change for this?"

The waiter shot him a sour look.

"Tell your boss," the American continued, unperturbed, "that I'm a Galicianer, just like him."

"Oh, Morty," his wife said, bubbling.

And the juicy salt beef sandwich turned to leather in Jake's mouth. It's here again, he realized, heart sinking, the season.

Come summer, American and Canadian show business plenipotentiaries domiciled in London had more than the usual hardships to contend with. The usual hardships being the income tax tangle, scheming and incompetent natives, uppity *au pairs* or nannies, wives overspending at the bazaar (Harrod's, Fortnum's, Asprey's), choosing suitable prep schools for the kids, doing without real pastrami and pickled tomatoes, fighting decorators and smog, and of course keeping warm. But come summer, tourist liners and jets began to disgorge demanding hordes of relatives and friends of friends, long (and best) forgotten schoolmates and army buddies, on London, thereby transmogrifying the telephone, charmingly inefficient all winter, into an instrument of terror. For there was not a stranger who phoned and did not exude warmth and expect help in procuring theatre tickets and a night on the town ("What we're really dying for is a pub crawl. The swinging pubs. Waddiya say, old chap?") or an invitation to dinner at home. ("Well, Yankel, did you tell the Queen your Uncle Labish was coming? Did she bake a cake?")

The tourist season's dialogue, the observations, the complaints, was a recurring hazard to be endured. You agreed, oh how many times you agreed, the taxis were cute, the bobbies polite, and the pace slower than New York or, in Jake's case, Montreal. "People still know how to enjoy life here. I can see that." Yes. On the other hand, you've got to admit . . . the bowler hats are a scream, hotel service is lousy, there's nowhere you can get a suit pressed in a hurry, the British have snobby British accents and hate all Americans. Jealousy. "Look at it this way, it isn't home." Yes, a thousand times yes. All the same, everybody was glad to have made the trip, it was expensive but broadening, the world was getting smaller all the time, a global village, only next time they wouldn't try to squeeze so many countries into twenty-one days. "Mind you, the American Express was very, very nice everywhere. No complaints in that department."

Summer was charged with menace, with schnorrers and greenhorns from the New Country. So how glorious, how utterly delightful, it was for the hardcore show biz expatriates (those who weren't in Juan-les-Pins or Dubrovnik) to come together on a Sunday morning for a sweet and soothing game of softball, just as the Raj of another dynasty had used to meet on the cricket pitch in Malabar.

Sunday morning softball on Hampstead Heath in summer was unquestionably the fun thing to do. It was a ritual.

Manny Gordon tooled in all the way from Richmond, stowing a fielder's mitt and a thermos of martinis in the boot, clapping a sporty tweed cap over his bald head and strapping himself and his starlet of the night before into his Aston-Martin at nine a.m. C. Bernard Farber started out from Ham Common, picking up Al Levine, Bob Cohen, Jimmy

Grief, and Myer Gross outside Mary Quant's on the King's Road. Moey Hanover had once startled the staff at the Connaught by tripping down the stairs on a Sunday morning, wearing a peak cap and T-shirt and blue jeans, carrying his personal Babe Ruth bat in one hand and a softball in the other. Another Sunday Ziggy Alter had flown in from Rome, just for the sake of a restorative nine innings.

Frankie Demaine drove in from Marlow-on-Thames in his Maserati. Lou Caplan, Morty Calman, and Cy Levi usually brought their wives and children. Monty Talman, ever mindful of his latest twenty-one-year-old girlfriend, always cycled to the Heath from St. John's Wood. Wearing a maroon track suit, he usually lapped the field eight or nine times before anyone else turned up.

Jake generally strolled to the Heath, his tattered fielder's mitt and three enervating bagels filled with smoked salmon concealed under the *Observer* in his shopping bag. Some Sundays, like this one, possibly his last for a while, Nancy brought the kids along to watch.

The starting lineup on Sunday, June 28, 1963, was:

AL LEVINE'S TEAM	LOU CAPLAN'S BUNCH
Manny Gordon, ss.	Bob Cohen, 3b.
C. Bernard Farber, 2b.	Myer Gross, ss.
Jimmy Grief, 3b.	Frankie Demaine, lf.
Al Levine, cf.	Morty Calman, rf.
Monty Talman, 1b.	Cy Levi, 2b.
Ziggy Alter, lf.	Moey Hanover, c.
Jack Monroe, rf.	Johnny Roper, cf.

Sean Fielding, c.   Jason Storm, 1b.
Alfie Roberts, p.   Lou Caplan, p.

Jake, like five or six others who had arrived late and hung over (or who were unusually inept players), was a sub. A utility fielder, Jake sat on the bench with Lou Caplan's Bunch. It was a fine, all but cloudless morning, but looking around Jake felt there were too many wives, children, and kibitzers about. Even more ominous, the Filmmakers' First Wives Club or, as Ziggy Alter put it, the Alimony Gallery, was forming, seemingly relaxed but actually fulminating, on the grass behind home plate.

First Al Levine's Team and then Lou Caplan's Bunch, both sides made up mostly of men in their forties, trotted out, sunken bellies quaking, discs suddenly tender, hemorrhoids smarting, to take a turn at fielding and batting practice.

Nate Sugarman, once a classy shortstop, but since his coronary the regular umpire, bit into a digitalis pill, strode onto the field, and called, "Play ball!"

"Let's go, boychick."

"We need a hit," Monty Talman, the producer, hollered.

"*You* certainly do," Bob Cohen, who only yesterday had winced through a rough cut of Talman's latest fiasco, shouted back snidely from the opposite bench.

Manny, hunched over the plate cat-like, trying to look menacing, was knotted with more than his usual fill of anxiety. If he struck out, his own team would not be too upset because it was early in the game, but Lou Caplan, pitching for the first time since his Mexican divorce, would be grateful, and flattering

Lou was a good idea because he was rumoured to be ready to go with a three-picture deal for Twentieth; and Manny had not been asked to direct a big-budget film since *Chase. Ball one, inside.* If, Manny thought, I hit a single I will be obliged to pass the time of day with that stomach-turning queen Jason Storm, 1b., who was in London to make a TV pilot film for Ziggy Alter. *Strike one, called.* He had never hit a homer, so that was out, but if come a miracle he connected for a triple, what then? He would be stuck on third sack with Bob Cohen, strictly second featuresville, a born loser, and Manny didn't want to be seen with Bob, even for an inning, especially with so many producers and agents about. K-NACK! *Goddammit, it's a hit! A double, for Chrissake!*

As the players on Al Levine's bench rose to a man, shouting encouragement—

"Go, man. Go."

"Shake the lead out, Manny. Run!"

—Manny, conscious only of Lou Caplan glaring at him ("It's not my fault, Lou"), scampered past first base and took myopic, round-shouldered aim on second, wondering should he say something shitty to Cy Levi, 2b., who he suspected was responsible for getting his name on the blacklist years ago.

Next man up to the plate, C. Bernie Farber, who had signed to write Lou Caplan's first picture for Twentieth, struck out gracefully, which brought up Jimmy Grief. Jimmy swung on the first pitch, lifting it high and foul, and Moey Hanover, c., called for it, feeling guilty because next Saturday Jimmy was flying to Rome and Moey had already arranged to have lunch with Jimmy's wife on Sunday. Moey made the catch, which brought up Al Levine, who homered, bringing in Manny Gordon ahead of him. Monty Talman grounded out to Gross, ss., retiring the side.

Al Levine's Team, first inning: two hits, no errors, two runs.

Leading off for Lou Caplan's Bunch, Bob Cohen smashed a burner to centre for a single and Myer Gross fanned, bringing up Frankie Demaine and sending all the outfielders back, back, back. Frankie whacked the third pitch long and high, an easy fly had Al Levine been playing him deep left instead of inside right, where he was able to flirt hopefully with Manny Gordon's starlet, who was sprawled on the grass there in the shortest of possible Pucci prints. Al Levine was the only man on either team who always played wearing shorts—shorts revealing an elastic bandage which began at his left kneecap and ran almost as low as the ankle.

"Oh, you poor darling," the starlet said, making a face at Levine's knee.

Levine, sucking in his stomach, replied, "Spain," as if he were tossing the girl a rare coin.

"Don't tell me," she squealed. "The beach at Torremolinos. Ugh!"

"No, no," Levine protested. "The civil war, for Chrissake. Shrapnel. Defence of Madrid."

Demaine's fly fell for a homer, driving in a panting Bob Cohen.

Lou Caplan's Bunch, first inning: one hit, one error, two runs.

Neither side scored in the next two innings, which were noteworthy only because Moey Hanover's game began to slip badly. In the second Moey muffed an easy pop fly and actually let C. Bernie Farber, still weak on his legs after a cleansing, all but foodless, week at Forest Mere Hydro, steal a base on him. The problem was clearly Sean Fielding, the young RADA graduate whom Columbia had put under contract because, in profile, he looked like Peter O'Toole. The game had only just started when Moey Hanover's wife, Lilian, had ambled over to Al Levine's bench and stretched herself out on the grass, an offering, beside Fielding, and the two of them had been giggling together and nudging each other ever since, which was making Moey nervy. Moey, however, had not spent his young manhood at a yeshiva to no avail. Not only had he plundered the Old Testament for most of his winning *Rawhide* and *Bonanza* plots, but now that his Lilian was obviously in heat again, his hard-bought Jewish education, which his father had always assured him was priceless, served him splendidly once more. Moey remembered his *David ha'Melech: And it came to pass in the morning, that David wrote a letter to Joab, and sent it by the hand of Uriah. And he wrote in the letter, saying, Set Uriah in the forefront of the hottest battle, and retire ye from him, that he may be smitten, and die.*

Amen.

Lou Caplan yielded two successive hits in the third and Moey Hanover took off his catcher's mask, called for time, and strode to the mound, rubbing the ball in his hands.

"I'm all right," Lou said. "Don't worry. I'm going to settle down now."

"It's not that. Listen, when do you start shooting in Rome?"

"Three weeks tomorrow. You heard something bad?"

"No."

"You're a friend now, remember. No secrets."

"No. It's just that I've had second thoughts about Sean Fielding. I think he's very exciting. He's got lots of appeal. He'd be a natural to play Domingo."

As the two men began to whisper together, players on Al Levine's bench hollered, "Let's go, gang."

"Come on. Break it up, Moey."

Moey returned to the plate, satisfied that Fielding was as good as in Rome already. May he do his own stunts, he thought.

"Play ball," Nate Sugarman called.

Alfie Roberts, the director, ordinarily expected soft pitches from Lou, as he did the same for him, but today he wasn't so sure, because on Wednesday his agent had sent him one of Lou's properties to read and—Lou's first pitch made Alfie hit the dirt. That settles it, he thought, my agent already told him it doesn't grab me. Alfie struck out as quickly as he could. Better be put down for a rally-stopper than suffer a head fracture.

Which brought up Manny Gordon again, with one out and runners on first and third. Manny dribbled into a double play, retiring the side.

Multicoloured kites bounced in the skies over the Heath. Lovers strolled on the towpaths and locked together on the grass. Old people sat on benches, sucking in the sun. Nannies passed, wheeling toddlers with titles. The odd baffled Englishman stopped to watch the Americans at play.

"Are they air force chaps?"

"Filmmakers, actually. It's their version of rounders."

"Whatever is that enormous thing that woman is slicing?"

"Salami."

"*On the Heath?*"

"Afraid so. One Sunday they actually set up a bloody folding table, right over there, with cold cuts and herrings and mounds of black bread and a whole bloody side of smoked salmon. *Scotch. Ten and six a quarter, don't you know?*"

"On the Heath?"

"Champagne *in paper cups.* Mumm's. One of them had won some sort of award."

Going into the bottom of the fifth, Al Levine's Team led 6–3, and Tom Hunt came in to play second base for Lou Caplan's Bunch. Hunt, a Negro actor, was in town shooting *Othello X* for Bob Cohen.

Moey Hanover lifted a lazy fly into left field, which Ziggy Alter trapped rolling over and over on the grass until—just before getting up—he was well placed to look up Natalie Calman's skirt. Something he saw there so unnerved him that he dropped the ball, turning pale and allowing Hanover to pull up safely at second.

Johnny Roper walked. Which brought up Jason Storm, to the delight of a pride of British fairies who stood with their dogs on the first-base line, squealing and jumping. Jason poked a bouncer through the infield and floated to second, obliging the fairies and their dogs to move up a base.

With two out and the score tied 7–7 in the bottom half of the sixth, Alfie Roberts was unwillingly retired and a new pitcher came in for Al Levine's Team. It was Gordie Kaufman, a writer blacklisted for years, who now divided his time between Madrid and Rome, asking a hundred thousand dollars a spectacular. Gordie came in to pitch with the go-ahead run on third and Tom Hunt stepping up to the plate for the first time. Big black Tom Hunt, who had once played semi-pro ball in Florida, was a militant. If he homered, Hunt felt he would be put down for another buck nigger, good at games, but if he struck out, which would call for rather more acting skill than was required of him on the set of *Othello X,* what then? He would enable a bunch of fat, foxy, sexually worried Jews to feel big, goysy. Screw them, Hunt thought.

Gordie Kaufman had his problems too. His stunning villa on Mallorca was run by Spanish servants, his two boys were boarding at a reputable British public school, and Gordie himself was president, sole stockholder, and the only employee of a company that was a plaque in Liechtenstein. And yet—and yet—Gordie still subscribed to the *Nation;* he filled his Roman slaves with anti-apartheid dialogue and sagacious Talmudic sayings; and whenever the left-wing *pushke* was passed around he came through with a nice check. I must bear down on Hunt, Gordie thought, because if he touches me for even a scratch single I'll come off a patronizing ofay. If he homers, God forbid, I'm a shitty liberal. And so with the count three and two, and a walk, the typical social democrat's compromise, seemingly the easiest way out for both men, Gordie gritted his teeth, his proud Trotskyite past getting the best of him, and threw a fast ball right at Hunt, bouncing it off his head. Hunt threw away his bat and started for the mound, fist clenched, but not so fast that players from both sides couldn't rush in to separate the two men, both of whom felt vindicated, proud, because they had triumphed over impersonal racial prejudice to hit each other as individuals on a fun Sunday on Hampstead Heath.

Come the crucial seventh, the Filmmakers' First Wives Club grew restive, no longer content to belittle their former husbands from afar, and moved in on the baselines and benches, undermining confidence with their heckling. When Myer Gross, for instance, came to bat with two men on base and his teammates shouted, "Go, man. Go," one familiar grating voice floated out over the others. "Hit, Myer. Make your son proud of you, *just this once.*"

What a reproach the first wives were. How steadfast! How unchanging! Still Waiting for Lefty after all these years. Today maybe hair had greyed and chins doubled, necks had gone pruney, breasts drooped and stomachs dropped, but let no man say these crones had aged in spirit. Where once they had petitioned for the Scottsboro Boys, broken with their families over mixed marriages, sent their boyfriends off to defend Madrid, split with old comrades over the Stalin-Hitler Pact, fought for Henry Wallace, demonstrated for the Rosenbergs, and never, never yielded to McCarthy...today they clapped hands at China Friendship Clubs, petitioned for others to keep hands off Cuba and Vietnam, and made their sons chopped liver sandwiches and sent them off to march to Aldermaston.

The wives, alimonied but abandoned, had known the early struggling years with their husbands, the self-doubts, the humiliations, the rejections, the cold-water flats, and the blacklist, but they had always remained loyal. They hadn't altered, their husbands had.

Each marriage had shattered in the eye of its own self-made hurricane, but essentially the men felt, as Ziggy Alter had once put it so succinctly at the poker table, "Right, wrong, don't be silly, it's really a question of who wants to grow old with Anna Pauker when there are so many juicy little things we can now afford."

So there they were, out on the grass chasing fly balls on a Sunday morning, short men, overpaid and unprincipled, all well within the coronary and lung cancer belt, allowing themselves to look ridiculous in the hope of pleasing their new young wives and girlfriends. There was Ziggy Alter, who had once written a play "with content" for the Group Theater. Here was Al Levine, who had used to throw marbles under horses' legs at demonstrations and now raced two horses of his own at Epsom. On the pitcher's mound stood Gordie Kaufman, who had once carried a banner that read *No Pasarán* through the streets of Manhattan and now employed a man especially to keep Spaniards off the beach at his villa on Mallorca. And sweating under a catcher's mask there was Moey Hanover, who had studied at a yeshiva, stood up to the committee, and was now on a sabbatical from Desilu.

Usually the husbands were able to avoid their used-up wives. They didn't see them in the gaming rooms at the White Elephant or in the Mirabelle or Les Ambassadeurs. But come Brecht to Shaftesbury Avenue and without looking up from the second row centre they could feel them squatting in their cotton bloomers in the second balcony, burning holes in their necks.

And count on them to turn up on a Sunday morning in summer on Hampstead Heath just to ruin a game of fun baseball. Even homering, as Al Levine did, was no answer to the crones.

"It's nice for him, I suppose," a voice behind Levine on the bench observed, "that on the playing field, with an audience, if you know what I mean, he actually appears virile."

The game dragged on. In the eighth inning Jack Monroe had to retire to his Mercedes-Benz for his

insulin injection and Jake Hersh, until now an
embarrassed sub, finally trotted onto the field.
Hersh, thirty-three, one-time relief pitcher for Room
41, Fletcher's Field High (2–7), moved into right field,
mindful of his disc condition and hoping he would
not be called on to make a tricksy catch. He assumed
a loose-limbed stance on the grass, waving at his
wife, grinning at his children, when without warning
a sizzling line drive came right at him. Jake, startled,
did the only sensible thing: he ducked. Outraged
shouts and moans from the bench reminded Jake
where he was, in a softball game, and he started after
the ball.

"Fishfingers."

"Putz!"

Runners on first and third started for home as
Jake, breathless, finally caught up with the ball. It
had rolled to a stop under a bench where a nanny sat
watching over an elegant perambulator.

"Excuse me," Jake said.

"Americans," the nurse said.

"I'm a Canadian," Jake protested automatically,
fishing the ball out from under the bench.

Three runs scored. Jake caught a glimpse of
Nancy, unable to contain her laughter. The children
looked ashamed of him.

In the ninth inning with the score tied again, 11–11,
Sol Peters, another sub, stepped cautiously to the
plate for Lou Caplan's Bunch. The go-ahead run was
on second and there was only one out. Gordie

Kaufman, trying to prevent a bunt, threw right at him and Sol, forgetting he was wearing his contact lenses, held the bat in front of him to protect his glasses. The ball hit the bat and rebounded for a perfectly laid down bunt.

"Run, you shmock."

"Go, man."

Sol, terrified, ran, carrying the bat with him.

Monty Talman phoned home.

"Who won?" his wife asked.

"We did, 13–12. But that's not the point. We had lots of fun."

"How many you bringing back for lunch?"

"Eight."

"Eight?"

"I couldn't get out of inviting Johnny Roper. He knows Jack Monroe is coming."

"I see."

"A little warning. Don't, for Chrissake, ask Cy how Marsha is. They're separating. And I'm afraid Manny Gordon is coming with a girl. I want you to be nice to her."

"Anything else?"

"If Gershon phones from Rome while the guys are there, please remember I'm taking the call upstairs. And please don't start collecting glasses and emptying ashtrays at four o'clock. It's embarrassing. Bloody Jake Hersh is coming and it's just the sort of incident he'd pick on and joke about for months."

"I never coll—"

"All right, all right. Oh, shit, something else. Tom Hunt is coming."

"The actor?"

"Yeah. Now listen, he's very touchy, so will you please put away Sheila's doll."

"Sheila's doll?"

"If she comes in carrying that bloody golliwog I'll die. Hide it. Burn it. Hunt gets script approval these days, you know."

"All right, dear."

"See you soon."

Permissions

The essay "A Real Canadian Success Story" first appeared in *Home Sweet Home*. Copyright © 1984 by Mordecai Richler. Reprinted by permission of McClelland & Stewart Ltd.

The essay "With the Trail Smoke Eaters" first appeared in *Hunting Tigers Under Glass*. Copyright © 1968 by Mordecai Richler. Reprinted by permission of McClelland & Stewart Ltd.

The essay "Safari" first appeared in *Signature* magazine, February 1983, under the title, "Africa the Great Adventure." Copyright © 1983 by Mordecai Richler.

The essay "You Know Me, Ring" first appeared in *GQ*, September 1986. Copyright © 1986 by Mordecai Richler. Reprinted by permission of *GQ*, a division of Condé Nast Publications.

The essay "Writers and Sports" first appeared in *Notes on a Endangered Species*. Copyright © by Mordecai Richler.

The essay "Gretzky in Eighty-five" first appeared in *The New York Times Sport Magazine*, September 29, 1985. Copyright © 1985 by Mordecai Richler. Reprinted by permission of The New York Times Company.

The essay "From Satchel, through Hank Greenberg, to El Divino Loco" first appeared in *GQ*, July 1989. Copyright © 1989 by Mordecai Richler. Reprinted by permission of *GQ*, a division of Condé Nast Publications.

Mordecai Richler wrote ten novels and numerous screenplays, essays, children's books and several works of non-fiction, most recently *On Snooker*. During his career, he was the recipient of dozens of literary awards, including two Governor General's Awards, the Giller Prize and the Commonwealth Writers Prize. He was made a Companion of the Order of Canada a few months before his death on July 3, 2001.

A NOTE ABOUT THE TYPE

Dispatches from the Sporting Life is the first book to be set entirely in "Richler", a typeface commissioned in 2001 in memory of Mordecai Richler and created by Canadian type designer Nick Shinn. RICHLER is an open, evenly spaced book face designed for sustained reading at text size, in the mass.

Like its namesake, RICHLER is a completely original face, full of personality in the details, yet smooth in the composite effect. It is the first known typeface to be designed specifically and exclusively for a single author's work.